THREE HUNDRED HOURS

THREE HUNDRED HOURS

Roderick Craig Low

Book Guild Publishing
Sussex, England

First published in Great Britain in 2009 by
The Book Guild Ltd
Pavilion View
19 New Road
Brighton, BN1 1UF

Typesetting in Baskerville by
SetSystems Ltd, Saffron Walden, Essex

Printed in Great Britain by
CPI Antony Rowe

A catalogue record for this book is
available from the British Library

ISBN 978 1 84624 295 3

For Chantal

The First Monday

David Grant walks out of the doctor's surgery at precisely ten o'clock in the morning. The time is hardly relevant, but he was always governed by time and he makes a mental note of it as he shields his eyes from the bright sunlight and opens the buttons of his pale-yellow lightweight summer jacket. It is going to be another hot day, just like yesterday, the sky straight from a Monet canvas, the lightest of breezes stroking his face as he passes the ends of the narrow streets running up from the riverside.

David Grant is exactly sixty-six years, five months, two weeks and six days old. He is unable to determine what time of day he was born so cannot be more precise than that. It is a question he had wanted to ask his mother before she died but she lost her memory long before her life and thus the detail eluded him. His birth certificate is equally and frustratingly inexact. As a consequence, the moment of his birth is the first event in his life about which he has no knowledge.

David Grant is a tall man; about six feet three, slightly stooped and extremely thin, such that his clothes hang around him as from hangers in a wardrobe. His face is craggy – once handsome perhaps but now drawn and sunken, which has the effect of making his eyes seem slightly protruding. His hair, still largely unchanged from its original black, is thick, rather too long and parted high

1

on the temple, the long side dropping over his eyes as it has since he was a young boy. There is something of the Jeremy Irons about him. He has a birthmark on his left cheek, about the size of a large grape. Over the years, it has altered its hue from deep purple to the brown of a liver spot. In a conscious effort to counter the wasted appearance of his body, he is immaculately dressed. I have already mentioned the jacket, which is more designer than High Street, but his trousers and shirt are equally smart in pale-blue shades with a cravat of dark sand at his scrawny neck. Clutched in his long, almost feminine, left hand is the doctor's prescription, neatly printed and signed, contrasting with the incomprehensible, handwritten hieroglyphics he experienced in England, together with a large white envelope, unaddressed and unsealed.

I apologise. I should really begin at the beginning. The place? Tournon in the Ardèche, a *département* of southern France. That river I mentioned? The Rhône – the right bank of the Rhône to be accurate. To know your right bank from your left bank, simply turn yourself around so that you are standing parallel to the flow of the water. If the river is on your left and you are watching the water receding into the distance, you are on the right bank. If it is on your left and advancing toward you, you are on the left bank. If you know the region, it would be enough to say 'Tournon in the Ardèche' because the habitation on the other side of the river has another name and, anyway, it isn't in the Ardèche at all. Not that all this matters greatly to the story but I am always governed by precision – not in terms of exact time it is true, but in all other particulars. It matters to me just as time and, clearly, personal appearance matter to David Grant.

If you have visited Tournon, you will say, 'I know Tournon! I remember the expansive car parks under the trees by the river, the massive and forbidding walls of the chateau squeezing one end of the town like the neck of a bottle, the number and variety of restaurants, the narrow streets of cheek-by-jowl houses, both winding and straight, level with the river or rising gently westwards, the little hotels all vying for business, the singing of the cicadas in the trees practically drowning out the sound of the traffic, the ancient suspension bridge built by Marc Seguin, the Thomas Telford of France' (the existing bridge was his second attempt, but everyone is allowed to improve on genius). Or, maybe, if you're into these things, you may say, 'Isn't that where we caught the little steam train that wandered up through the hills whistling at every farmhouse and waving bystander; that stopped somewhere for half an hour there and back so we could buy honey sweets and pots of home-made preserves at hurriedly erected stalls and quaff quantities of Pelforth and "33" and red wine at the lineside bar; that sat at the terminus for hours to encourage us to take a four-course lunch in one of the Lamastre restaurants *and* still have time to sleep it off before the engine's whistle summoned us back to the station?' You'd be right about all that, too.

Tournon, as you can tell, has much to commend it.

David Grant pauses at a street corner and looks at the prescription, sighs and then folds it neatly before unzipping his French-style wallet and sliding it between his *carte de séjour* and his driving licence. It is a Monday, and most of the pharmacies are closed. Oh, there will be one in the area open for cases such as his, but where? This end of the town or the other? Over in Tain perhaps? Tomorrow will do. Or the next day. It will be easier than usual to get the prescription made up with his wife away, he reasons.

He likes his wallet, a thing of many zips and pockets, some he never uses and probably one or two remaining unknown to him, a thing the size of a substantial paperback and therefore too large for any pocket of his. His life is in

3

that wallet – his credit cards and chequebooks, his car papers and money, his receipts and addresses, his family photographs and his spare keys. He knows, if he loses it, there will be parts of his existence that will become irrecoverable. Years later, his wife might say, 'You've got so-and-so. Come on, you keep it in your wallet.' And that brief but accurate request will open a hitherto sealed door to an aspect of his life long forgotten. If that ever happens, he will fumble impotently with the replacement's zips, trying one and another as his brain winds back to beyond the loss and the realisation that he has lived for years without something so important that he had felt it necessary to carry it around with him constantly.

He checks the presence of his credit cards as he does every day, several times a day, and closes the wallet before letting it slip though his hands until only the strap prevents it from falling to the uneven pavement. He transfers the envelope to his other hand and turns down one of the roads to the river, crosses the main street, and locates the elderly and battered Opel Corsa with the local '07' plate. The engine fires first time and he pats the steering wheel by way of a 'thank you'. 'What does Jeremy Clarkson know?' he asks himself, 'Chortling like a lunatic schoolboy over slivers of Italian steel with engines more powerful than five London buses, at the same time as being creatively sarcastic about the products of General Motors? This is what matters: it starts at the first turn of the key, it is utterly reliable and it costs very little to run.' He does pull a rueful face, however, as the heat builds up in the cabin. 'No air conditioning, though.' He has promised himself that the next car will have air conditioning, but the Corsa would have to break down irreparably for there to be a 'next car' and that seems highly unlikely. So, he fumbles his way out of his jacket before clipping the seat belt, winds the window down, and starts to perspire. For a slim, spare man, he is a martyr to perspiration.

David Grant noses out of the car park, turns right, pauses as a woman with an oversized buggy containing an under-sized infant shambles over the road at a crossing still showing red for pedestrians, and accelerates northwards, the river disappearing behind a row of shops and apartment blocks. The petrol station is open so he glances at the petrol gauge and decides to fill up. It isn't strictly speaking necess-ary yet but it brings trade to the local garage. He is a creature of habit and, anyway, he is loyal. Besides, there are other attractions. He serves himself, wipes around the spilled fuel making muddy streaks down the dark-blue paint with a piece of paper torn from the conveniently placed kitchen roll, unnecessarily notes the number of the pump – there are no other customers on the forecourt – squints at the price and takes his wallet from the passenger seat.

The girl, perhaps twenty years old and no more than five feet tall, tanned breasts forming their own gently sloping valley in the V-neck of her T-shirt, bared flat midriff and loose white shorts that reach her knees, turns around, stops loading a biscuit and sweet rack, returns to the counter, and smiles in recognition.

'Ça va, Monsieur Grant?'

'Yes, thank you, Cécile. Pump number five, please. Thirty-six euros, eighty cents.'

She nods, takes the proffered bank card, inserts it into the machine and presses some keys on the register. She passes the hand-held device to him.

'OK, Monsieur, your code please. And Madame Grant? She is well?' She peers past him to see if his wife is sitting in the passenger seat.

He keys in his code, remembering to push the nine particularly hard. He's had trouble with it before. 'Yes, thank you, Cécile. She is away from home on a retreat this week. Next week too.' The little screen displays 'Code bon. Patientez'. He twists the pad around and hands it to Cécile. She takes it from him and waits for the confirmation.

'Really? Where has she gone?'

'To the Yonne, near Auxerre. Not far from Paris. It's a special retreat called Vipassana. I believe it's a Buddhist centre. It's a very hard regime – too hard for me. Lots of silence, concentration, contemplation and meditation. But she loves it. Apparently it's very good for the equilibrium and for the spirit. As a consequence, when she returns, she is very different. There you are! She's happy but, for the moment, I am alone.'

Cécile listens politely, her mind drifting before being brought back to earth by a sharp electronic signal from the till. She tears off the ticket and hands it, together with the card, to David Grant.

'What a shame, her being away, Monsieur Grant! But absence makes the heart grow fonder, isn't that true?'

David Grant grins and nods in agreement. He does miss her, misses her chatter filling the air, misses her energy, misses her eccentric enthusiasms, misses her confidence, misses her gregarious nature – so different from his own – and misses her certainties.

'Yes, it's true. I do miss her,' he confirms, nodding sagely as he turns to leave, 'Au revoir, Cécile.'

Cécile smiles. 'Until next time, Monsieur Grant. Bye-bye.' Funny how that colloquial form had moved inexorably into the French language. It sounds sweet and tight with a French accent. Not at all like what verges on sounding like 'boy, boy' in the English.

Cécile moves back to her display and squeaks as she knocks some no-doubt breakable biscuits to the concrete floor. He grins as she utters a 'merde' before clasping her hand to her mouth in embarrassment.

'Oh, pardon, Monsieur Grant!'

He laughs and shakes his head.

It isn't as though he has ever learned French formally, not even when they decided to move to France eight years ago. He was never very good at sitting down with a book and learning anything by rote. His wife – her name's Élodie by the way – is French, making the transition so much easier, but she had revelled in using her mother tongue again after twenty-five years in England, and gradually, almost imperceptibly, they had used French more and more until it had become their main means of communication. His quiet manner and ability to imitate make him seem a better linguist than he, in fact, is, so when there had been a bit of trouble over the English diaspora in the area, with all the emotional ballyhoo about incomers pushing up the price of property, he and his wife had been spared from a series of random outbreaks of minor vandalism. She was French and he was accepted. End of story.

Once again he blinks as he steps into the sunlight. His sunglasses will help, he thinks. He hopes they will be in the glove compartment but, by the time he is installed in the car, he has forgotten to look, and as, once again, he turns into the traffic, it is too late to hunt about for his glasses. That will have to wait until he gets home.

David Grant feels oddly light-headed. Although it is warm, it is not yet too warm, and by driving quickly with the window down, he is able to keep the temperature in the car at a tolerable level. Soon he arrives at the main road junction and turns left in the direction of Lamastre and the house in Le Crestet. With the sun to his left and partly hidden by the hills, he folds the visor to the roof and turns on the radio. His wife, who used his car last, had left it tuned to a pop station they both enjoyed, so he hums along to something new and haunting by Natasha St-Pier.

As he drives, he thinks about his situation. His wife has

7

gone to the Vipassana Centre near Auxerre for the fifth time and that means no contact of any sort from either of them for the duration, except in dire emergencies. She is going to be away for ten full days' retreat and left yesterday morning.

'What', he had asked her at the beginning of her new preoccupation five years before when the subject of her inaccessibility was raised, 'would constitute a dire emergency?' His wife had stopped washing the salad for a moment while she thought, her hands clasping the green leaves under the cold water, staring out of the window at the garden sloping down towards the river and then up at the hills beyond.

'The death of a pet, perhaps?' he had prompted her.

'Well, we haven't got a pet.'

'No, I know.' The death of their small terrier the summer before had been more of a blow than either of them could have imagined, but Queen Elizabeth had been much more than a dog – more a friend, a presence, an extra limb, a late child they could share – and the question David had asked was academic and narrow.

Élodie resumed her washing of the lettuce. It was easy for her to say, 'No, if a pet died, you'd just have to give it a full Christian burial, or whatever, and then tell me about it when I returned.' He didn't want to labour the point by asking, 'But a pet like Queen Elizabeth?' because, even to him, she wasn't a pet at all, not at the time and certainly not in recall.

'The roof leaking perhaps?'

'Absolutely not! You're as capable as me of getting someone out to fix a leaking roof.'

'The death of a family member then?'

'Yes, all right. The death of a family member.' She had smiled as she loaded the salad into the spinner. 'But only a death, mind. Your family has a habit of taking a very long

8

time indeed over dying and I'd hate to be called back at the beginning of a process that took a year or more to complete.'

He pulled a face. 'Ouch! That's a bit below the belt!'

'Sorry, but you know what I mean.'

'So it would have to be a real, complete, heart-ceased-beating death then?'

'That's right, a real complete, authentic death. With a death certificate *and* the funeral booked. Boxed and lidded. Yes, nothing less than all that.'

They had laughed at the time.

To say that the courses at the Vipassana Centre are hard and involve a lot of meditation and contemplation is a sanitisation for an uncomplicated, worldly, neo-teenager. Cécile's time for truth-seeking, for explanations, for facing her ghosts will come, although David hopes the thorns of life will never seek out her vulnerable flesh. For now, Cécile is drunk with the beauty of her reflection; amazed at her good fortune; a little smug that it is she who has all the desired attributes and not her best friend from school or, for that matter, her elder sister; content that it is she who has caught the eye of the best-looking *gars* in Tournon, one Jean-Pierre; and privately satisfied that he is as good a lover as he is a trophy companion on summer nights when Tournon's youth parade the *terrasse* by the river or hang around customised cars and ear-piercingly noisy scooters.

For a brief moment, David Grant wonders if his treatment of the Centre's work has, in some way, diminished it and the validity of his wife's attendance and devotion as a consequence. But no, he thinks. Explanations are shaped as much by the enquirer as by the need for a precise answer, and what he had said to Cécile would suffice for now. Perhaps for ever. Maybe, at some future time, his wife will sense a need for more from Cécile and explain in her own way. Perhaps she'll tell Cécile more than she has told him.

9

That's how it is with Élodie: she has an instinct for how much to give and how much to withhold.

While he respects her choices and recognises the good it has done, David Grant is not himself an ideal candidate for a Vipassana Centre. He thinks he knows his ghosts and has largely confronted them, and anyway, with one exception, they have been of little consequence and mostly self-induced. It had been very different for Élodie, and his shallow explanation to Cécile had masked a great struggle and what had probably been Élodie's greatest journey of all. Humming mantras and eating wind-inducing pulses had not been even a quarter of it.

David Grant drops a gear as the road steepens. Now he is climbing out of the Rhône valley and crossing the ridge before dropping down towards the river Doux. The famous vines of the Côtes du Rhône are behind him, replaced by steep fields of fruit trees planted after America's weapon of mass destruction, the phylloxera aphid, had arrived in the 1870s on imported vines and ravaged the admittedly poorer vineyards of the Ardèche hinterland. Where it hit in the Rhône valley, the climate, soils and wealth of the *vignerons* ensured the vines' replacement and a continuance of the traditions of hundreds of years, but for the Ardéchois, wine-making was, to all intents and purposes, over. That's why the railway was there in the first place, for soft fruit couldn't go to market on the backs of pack mules and arrive other than damaged beyond eating. He can see the railway track twisting and turning below him as he reaches a slight downhill slope, but the train is far ahead of him, no doubt pausing for breath as the tourists slake their thirsts at the wayside station.

The road climbs again, twisting on and on between rocky outcrops and glades of trees crowding down to the road. He keeps his speed down, negotiating troops of cyclists as they energetically climb the hill. 'Many of them are older than me,' he thinks, rather admiring their fine physical shape and the startling contrast of muscular legs and narrow hips with their lined faces. He had thought of buying a bike when they first moved to France, but the level of fitness and ability he encountered was too intimidating and he stuck to the car. Anyway, he had reasoned, on every cycle ride he took from Le Crestet, half the trip would have been on foot – pushing the bike up the hill. So unlike the locals.

When he reaches Le Crestet, he turns off the main road and drops down to the village. He picks up a *pain artisanal* at the bakery, explains his wife's absence to Madame Blanc behind the counter, and takes the loaf home for lunch. Letting himself into the house, he drops his keys as usual on the corner table at the front door, places the bread and the envelope on the kitchen table then runs upstairs briefly to puts his wallet into its accustomed drawer in his bedside table. For kitchen table, think French rather than English. This is not a small eyesore of checked primary colour, Formica-topped, thick Swedish plywood and bent chromium tubing with uncomfortable chairs to match pushed inconveniently up against a rare corner devoid of fitted units. It is, rather, a trussed and pegged construction of colossal weight in solid oak about four metres long bounded by matching monastery benches and topped and tailed by a couple of rustic French carver chairs. The table takes pride of place down the centre of the kitchen and, as there are normally only two of them in the house, less than a quarter is devoted to the process of providing and consuming meals. The rest is piled with the temporarily homeless effects of life – bottles and jars for jam-making, unconsulted post with that hopeless air of strongly denied unimportance, washing not put away, small coins for visiting tradesmen and bread-buying, past copies of the local newspaper kept for a recipe or an uncompleted Sudoku, and opened packets of seeds that should probably have been discarded but would almost

11

certainly be sealed up and taped shut during a spare moment for planting the following year.

What to do? He weighs up the possibilities. He has promised to re-lay a short path to the vegetable patch – he has even bought the stone slabs – but can't face starting the job, even though there is some merit in doing the physical work while she isn't present. Effectively, it will be ten days before he sees Élodie again and disregarding his planned project leaves a void stretching out before him that instils a feeling akin to agoraphobia. If he puts it back into his head – the days of measuring and cutting, of mixing cement and carefully levelling, of replacing soil around the edges and carefully replanting border plants to make it look as though it has been just so for ever – the fear of nothingness disappears. But he doesn't want to do it. It isn't as though he is being deliberately rebellious. He just doesn't want to do it. So, the agoraphobia returns.

He cuts some thick wedges of bread, thickly spreads them with unsalted Breton butter and takes anchovies and a home-grown tomato from the fridge, cracking open a *blonde* "33" to wash his lunch down. Nine totally empty days, with the tenth spent feverishly getting things straight for Élodie's return, a man/guilt thing. Nine days when he could please himself entirely.

'I can get up exactly when I want to,' he says out loud. 'I can do exactly what I like. I can just go where the mood takes me.'

This is a conversation he has with himself every time she goes away. He lifts his shoulders and sighs before forking three or four oily little fish onto his bread, laying them neatly in rows, and taking a mouthful. It is always the same. He will not set the alarm (as he had to that morning, having the doctor's appointment), only to find himself waking up at the usual time. Or earlier. And he knows his new-found freedom will be squandered in doing little jobs and pining for her.

He has always set himself projects to be accomplished during her retreats – a new cupboard or some replacement lights in winter, turning over the vegetable patch or painting the shutters in spring, picking, blanching and freezing French beans in summer, tidying the garden in the autumn.

Élodie has only been away a few times, but usually at different times of the year. She has reached the stage where she is a 'helper', metaphorically and sometimes actually holding the hands of new attendees finding that the process is very different from what they had imagined. Resting, relaxing, eating simply, being alone, and the discipline of rising and going to bed early has the effect of unravelling the mind, and she has seen so many people rediscovering aspects of their past left buried. Some might say best left buried, for the mind heals itself as best it can, builds a bypass around the extremes of good and bad, blots out the pain, renders it inaccessible, makes the best of a bad job. But nothing ever removes those memories. In fact, they are all there, just as they were learned in the first place. The imperfections on a mother's countenance and the cruel words uttered from her pursed and angry lips. The hair on the back of a father's hand and the sound of it as it came into sharp, unexpected and bewildering contact with childish flesh. The time of the bus caught on a holiday-time trip to the seaside when eight years of age, and the sickening smell of moquette and creased leather and sweat and cigarette smoke as a request to travel upstairs was granted. The colour of the ink in a long-lost uncle's fountain pen and the memory of his long-expected death and the prayers finally answered for him to be released from his suffering. The smells and sounds and images of life, good, bad and indifferent. To make sense of it all, some believe it is necessary for the mislaid remnants of a life to be brought forward one by one into the conscious mind; to be relived, re-experienced so that, hopefully, the emotional scar tissue will be rasped away to reveal the totality within. This was the outcome for many of the Vipassana experience, even though no promises were made, no objective set, no outcome guaranteed. Most of the people Élodie helped benefited, but many had to suffer a breakdown on the way. To Élodie that was fine. Par for the course. It had happened to her.

David Grant grins. 'Perhaps,' he muses, 'I'd find out the precise time of my birth if I went to Vipassana.' And perhaps he would have. Secrets are always important to those who keep them but when the secret concerns someone else its importance increases.

He pops the last of the bread into his mouth, drains the bottle (there would have been a glass if Élodie had been present – fertile food for the man/guilt thing), puts the plate and cutlery into the dishwasher and goes into the bathroom to wash his face. 'The trouble with anchovies is the aftertaste,' he thinks, and proceeds to brush his teeth. As he finishes, he catches sight of his reflection in the mirror. Same old David Grant, perhaps a little older, a little more drawn, but wearing his age well he flatters himself. He wonders if the birthmark is a little larger but decides, after close examination, that it is not. He and his birthmark are old companions, together too long for either to take advantage of the other.

David and Élodie's move to the Ardèche was something of an accident. Not long after they married, the second time for both of them, they had been on holiday in Avignon and left a few days at the end unplanned. Never having been in the Ardèche, they crossed the Rhône in order to travel up the right bank as far as Lyon and then thought they'd spend a couple of nights in Dijon before making for

14

Calais and the ferry home. They decided they would wander about exploring the countryside, so their first port of call was Vallon Pont d'Arc. They found it not to their liking – too many tourists catered for by too many tat-selling tourist shops and pizza bars – so drove north and stayed in a hotel on the main road in Tournon. Although they slept little due to the traffic, they liked the town and liked the hinterland more. They booked into a quiet little hotel in Le Crestet, fell for the young couple running it, and never saw Dijon. Always being gazers in estate-agent windows, one thing led to another, and they moved as soon as family responsibilities had abated and he had managed to convince his employer to make him an offer of early retirement he couldn't refuse. Élodie was overjoyed at his success and staggered at the amount offered.

'They're a bank, remember?' he had said. 'They've got oodles of the stuff and too many people.'

It never entered their heads to look elsewhere. Their life, after his mother, his children and his work, was inextricably tied into that happily thwarted holiday and the little house in their lost corner of France . . .

But this ruminating on David Grant's part, left staring into his bathroom mirror and minimising his imperfections, and my brief explanation of the circumstances surrounding his and his wife's uprooting from sylvan Cockfosters to an obscure part of France, has in no way helped him with his dilemma. So, to repeat, what to do with his freedom?

His first decision is to do nothing. It is two o'clock and the temperature has reached thirty degrees Celsius. He will sit down and have forty winks, maybe fifty, and then go out for a short walk before ambling along to the hotel at about seven o'clock for a chinwag and a menu, washed down with a rather more expensive than usual Côtes du Rhône. So, at about four o'clock he walks out of the house and down the steep hill to the railway line, shushing a neighbour's dog

15

that couples a poor memory for faces with a hysterical desire to guard what he feels is his. There is no sign of the train, so he takes a fifty-centime piece from his pocket and puts it on the track, carefully choosing the rail on the outside of the curve where most of the train's weight will be thrown. Repeated soprano whistles announce the train's imminent arrival, so he returns to his vantage point by the hedge and watches the little train rounding a corner; green engine on the front doing more to inhibit speed on the descent than actually providing any traction. He feels the heat as the locomotive passes, smells the hot oil and the sweet, sulphurous smoke from the burning briquettes, admires the shining paintwork and polished brass, acknowledges the 'bonjour' from the driver and then the guard in the old, wooden *fourgon* who recognise him from previous encounters, and waves weakly at the animated and replete tourists hanging out of the windows as the carriages clatter past. Some of them in the last vehicle are singing old French folk songs which become louder at the appearance of an audience of one. In no time, the train is away down the line, the sight and sounds diminishing, the melodious voices carried away on a slight breeze. Soon, only the whistle, echoing off the hillsides, betrays the passing of a train.

When he returns to the track and puts his hand on the rail, he can feel the faintest, rhythmic vibration as the wheels clatter over the joints in the track more than half a kilometre away. A short search rewards him with the return of his coin, suitably flattened. He can tell by the fact that it is more than double its original size that it had stayed put for much of the train's passing before being spun off into the ballast. It is still warm from its illegal re-engineering.

When he gets home, he puts the coin on the kitchen table and watches some early news on the television before sauntering down to the hotel.

He tells his story of temporary separation, and the germ

16

of an idea for what he could do for the next week is sown by the owner as he dries glasses in the little bar straight off the road. Michel likes the visits of the Englishman and uses them as a golden opportunity to practise his English, quite the opposite of what David Grant really wants. Frequently, Michel will speak in English while his guest replies in French. David Grant has never tried to explain the specifics of the British Isles and the fact that he is, strictly speaking, Scots, although he has spent half his life in England. To the French, all Brits are *anglais*, and any attempt at precision usually draws blank expressions or total indifference.

'You could go away,' Michel says, holding a glass to the light and peering at a speck before giving it another desultory wipe, 'take a little holiday, and still be home long before Madame Grant returns.'

At first David Grant shakes his head, and then nods when another pastis is offered. Going away without Élodie knowing would be like skiving off school – playing hooky. Besides, he wouldn't enjoy himself on his own, would he? They always do things together, and much of the enjoyment in his life comes from sharing experiences. He has no idea what it would be like to take something as significant as a holiday without her. And then, how would he explain his actions afterwards? What would she think if he said he'd been down to the coast, or over into Italy or perhaps to Switzerland? They can see the French Alps from quite near their house in winter – snow-covered, ethereal, glinting in the sun, almost always a season displaced. Perhaps he could go there?

'What about it?' Michel encourages as he spins the top back on the pastis bottle and puts it on the shelf behind the bar.

'I don't know.' He shrugs. 'Perhaps. On holiday on my own? It's not easy.'

'No, not the obvious or easiest thing to do, I agree. But it might be interesting, no?' He resumes his glass drying and then pauses again, stepping out from behind the bar and peering down under the luxuriant vine towards the restaurant. 'I think they'll be ready for you on the *terrasse* in a few minutes. You and Madame's favourite table.'

One of the summer students serves him, telling him her life story between courses. When he reaches the dessert, and the bottle of fine, local red is three-quarters empty, the contents resting slightly uncomfortably on a bed of Pastis 51, he has decided. He will go away and tell Élodie in amongst all the other stuff when she gets back. He might even have time to do the little garden path upon his return. Setting himself the double task of going away and a spot of civil engineering certainly banishes the agoraphobia. He will pack in the morning and he guesses that, when he awakes, where to go on his clandestine holiday will be clear to him.

As he leaves, he thanks Michel for the meal and the idea.

'You're going then?' he asks as he returns his credit card.

'Oui, bien sûr,' David Grant replies, and then lapses into English. 'I don't know where, but I'm going to go away. Perhaps a week. Perhaps less.'

He returns his card and the slip to his wallet, and stands up, slightly unsteady on his feet. Must be the wine, he thinks. That and the pastis. There was a time when what he had drunk that night would have had no effect at all. He smiles at the younger man.

'I'll tell you where I went when I get back,' he says as he pushes open the door and steps out into the warm, summer night.

The First Tuesday

David Grant wakes at ten to seven, just ahead of his alarm clock which he had set, contrary to the seductive freedoms of solitude and choice. He flicks the switch after the first four beats to the bar, top C, about the same pitch as the whistle of the steam engine. He had hoped the night would bring clarification but it has not. He is no further forward on the where, even though the what is now beyond question, any semblance of choice regarding staying or going far behind him. So he rises, showers and packs a bag sufficient for eight nights (much more than he'll need); collects such things as a light coat, a small umbrella, his mobile phone with the car cigarette-lighter charger; and makes a simple breakfast of French cereal – he likes Reva flakes best – and bread from the day before, lightly toasted, with the much-loved butter and some home-made gooseberry jam. So long as he has his wallet, he reasons, he has everything the trip requires. Thinking of his wallet, he returns to the bedroom and takes it from the drawer in his bedside table and checks the presence of his credit cards before tidying up the breakfast things. Returning the butter to the fridge, he catches sight of a mustard pot which, used so rarely, he and Élodie keep on the shelf in the door, and the first stage of his adventure is decided. Of course! Dijon! The Dijon usurped by the Ardèche years before. Dijon, home of French mustard. A shadowy, tenuous connection to a long-lost ambition. Flimsy associations such as this often determine the big decisions in life.

The map is already in the car but he knows the way in terms of the autoroute network. Cross the river to Tain, follow the blue signs, go over the autoroute, turn north and down the slip-road, through Lyon, head for Paris and then take the split from it, veering off for Dijon rather than the capital. Easy. He wonders if he should leave a note for Élodie but he plans to be back days before she returns. Then he worries about it being her who has the 'dire emergency' but dismisses the idea. One can't go through life worrying about things that might happen. Anyway, if she phones and he isn't in, she'll eventually call the hotel and Michel will tell her what her husband told him – that he was going away for a few days and that he'd be back before her return. It isn't that David Grant is a permanent fixture at the hotel, only that it is his second-favourite place in Le Crestet and she'd know, the phone at home unanswered, where he'd most likely be. Then he smiles. He knows she'll try his mobile, even though his amnesia as far as mobile phones are concerned has often been a source of conflict. How often had she wondered where he was and resorted to calling his mobile, only to hear it ring in the next room, and him caught in traffic miles away.

'What use is a mobile if it isn't on you?' she'd ask.

He would shrug.

'I forgot it. I never remember it until it's too late. Besides, I didn't think I'd get delayed.'

'I don't know why you don't keep it in that wallet of yours! There must be space for that new one? Look at it, it's so small.'

But he never did find a permanent home for the phone in his wallet.

He then goes through an agony repeated again and again. Quitting the house – how should he leave the shutters and gate? Even when it was both of them going out together just for an evening, they would go through a ritual which only varied with the seasons.

Witness the summer machinations. 'We'll be back before dark – or soon after, so leave it all open,' Élodie would say. 'Close the windows, lock the doors . . .' Why did she so often state the obvious he wondered? '. . . But leave the shutters open. And the gate.' Or, if it was getting towards winter, deep winter, or spring was still some way away, it would be 'Leave the kitchen shutters open, the *séjour*'s closed, the bedroom ones open and the light on in the kitchen and on the stairs. And close the gate. Oh, and close the windows and lock the doors.' He would slightly shake his head, trying to avoid outward evidence of his irritation at repetition of the one part of his task he didn't need reminding of.

But Élodie's absence and his freedom of choice over the matter of how to leave the house are spoiled by the uncharted waters of his situation. He has never before left the house empty for a period of several days, alone. And so, as is so often the case with husbands who find asking their wife's opinion preferable to thinking for themselves, he asks himself what Élodie would do had she been at home. Would she treat it like a summer evening outing, effectively owning up to their absence but implying that they would be returning instantaneously, or should winter's message of being tucked up inside the house watching TF1 or Arté, and armed to the teeth with defensive and, as this is France, offensive weapons, be conveyed?

In the end, he devises a strategy that will convince no one of anything. He closes all the shutters and leaves the gate open. And, of course, he closes the windows and locks the doors. This is achieved after several practices in which every permutation is exercised in his mind and a good few are actually tried on the house. But, in the end, he leaves it as described, getting out of the car as it purrs happily in the road and looking back at his handiwork before moving off.

He drives past the hotel but there is no one to wave to or hoot at. Madame Blanc follows his passage with her eyes as she wedges another batch of baguettes into the wicker basket designed for the purpose but doesn't lift her hand to acknowledge his progress. The thing about owning an Opel Corsa is that it provides instant anonymity. Diana should have been chauffeured in an Opel Corsa on that fateful last night in August 1997. Had she done so, she'd probably still be alive, the paparazzi bashing off at great speed after a decoy Mercedes that could have rushed dementedly up and down the Champs-Elysées like the last day of the Tour de France, with the Corsa soon losing itself safely in the good-natured rivalry of the Paris traffic on that dark and balmy night. So long as she'd put on her seat belt, of course, because celebrities masquerading as ordinary people can still get themselves into car accidents occasionally.

David Grant gains the main road and begins the slow descent to the Rhône Valley. There has been a light rain shower overnight, just enough to puddle the uneven stretches of road and add arrhythmic staccato hissing to the more familiar sounds of the car. He lets his right hand glance over his wallet lying on the passenger seat, decides against opening it to check his credit cards whilst on the move and settles back to enjoy the scenery. Momentarily he sees the little railway line winding along near the bottom of the Doux valley before he crosses the ridge and drops down to the outskirts of Tournon where the roadside is graffitied with cheap signs encouraging holiday makers to choose their campsite over any other for the 'holiday of a lifetime'.

In Tournon.

Tournon, I should point out, is extremely nice, but elderly French couples, on winter nights in Lyon or Lille or

Lens, with the photo albums spread across their knees, the central-heating radiator ticking like the approach of the end of the world in a James Bond movie, and the dog folded into two and absent-mindedly licking its testicles on the tiled floor, would revisit Tournon affectionately as the place where they holidayed during their children years: the sickening heat of the tent; the evil sliced sausage on the hottest of days which sired the food poisoning that laid them all low; the overweight woman – dangerous white thighs and too short dresses – who played her crackly radio full blast in the caravan shaped like a torpedo with the door clipped permanently open; the long and sometimes unsuccessful night-time rush to the toilet block with children too tired to hold their waste; the evening ritual of sitting quietly outside the tent with a cardboard plate of *frites et mayonnaise* – the smell so much better than the taste and the taste impossible to improve upon – all would be rendered vague and indistinct by the photographic reality of small children squinting at the camera or sitting astride a playground toy, playing *boules* or up to their knees in the shallow, slow-flowing river. In time, they would remember only what appeared in the photographs. Even the year might need an approximate guess. Unless, of course, the children, on duty visits to their aged parents, had better memories or they had been on a Vipassana course and were in touch with their inner selves. They certainly wouldn't, however, remember Tournon as the holy grail of their holiday of a lifetime.

Probably not anyway.

Hopefully not.

Nearing the river, he picks up the blue signs for the autoroute and crosses the Rhône on something more practical but infinitely more anonymous than the work of Marc Seguin. He then climbs gently past Tain and heads east until he sees the sun glinting on a thousand fast-moving windscreens that is the nightmare of the Route du Soleil. A short link road brings him to a flyover and the slip-road, down which he coasts to join a short, nervous queue, cars forever changing lane in an effort to get through the *péage* in the shortest possible time. David Grant holds back and waves an Espace, its windows filled with animated Arab children's faces, into the queue in front of him. The driver seems surprised at this passive generosity and raises his hand in gratitude. The queue moves forward, car by car, and, for a moment, a curious child looks back, half smiles and then turns to face another on the seat beside him. By the time they reach the momentary shade of the gate, even that child has forgotten the elderly car and the man in the short-sleeved shirt who had let them through. David Grant watches the Espace dip its rear end down on its suspension as it speeds off into the sunlight and he, too, forgets his brief encounter as he winds the window down fully and extracts the ticket from the machine. Then it's his turn to gun the accelerator and feel the heat from the sun again. He turns down the opportunity for a free check of his tyre pressures knowing that the *gendarmes* often hover about places of official generosity looking for people to pinch.

It is running up towards lunchtime but he isn't hungry, so decides he'll put Lyon behind him before he stops. Plenty of petrol; he remembers he filled up only yesterday. Engine temperature gauge at most a point or two above the minimum. Vibration from what passes for a rear axle nowadays much the same as usual – no better, no worse. He winds the window up against the irritating roar of air and the smell of hot rubber and tortured engines and starts to perspire. He lets the speed rise to 130 and holds it there, amazed at the number of trucks gaining on him.

As he nears Lyon, he ignores the advice to use the bypass to the east. He'd done it once and been upset by the proximity of Switzerland after about an hour's driving, only to be brought back where he wanted to be, north of the city, but still firmly in its suburbs. The road twists and surmounts a small rise before squeezing itself between an urban road and the river. As always in Lyon, simultaneously the sun goes in and the traffic grinds nervously to a halt. The overhead signs have been joyfully announcing a *bouchon* for the previous twenty kilometres. How very French to use a word associated with wine (a *bouchon* is a cork), conviviality, good food and all-round pleasure, rather than the more prosaic English 'jam' – redolent of tea, sweetness, gossip and rotting teeth.

He decides to stay in the lane nearest the river and crawls forwards, forced to admire the view for about half an hour. Every so often, he passes under a bridge and sees slow-moving trains or crawling trams with down-turned, sad countenances creeping from bank to bank. It is as though all Lyon is a theatrical performance in slow motion – everyone and everything having all day to gaze around them and yet not gazing, instead looking steadfastly ahead. Even the pedestrians crossing the river and its confluence with the Saône, walk slowly, deliberately, trance-like, looking neither to the right nor to the left. Only a lone Mobylette ridden by a young boy wearing an insect-inspired helmet scoots noisily along the parallel road, weaving in and out with the skill and foolishness of youth, once jumping a light perilously close to red and needing to save his life by chicaning around an unmarked white van whose driver is clearly also suffering from colour-blindness. A toot from the van. An upturned middle finger from the bike. French courtesy.

At last, the road leaves the riverside, climbs a little and enters the tunnel. He hears the roar of the ventilation fans and is briefly appalled by the layers of monoxide dust rendering every feature at the tunnel mouth indistinct before the traffic starts to accelerate in the comparative darkness. By the end of the tunnel, speed has risen to sixty kilometres an hour and, within ten minutes, he is up to the local limit of one hundred and ten.

Feeling distinctly peckish by now, he looks out for a service station with a proper restaurant and finds one after a short while. He hopes to find a parking place under the trees as the temperature in the car is approaching forty degrees but *Joe Publique* has beaten him to it, the serried ranks of carelessly parked and shaded cars stretching almost to infinity. He has to settle for the compensations of a space much closer to the restaurant but in full sun. He retrieves his wallet from the passenger seat, winds the window down slightly and locks the car before walking to the low-lying cafeteria. Pushing the door open, he feels almost cold in the air conditioning, holds two hands, palms outward, up to his chest at the girl on the desk who half expects him to approach her and pay for petrol, gazes about him to gain his bearings and aims for the WC.

Some disaster has befallen the gents' facilities. Two brushes forming a St Andrew's cross effectively block the way, with a bucket of water placed between them for good measure. Had it been in Britain, every male would have clenched his knees together and found alternative arrangements, almost invariably on the other side of the autoroute or even forty kilometres up the road. But this is France and, being a practical people, the men, deprived of their loo, shrug dismissively and, without hesitation, push open the door to the female toilets where they queue impatiently for the cubicles before liberally spraying tiled walls, seats and floors, emerging satisfied and carelessly doing up their flies as they head, unwashed, for the doors. The women shake their heads at this desecration of their most private space but remain aggressively silent.

At the same time as David Grant entered the cafeteria, but unnoticed by him at the time, a coach-load of blind Parisians has disgorged itself onto the melting tarmac and forty or more middle-aged people, link-armed, stepping uncertainly, brandishing white sticks and chaperoned by, at most, four talkative young assistants, crocodile in a none-too-straight line across the tiled floor with the same call of nature to satisfy. They are led by a man and a woman with minimal tunnel vision and a carer who is walking backwards, more concerned with the peloton than the yellow jersey. The file of visually handicapped makes its uncertain way to the toilet corridor just as David Grant approaches from a slightly different angle. The two with minimal vision reach the barricade at the same moment as David Grant and all three stop to assess the situation. Our hero hesitates, inhibited by his essential Britishness and the presence of such a crowd of blind toileteers, while the leaders also pause as they focus narrowly on the crossed brushes and the bucket. The main body of the party, however, are not aware of any problem and they cannon softly into their compatriots like the segments of a caterpillar ready for the next surge forwards.

David Grant holds open the door of the ladies loo – he has lived in France long enough not to cross his knees – and ushers the first two though. Then, realising the long-term consequences of generosity on his schedule, he steps quickly in behind the two he has assisted and holds the door open behind him for the rest of the party to enter. This they do, occasionally punctuated by a hurriedly exiting, head-shaking female. The party helpers, aware only that their charges continue to advance, concentrate on one or two of the more severely handicapped members who stray this way and that, clattering noisily into shiny display shelves and fridges full of ice creams. Panicked by the incoming throng, David Grant hastens across the tiled floor of the vast *toilette* and is fortunate to reach the bank of cubicles just as a woman emerges with a little girl. Without a backward glance to see if it is really his turn, he disappears inside and commences doing what is necessary. As he sits there, he is aware of raised French voices – not an entirely unusual phenomenon but noticeable in that it starts suddenly and does not abate.

On emerging and heading off to wash his hands, he is regaled by the sight of three blind Frenchmen peeing into washbasins, much to the chagrin of most of those present and the evident amusement of their helpers. No one has told them of any change in the arrangements and to a Frenchman, even a blind Frenchman, the most important facility is the *pissoir*, followed by the cubicle. Washbasins are 'fancy' and, anyway, nothing is traditional anymore. At one time a place for a pee was uniform in design and uncompromising in its functionality and lack of privacy. Now, they can be shaped like a washbasin and often are. Especially confusing to someone who can't see.

David Grant chooses casseroled beef, *épinard*, *frites* and a small beer. He also buys a token for the espresso machine for later and pays for it all with his bank card. He sits down at a table near the window and looks out onto a small children's playground where he can watch embryonic male egos and female temperaments forming among the brightly painted blocks and slides and see-saws and gaudily painted sprung cockerels. A small boy defiantly sits astride one of the cockerels, jigging back and forth, legs stretched straight ahead like a rodeoist, as a little girl, presumably his sister, screams for his abdication. A small row of similar devices stands unoccupied.

Eventually a woman lifts the boy off the toy by hooking her arms around his chest from behind, his head momentarily thrashing in frustration between her breasts. She whispers something in his ear and the thrashing stops as he stands quietly and takes his mother's hand, half leading her back into the restaurant and towards the shop. The little girl, meanwhile, climbs aboard the cockerel but the pleasure of triumph is brief. Without an audience and with something a good deal more satisfying in prospect, she slides off almost as quickly as she had mounted and pursues her retreating family. David Grant eats his dinner and thinks about the woman. Something is familiar but he can't quite place it.

Moments later, the little group returns and makes its way via the restaurant back to the children's playground – both children brandishing frozen chocolate bars on sticks and the woman taking the top off a bottle of still water. The children wander about, a competition over who can lick the quickest rapidly replaced by one in which the child who can make the treat last the longest will be the victor. The woman sits down on a bench, crosses her legs and swings around sideways so that she can keep an eye on her charges. She is pretty and slim – almost coltish – with that characteristic French build of narrow, almost boyish hips, an almost non-existent waist combined with a flat stomach, but generous breasts. Her hair is cut short but very neat – her natural brown lifted with subtle blonde highlights around her temples. She wears trainers, well-cut jeans and a white cotton blouse with a deep V-neck. Her skin is the colour of a rich tea biscuit and it is flawless.

Then what is familiar occurs to him. It is her eyes.

David Grant had worked for three months in a consultancy role for his old employer a couple of years before. It was one of those silly things, a business design job he had done during the last few months of his career had come up for replacement but nobody really knew what they had in the first place.

'A lot easier to know what must be done if we know what must go!' an old colleague chortled down the phone. 'What about three months?'

'How much?' had been David Grant's circumnavigated reply. He and Élodie didn't really need the money but if the price was right he knew his wife would be amenable. And he wanted to do it. He had always needed recognition, having realised long before that outrageous success would never come his way. Recognition, and the essential respect that goes with it, is the ordinary man's opiate.

'Name your price,' the voice responded, and then added quickly, 'as long as it's not too high.'

They settled on an excessive, Élodie-convincing figure, and he had his flights paid and the use of one of the bank's flats in Kensington, so for that brief period he lived as he never lived, lived as he might have always wanted to live. The bank's largesse didn't run to taxis (although he could have well afforded them on his daily rate) and he had always used the Underground in the past, so he commuted daily from his prestigious address by way of the Piccadilly Line and the Met and Circle to Liverpool Street or some-times used the District and Circle to Monument and walked to the office in Broad Street.

With nothing much to do in the evenings, he often worked late. He liked to appear keen and unaffected by advancing years. He nursed a forlorn hope that they might repeat the invitation; that they couldn't, after all, do without him. The trouble with opiates is that one constantly needs another fix. Besides, this was a bank in London at the beginning of the twenty-first century. When going-home time arrived every five-thirty, the only sign of anyone having a life other than deals and stocks, derivatives and data networks, Bloomberg's statistics and the lure of annual salary-exceeding bonuses, was the little bevy of status-con-firming secretaries emerging from glass-walled sanctums around the perimeter of the open-plan office, shrilling their farewells over their shoulders, joshing with the younger traders and IT specialists, and propelling their neatly dressed figures on high-heels towards Liverpool Street station and the uniform commuter sprawl of inner Essex.

The rest worked on, some absorbed in their tasks, all absorbed in self-advancement, until home or the local bars beckoned or exhaustion took its toll and, one by one, they leant back in their chairs, yawned and stretched like the crucified, exchanged a few words, logged off their terminals, pushed their arms into tailored and designer jackets, and made for the lifts, releasing state-of-the-art mobiles from bags and pockets, quick-dialling friends and loved-ones.

An advantage of travelling back to Kensington at eight in the evening was the occasional occurrence of an empty seat on the train. On a typical day during that autumn, he left the office and chose to walk to the Monument station instead of catching the Circle at Liverpool Street and having to change at King's Cross.

He walked slowly, looking into occasional bars where the over-rich paid dearly for warm beer and good-quality but ill-served wine – the red too cold and the white too warm. At the Monument, he headed for the westbound platforms and waited for the train. When it came in, he pressed the button to open the door and was pleased to see an empty seat with its back to the window.

He saw her almost immediately and that's where he spotted the resemblance with the woman at the service station north of Lyon. She had the most sunken eyes he had ever seen. Deep and half-hooded, she was almost like a subspecies, beautiful in a new category of beauty he had never considered before. He found himself smiling at her – not a thing that usually went down well in London – but she smiled back at him, probably as a young acquaintance would smile at one of her father's contemporaries. She was probably in her mid to late twenties. He stared at her, then looked away out of embarrassment, feigned an exaggerated indifference, did that older-man thing of seeming to be animated and a little lost and confused, his mouth pursing,

dry lips bitten, his glasses requiring to be cleaned ostentatiously with an outsized cotton handkerchief and his nose
needing to be blown, but his eyes kept moving back to hers
as if hooked by the line on a fishing rod. She also seemed
locked onto his eyes and didn't seem to mind his attentions.
Whenever he returned his gaze to her face, she was looking
at him, confident, expressionless, without intention or any
sense of the exhibitionist, without invitation or rejection, a
steady inscrutable gaze. She seemed to know it wasn't lust,
that she simply attracted him, perhaps reminded him of
someone from his past. But she didn't. It was she whom he
would be reminded of, *she* who would be part of *his* past,
this day on the autoroute when he clatters his token into
the espresso machine and returns to his seat to watch the
young mother . . .

At the next stop some rowdy young bucks got on, very
much the worse for wear. Attracted by the lone girl and
emboldened by alcohol and their numerical superiority,
they started to make lewd comments which quickly moved
on to lunging at her unnecessarily as the train accelerated
and swayed.

'Sorry, darling,' one of them said, resting his hand too
long on her leg to steady himself, 'these trains don't half
rock and roll, eh? Nice thigh, though.' He sucked air
through clenched teeth and rubbed his hands together.

The others giggled.

David Grant caught her eye and saw just a moment of
fear coupled with disgust. He motioned her to sit in a seat
fortunately just vacated beside him. She quickly got up and
crossed the train.

'You er dad then?' He remembered thinking how it was
funny that these products of Eton and Harrow seemed to
have honed their accents on the municipal shabbiness of
Albert Square.

32

'I could be,' David Grant replied, pulling his shoulders back.

'Sugar daddy, more like,' one of them quipped and they lost interest, which was, however, quickly restored when David Grant and the woman stood up simultaneously as the train slowed for South Kensington station.

If he had spoken to her, David Grant would have undoubtedly said, 'Your stop, too?', surprised at the coincidence and worried for a moment that, following her recent experience with the Hooray Henries, she would now fear the threat of an aged stalker. If she had spoken to him, she'd simply have said, 'Yes,' and thought nothing more about it.

As it was, they left together, closely followed by the cavorting mob, one moment intensely curious about the odd couple and the unanswered questions of their chance encounter, the next applauding the athletic antics of one of their number as he threw himself sideways, both feet on the tiled wall or a pillar, effectively and, it has to be said, impressively imitating the gravity-defying moves of Spider-man. The girl, who was probably five feet eight inches tall, looked up into David Grant's eyes and slowly took his arm, a whisper of hand and coat on his. He squeezed hers into his side gently to acknowledge her move. He wanted her to know he had noticed. The lads all roared their approval.

'I was right, see?' one of their number bellowed. 'She's giving him one once a week in return for a fancy apartment! That's if he can still get it up!'

David Grant stopped and wheeled the reluctant girl around to face the throng.

'Any of you got children?' he asked.

'Not that I know about,' said one, and the others laughed in affected falsettos.

'Well,' said David Grant quietly, 'When you do, and if

you manage to have a daughter, and if she grows up as proud of you as you are of her, one of the compensations of growing old will be your daughter taking your arm occasionally, without bidding, without pressure on your part, or a desire to please on hers. I do hope it happens to you because, if it does, you'll never forget those moments until the ends of your lives. Now, why don't you go on ahead and think about what I've said.'

The lads listened, paused and then did what they were told. One of them even apologised. They almost ran up the stairs without a backward glance, fed the ticket machine and were gone.

She didn't remove her arm from his but inclined her head and whispered a 'thank you' as they also ascended the stairs. She laughed when, instead of using her ticket at the barrier, she stood close behind him and tricked the machine into thinking they were one person.

'Here,' she said, passing her ticket to him, 'a souvenir from today for a White Knight.'

He took the ticket, looked at it for a moment and then put it into his pocket.

'How did you know you could get away with it?' she asked when they had reached the street and, to his surprise, set off in the same direction.

He laughed, almost out of relief. 'I didn't,' he confessed, 'but I guessed they would treat me differently than you and that actual fighting was not on their agenda. Aggression, possibly. Towards you, I mean. But not fighting. Anyway, they weren't bad. Did you hear that one say sorry? They were just a bit drunk and bold and unpredictable.'

'You could have left it with the sugar-daddy story.'

'Neither of us is the type,' he replied.

'I was, once, years ago,' she said.

'And if I'd been wealthy and I'd met you, I could have been the type too,' he replied, almost in a whisper. He said it because he didn't want her to think he was sitting in judgement of her – that it was necessarily wrong to be either the daddy or the sugar. But he also said it out of exquisite envy.

'He was married, in his fifties and terribly distinguished,' she continued as if she hadn't heard his confession or its hidden declaration. 'I was twenty-one, just at the sore stage of a broken love affair and, for a while, I lived in his London flat all week while he went home to Dorset and his family at the weekends.' She took his arm again. 'The first Christmas finished it for me. All the shopping for his family and me taking days off work to receive deliveries from Harrods. And then the awful quiet for ten days while he was away.'

'Did you leave him?'

'Yes. I just left a note for his return. I did love him, you know. It wasn't that I was using him. It was just the timing. I suppose I was homeless after Giles and panicked a bit.' She laughed quietly. 'But then I was homeless after my "title" too.'

'He had a title?'

She laughed and looked at him. 'Yes. Are you shocked?'

'No. Not at all.'

'Oh, I suppose I was flattered. But he was very attractive. He was warm, too. He held me as if he was a big teddy bear. I just dissolved into him. But I don't think I used him, do you?'

David Grant shook his heady vigorously. 'No, not at all. You were both adults. There was a need there. I suppose we are all needy in some way. But used? No.' He wanted to change the subject, knowing that if he said more she might doubt his sincerity. 'But you've someone else now?'

'Yes, he owns a club. A nice nightclub, quite near here. My "title" took me there one night, funnily enough. He was a member. It's one of those members' clubs for writers and

35

entertainers. Politicians seem to like the place, too. It's discreet. I met him there but nothing really clicked until long after I had left ... you know ... him. But he always works late so I have plenty of time to myself. I like it that way. Time to think. I work in advertising near the Post Office Tower but I've been down to St Katherine's visiting a friend. She's got a baby. Sweet. Hard work, though.'

'You've no children?'

'Not that I know about,' the girl echoed, then laughed.

They walked on in silence, she still with her arm in his. He looked at her once under a street light and she looked back up at him, her eyes almost hidden by the shape of her head and the play of the shadows. She smiled a half-smile that was already familiar and which melted him every time he saw it cross her face. He felt flattered by her attentions but knew that, to her, they were probably unconscious, his churning mind and curious elation unmatched by her comfortable, uncomplicated trust.

'This is me,' she said, suddenly stopping, and quickly adding, 'I hope you haven't come too much out of your way?'

'Not at all,' he replied, 'I'm just up at the end and on the right.'

'That's good then. Thank you very much. You've been very kind.'

'It was nothing. Can I say something? Don't get me wrong, I don't want you to misunderstand me.'

'OK.' She removed her arm from his, an almost imperceptible whisper of hand separating from coat, just like its first arrival – a change in their relationship unconsciously signalled.

'It's just that I think you have the most interesting eyes I have ever seen.'

'Interesting? Not beautiful?'

'Yes, beautiful as well. But "interesting".'

'Is that what you were looking at on the train? My eyes?'

'Now I feel ashamed.'

'Why should you?'

He shrugged, unable to answer, stepping slightly away from her. Aware of his discomfort, she spoke.

'I found you attractive, too. Kind. Aware. Most people on the Tube switch off; just exist.' She changed the subject again. 'You don't think I was using my "title", do you? Really?'

'No. In any case, if we are used, we choose to be used.'

'Well, goodnight then. Thank you again.'

'Goodnight.'

She kissed him on the cheek and, for a brief moment, he caught the scent of something expensive. He put a hand lightly on her waist but did not kiss her back. She stepped up onto the stone steps leading to her front door.

'Perhaps you'll rescue me again some day?'

'Perhaps,' he replied as he set off again. He looked back and she waved as he heard a clink of keys.

'I don't even know your name?' she suddenly shouted.

He stopped and turned around. 'And I don't know yours,' he said. 'Mine's . . .'

'. . . No, don't tell me. Not unless we meet again. Let's leave it that way. I wish it had been you, by the way, my "title".'

'I'll never forget you,' he blurted out, and then regretted his incaution.

She waved and was gone.

David Grant walked on up the road, his head full of might-have-beens and memories of unfulfilled encounters when he was young, and the already fading image of the girl.

Back in his flat, he thought again about her as he heated some soup for a late supper – too confused and upset to bother with making a proper meal.

He thought about her strangely intense anxiety about using people, or more precisely the man she called her 'title'. 'You don't think I used him?' she had asked. Why ask me, he wondered. Why was it so important to her to obtain the affirmation of someone whose name she didn't even know? Had he, her 'title', said that to her when the inevitable 'whys' and 'you knew the scores' and the 'I love you stills' were traded? No break-up is ever clean. He didn't know, but he didn't believe it just ended on her departure, the empty flat or her tear-stained note. No one could lose her without a backward glance, he thought. Not even a man who had it all, wealth, position, a family in prosperous Dorset, a title. David Grant had known her for, perhaps, twenty minutes and already she was sewn into him, altering him. And, he thought, in the end it actually had nothing to do with her eyes, beautiful, strange and interesting though they were. She had a presence, an innocence and honesty, a persona that was unique and captivating.

He stirred the soup and took some Tesco Metro baps out of the fridge.

'I don't think she uses people,' he reasoned. 'It's a choice to be used; to be in someone's sway, to be locked into an emotional prison of one's own making.' A choice that he knew he had already made with the beautiful girl on the District Line train to Richmond.

He never did see her again. He couldn't even be sure of the door at which they parted. He began to wonder if the event had even taken place. But then, there was the ticket. 'Tower Hill' it said, where she must have walked to from St Katherine's Dock. He had put it into his wallet that same evening, imagining he smelled her hand cream or the expensive perfume he didn't recognise.

As he sits watching the woman taking infrequent sips from her water bottle, it becomes imperative to find the ticket. He knows the memento will still be there, in his wallet, but where? He starts a laborious search, left-hand side or right-hand? Or perhaps not in the main part but in one of the peripheral pockets on the outside. Eventually, he finds it. It is still quite flat and uncreased; a sickly pink colour that had been so everyday and familiar in his London days but now only seems strange. He smiles to himself and puts it back in the same spot.

When he looks up, the woman and her children have gone. There is no sign of any of them; no discarded water bottle, no melting ice creams, no voices carried on the breeze. Just a children's playground; spring-footed cockerel gently rocking. He stands up, stretches his legs, and drives to Dijon without stopping, booking into the Campanile just off the autoroute and availing himself of the Chef's Special and a carafe of house red before turning in.

The First Wednesday

David Grant awakens with a headache. He stands up and sways for a moment before rubbing his eyes and shuffling into the bathroom.

'Must have been the wine,' he thinks, and remembers he drank the same-sized carafe he habitually ordered when Élodie was with him. 'Not the Campanile's fault then,' he admits. And there had been the long journey. He takes one of his rather ineffective Aspirine du Rhône which at least has the merit of tasting palatable and remembers his prescription. He decides he will go into Dijon, find a *pharmacie* and get it made up. He rakes around in his wallet, finds it, and pairs it with his *carte vitale* that will probably pay for most of it, and begins running a bath. He turns on the television cantilevered out from the wall next to the window and zaps though the channels looking for anything other than cartoons. Eventually he finds an American news channel that would probably have shown Adolf up in a good light had it been around seventy years before, and lets it propagandise away happily while he bathes and washes his hair under the shower.

By the time he walks across the car park to the restaurant for breakfast and the television channel has settled the world's ills by separating us all into, on the one hand, America's friends and, on the other, the bad guys, his headache has virtually gone.

A waitress intercepts him as he makes for a table by the window, looking past him for any dawdling family member.

'Bonjour, Monsieur. You are alone?'

'Yes.'

She waves her arm vaguely in the direction he had been travelling anyway, indicating he could sit anywhere. It is just after nine o'clock and the rush of business people is over. A few families sit eating their fill, the parents making the most of the generous buffet while the children, bemused by their parents' unusually prodigious breakfast appetites, either sit obediently but demonstrably bored, or, deliberately unnoticed by their gorging parents, systematically break hard rolls into brittle crumbs that shower thickly to the floor like camel dandruff before running around the table trying to pick fights with their siblings.

David Grant sits down at a window seat and then immediately rises to look at the buffet. He, too, will eat more than usual as someone else is doing the work and the amount he eats will make not a jot of difference to the price. On the whole, he is a careful man with his money. Not mean, as the clichéd Scotsman is often portrayed, but careful. This he inherited from his father who was also careful and frequently mean. He puts cereal and yoghurt onto a tray, boils an egg in the strange contraption beloved by the Campanile chain, selects some hunks of baguette and helps himself to far too much butter and marmalade. Back at his table, he makes almost as much mess with his baguette as the children had with their hard rolls.

Not knowing the idiosyncrasies of the machine, he finds the egg is undercooked. Still, he eats it, and indulges in a childhood pleasure of breaking bread and dipping it into the aqueous mess inside the shell.

He settles his bill with his card and crosses over to his room to pack. By the time he has returned the key and driven out of the car park, his headache has completely

41

gone and what had seemed his most important mission in Dijon is forgotten. He parks near the centre and plays holiday visitor for a while, looking in the tourist shop windows at the infinite variety of mustards, visits a museum dedicated to the grain and wanders about the old town. The city soon bores him, however, so he goes back to his car and drives out towards the autoroute without a clue as to where to go. He fills up with petrol at the first opportunity and realises he is heading north, rather than north-west towards Paris and, incidentally, close to where, at this very moment, Élodie has already been up for hours, sitting silently, cross-legged on the floor, in a room full of similarly silent people whose blank expressions are closed doors on a pandemonium and chaos only they experience. In the days when the autoroutes around Paris had been incomplete, and a veritable nightmare to boot, he had used this route via Reims to get to and from the South of France and, without thinking, he begins to retrace his steps towards the Channel.

This wasn't his intention, of course. He is feeling melancholy without Élodie and doesn't want to pass the road to where she is taking part in her course. He is incredibly proud of her and her 'other life', as he sometimes calls it, but from time to time, when his frail confidence has taken a battering, he looks upon her discovery of Vipassana and, by definition, of herself, as a child might upon the arrival of a younger brother or sister – something or someone diluting focus on himself. He knows he is foolish and that he awards himself places she cannot visit, but that is him – he knows how small a place his personal things really occupy. But she is different. With Vipassana, she became absorbed and frequently lost in thought, distant and abstracted, and he felt excluded. His melancholia transfers itself from his wife to thoughts of the killing fields of northern France and he decides to fulfil another long-held ambition – to visit some of the war graves. So he rumbles on into the Champagne and round by Reims before heading north-westwards into the battlefields of the First World War, picking up a sandwich on the way. As he drives, what had started out as a cool but bright day turns hot and close.

From the autoroute there is virtually nothing to see. It's as though the road builders have carefully picked a sanitised route through huge fields and past vast colliery spoil heaps, avoiding the dreadful reminders of European conflict. A new road for a new, forgiving, forward-facing Europe. It isn't how he remembers his first holidays to France by car. Then, in the days before the cat's cradle of northern autoroutes, the roads threaded their way past cemetery after cemetery. To start with it was a surprise – a triumph even. 'Look, there's one!' It was rather like when they espied Mont St-Michel from miles away across the countryside, their first vineyard or corrugated-iron Citroën van; it was something new, something sometimes anticipated, sometimes a surprise, read about, singled out for spotting, if possible, as confirmation of France's differences, to boast about or report back to family or friends . . . But the sheer numbers of cemeteries quickly replaced that novelty of discovery with an awful, monotonous, horrifying, endlessly repeated inevitability. The nameless living in those parts were outnumbered a hundred, a thousandfold by the celebrated dead. It is a land that can never really recover, never move beyond the accident of geography, never discover a definition of life in the presence of such a host of dead. Can never. Perhaps *should* never.

Then they had noticed their first German cemetery, the stones black and forbidding.

'That's because they were the bad men,' chirruped his daughter, aged about seven at the time. 'White stones for our good people, black for the enemy.' The clarity and simplicity of American television news channels in the words

43

of a young Scottish child. He and his then wife had exchanged glances at their daughter's certainties. They were, when all's said and done, all dead – whoever was right. Both sides had God on their side. And they had all been told to get back to work when they emerged that Christmas to find that they looked the same, sang the same carols, played football by the same rules, shared the simple hopes of life, love, parenting and homeland, and a lasting hate of Flanders.

But after a while, driving along that endlessly straight road into the dusk, the white stones of the Allies seemed incongruous and the black more appropriate. Black for the night, for the hell they were all in. Black for the wilful destruction of human ambition. White was a virginal colour, white for sanitisation – for sanity perhaps – a colour rightly or wrongly associated with being clean, with being unblemished, with innocence. Picasso's white dove of peace, probably his lasting legacy, forever underlining the virtue of white in the war-and-peace stakes. And he remembers how the sight of the cemeteries palled and appalled. One, two, three perhaps. Then a German one or two. They must have been crossing and recrossing the wavy line of the battlefront, the Allies burying their dead and the Germans theirs. After fifteen, twenty, twenty-five cemeteries, an almost forgotten one for every one that was well kept; they wanted them to go away, or for there to be a way to drive out of this immense, endless and inevitable repetition.

'How does anyone live hereabouts?' his wife had asked, gazing out of the window at yet another study in primary colour, geometry and perspective. The question hung unanswered in the warm stale air of the car because it was unanswerable. But it still had to be asked.

He had always wanted to go back, just as he had wanted to visit Oradour and Auschwitz, to see the appalling residue of unspeakable error, to grieve at man's folly, but not to try

44

to learn the unlearnable. Seeing such things may be a pilgrimage but they are not revealing. One doesn't find any answers. These are not Jerusalem to the Jew or Christian, Mecca to the Muslim, Mother Ganges to the Hindu, where the faithful are rewarded and inspiration is gifted by the bucketful for those who seek it. These are at the other end of the scale of human endeavour. These are the black holes of despair, the pits of the world, the sewers and the landfills, the places where the sun should never shine and where birds should refrain from singing.

As he drives along, his thoughts turn to Élodie and to the first time he had taken her to the Vipassana Centre. It might have later become a crisis for her but his, at their parting, was almost as profound. Not being able to contact her had made him think of it in terms of her death. 'This is how it would be if she ever died before me,' he pondered. And as he contemplated that possibility, he began to believe she was dead. To start with it was simply 'dead to him' – carried off by a belief system that would render him trivial, irrelevant and a distraction. Then, as he drove the endless miles through pouring rain, his sense of loss became real. It was as though she was actually dead and he started to think in terms of bereavement – of how he would feel if he never saw her again.

He was surprised at how soon he lost his temper with her.

It was still on the way back home. Strange city, rain pouring down, wipers ineffective on the oil-smeared windscreen, signposts ignoring the one place he needed to be. And she was not there to navigate. It had always been like that, him perusing the map and anxiously looking for landmarks for her, or the other way about. No fancy GPS satellite navigation system for them. Only the Michelin map and a misplaced confidence that he could find his way back on the same roads that had brought him without a hitch.

Why wasn't she there? She was always there and even when she was unsure and they argued and he took it onto himself to drive on regardless, she would always get them back where they should be. Her approach, when driving, was to stop anywhere and look at the map herself, disregarding the unnecessary toots from irritated motorists who could tell quite clearly, from the number plate if not by the hesitant driving, that this was a car well away from its normal hunting ground.

At last the autoroute signs had reappeared, so he drove north to turn south onto an autoroute about three metres deep in spray thrown up by Norbert Dentressangle, Globetrotter and Willi Betz. His heart stopped racing, he apologised to his wife, thanked his God and settled down to the long journey. As it grew dark, tired of the tapes he had brought with him, he put the radio on and tuned into 107.7, the autoroute traffic news channel. There being nothing to report, France Gall was singing. Distinctive, timeless, beautifully executed, pitch-perfect, the clearest diction and somehow tragic whatever the message. You could hear it in her voice, the woman who had been in at the beginning of French pop, who should now be fêted regularly on every TV music programme, but who had suffered the double tragedy of the loss of husband and daughter at different times and for different reasons, and was now considered reclusive and seemed, to all intents and purposes, invisible. The girl who had been to her namesake country what Sandi Shaw, Cilla Black and Dusty Springfield had been to Britain and Brenda Lee to the USA; who had matured and survived throughout the seventies and eighties and even into the nineties; the woman who had broken hearts and had half a dozen songs dedicated to her by admirers and bereft lovers, now faded from view. But still she was on French radio every day, as now. ''C'est bon que tu sois là', she sang, the keyboard and guitar answering France Gall's slow message, the percussion forcing the pace towards the inevitable conclusion, the brass section overpowering everything to be quickly defeated by a soaring, twisting, goose-pimpling guitar solo; France coming back again to be finally defeated by the brass and a single guitar note.

At that point the tears came. He sniffed, coughed and wiped his eyes with the back of first one hand and then the other, but he couldn't control himself. With the tears came a sobbing that, momentarily, he thought must be someone else, the sound unfamiliar to him. He rarely wept but was making up for a recent past of emotional restraint. He considered stopping dangerously on the roadside, his little car virtually invisible in the dusk and spray, but resolved to continue, at least until the next services. There, he would refill the car, knowing that standing in the wind and rain with the hose in the spout, watching the litres and euros racing each other on the meter, his head would clear and make his loneliness more profound.

They had often been separated before. Indeed, his memories were full of leave-taking and greeting. Railway stations and airports, her face bobbing about trying to catch a first or last glimpse, the broad smile of recognition, the raised hand waving, the heedlessly blown kiss. But that was it. For every parting there was the certainty of reconciliation. He thought it could last for ever. In his present frame of mind, he considered a different equation, one that did not resolve.

He pulled into the overtaking lane, cursing a Dutch-registered car that seemed to lose its bottle every time it performed the same routine, its brake lights once again shining brightly as the driver hesitated before plunging into the wall of spray. 'Is the silly sod afraid of becoming a statistic?' he shouted, his anger dispelling his sadness for a moment. He shrugged. We'll all be statistics one day, he thought. Born, married, dead. Records kept. Entries opened, updated and closed.

At the service station he filled the tank and parked up, paid for his fuel, dropped his euro into the coffee machine, pressed the wrong button and justified his choice with sugar on the grounds that he needed the energy. When at last the coffee had been made and the little stage in the machine had elegantly dropped to let him retrieve the polystyrene cup, he caught sight of himself reflected dully in the painted glass on the front of the machine. In amongst the exhortations to enjoy a perfect cup of coffee, the sinuous curve of white steam rising from bone china, a pair of parted female lips reaching for the sensual liquid of a thousand advertising campaigns was a haggard face perched at the top of a darkened, stooped frame. A reflection of one. Alone. He turned away, conscious of a small child peering up at him curiously. He aimed for a tall table surrounded by four tall chairs, clearly designed to be virtually unusable to anyone other than a basketball player and, even with his lofty frame, struggled to reach a sitting position which firmly lifted his feet off the ground. His lower legs swung around crazily as they had when he was a child at his parents' dining table. He remembered how, without feet on the floor giving purchase, it had been difficult to talk to the person sitting next to him without a violent and vigorous twisting action that inevitably ploughed his loosely hanging shoes into any adult seated in close proximity.

He smiled at the memory, even though it had unjustly earned him sharp reprimands from parents and injured alike, and then frowned as his dark thoughts returned to his imagined widowerhood. He had never minded being alone in the knowledge that his wife was in the background. He hadn't even minded when he had been between wives – such had been the hectic shape of his business and personal life at the time. But now, with the reflection in the coffee machine confirming his advancing years and the instance of Élodie's first visit to Vipassana, premonitions of death and permanent separation invaded his consciousness. He would be returning to an empty house, empty save for Queen Elizabeth who was not keen on long car journeys and much preferred solitude to the delights of the auto-route. 'God save the Queen,' he thought. 'At least she's at home; she'll be pleased to see me.'

But the thought of the dog wasn't enough. He looked around him at the couples – the threes and the fours, the pair nearing his own age with an ancient and bewildered crone in tow – before shuffling his body into freefall for the floor, searching unsuccessfully for a France Gall 'Best of' album in the boutique and heading for the door and the persistent rain.

He felt calmer and sadder as the rain lashed down and the wipers beat their mindless rhythm on the screen. On would go 107.7, then off again. On to counter loneliness, boredom and fatigue, off to allow time to think and to sharpen the wits. More France Gall, then Julien Clerc – he with the voice like a clarinet, the Beatles' 'A hard day's night', Queen's 'The show must go on'. That would have brought back the tears were it not for the announcer talking over the end of the track and quickly spoiling the moment, revealing details of bad weather conditions that were plainly self-evident. How many British radio stations would have been so generous with air time for French music, he wondered. The only French songs he could think of hearing in the UK since the days of Piaf, Charles Trenet and Maurice Chevalier – they were often on the BBC Light Programme of his youth – was something called 'Joe le Taxi' and 'Je t'aime . . . moi non plus' by Serge Gainsbourg and Jane Birkin, and the latter was more about the fact that it was sexy, outrageous and a bit mucky-sounding, which fed an English perspective on France at the time, than because it was French. Anyway, Jane Birkin was English, the archetypal English rose, all white-skinned and virginal, with a perfect accent and floaty dresses, a slim boyish model's figure; ravished by that brilliant, sinister foreigner Serge with his ugly face and unkempt appearance. Good and evil. Light and dark. The white and the black, again. And it wasn't as though French music was bad – far from it. Nor would the language excuse wash. Contrary to arrogant British parochialism, the average French person was no more able to understand the words, let alone the nuances and half-disclosures of English lyrics, that the other way about.

About fifty kilometres from home on that long haul from the Vipassana Centre, the rain finally stopped and the wipers could be turned off, other than when he was overtaken by the odd fast-moving car and the screen coated with spray. Long before time he pulled into the overtaking lane when approaching slower-moving trucks for the same reason. A bright moon lit the road sporadically as it leapt, an almost perfect circle, from one side of the twisting Rhône Valley to the other before hiding behind black-shadowed rocky outcrops or clouds like smoke from a forest fire. He gratefully paid his last toll and hissed up the link road, slowing unnecessarily at a deserted roundabout and moving quickly through a silent, sleeping world.

When he finally reached home, Queen Elizabeth hardly raised her head from her bed before yawning, biting the claws of one paw for a moment and then falling asleep again. He wandered about, stumbling into furniture and mislaying things – moving unconsciously into the role of an old man losing more than just his wife. Then he saw the light on the answer phone flashing. It was Élodie. Moments before the Vipassana self-imposed rule of silence was applied, she had sent a message hoping he'd had a safe journey and telling him she loved him. He played the message three times, answering her out loud, saying the same things back to her, his voice incongruous in the empty house as if she could hear him better that way, before erasing it, embarrassed at his fanciful depression. Then he wished he'd kept the message for the days ahead before going to bed and sleeping unremembered dreams . . .

He eats his sandwich at one of those *aires*, café-less, service-less stopping places – little more than a fly-strewn toilet, a trashed telephone, a herd of refectory bench-tables and a map of the area – before leaving the motorway and moving along straight roads into Picardy and the Pas-de-Calais. To start with he finds nothing, but then, almost by accident, in a small wood he sees a rusty gate and a footpath leading thirty metres or so towards a walled square of grass and stones. It is one of those cemeteries that no one nation can claim to be truly their own, so evidence of ownership and pride manifested in immaculate maintenance is absent. There is no sign explaining its history and, having parked on the verge, there not even being a lay-by, David Grant has to half lift the gate as he pushes it open very much against its will. The rusting hinge squeaks and groans at the unwarranted intrusion. At the noise, two magpies flap black and white from a tree on the edge of the wood and perch clumsily on the wall at the far side, regaining their balance after rocking to and fro for a moment and facing away from him, ready for a hasty withdrawal should that prove necessary. They turn their heads around and look over their backs, eyeing the stranger suspiciously, their long tails flicking up and down as they stretch their wings momentarily before folding them neatly against their bodies.

He makes a slight kissing sound, a sound he has found to almost always comfort nervous garden birds, and then turns his attention to the rows of stones. The birds hop into the air and turn to face him but make no attempt to leave. Judging by the long grass and the cemetery's air of sad neglect, human visitors to the dead community of two thousand or more sleeping youths are few and far between. Many of the stones look official – regulation size, regulation shape – names carved using the same neat characters. They are mostly French, although there are some Belgian and British stones, a few Canadians and one or two American. Many say 'A British soldier' or 'A French soldier', rather than quoting a name. One or two have numbers that have become indecipherable over the years and, in one corner, there is a small sad row of six-pointed stars and purposefully non-Christian edifices with 'A soldier from an Indian regiment' carved in scarcely readable characters. Could it be that some of those 'Indians' were Hindus and Muslims, laid uncharacteristically in the ground, alongside Jewish fallen long before Jew and Muslim, Muslim and Hindu learned to really mistrust each other and found history within living memory to justify those doubts? Before bigotry became king and threatened the world, had they fought shoulder to shoulder on the same side, intolerant of an intolerant enemy in a war that they were told threatened the world? It is as though, in that little, sleeping graveyard, the answer to everything about man's stupidity and salvation is there for the taking.

David Grant strolls around, crouching down to run his fingers over worn and mossy lettering or standing back to deliberately shield the text from the sun better. He thinks of this little cemetery in the wider context, a taster for a thousand, an unrepresentative crumb in the bakery of folly, and his heart sinks at thought of the atrocities committed since then all over the world. From time to time he catches sight of the curiously indifferent magpies who have forgotten all they had been doing before the stranger pushed open the rusty gate. They squawk occasionally and groom each other, even hop along the wall flapping their wings impatiently, but they stay put, sensing no danger from the intruder. The sun is strong and his head begins to hurt. He has 'done' the cemetery, his crushing of the grass indicating his thorough investigation of the whole area, but something makes getting back into the car an unattractive proposition. He feels drawn to the place, that to return to the twenty-first century via the battered old Corsa and a local commercial radio station is a form of betrayal – like visiting a cathedral and then going too quickly to a pub for lunch. There has to be a decent interval between reflection and modern life, between reverence and reality.

He walks out through the gate and pulls it shut behind him. As he does so, the magpies fall forward from the wall and start to flap their wings, almost hitting the stones as they gradually gain height like two planes flying in formation. They wheel around in a long climbing curve as they head back to the woods, landing again fifteen metres or so up in some hidden branches. He hears their giggling, chattering call once, maybe twice. 'Show's over,' they seem to be saying.

David Grant takes his time over re-entering the twenty-first century by leaning on the wall and looking up and down the deserted road. He hears the slightest sound about a hundred metres from him and sees a small deer break cover and look this way and that before skipping lightly over the tarmac and disappearing into the trees on the other side. His head hurts and the sun beats down upon the country road, softening the tar at the edges and making the road shimmer in the distance. He remembers that he and Élodie keep two cushions in the back of the car and decides to fold the front passenger seat almost flat and take a rest. At first he can't find the cushions but eventually realises they have fallen to the floor and half slipped under the front seats. He retrieves them and absent-mindedly pats any dust from the pseudo Jackson Pollock splatter of colours, useful for masking spilt wine and carelessly dropped crumbs of tuna from long-forgotten sandwiches. He attempts to make himself comfortable in the car but it is stiflingly hot, so he resorts to arranging the cushions on the grass verge between the car and the wall surrounding the field containing the cemetery and lies down.

He stares at the sky, watching a silent aircraft leaving a vapour trail that cools and spreads into fluffy billows against a sea of blue before he begins to ready himself for sleep. He stiffens and lies still as he hears the sound of an approaching tractor. Its powerful engine momentarily hesitates as it draws alongside the parked car, but then the note returns to its normal cruising pitch as the machine passes the cemetery gate and crosses the invisible track taken by the deer. Gradually the clatter of the tractor's engine fades and merges with the other sounds of the countryside, rustling leaves and birdsong, the intermittent screech of a chainsaw in the woods, the hoot of a passing train a kilometre or more away. David Grant closes his eyes, wincing at his throbbing head and breathes deeply.

Whatever it is, the heat of the sun, his aching head or heightened emotions as a consequence of visiting the cemetery, he begins to dream vividly, moving in and out of sleep; the reality of his waking moments and the creative imaginations of his unconscious merging and separating so that he can no longer segregate sleep from wakefulness, truth from fiction. He hears a vehicle engine which could be something new and real, a part of his dreamland or merely a recall of the tractor. He sees another vapour trail, now widely spread and vanishing slowly like clouds on a hot day, now two thin pencils of steam erupting from the rear of a plane, a mere dot, ten kilometres above him. He hears a dog bark and imagines the sound of gunfire, sometimes light and sharp like a twig snapping, sometimes deeper like a twenty-six hundredweight howitzer, sometimes rapid and repetitive like a machine gun. He hears the staccato chattering of the magpies and sees them again on the wall of the

54

cemetery, a thing he patently cannot do from his horizontal position in the warm grass beside his car. He sees the gravestones again, straight lines to left and right and away yonder to the far wall recently vacated by the magpies. He notices the wobbly V-shape of the stones' patterns as he lets his eyes follow their symmetry to the walls to his left and right. He sees flashing that might be the effect of his drumming headache or the crazy firework display of war. And, as he watches, he sees the gravestones stretch and twist, lengthen and narrow, their pale sandstone, cold granite and darker basalt metamorphosing into what might have been creased and shapeless sleeves, still stiff and uncompromising but seemingly capable of movement, of concealing articulated shoulders and elbows and wrists within . . .

A sudden sound brings him to consciousness as a car passes and he feels irritation at the interruption and an overwhelming desire to return to what has begun to seem more real than reality itself. He is rewarded by another sharp outburst, this time from two beaky-faced teachers dressed in the old-fashioned black and white of perhaps a century before, sleek and almost identical in their long dress jackets with dusty tails, waistcoats with looped watch chains and white shirts with stiff stand-up collars. The two strut back and forth between the serried ranks, brandishing sticks that are clearly badges of authority and a counter to breaches of discipline. These they sporadically clatter on an invisible floor before waving them in crazy arcs over the tops of the outstretched arms. Their charges are not visible, other than those arms that still hold only the vague promise of sinew, flesh and blood. To and fro the old tutors move, still no sign of the bodies of their pupils other than the slight mounds that lie behind each arm held aloft; horizontal six-foot truths with still hands raised, prepared to provide an answer to any question posed when bidden to do so, buried answers to two thousand or more questions, or two thousand different ways of phrasing the answer to a single question. But the question never comes and none can answer. Many don't even have names so they cannot be summoned to their feet to tell all they know by either of the strange schoolmasters. How can they tell their story with their identities hidden behind such imprecision as 'A soldier from an Indian regiment'?

But still the teachers parade, up and down and through the throng, clattering their sticks and making indistinct comments. And still the arms are outstretched, demanding attention, wanting their say, their moment of recognition, a word of praise, of encouragement, of glory. For whatever the masters ask, they will know the answer; know so much more than the living if there is anything more to know. It is as though, for all their pontificating, the teachers are secretly aware that they will be diminished by the posing of a question whose answer they do not know, their authority swept aside by superior intellect or an inside track to wisdom, or a redefinition of what matters and what does not. So they hold back, inhibited by that sea of outstretched arms, and retain their superiority by that very reticence. Their power lies in revealing nothing and disallowing revelation, in strutting and clattering their sticks on an invisible floor, on restricting their instruction to the haves and have nots. And still the guns pound, the lights flash and the raised hands remain still and silently accusing . . .

David Grant opens his eyes, shivers and feels an ache in his shoulders. For a moment he wonders where he is, aware only of a long stem of grass tickling his cheek, the smell of warm tyre rubber and of melting tar. His head spins and he closes his eyes again, rubbing his forehead and scratching his ear. Slowly his world expands and he spots the stand of trees at the top of the field. Turning over stiffly, he sees the road dropping down into a hollow and up again, a fraction of its former width on the other side before diminishing into the countryside, a thin deserted line between fences and short runs of wall. He stretches himself and yawns. He feels in his pocket for his car keys and drags himself slowly to his feet. Gazing around, he sees the cemetery just as he'd left it, the gate closed nicely to prevent intrusion by animals, the grass already recovering from his brief and reverential invasion, the standing stones tidy, upright, inanimate. He can see and hear nothing of the two magpies but sees instead a small flock of sparrows moving in and out of some bushes, too involved in a frantic flit back and forth, no doubt mobbing one of their number, to take much interest in the gangling human brushing his hair back, dusting off his trousers and retrieving the cushions from the grass.

A cool breeze suddenly picks up, first rustling the trees bounding the cemetery and then making a prematurely fallen leaf chatter and hiss along the road. David Grant shivers again, in spite of still feeling the heat of the day, and carefully replaces the cushions in the back of the car. He turns the car around; looking one last time through the gate at the serried ranks of stones imitating the inmates' last passing-out parade, and drives to Laon. There, on the hill, he finds a hotel with a comfortable room affording breathtaking views out over the plains to the north. After a relaxing bath to take the ache of his afternoon rest out of his back, he finds a chemist where they quickly make up his prescription and spends an hour in the bar drinking fizzy water to wash his medicine down ('Not to be taken with alcohol, it diminishes the effectiveness,' his doctor had warned him). Feeling much better, he goes into the restaurant where he sits alone by a panoramic window, trades effectiveness for pleasure by ordering a bottle of St-Émilion and eats a delicious *pot-au-feu* followed by a Breton-style *tarte aux pommes* with a hundred slices of apple carefully laid out in a beautiful pattern before stumbling off to bed.

He makes no sound other than gentle, even breathing,

He sleeps well and will remember nothing of any dreams he may or may not have in his vast bedroom on the top of the hill at Laon, the curtain moving restlessly by the open window. Maybe that's how it should be, in contrast to his strange visions beside the deserted road out in the battlefield.

The First Thursday

David Grant looks at his watch. It is half-past seven. A fitful wind rattles the window and the curtain flicks back and forth marking little victories and defeats in its war with the elements. He turns over and yawns, rubbing his eyes with the back of his hand. Before he remembers where he is, he thinks about Élodie and wishes she was with him. Suddenly, he needs her very much. He looks across the room and sees his suitcase, open, on the luggage gurney next to the shower. The window rattles again, followed by an almost soundless flick of the curtain like a matador taunting a bull. 'That's what must have woken me,' he thinks, and then he is glad of it. If he sets off early enough after breakfast, he can get back home to the Ardèche by the evening. He feels lonely and sad and his head is giving him trouble. Why attempt to solve the problem of one's wife's absence, he reasons, by separating himself from practically all he knows?

He breaks open a bottle of Vittel provided by the hotel and puts a pill in his mouth before washing it down straight from the bottle. It takes the best part of a third of a litre to get it down. He remembers his father's pill-taking abilities with a degree of envy: accompanied by the sounds of choking and with his thumb and forefinger pushed way down his throat, it was achieved without the assistance of water or any other liquid. An unconscious, virtuoso performance remembered a third of a century after his death.

And now he himself had come to this, old age and habitual pill-taking.

He showers and dresses carefully, discarding most of what he had worn the day before. His shirt is streaked with grass stains from his siesta and the trousers are far too creased for him. He considers ironing his trousers using the equipment provided in the room but he has three more pairs in the case and knows that, if he goes home, the need for 'keeping up' will disappear. He can do all that later in the week. Or just put them all to the wash.

At about eight-thirty, he goes downstairs carrying his wallet, having checked the presence of his credit cards before quitting his room. He finds his way to the restaurant, nodding at early risers eating their croissants and slices of baguette and drinking coffee from old-fashioned soup-bowl cups. Some, who have chosen the tables overlooking the view and who are clearly tourists, have little espressos and even the odd pot of tea with lemon, but he is surprised and charmed by the idea of the coffee bowl and when the waitress arrived at his table that's what he orders.

Cradling the coffee in both hands, he wonders that he would ever want to start the day any other way. There is something deeply comforting about lifting the steaming hot black liquid to the mouth, an aromatic drowning that restores life like nothing else. Being watched by an English family who discreetly point him out to their two young children, he rather plays to the gallery by dipping his baguette into the coffee before popping it, dripping and stained, into his mouth with an ostentatious smacking of the lips.

'It's a French habit,' the man whispers, and David Grant remembers his mental 'list of things to spot in France' all those years ago. Was he now part of the sideshow? An ancient, dipping his bread in his coffee? First World War cemeteries, road signs in different colours and rude old

Frenchmen? The smaller boy tears a piece of bread from his plate and, watching David Grant carefully to see if there is some secret step in the procedure he might have overlooked, sinks his morsel into his tea cup. The boy's eyes connect momentarily with those of David Grant and a flash of empathy precedes a look of concentration as the deed is done. His mother quickly intervenes and, using a spoon, puts the dripping bread onto her plate.

'It's a bad French habit,' she murmurs, casting a brief angry glance at her husband, who is now a part of a conspiracy with the supposed Frenchman in the undermining of good table manners and family authority. The boy looks briefly in David Grant's direction, who smiles before repeating the unacceptable behaviour with obvious relish and a trace of deliberate provocation.

In time the English family get up and walk past David Grant's table on their way to the door.

'Good morning,' David Grant says in his impeccable English accent.

The children stare at him and the parents looked slightly abashed.

Perhaps he hadn't heard.

The decision to go home gives his adventure scale and form and removes the unknown. It makes infinity finite, ties up loose ends, adds an end to its beginning and middle. This in turn gives him courage. There is no urgency and he doesn't have to try to retrace his steps all in one day. He thinks he might just take a look at Calais and then, perhaps, spend the night in Paris before returning to the Ardèche by way of the Massif Central. That way he'd be back by Saturday night and have a few stories to tell Michel. If he gets on with it, he'll be back in time for dinner. It being six hours or less from the south of Paris direct, he could easily leave at just after nine and dawdle through the beautiful countryside before fetching up in Le Crestet at about seven.

So, he presses his creased trousers up in his room after all and then packs his bag carefully before paying his bill using his French credit card for a change and going out to the car. Up on the hill it is extremely windy and quite chilly. He is glad to throw his case into the boot and quickly draws some cash from a machine before letting himself into the car. Within moments he is nosing out of the old town, slipping down past the sinuous arches of the Poma and making for the autoroute.

The autoroute to Calais is, to Frenchmen, largely a motorway to nowhere. The closer you get to Calais the percentage of British registrations grows, particularly in summer. Even the trucks seem to whittle down to large fleets with British and Spanish plates, the French having mainly veered off for Lille or the towns ranged along the Belgian border. Within a few kilometres of England's last French possession, the only things left that are truly French are the fact of driving on the right and the road signs.

David Grant pays his way off the autoroute network and aims for the impressive tower of Calais's town hall before parking along the front. It is too early for lunch, so he finds a beachside café and sits down with an espresso. It is still windy and he watches litter being played with by the wind on the broad pavement. He sips his coffee and the breeze and the troubled, restless litter take his mind back to a time that might have been yesterday or might have been long time ago, might have happened just as he remembered it or become a fiction drawn from base events or even a complete figment of his imagination. For the first time in his life, he finds he is letting things be what they want to be in his mind, their veracity becoming irrelevant, their detail now of the utmost importance . . .

He had watched her go.

As she made her way across the car park, she moved in and out of the pools of light radiating from the lamp posts.

One moment it was not at all clear that anyone was there – just a sense of movement that was so ephemeral it could have been a trick of light or of the imagination. The next, though, under the yellow glare, she was clearly to be seen, restless blonde hair brushing her shoulders, coat buttoned tightly around her slim body, her athletic walk taking her quickly back into the darkness.

He kicked at a stone that was spoiling the studied perfection of the tiled entrance. A chill breeze played with a discarded Snickers wrapper that hid behind a concrete pillar, only to be flushed out and toyed with again. Behind him, a low murmur of voices issued from a large room in which a business conference was winding up. He imagined the vaguely ridiculous sight of eager-faced, unguardedly enthusiastic, uniformly suited businessmen with blue ties, shiny black shoes and ludicrously large name badges hanging untidily from top pockets, and aggressive female executives treating their identities as a newly acquired fashion item, the slim girls wearing them at their waists, the fatter ones clipping them to their handbags or the thrusting lapels of jackets left unbuttoned to reveal monumental bosoms under stretched white cotton. But the conference and the revved-to-a-frenzy delegates were not his preoccupation.

He remembered the saying that they looked around if they loved you, so he waited and watched. Once, he thought she waved, and he waved back, but she was in the darkness and he knew he could have been mistaken. So, he waited a little longer and, as she reached the end of a line of parked cars and would, in a moment, be lost from his gaze, she did turn and stretched out her hand, holding it silently above her head, awaiting a response. He waved back, a silly wave, frantic and childish, conveying no message at all, betraying nothing of his feelings. And yet his mind was overflowing and in turmoil and he wished she'd wait in order for him to at least get his ideas in order – to have the luxury of saying, 'There she is and this is what I feel.' He knew, however unclear his feelings at that moment, they would be even more confused when she turned away. But of course she turned on her heel and, with a last flash of her pale coat in the streetlight, she was gone.

His life had been tormented by love, the lack of it as a child, and too much as he pursued and broke hearts, his and others, in and out of marriage in his maturity. By the time he was in his early fifties, and well into his second marriage, he knew enough of himself to know that he was good at friendships, average at intimacy, and poor at sustaining lasting relationships. He hurt people who were close to him by his impatience and an indifference that, no matter how hard he tried to combat, kept invading his personality like a cloud covering the sun. He enjoyed friendship, craved intimacy, and was groundlessly proud of his relationships, but found the first easy, the second necessary and the third hard work – rewarding on the odd occasions he managed to put all the pieces into the right places at the same time, but hard work.

He waited, looking out into the darkness, and fancied he heard her car pass the end of the approach road. It could have been her, so recently his companion in the bar, telling him about her life; her husband, with whom she was happy and content after a marriage that had outlasted those of so many of her friends, her holidays which meant so much to her, her increasingly fulfilling job, and her dreams – or at least those of her dreams she was prepared to share. On the other hand, the car powering down to the roundabout could easily have been someone else or even a figment of his imagination. What sounded like a quiet car engine and hissing tyres might have been nothing more than the wind tiring of the chocolate paper and turning its attention to the hedgerow and leafless branches of the trees in winter slumber.

And there, alone, and in that place of compromise on a cold night, an unexpected wave of contentment surged through him such as he had never felt before. He breathed deeply and felt completely whole, wanting to hold the moment for ever, to remember how he felt, even to die at that moment in the knowledge that nothing could ever be better. This had been a moment of discovery without really knowing what he had discovered. An arrival at a place he could not name by a means he could not describe. Lost and found at the same moment. The only thing he was sure of was that he knew for certain that this had been what he had sought all along. In the camaraderie of the school playground, the rugby club and the friendship and support of work colleagues; during his teenage fumblings at the cinema, his glasses so steamed up he could barely see Doris Day sitting in the bath surrounded by a cloud of improbable soap bubbles; in marriage and the hysteria of child-rearing, moneymaking and building dodgy wardrobes; in divorce and guilty loneliness; in a true love that ultimately destroyed both of them; in a string of ultimately unrewarding love affairs and in a second marriage where common purpose and bottomless generosity on her part were repaid by him with his demons – all had failed to open the door before which he now stood. Here, at last, was what he had always wanted. A nameless something, a feeling of inexpressible joy, a destination where, for the first time in his life, there was no language to adequately describe his homecoming.

Of course, it was not that he sought another conquest. The idea would have been ludicrous and insulting to both of them. He loved his wife, probably even more than the girl who broke his heart and haunted his dreams. It was as well the recently departed did not see him that way either, her marriage as sound and certain as faith. Had they both been unhappy, of course, and he had made a move, and that move had been reciprocated, the contentment he now felt would have drifted away, to be replaced by the surge of passion and the headlong rush into a relationship skewed by need and longing, loneliness and desire. And he knew he would have been the poorer for it. He knew that, had they both been unhappy, or free, they would almost certainly have had a love affair – such was the silent intimacy between them. But, while that was not the point, that understanding, too, was a part of the contentment he felt. With her, he was able to communicate at two levels at once; the one, an easy conversation lacking a fear of misunderstanding, knowing instinctively that he would choose the right words, that he wouldn't offend, that he would set her at her ease; the other, a strange language of gestures and smiles, of words and thoughts and silences, of certainties and ideas unspoken, of keen observation – at least on his part – of her proud head, her penetrating and fearless green eyes and her long, pale hands as they emphasised a point or sought subtle meaning in her own words.

He remembered another appointment, another colleague waiting inside the building, and felt torn between the prospect of jovial conversation well into the night and the need to be alone, to hold the moment, to try to order his thoughts as they jangled against each other in his mind. Of course, it was a form of love that he felt for her, there was no other word, though it was so dreadfully inadequate, and he felt a sense of loss now that she was gone. That much was true. And, she had looked around but, as the seconds had ticked by since her departure, an insidious voice inside questioned his former certainties concerning a lover's last look. Her gaze and that up-stretched hand might just have been politeness or a simple farewell. He cursed himself. This was not what was happening or what he should be thinking. This was not what he wanted to remember. He didn't want to analyse it in terms of 'Do I love her? Does she love me?' He needed time to order his thoughts and to

66

try to explain to himself how he felt. And time was not on his side. The door behind him opened and, for a brief moment, he thought it was his colleague, impatient at his absence, looking for him. But it was not, and he had a few seconds more to analyse his feelings.

It came to him in the end. For the first time in all his encounters with women, he felt no sense of selfishness, no urge to want against the odds, at all. Perhaps she had taught him this; opening up to him; trusting him; sharing herself with him; becoming that rarest of gifts, a real friend. Perhaps he could only feel this way about her in the sure knowledge that they both shared another gift, sound marriages to other people. Perhaps, for the first time in his life, he felt exactly the same at exactly the same time as someone else. Utterly at one with each other, without vacuum or a gulf, without the need for the confessional or the cloying treacle of guilt, without one of them misunderstanding and ahead of the other in an emotional marathon, one seeking what the other could not reveal, one demanding what the other could not give.

He had thought himself caddish in not walking her back to her car but that would have spoiled the moment. Had he done so, it would have resembled what it was not. Either a father seeing off his daughter – he was, he mused, just old enough to be her father. Or worse, a repetition of those days long ago when the imminent departure of a train, bus or car inexorably depleted the time for making dates or expressions of love. And, anyway, it wasn't like that. He didn't want, and knew he wouldn't get, conversation on that level. What they had was unsaid, a kind of unexpressed and inexpressible way of being. Indeed, he wondered if he should ever tell her how he felt for fear of breaking the spell; of bursting the soap bubble. She might take it the wrong way. And so he had resisted the trap of the fond farewell, the cliché of sweet-sorrow parting, the danger of cheapening his feelings and, greatest risk of all, of frightening her away. If, in that moment on his own, he could not find the language of how he felt, even though his feelings were clear and unequivocal, how would it have sounded if he had said anything to her?

And there was another discovery. Not only had he realised a dream and found a fusion of minds and ideas for the first time in his life. He also discovered the limitations of language, the bluntness and inadequacy of words. While he could say, and mean, that he loved his wife, there were no words he could remember hearing that fitted how he felt about this other woman or, perhaps more importantly, how she made him feel.

He turned to re-enter the building, slowly, reluctantly, and as he did, he analysed his feelings in the language he knew. He liked her. Of course he liked her. He was a man who liked a lot of people, always getting his fingers burned when his liking was betrayed. He loved her. Well, of course he loved her but, once again, his six decades on earth had taught him many kinds of love and he knew, furthermore, that he could choose to love many people at once. Beyond that, what? He thought she was beautiful but, he thought wryly, at his age most young and younger women looked beautiful. He thought she was endearing; he remembered her little mannerisms and imagined he could still see the little girl in the grown woman. And as he made his assessment, he realised he was driving away the essence of it all. Language, inadequate language, was obliterating that core feeling he had felt as she turned away and disappeared into the night.

And he knew he must never try to analyse it again . . .

Of course it happened, just as he remembered it, his recollection as he sits sipping the last dregs from his cold coffee cup just a few stanzas ahead of his reliving of the moment. And he had told her, against his better judgement but scared of the alternative of her not reading it (for he wrote it down), shown her his clumsy jottings and waited heart-in-mouth for her response, recognising the risk he had taken by its revelation. And when it had come, it had been measured, wise, distant, objective and careful to protect what they had by treating it as a piece of prose rather than as a confessional. Probably as a consequence of her response, they were still friends and he knew that, as he had thought at the time, it was where it should be, beyond analysis. But, from time to time, still he wondered . . .

The waiter drifts around the terrace collecting payment in that trusting French way from the tables of the recently departed. He approaches David Grant.

'More coffee?' he asks.

'No thank you. But . . .' The waiter is about to collect the bill from the counter, but pauses. '. . . It must be midday. Let me have a look at the menu, please?'

'Of course. Two minutes. Would you like an aperitif?'

'Yes, a *blonde* and a glass of water, please.'

David Grant proffers two euros for the coffee and the waiter whisks away, his laden tray describing skilful swoops and arcs between customers' heads as he rushes for the smoky interior of the café.

'One beer and one glass of water,' the waiter says unnecessarily as he drops the glasses to the table with a flourish, 'and, here you are, the menu.'

'Thanks,' replies David Grant, and adds. 'The beer is for pleasure and the water to help me swallow a pill.' He grimaces, touching the side of his head with extended fingers.

'Ah yes, you have a headache?'

'Yes, sadly.'

The waiter tuts an appropriately limited sympathy to the open stranger and motions towards the menu before bounding off to another table at the far end where a couple

69

are just sitting down. David Grant sips his beer and then goes through his ritual with the pill, managing a successful swallow just before he drains the glass of water. He'd have hated to use the beer for medicinal purposes.

He scans the plasticised and rather grubby made-for-tourists menu. Nothing appeals except, possibly, the undisclosed secrets of the *plât du jour*. On enquiry, this turns out to be rabbit in a provençale sauce, served with fried sliced potatoes and green beans, which he eagerly orders, along with a fifty-centilitre carafe of house red.

He looks around the restaurant. It is easy to tell the tourists from the locals simply by their choices for lunch. The former range over the delights of the menu, *frites* being the common denominator, while the French restrict themselves to a salad, the *plât du jour* or the occasional very rare steak. The differences are not as extreme as at the time of David Grant's first visits to France but they are still there. And whether he feels it or not, David Grant is now as French as anyone, in spite of his rather careful appearance. To those in the Ardèche, and probably here in Calais, he is identified simply as a *parisien*, a catch-all for the seemingly moneyed. Even the way he holds his knife and fork. That's not the way his parents would have told him to grasp his cutlery. Perhaps he is more chameleon than *parisien*. But certainly more French than British.

He follows his rabbit with a generous *île flottante* and another coffee; then sits back in his chair. By twisting around, he can see the blue Channel reflecting a cloudless sunny sky and watch the ferries processing back and forth like waterborne buses through a sea whipped into restless turmoil by a strong south-westerly. The sun glints on white crests streaming out like the manes of countless racehorses as they pass and repass each other rushing northward, rising and falling in contrast to the steady movement of the ships too big to be noticeably affected by the swell. He remembers

70

his first trip to Ostend in 1960 on a ship a quarter the size of the modern cross-Channel ferries: the *Marine*, the frayed and forgotten edge of Belgian Railways, a thing of rust and flooded toilets, of vomit swilling about in the saloons and on deck and, on that day of high seas, strange metal contraptions to keep the plates on the dining tables.

Having paid his bill with his credit card, he makes his way back to his car, his mind made up as to his next journey – to the capital. He has the Campanile guidebook and remembers a hotel on the south side of the city that would set him fair for the next day's trip. He knows the road as far as the Périphérique and will stop just short to decide whether his best course would be clockwise or anticlockwise, or even through the centre. Paris still worked, and there was as yet no complicated congestion charging, so going through the middle might even be quicker.

He knows something is wrong as soon as he sees his car. It is not that the damage is extensive, but the shape of the bonnet, so unconsciously familiar, jars. Someone has reversed into it while he was eating, drinking and dreaming, and the front of the car is no longer quite as it should be. Needless to say there is no note or a penitent driver standing by. He imagines the vandal cursing his careless-ness, the startled and guilty look up and down the road anticipating a furious owner returning hot-foot and, realis-ing there was none, setting off quick-sharp into oblivion.

David Grant opens the car door and releases the bonnet catch. It takes him a moment or two to open the lid but the catch still seems to work. The radiator appears to be intact with no tell-tale liquid on the road, but the fan assembly and a bracket that holds the horn are stove into the outermost fins and the grille is misplaced and broken. Everything else, the bonnet and the steel framing the grille, is dented, but these are only decorative and the poor old Corsa has suffered many bruises and scrapes over the years, the imperfections that all objects inherit as a reflection of those acquired by their human owners. Miraculously, the headlights are undamaged.

He starts her up and knows she will be fine until the engine warms up to the point that the cooling fan will kick in. What would happen after that he couldn't predict. The fan motor is powerful and he had visions of it starting to spin and breaking into the radiator itself. That would be a show-stopper – a forced sojourn in Calais and a lot of money as well.

David Grant curses his luck. It is as though he feels his decision to return home should be rewarded, the prodigal returning, no harm done, a nice balance between doing right by Élodie and not appearing a wimp to Michel. He has even resolved to rebuild the garden path. Now what?

He puts the bonnet down but needs to drop it two or three times before it snibs properly, and then drives out of the town towards an area of commercial buildings and motor concessionaries he spotted on his arrival. Perhaps there will be an Opel dealer with a workshop that could rescue him. Within a few moments he sees what he is looking for and swings the car into the forecourt. A cursory glance at the thermometer gauge just before he turns the engine off alerts him to the fact that the needle has moved off the bottom ninety-degree position. At ninety-five degrees, possibly lower, the cooling fan will start to operate.

The garage man looks at the damage and scratches his head. He would need a new bracket, a new fan, a new bonnet lid, a new grille and a respray to match the dark blue of the car. The man expertly checks the colour code on a plate in the engine and makes a note of it on a small pad he keeps in the top pocket of his immaculate overalls. The quotation comes to something over a thousand euros and will take at least a week to complete.

David Grant thanks him for his time but walks away. So

different from his garage at home where make do and mend are the order of the day. He drives out of the shiny forecourt and makes his way out of town, watching the temperature needle rise slowly again. After a couple of kilometres, he comes to what looks like a scrap yard, with a long, low barn of a building made of corrugated asbestos, windowless but lit from within by occasional, drooping strip lights, and surrounded by a cluster of rusting and partially dismantled vehicles. He draws up and turns the engine off as quickly as possible. A large Dobermann barks and swings about crazily on its back legs, only a stout chain preventing it from making David Grant its next meal. A flashing of oxyacetylene from deep within the building ceases, due, no doubt, to the fusillade of insane barking from the tethered dog. An old man, skin brown and cracked like old car-seat leather, his head second-skinned by a shapeless beret, emerges, removing one thick oil-stained gauntlet to retrieve a crushed cigarette packet from the top pocket of his greasy overalls. He forces a cigarette into a handy gap in his teeth next to a remaining incisor and lights it with a grimy Bic lighter.

'Monsieur?' he enquires.

'I have a problem,' David Grant replies, indicating the front of the car.

The man shrugs.

'You have lots of problems, Monsieur' is the reply. 'Open the bonnet.'

David Grant does what he is told.

The old man puts his ungloved hand into the engine and shakes various parts of the damaged interior.

'There is an Opel dealer in the town,' he offers.

'I know. I've been there but it's too expensive and the repair will take too long.'

The old man sucks on his cigarette and coughs.

'Saturday,' he says.

David Grant shakes his head slightly; waiting until Saturday will spoil his immovable yet brand-new plans.

A look of realisation crosses the old man's face.

'Ah, you are on holiday?'

'Yes,'

'England perhaps?'

Now, whether David Grant isn't paying attention and assumes his accent has given him away, or he hasn't been listening properly and heard *anglais* for *Angleterre*, it doesn't really matter, but he nods.

The old man shoots into action. He drops the bonnet lid with a resounding crash and motions David Grant to drive into the entrance to the shed. Encouraged by a hysterical outburst from the dog, he does as he is bidden.

'It's going to be provisional, Monsieur. Like a "quick-fix".'

'That's exactly what I want. Thank you.'

'It's nothing.'

There follows a piece of automotive engineering that would never find its way into a car manual or be taught at a car-maintenance evening class. A large hammer brings the bodywork back to something resembling the original intentions of the manufacturer; the bracket is removed and straightened by a combination of the hammer and the man's booted foot; wires for the horn, disconnected in the accident, are hurriedly replaced, the fan tested and refitted and the whole thing reassembled in less than half an hour. When asked how much, the old man shrugs and puts his hand up dismissively, wedging another cigarette into his conveniently shaped teeth.

'That's fine, Monsieur.'

'No, no,' implores David Grant and presses thirty euros into the old man's hand. The man firmly returns a ten-euro note and points out the quickest way to the port. David Grant knows that it is left for Paris and right for the town

74

centre and the ferry terminal, but the old man stands watching him, expecting to see confirmation of his assumed destination in return for his good deed. David Grant glances in his rear-view mirror as he drives away to see an immobile figure, smoke scudding from his clenched jaws, in dramatic contrast to the violent animation of the frustrated dog. He feels compelled to turn right and, unthinking, follows the old man's advice to the letter until he is parked outside the Sea France late-booking ticket office just ahead of the barrier on the dock.

Quite why that happens he doesn't know. His head is hurting, almost at the pitch of a migraine, and his one thought is to lie down and rest as soon as possible, but why he ends up on the dock he could never have explained. On the other hand, it is a case of 'why not?' His passport is, as always, secreted in his wallet, and he can afford a little diversion. Besides, he is a free man, able to do as he wishes, even if the choices he so often makes come from misunderstandings and willingness to respond that sometimes has been construed as weakness or at least indecision.

He buys a twenty-four hour return and reasons he can find a hotel, enjoy an early lunch in a Kentish pub the next day and, by reorganising his return across France, still arrive in the Ardèche by Saturday night. Or even include his brief visit to Paris and have dinner in Le Crestet on the Sunday. He proffers his ticket at the gate and trundles through the unattended customs post before being waved into one of the serried ranks of parked cars. The man in the ticket office thought he'd get the next boat and the short length of the queues make this prognosis extremely likely.

Taking the wait for an absent ferry as an opportunity to visit the lavatory, he has to push his way through a group of five or six men in their twenties or thirties who hover outside the door. They could be fellow travellers, but are too untidy – even truck drivers are smarter. They could be

French dock workers but they speak not a word and no group of Frenchmen is ever silent. They could be illegals looking for a lift but they don't ask him. Then he guesses they *are* illegals but are waiting for a pre-arranged lift that will land them in Dover under the cover of darkness. David Grant's ferry will be too early for that. In the dark, two under the wind deflector on the cab roof, two behind the cab in the narrow gap before the trailer, another two in the toolbox under the trailer, the driver politely getting down to show his papers and fend off any close inspection, a short pause on the dual carriageway at the top of the hill out of Dover, the balance of the two hundred euros per head paid and everyone will be happy. Within a week they will be living in a stolen and rusting P&O Nedlloyd container in a farmyard in Cambridgeshire and picking lettuces overnight for some local Tesco's. Happy days. As Mrs Thatcher said, 'You can't buck the market.' So, until their lift – a lorry driver with an expensive wife or a 4x4 to pay for arrives looking out for a cargo in human ambition – they hover around the toilet block, at a distance blending into the anonymity and windswept acres of concrete and tarmac at Calais Ferryport. Periodically, they feed euros into a coffee machine, avoiding eye contact with other travellers and giving way rather than opening their mouths for fear of detection.

An hour later, David Grant joins the queue of all different, all identical cars as they file obediently onto the ship, merging with lines of trucks and a cluster of garish coaches on the cross-Channel Noah's Ark, and parks David-like amongst the Goliath trucks, buses and cars, air-brakes hissing with exhaustion, doors slamming, families disgorging themselves in the darkness, a headlong rush to be first for what? – a queue to the unopened restaurant or a barred non-duty-free shop? The car deck is full of noise and diesel fumes. Noting the number of the door, he makes his way quickly to the staircase, a welcome relief from the car deck, and somewhere to lie down his objective and an excuse for his haste, joining the mass of bag and coat-carrying adults and hyperactive children determined to be first to the top and then just as determined to return down through the upward throng to universal irritation and their slow-moving parents.

He half lies down on a bench by the window, closes his eyes and doesn't move until the boat, which rolls more than most would wish, is drunkenly pointing its prow between the twin moles of Dover harbour. He just has time to wrest a bottle of Volvic from a chiller in the self-service restaurant before it closes, pays the idling lad on the cash desk and takes another pill, carrying the practically empty bottle down the companionway to his waiting car.

His head is hurting badly, to which must now be added periodic flashes of light in his eyes, open or closed, so he decides to find a room near the front in Dover and get some sleep before finding something to eat. He achieves the former in no time, climbing a staircase of peeled wallpaper and chipped banisters with over-zealous gratitude and a polite refusal for a kindly offered cup of tea, but never manages the latter as he sleeps the clock round.

And some more.

The First Friday

David Grant awakens completely worn out. He's had one of those nights that seem endlessly busy, the act of waking coinciding with the welcome conclusion to a turbulent, hectic and exhausting dream. Élodie had been there, the chief character in an overpopulated drama owing more to Peter Greenaway than to the director of *Sleuth*. A cast of thousands had criss-crossed his mind's eye while all the time he was trying to talk to her, the interruptions so frequent and so forceful that he could no longer remember what was so crucial that it had to be discussed without delay. Only that there was something. So he was left with the anxiety of conveying nothing in a conversation that seemed to span his sleeping hours.

Just as the thunder of footfall and rustle of a thousand conversations abated, just as the endless pushing and stepping aside and excuse me's and thank you's reduced, Élodie would turn to him with that slightly head-on-one-side quizzical look he loved so much, as if to ask, 'What did you want to say?' And he would look this way and that to see if they had a moment to themselves, hesitate as he gathered his thoughts trying to remember what was so important, remember at last, open his mouth, and the cacophony would start again, a thousand, ten thousand, a hundred thousand people, some he recognised, some he didn't, shambling and marching from left to right, right to left, towards him from the front and brushing past him from behind, bumping and squeezing, stumbling and shoving, until the moment was lost and Élodie looked away, assuming he wanted to say nothing, that she had been mistaken, that this was how he wanted to conduct his own dream, hopelessly busy, endlessly frenetic but ultimately without purpose . . .

Élodie looked as she had first appeared to him. Younger, of course, her hair unfashionably frizzy (at least unfashionable in the London of their first meeting), permanently looking as though she was just back from a holiday in the West Indies (a product of her Mediterranean ancestry, she had told him later), taller than most women who attracted him, a woman with a style all her own that was certainly distinctive if not always entirely successful, a woman who understated her femininity, wanting to be judged professionally for her abilities and personally for her spirit and her humanity. She kept her femininity private; her allure a well-concealed promise rather than a seductive, in-your-face trailer for the big picture. He remembered that, when they had first gone to bed together, he had been surprised, shocked even, by what he saw. Until that moment, he had thought of her as a face crowned by the shock of curly hair, a face angular, high-cheekboned and obviously not British, a face dominated by two sad, beautiful brown eyes, a long neck and, beyond that, mere extremities of limbs clad in sleeves to the wrist, and skirts reaching her mid-calf or jeans hiding all that flopped onto the top of her Doc Martens.

Her ploy had worked, of course. He had been attracted to her by her professionalism, her mind, her spirit and her clothes. And now, he had to come to terms with this new stranger, an ardent lover with a generous, giving, demanding body; a body of terrifying curves and large dark nipples, of softnesses and hardnesses, of a long sinuous back and a flat stomach unaltered by childbirth, a body that delighted in his pleasure and encountered its own orgasms as though they were a new and total surprise each time, a holding of the breath and a sharp sigh that reminded him of running pell-mell into the surf at North Berwick as a child, and a cry that sounded as though she had burnt her hand in an open fire. He remembered the beads of sweat on her forehead and gathering between her breasts, her long sighs, her arms surrounding him, her machine-gun fire of little kisses on his cheek, her reluctant wriggling free, the almost childlike mopping with a corner of the sheet and her thoughtful expression as she puzzled over when it would be acceptable for her to get up and light a cigarette. Eventually, he learned to put her out of her misery by turning over and knocking one from its packet, putting it into his mouth and lighting it with any one of a dozen or so throw-away lighters that were strategically placed all over the house. He, a non-smoker, became at least a five-a-day man, but only one draw per cigarette before he tantalised her by taking it from his mouth and making to place it between her eager lips, only to hold it to one side while he gave her a passionate kiss that challenged her, by now, divided loyalty.

When, with her lungs crackling with a new voice during sleep, she finally gave up smoking (and she had been a two-packs-a-day woman for twenty years), he was glad for her, glad for him, glad for their house whose rooms he could now see across, but something that was deeply her was lost forever. Smoking gave her a hundred little customs and mannerisms that breaking the habit rendered obsolete. It was a loss he could never express, certainly in those first two years when withdrawal was so hard, the new habit of not smoking fragile and shallow-rooted, and after that time it rarely entered his consciousness, but during that dream, where she was smoking feverishly just as she had when he first knew her, they all came back to him: the cupped hand around the flame on a windy day; the rare sight of it held

80

between her lips; the almost ashamed way she took a final drag, head down, before stubbing it out or grinding it under her shoe; her fragmented side of a conversation as she interrupted herself to take another lungful; the way the smoke would curl from her mouth and nose slowly rather than being blown thoughtlessly across the room; the relaxed way she would smoke sitting in his lap watching television, her concentration moving from the screen to the cigarette and to kissing him by turns; and the high anxiety over a last half-empty packet on a wet night with the shops closed.

I suppose if you are reading this and you are a non-smoker or, worse, an ex-smoker, you will be appalled. 'None of that sounds attractive at all!' you will stutter. And, set down in black type on white paper, I would have to agree, it doesn't. But it was, at least to David Grant, although he never went there in case she took it up again 'for him' and killed herself as a result. So, her endlessly restless hands, her dexterity with cigarette in conjunction with cup, pen, telephone, door key, using a wooden spoon to stir soup, manipulating camera or binoculars, became nothing but memories as she adjusted from the habit of decades and became uniform with most of the rest of us. A bit of Élodie that he had so hoped would change changed and, as a consequence, he lost a part of the Élodie he had first known and loved. And not only for him. She regretted giving in to reason; regretted arrival at a place called no alternative; gained no reward from the application of received common sense. She had lost a part of herself.

But now the mists of his cluttered night clear, the legions fade, their clamour replaced by instructions shouted from below to a Ukrainian chamber maid nervously tapping at doors down the corridor; the centre light with its cheap, square, paper lampshade hanging still and dusty taking the place of Élodie's fading face. The tapping reaches his door.

'Am I too late for breakfast?' he shouts as he sits up.

The girl tries the door but finds it locked.

'Yes, sir. Breakfast finish. All gone. All the foods gone. Nobody.'

'OK.'

'Can I do room?'

'No. Not dressed yet. Half an hour.'

The girl does not reply.

'OK?'

The girl still does not reply. He thinks he hears her light step as she moves down the corridor.

He clambers into the shower which, at about three feet square, might have been reported to some earnest and humourless organisation for being sizist, and wrestles with a tap that knows very little graduation between stone cold and lukewarm. Emerging shivering into the room, he towels himself damp with a square little bigger than a facecloth. Outside the windows, way below him, the road is filled with a convoy of big trucks making for the M20, the sun glinting on their windscreens momentarily as they cross a road-end, and small herds of asylum seekers joining and parting on the pavement, shaking hands formally with each other or staring suspiciously at the new arrivals, the so far unrecognised or the instantly recognisable homeland enemies thrown together in uneasy union by oppression, poverty or ruthless ambition. They are uniformly dressed in cheap, flashy trainers, old washed-out jeans and padded jackets, even though the weather is warm. These are the law-abiding illegals that have run the curiously passive British Labours of Hercules. How did they go again?

'Please don't come.'

'You really shouldn't come, you know.'

'I know you've heard it's great but don't come anyway.'

'We have insisted that the French close the temptations of a refugee camp at Sangatte within sight of the Promised Land, so don't come.'

'Let us tell you about the tragedies of the frozen-to-death in refrigerated lorries, the suffocated in mislaid containers and the cut to bits on the railway lines in graphic detail and in every language in common use east of Austria, so don't come.'

'We'll send you back on the first train if you do get through, so please don't come.'

Then, when they do get through, they're picked up by a kindly plod who tells them their rights, assumes they have been mistreated wherever they come from, obtains cheap, flashy trainers and, from a charity, old and washed-out jeans and padded jackets, even though the weather is warm, finds them a recently rich duty lawyer, takes them to one of the shabby and now redundant hotels in Dover and all the surrounding faded holiday resorts that have never in their entire histories done better business, and they begin the long and fearfully stressful experience of British red tape and apathy.

Better to stow away successfully, be offloaded on the approach to the A2 handing over the few euros or British pounds that cost you so much, hide during the day, walk at night, get an English-speaking compatriot to buy a mobile phone, call a number you were given back in Tbilisi or Istanbul or the village where your distraught mother put back her veil to give you a last tearful embrace as you climbed into the ancient and dirty minibus, and work your way into a system as leaky as the one you left was watertight, picking lettuces for mothers of two point four children driving high-wheeled four-by-fours.

As they say, 'Every little helps.'

He dresses and stumbles down the stairs. His head has stopped hurting but he feels light-headed, due no doubt to a lack of food. He looks at his watch. It is half past eleven.

'I'll have to charge you for the breakfast even though you weren't up in time.' The woman, wearing masculine horn-rimmed spectacles, her grey hair raked back into a tight bun and dressed in a flowery pinny over a long-sleeved cardigan with a full, three-quarter-length tweed skirt, is writing a receipt on the little painted shelf in a hatch between her private quarters and the corridor in anticipation of being paid. She is roughly square in shape, smells slightly unwashed and licks the end of her biro, a habit he always associated with pencils years before. He stands and watches her and then takes in the plethora of dire warnings drawing-pinned to the cream-coated Lincrusta about guests' behaviour in the rooms and what she jauntily calls 'Key Kourtesy' which concerns not poddling off home with her room keys. As she licks her pen yet again and gives it a frustrated shake before resuming her laborious shaping of the letters, he thumbs through the tray of creased leaflets advertising Dover's splendid attractions and eateries, and touches the cold brass summoning bell that he figures nobody will dare to use, before replying.

'That's fine,' he murmurs.

'It's all in the price,'

'No problem. My fault. Needed the sleep.'

'If,' the woman continues, swinging her wrist around ostentatiously to reveal a large manly watch, 'you had been half an hour longer, I'd have had to charge you for a further night.'

'Oh.'

'Yes, as it is, the girl should have gone off for her lunch break before now.'

He doubts this premature timetable but leaves the point unchallenged as the woman is clearly enjoying being on a roll. He apologises again. The victory brings a measure of magnanimity.

'Were you the gentleman who turned down the cup of tea last night?'

84

He apologises again, pleading a headache and exhaustion.

'Would you like it now?' she asks, adding, 'There'll be no charge.'

He accepts gratefully. He feels he ought to take another pill, suspecting the light-headedness is probably part of the same problem as his headaches of the previous days. She shows him to the empty dining room, already laid for the next morning, the view of the street obscured by plain lace and a frame of heavy curtain and deep pelmet in navy-blue velvet.

'Sit where you like but please don't disturb the cutlery.'

He nods, whispers a thank you and sits near the window before he remembers he is without any English money. The woman is making for the dining-room door as he speaks.

'I'll have to get some cash. Can you tell me where there's a cash machine?'

She looks at him suspiciously and then gives him the benefit of the doubt.

'Out of the gate, turn left. There are about three banks on the crossroads about two hundred yards away. One of them's bound to have a hole in the wall. Or there'll be one open I s'pose.'

'Thanks,' he replies.

'You'll leave your bag and car keys here?'

Not quite giving him the benefit of the doubt then.

He puts his keys beside his chosen place at the table in the window and leaves his suitcase untouched, standing like an obedient dog at the chair's side, its towing handle lying like a lead on the chair, before making for the front door. In his hand he clutches his wallet, having first checked that his cards are present. Without them the woman's suspicions would have been well founded, hence the need to make the check.

It is another sunny day but much cooler, with a breeze coming in off the sea and whipping grains of sand and grit into his face, making him screw his eyes up against the discomfort. He regrets not taking a jumper but, within a few yards and with the sun on his face, the cold goes from his frame. He swithers over whether to use the French card and take the hit on the conversion or use the English cards he and Élodie had retained for trips such as this and opts for the latter course of action. He takes out enough for a good lunch and petrol as well as the anticipated cost of the room in the boarding house.

In no time he returns, choosing to ignore the woman's face peering at him from the dining-room window as he turns in at the gate.

'I've put your bill beside your tea on the table,' she announces.

'Fine. Thank you.'

'Successful?'

'Getting the money?' he asks unnecessarily. His turn to play.

'Yes,' she retorts, again unnecessarily.

'Oh, yes,' David Grant says in an absent-minded, unconcerned fashion.

'Good,' she replies and again says, 'good,' as she leaves the room.

He sips the tea and, it being cool, takes one of his pills. For once it goes down without difficulty. He looks at his watch. It is just after noon. If he is to make it into deepest Kent for lunch, he will have to go soon. He finishes his tea and then takes his cup obediently to the hatch with the necessary cash and the bill.

She takes the cup without a word and counts the money carefully.

'I owe you three pounds,' she says reluctantly but makes no move to complete the transaction.

'Give it to the girl. To apologise for being a late-riser,' he replies.

'I'm sure she'll be very grateful,' the woman says, putting the notes into a locked drawer beneath the hatch.

'Do you want a receipt?' she asks.

'No. That won't be necessary.'

She nods, smiling slightly, before watching him collect his suitcase and make for the front door.

'Where are you going to next?'

'Back to France,' he replies. 'Just going to have a real English pub lunch first, then I'll be off on the first boat that'll have me.'

She shrugs in indifference, displaying no curiosity about the reference by this Brit to 'going back to France', before wishing him a safe journey. Asking their next destination is a question expected by the public and it always keeps the conversation going as they make for the door but, after thirty years of running the boarding house, she is indifferent to the responses she receives and rarely listens to the answers. He feels that if he had said he was going to the moon or Hesikos, she would still have replied wishing him a safe journey and asking no subordinate question.

As he walks to his car he wonders why he still harps back to Hesikos when he needs to grasp an analogy for somewhere remote. Hesikos was a fictional planet in a *Children's Hour* radio drama of his childhood, a mystical place as far away as one could imagine and beyond the world dominated by his elders and betters. He can remember nothing of the story or the characters. Only the name sticks and, with it, a vivid and probably by now inaccurate picture of the planet with its young people who mattered and made things happen, its strange vegetation, bright colours, smooth red-hued rocky terrain, the bluest sky and everything familiar and comforting reinvented, but still familiar and comforting. On Hesikos birds sang and no one had to walk around wearing forties-style deep-sea diving gear masquerading as a space suit. It wasn't like *Journey into Space*, a much more uncomfortable and sinister creation. Hesikos was entirely satisfactory, a place his parents could never be a part of that was, nevertheless, superimposed upon the securities his parents represented. As a child, just saying the word made the hairs on the back of his neck stand on end and even now he could remember that other-worldly effect, the sense of conspiracy, superiority and power living on that planet in his imagination gave to the mediocrity of his life. It was probably the beginning of his living within himself, a thing he had always done to a greater or lesser degree when the world was too hard, too mundane or too unpredictable. He might have made a writer.

'It's not permitted.'

He looks up. A parking attendant is gesticulating at the single yellow line and a number of signs he'd not noticed the evening before. He says nothing. She repeats her observation and then shrugs. Bloody Frenchman, she thinks, coming over here and flouting the rules. David Grant senses her assumptions about his ignorance of the language and the proximity of her lunch break might save the day. He shrugs as Gallic a shrug as he can muster and mutters a 'desolé' before shrugging again and loading his car.

'I should give you a ticket!' she roars, tapping her pencil on her pad to convey the message more strongly to the foreigner and then walks off down the road past a group of young men watching the mini-drama unfold. As soon as she has gone, the men laugh and put their thumbs up to David Grant. He grins covertly and gets into the car before driving past them and returning their upturned thumb. He has more in common with the dross of society than the incumbents. A bond between the lost and the almost lost.

Half an hour later he is away from the main roads and slipping past oast houses turned into priceless homes and fields of everything but hops. He eventually finds a pub that looks suitably chocolate-box with a half-thatched wobbly roof that comes almost to within reach of his upstretched hand and an ancient climbing rose poised beside the door, waiting to ensnare careless visitors. He steps gingerly inside, stooping to avoid hitting his head on the sun-bleached, deep-grained lintel, orders a pint of Directors in lieu of a local brew and asks to see the menu.

'S'on the wall, sir. The board over there, see?'

He nods and, as his pint is pulled, he wanders over to the chalk board that turns out to be cleverly painted to look like chalk.

'We stop taking orders at a quarter to two, sir,' the barkeep adds petulantly, following his latest customer with his humourless eyes, 'so if you want a dessert you should order it with your meal.' He can't pronounce his tee-aitches and says 'me-all', but David Grant gets the gist.

To give the menu justice he should have arrived about an hour before. There are approaching sixty items spread between what the board calls 'starters', 'mains' and 'deserts', the latter having little to do with the Sahara or Gobi. He had hoped for a traditional roast dinner, even with the beef cooked to death, sliced as thin as shoebox cardboard and hued a universal grey in a puddle of corn-flower-thickened gravy. That, and bullet-hard roast potatoes with waterlogged Brussels sprouts and green cabbage, would have been appropriate; what he'd have expected. But roast is only for Saturdays and Sundays, the board announces. Instead, he chooses chicken tikka and rice with poppadams and banoffi pie. The former because rural France is indeed an Indian cuisine desert and from time to time he misses a good curry, and the banoffi because it sounds suitably indulgent.

'That's thirteen pounds sixty, not including tip. Which table you sittin' at?' the barman asks.

'I don't know,' he replies honestly as he pays the man fifteen pounds and obediently holds up his hand to refuse the change.

He looks around at the three-quarters empty pub before pointing to a group of tables in the window. 'That one over there, in the window?'

'I need a number' comes the reply. The barman stops writing the order and slaps his biro down on the bar with an impatient clatter. 'It's on a metal plate on the table.'

The conversation seeming to be over, David Grant assumes he'll have to cross the pub and make a detailed examination of the table he indicated. He isn't even sure where the table number is to be found but uses his time taken in crossing the pub to carry out the necessary research. He sees that rather tasteful brass plates are screwed to the table tops.

He returns to the bar. 'Fifty-three,' he announces, and then realises the barman has watched his progress and managed to enter the number on the food order before his return.

'Cutlery over there on the sideboard,' the barman orders. 'Sauces. Napkins. Mustards, English and French. Mayonnaise.'

'He could have had a job in a department store elevator back in the fifties,' thinks David Grant as he makes for the sideboard and collects his cutlery. As he walks back to his table, he is aware of someone following him. It is a young girl carrying his lunch with a plate of poppadams on a large tray.

'There now,' she says pleasantly as she unloads the tray even before he sits down.

'That was quick!' he replies, before thanking her.

'Yeah,' she says, beaming. 'It's ever so quick, the new microwave. Done in a flash. Normally it's them big crisps what takes a while but we had a few on the go.'

David Grant surveys the scene.

'Got everything you want? Sauces and that?' she asks.

'Yes, thank you,' he replies, releasing his knife and fork from their paper napkin shroud.

'Enjoy your meal,' she chirps as she accidentally clatters her tray on the back of a spare chair heading back to the kitchen.

He doesn't reply.

If he'd wanted a curry he really ought to have gone to an Indian restaurant. This offering is as mild as a stew, buried in a slurry of vomit-coloured goo and could have done with a few more moments in the new, miracle microwave. The girl brings his banoffi pie five mouthfuls before he has finished his main course.

'That's my favourite,' she grins as she puts the dessert down and waits, twiddling her tray around in the air impatiently as David Grant forks the last of his rice into his mouth.

He nods; his mouth too full to reply. As soon as his plate is empty and while he is still wielding his fork, she whisks his plate onto her tray and waits for him to put his fork onto the hovering plate.

'That's good,' she says, almost patronisingly as if speaking to an inmate in a rest home and leaves him to enjoy his factory banoffi.

He orders a coffee from the girl, who contrives to retain most of the liquid in the cup, and feels suddenly tired. He knows he has to head back to Dover quite quickly to be able to use his twenty-four-hour ticket, so he pays for his coffee, lies when asked the ritualistic question about whether or not he enjoyed his 'me-all', and makes for the car looking quite lost in the empty car park. He turns onto the road and begins to retrace his steps but a feeling of fatigue begins to overwhelm him and, at the first lay-by, he pulls off and winds the seat back for a few minutes' rest, dropping the window part-way before turning off the engine.

When he awakes it is getting late and he has no idea where he is. For a moment he thinks he must be in France and, the road not being dissimilar, he looks up and down for the familiar landmarks around the cemetery of two days before. But there is no rusting and reluctant gate, no stone enclosure, no serried rank of tombstones and there are no chattering magpies, although gulls shriek and swoop in the still air. Still, he thinks he must be on the homeward road and drives for a few moments with his car firmly on the right-hand side of the road before a looming road sign dashes any hopes of a simple solution to his dilemma. It tells him where he is and that realisation increases his bewilderment. Better before in his ignorance. The knowledge conveyed by that isolated road sign makes things immeasurably more complicated. He stops the car and looks at the sign with its little Kentish Invicta motif and its mention of half-remembered villages and the indisputable certainty of Canterbury.

He drops his forehead into his left hand and tries to remember what has happened since the last time he remembers terra firma beneath his feet. That has to have been the cemetery with the raised hands and the strutting schoolmasters. That much is solid and reliable, if as far away now as a distant memory, but what has happened since? Then, from that far off certainty, little flashes of experience begin to link him from what he knew to his present doubts of where and why. His memories play tricks, however, for the obvious takes second place to misplaced images rather than reliable geography. The boy with his expression of complicity as he drowned his bread, the odoriferous woman sucking her pen, the clattering children's feet on the ship's companionway, the waitress and the coffee in the saucer, the stooped huddle of men on the dock at Calais, the fraternity with the displaced in the face of officious authority, the old man somewhere with a cigarette stuck between yellowed teeth who had done him some forgotten good deed. He looks in his wallet to check his cards and the ferry ticket, folded and damaged, reminds him he has to get back to Dover. Then he looks at the time and realises his crossing ticket has expired. The best thing to do would be to drive back to Dover and appeal to the better nature of the shipping company, or pay an excess. Ironically, he has compared the time on the ticket with the car's clock which still shows French time, so he might even have made it without the need for much negotiation. But something prevents that option from entering his head. Instead, the road sign becomes dominant in his mind and he crosses over to the left-hand side, studiously indicates his intention to turn left to a deserted world, and heads smartly up the main road to Canterbury. There he finds a three-star hotel that could have been anywhere in the world, orders a sandwich and a beer at the bar and consumes them in silence before turning in.

The room is equipped with everything one could ever want in the obvious place and put together with studied blandness that neither jars nor charms. He takes a shower, not the normal end of the day for him, flicks on the television and looks at the pictures on the wall. They are mostly prints of chameleons, as bland as everything else in the room. Even someone who has a distinct antipathy for chameleons and all things lizard-like couldn't have taken offence.

He turns his attention to the box and recognises Jonathan Ross. Yet another Friday, yet another chat show, yet more expense on pricey personalities, yet another worthwhile public-service drama spiked. Come back, Auntie, where are you? It's true, you don't know what you've got till it's gone.

First he silences Jonathan with the mute button. Then he puts his image out of its misery, the heroically dominating double-breasted jacket diffused to a pinprick of light in the middle of the screen, the screen crackling to a deafening silence, the sound and vision replaced by a single red standby light at the foot of the glass. He looks again at the chameleons before taking off the dressing gown and crawling into bed. He strains around and finds the light switch and lies in the dark thinking of the chameleons with their long tongues reaching for sanitised insects and remembers another place with a lizard this time, and another patient wait unrewarded . . .

She stood at the upstairs window, arms folded, watching him. The short brown hair merged with the darkness of the room beyond, exaggerating paleness in the face he knew really to be tanned a deep brown by the Riviera sun. At that distance, she seemed expressionless and he guessed proximity would alter nothing of that. For a while now, she had only looked at him that way. Pain, puzzlement and a need to protect deaden the face and, at best, make friends of ex-lovers. Before, he had never known what was going on behind those grey eyes that shone blue in the sunshine – only that she loved him intensely, passionately, completely. Now that the intensity, passion and commitment had gone, sadly, he knew only too well.

She was there because he wanted it and she liked the sun. Perhaps she was also there because he was a sort of habit – a first lover with whom she had shared so much that the death of passion made orphans of them both, deprived of so much of each other and the things they shared in common that they both still craved – a yearning that he hoped would raise her love from the dead to join the muddled constancy of his own feelings.

She continued to watch him until, with the slightest turn of her head, he knew she had been distracted by something across the high wall that surrounded the house. He smiled to himself. It was probably the two black cats that amused them with their antics along the side of the pool – teetering along the brink, letting one lazy leg cantilever out over the water during an essential but ill-timed washing spree. She loved cats more than people, he thought. She certainly loved cats more than she loved him.

He thought all this, saw all this through his rear-view mirror, as he steered the car between the stone pillars and turned out onto the hot, grey road. Apart from the girl and a long, dusty lizard who eyed the car cautiously as it drew hot draughts past its pillared hunting ground, no one saw his passing. The rhythmic percussion of the *cigales* went on uninterrupted, most of the villas' shutters were closed against the heat and he assumed the cats would still be entertaining the girl with their cavorting. Perhaps their owners would be back from work, changing quickly for a swim before dinner, getting cupboard-love rubbings from the cats at the prospect of treats from the table. Adding insult to injury, he had caught sight of them one day, his innocent glance out of the window at the pretty garden, the pool and the two black cats being rewarded by seeing the two of them making love on a sun-lounger, her long hair reaching down to the tiles, her legs locked around his back while he thrust into her with a violence he abhorred and envied simultaneously. It was her question as to his where-abouts that dragged him from the window and assuaged his feelings of guilt at accidental voyeurism. But the image lingered on and disturbed him constantly, especially alone at night, as he compared his lot with theirs.

At the end of the deserted street, he turned left and made his way to the busy autoroute approach road. Under umbrella pines and alongside spindly Mediterranean oaks, he accelerated the car and wound back the sun-roof, turning on Riviera Radio for some decent, familiar music and the comfort of a language he understood. It shouldn't take him more than about twenty hectic minutes to reach the Grasse/Cannes junction and then, depending on the traffic, another twenty minutes before he was in the shop – no time at all, really.

The trousers were her idea. To him, they resembled too much the school cricketing whites of his youth, but her yardstick was more sophisticated, less trammelled by unsatisfactory memories of the past. That was something she had made him aware of more than anyone else. Style. She had style in abundance and, as far as her modest budget allowed, was able to mix the high street with designer chic that continually surprised and delighted him. But this time, he was the object of her attentions. Hence the cricketing trousers. No, wrong, he thought. These had nothing to do with cricket, these off-white trousers styled by Guy Laroche. He had raised his eyes at her perspective and at the price. But even he had liked the belt.

'That belt says something,' she had said.

'Yes,' he had replied ruefully. 'It says I'm too fat. They've got to punch three new holes in it to get to the point where I can do it up without looking like the "before" in an advert for slimming soup!'

'It's made for the Riviera Set,' she had said kindly. 'They are all . . . slimmer than you.'

'Thanks,' he said sarcastically. But he knew it had been meant well.

Like most trousers sold in France, the shop had left the hems open. This, he was glad of, since it had masked the fact that his waistline was probably about right for a man at least four inches taller than he. Had they been ready-made, the need for substantial letting out would not have been restricted to the belt. So, there he was, dodging in and out of British coaches, Spanish trucks and hundreds of suicidal

Renaults, Citroëns and Peugeots on his way back to Cannes to collect his new purchase.

He arrived too early. He always arrived too early for everything. The assistant looked at his watch and reminded him, in impeccable English with just a hint of an American accent that was thought so trendy in the South of France, that he had been told they would be ready at four-thirty and it was only just four o'clock. The alterations lady, he said firmly, but with a smile on his face, would have them in the shop by four-thirty. As promised.

He shrugged, smiled a little self-consciously and left the premises. What to do for thirty minutes? Most people with thirty minutes on their hands in Cannes in August would, at the very least, make their way down to the rue d'Antibes and window-shop. The more athletic might leg it down to the Croisette and spy out the talent. After all, that's why it was there. It wanted to be seen and, without the reproachful glances of anyone in his company, he would be in a perfect situation to give it, and him, what they both wanted.

But no. He went instead to the railway station. He struggled through the throng of perspiring holidaymakers and risked a lightning strike by roving ticket collectors to take himself onto the low platform under the roof formed by the elevated roadway to watch the world go by. He had done this sort of thing since childhood. Then, it had been the lure of steam engines, their numbers in grubby yellow paint quickly transferred to his little red lined notebook, but now there was a strain of pathos in a railway station that matched his mood. To him, stations were sad places where the tears of farewell always seemed to make more of an impression than the cries of greeting; where holidays ended so much more definitely than they started; where any brave attempts at architecture (totally absent here) were blighted by untidiness and the detritus of humanity.

97

As he took up his position near the eastern end of the station, a powerful howl announced the arrival of a TGV near the completion of its journey from Paris to Nice. The train slid to a halt on the track furthest from him with a contented hiss of its brakes, the driver's cab opposite his point of observation. The lights by the doors illuminated and, one by one, the doors slid open to reveal eager arrivals that started to tumble to the platform below, dragging their cases and large numbers of small, awkward-footed children behind them.

He had been aware of three or four railway officials who had gathered on the platform in advance of the train's arrival, but their purpose had eluded him. Now, their curious actions made them the centre of his attention. At the first door of the train, instead of passengers eager to start their holidays, he saw a stack of extremely expensive-looking luggage. This, the officials swarmed over, lifting piece after piece delicately from the train and loading them all onto a hastily obtained barrow. Soon, with the barrow practically full, the train doorway was clear, and the staff turned their attention once again to the train. Several of them disappeared inside to return to the doorway with an extremely frail old woman in a small invalid chair. With infinite care, they lifted the chair with its fragile load to the platform below. The figure in the chair was motionless and, he thought as he watched, could well have been dead – such was the careless way in which she sat. Once it had been safely lowered onto the platform, one of the station staff took up his position at the handles of the chair whilst the others took charge of the luggage barrow and prepared to follow in convoy towards the exit. The others stood about and talked. The driver hung out of his cab awaiting the signal to start on the last leg of his journey.

He almost lost interest in the old lady, the barrow of Louis Vuitton, and the sweating railwaymen, especially as they became partially hidden from his gaze by the station name board. But, at that moment, he spotted a bony arm bursting from the wheelchair and slicing through the air like a scimitar. The figure of the woman remained awkwardly prone but the arm continued to sweep animatedly back and forth. A railwayman leant over the chair and then stood upright quickly as the whistles blew and the driver disappeared from the window of his cab to take up position at the controls. All at once, the platform was boiling with running, shouting men – one towards the driver's cab, one in the direction of the guard towards the back of the train. The pusher of the wheelchair swung it around with undignified haste and the barrowmen described a hasty U-turn as they made for the door they had so recently left. The departure of the train was prevented by the efforts of the men on the ground and the alertness of the driver, who stuck his head out of the window once again and watched as, firstly, the old lady and then all the luggage were returned to the train. Safely stowed away, the doors slid shut and, with a howl, the train moved swiftly out of the station, the railwaymen dispersing after more animated chatter.

Clearly, the old lady was very much alive and in full possession of her faculties for it was she, and only she, who had realised she had been put off at the wrong station. But how was it that so many railway staff had been assembled at the wrong place for the purpose of detraining what must have been a very important passenger? And what would have happened if the train's departure had not been prevented? He smiled as he imagined a silver Rolls-Royce cruising to a halt outside the station to overcome the embarrassment of French Railways.

Only in France, he thought, would such a thing happen. He had read too many Peter Mayle books and itched to see the eccentric and the charming for himself. Now he had. And he knew, if he could tell it well, she would laugh at its retelling, admire his pace and humour, see his qualities and perhaps, just perhaps, move into his arms to kiss him. He knew, if only he could get it right, this period in the wilderness would be over and they could move forward together. And he had it, too. He knew just the right things to say to submerge his own eccentricity in being at the station at all. He could find the words for a slow build, like Peter; a gradual realisation that something that appeared perfectly normal was simply not so – that a deus ex machina would elevate the mundane to the surreality of a Man Ray photograph. He knew that, if he told it well, she would laugh and laugh as she could, with uncontrollable giggling and tears in her eyes, and he would make sure, for once, his advances matched her receptiveness. He would let her lead, let her decide. For once he would get it right. He just knew it.

But by the time he had returned to the shop, had a final fitting, pronounced the trousers 'fine', retrieved his car and joined queues of homeward-bound vehicles at the beginning of the rush hour, his confidence began to drain away. By the time he joined the autoroute, he was in a panic. Why wouldn't the words come as they had done? Why did it now sound like straight reportage when it had been so fresh and funny?

'Got them then?' She stood by the door as he opened it, her perfect, bronzed shoulders contrasting with the white strapless sun-top he loved so much.

'Yes,' he replied.

'Good fit?' She took the fancy bag from him and opened it carefully for a brief inspection. He might have the trousers but when they got back to England, she thought, she would have the bag.

'Fine. Still look like cricketing trousers, though.'

She clicked her tongue impatiently. 'You've got no style. Cricketing trousers, indeed! That's Guy Laroche, you know.

Seriously good stuff. Trendy. And amazing quality.' Then she added, 'You were a long time?'

'Yes, a bit. They weren't ready, so I went off to the station.'

'The what?'

'Er. The railway station?'

'You are on the Côte d'Azur and you went to the station? You must be barmy.'

'No, just to put off time . . . thought I might.' He shuffled around a bit.

She snorted. 'Phew, glad I didn't come. The station!'

'Saw something funny, though.'

'Yes?'

She walked ahead of him into the kitchen, not really listening.

'There was this old lady.'

'How old?'

'Oh, I don't know. Old. Perhaps in her eighties?'

'Yes?' She started to break open a packet of crisps and pour them into a bowl before pulling a bottle of rosé from the fridge. 'It's salmon tonight, by the way.'

'I like salmon.'

'Thought I'd do it with a provençale sauce since we're down here. And oven chips since I come from the north of England and like them!' She made a sound like a short trumpet fanfare. She was very happy in the security of her emotion-free relationship. She poured the wine and abstractedly picked a piece of floating cork from a glass before handing it to him.

'Great!'

'It will be. Oh, you were saying?'

'Yes, the old lady . . .'

'. . . Eighty, you said?'

'. . . ish.'

'What was she doing?' She opened the fridge and

101

removed a paper packet before smelling its contents. 'Mmm, it smells so fresh. Salmon is so good, isn't it?'

She drew a kitchen knife from a drawer and started to cut the skin away from the flesh.

'She was put off the train in Cannes by mistake,' he said.

'Really? How do you know?'

'She was waving her arms about and insisting on being put back on board.' He knew Peter Mayle would have put it so differently.

'Oh well, I hope she got off at the right station in the end. SNCF just as bad as British Rail, eh? Oh, you'll never guess!'

'What?'

'You know the villa next door where the cats are?'

'Yes.'

'There was a couple there, about the time you left. You'll never guess what they were doing.'

He knew perfectly well. She didn't have to tell him. He gritted his teeth for the inevitable and felt his eyes unexpectedly fill.

'They were screwing right there, beside the pool. Don't they know they are overlooked?'

He tried to sound surprised. 'Must be the weather. It's very hot. Must make them feel . . .'

'. . . Randy? I suppose so.' She stopped cutting the silvery skin and spun the knife unconsciously in her hand before putting it down on the surface. 'It made *me* feel randy, seeing them.' She put her hand unconsciously, momentarily, on his shoulder as she relived what she had seen. 'They were so, you know, up for it. It was really abandoned.' She shook her head, almost as if she was shivering from cold.

He ached for her hand to return to his shoulder. If only he hadn't gone to Cannes. Maybe she'd have still peered out of the window, seen them, felt as she had admitted she felt, turned to him for relief, for whatever she wanted at that brief moment. But he was away down the road while she was so close to needing someone. If the timing had been right, it wouldn't have needed his slight tale, carelessly told.

He moved over to her, casting his sensitivity aside. He put his arm loosely around her waist.

'So, you felt randy, eh?'

She tore away from him. 'Get off,' she snarled, 'you know the rules!' She softened and smiled at him as she lifted the knife to continue her work. She was very fond of him but not – not now, not ever again – in that way. 'Anyway I don't feel randy now. Only hungry. Do you want to open another packet of crisps? I'm starving!'

David Grant, her voice in his ears, turns sadly onto his side and falls asleep.

The First Saturday

David Grant opens his eyes and, reminded by the pictures on the wall, recalls the final thoughts of the night before. Sunlight and the promise of a new day put those notions where they belong, an archway, richly carved with half-remembered faces, leading to a darkened cathedral of fond memories, a place he can go to in his imagination whenever he likes, a sometimes indulged keen sense of loss and of what might have been, but belonging firmly, if occasionally reluctantly, to the distant past.

He feels in good humour, elated almost, and surprisingly well. In spite of showering the night before, he decides to repeat the process. It is only half-past seven, plenty of time to get himself thoroughly organised and more or less packed before going down for breakfast. The room being prepared for two people, he squanders a second bath towel after the shower and the last small hand towel while he shaves. He gives in to the only serial thievery he has ever indulged in and packs the liquid soap and two-in-one shampoo he hasn't used. He even takes the shower cap for Élodie and the little sewing set thoughtfully left, presumably as justification for the outrageous nightly rate charged by the hotel.

He carefully selects a pair of cavalry twills, still remarkably crisp from the case, and unfolds a cotton shirt with a designer motif on the top of the pocket. Another squint at the weather confirms it will be dry and warm, at least to start with. He goes down to breakfast and eats well before settling his bill with a sterling credit card and retrieving his car. He is in a hurry, almost running from another piece of illegal parking to obtain more sterling from the cash machine at a branch of Barclays (he argues that, as far as he can tell, the only legal places to park in England are in a multi-storey car park or your own front garden; most front gardens seem to him to have become car parks), before loading the maximum it will give him into his bulging wallet. With the balance of the previous day's withdrawal, he now has about five hundred and twenty-five pounds on him, together with a couple of hundred euros and, of course, his small collection of plastic. Plus the rest of his life secreted away in the numberless pockets of his wallet. Mustn't forget that.

Yes, he is in a hurry, expertly swinging the little Corsa out from behind an also illegally parked police car, its occupants in a next-door sandwich shop getting late-breakfast bacon rolls and eyeing the driver of the French car as an easy cop. But the sandwich maker is slow with the bacon; his observations on the weather, crime, politics and Britney requiring long pauses and excessive reversals of the rashers in the greasy frying pan, each scrape and swing of his spatula emphasising a point. Besides, there will be all that gesticulation and French babble to deal with. David Grant's rapid departure removes thoughts of duty, complication and the prospect of cold bacon in a doughy bap while offences are explained and tickets written.

He *is* in a hurry, quickly reaching the point where the policemen might have had another reason for professional interest, but why? And why the need for more of the UK's stubborn pounds? I don't know and neither does David Grant. He is living in a bubble, with the now paramount, the future a remote trailing second and the recent past faded and mendacious. He no longer ponders on the path-laying and his earnest intention to return to Le Crestet today or tomorrow. He still knows he must be back before Élodie and thinks in terms of a day or two to settle things but, having lost his cheap return trip, it's as though the obligation to cross the Channel has been cancelled by the ferry company's terms and conditions. Their restrictions have released him from a pledge, broken the chains that bind and left him utterly free. He is enjoying himself, and the reconnected familiarity of church spire and tower, red letter boxes and English-language advertising hoardings, driving on the left and kerb-stones everywhere, please him and bring a smile to his face, in spite of his oft-voiced commitment to and love of France. He makes a point of over-exaggerated courtesy at zebra crossings, grinning and nodding to the surprised and grateful, and the knowing-their-rights and surly alike, before scooting off as quickly as the little car will go.

He swings the Corsa out through the suburbs of Canterbury and soon turns onto the A2 signposted for London. He remembers their old house in Cockfosters and this becomes the focus of his mind. He turns on the radio and lets it search for a channel, smiling at the sunlit road and amazed at the weight of traffic coursing along the dual carriageway. That house had been a happy place, tucked back behind the main road through from Hadley Wood to Southgate, near, but not too near, the junction with the road coming up from Barnet to Oakwood. He remembers the two of them striding up to the station fifteen minutes away at the most and always getting a seat into town, living as they did at the end of the Piccadilly Line. Going home was more problematic and the short link between Finsbury Park and Moorgate was usually a stand but what he remembers most is a seat in the mornings and a chance to read the paper or chatter to Élodie during the adjustment between home and work, the overlooked advantage of commuting.

The only sad connection with the house had been his mother's descent into dementia a year or two before they moved to France. His face darkens as he remembers those difficult days of travelling increasingly frequently the long journey to her home, the short period she was with them, then the visits to the hospital and finally to one of the few nursing homes that would take a new resident who had not at least arrived with all their faculties. Still, it hadn't lasted long and she was a good age. One has to keep a sense of proportion about these things, see the big picture of her life of eighty-five years with only just over two where her memory had become unreliable. He thought of what he'd just said to himself. 'Her memory had become unreliable.' That's what it would say in an obituary, if even that. He might have used those words to an acquaintance. But they in no way reflected the reality and did his mother a disservice because there is no learning implied in those words and, in many ways, he learned more from his mother as she descended than he had since he was a small boy.

He calls in at a service station before he reaches the M25 and then plunges across the ring of insanity and heads into London. He would have been better to go anticlockwise on the M25 and turn down at Potters Bar but it is as though his mental map of the road system has not been updated for forty years. He follows the signs for Central London, only vaguely aware that he is on a motorway at all and perhaps a little surprised that he has not encountered a *péage* before it all comes back to him, the doubtful pleasures of the Blackwall Tunnel and the mean streets of the East End versus the glories of the Tower, Westminster and The Mall and perhaps a wander around his old haunts before a brisk commute out to Cockfosters. That's what he'd done when he was younger and the traffic was not so heavy; he had enjoyed London by car, enjoyed how compact and neat it all was. So, his memory acute and some trick of the mind coping with new road junctions and unfamiliar buildings, he instinctively races the little car without reference to any map ever-westward until he is speeding along the Old Kent Road, wheeling around the Elephant & Castle and crossing the Thames by means of Waterloo Bridge. I don't use the word 'speeding' lightly. On his way in he triggers two speed cameras that, in spite of the flash, he appears not to notice. Perhaps he thinks they won't be able to follow up a French plate but I don't think even that enters his mind. Everyone around him notices the flash, some think *they* triggered it and drive extra carefully for the rest of the day, damning themselves for being careless and hoping against hope that they had been mistaken, but only he, the true culprit, seems completely oblivious.

He finds a radio channel playing sixties music and he is driving his old Ford Popular again, bright blue, three forward speeds, pedals that need a clown's long shoes to reach them from the floor, but very quick and very thirsty. And she was there beside him, his first proper girlfriend with her panelled plastic coat inspired by Mary Quant, her white crocheted dress that ended four inches above the knee at best, her vastly expensive tights, her heavy eye make-up, the short, almost cropped hair flicked forward and lacquered ('Don't touch, you'll spoil it') and the gold cross around her neck that meant a lot to her and told him no for ever until he found someone else who said yes. He'd rather have stayed with the one who said no and she might have said yes to get him back, but he'd have felt a heel forcing her into something she didn't want and the one who said yes just kept on saying yes, yes and yes again and he was young and his priorities were suddenly all wrong. But the music is just what they'd listened to, not on the car radio because it had none, but on her little Dansette with the metal contraption that allowed a dizzying and somewhat lopsided pile of 45s to drop onto the turntable, usually after the playing arm had been retracted but not always, and if her parents were out they could set the thing up with the Everlys and Elvis, Cliff and Eddie Cochrane, the Bachelors and Marty Wilde and challenge themselves and their God to a contest to see how far they could go before conscience and the risk of babies pulled them back from a delicious and agonising brink. And they got so close, making a cup of tea when her parents were due to return and, in embarrassment, comparing notes, a post-mortem not unlike pundits pontificating after a football match. He shakes his head and smiles. He supposes that, nowadays, they just do it, no discussion. How it was for him later, in fact, without the inhibitions of faith or fear, and not how it was when he was young. They didn't do it, well he didn't do it with her, but they got close and then discussed it as their little secret; intimacy born out of restricted intimacy.

When the time of her parents' return drew near, she would tap him on the shoulder and he would lift himself gently off her and drag himself to his feet, frantically adjusting his erection that never seemed to be left tidily north and south and down the middle. She would wriggle about, lifting her bottom to get her dress or school skirt down over her legs again into something approaching the right place.

'Shall I put the kettle on?' he'd say, turning away from her and exaggeratedly admiring her mother's collection of Capo di Monte in the glass-fronted mahogany display cabinet to conceal his feverish rummaging in one trouser pocket and then the other to restore a little of his fragile dignity.

'Yes please,' she'd reply, standing up to smooth herself down before forking her fingers and running them through her hair as she peered in the mirror with the plaster gold frame over her parent's never-laid fireplace with the coal-effect electric fire, and adding, 'Lay a tray with four cups and saucers for Mum and Dad too, please. As usual.'

After she had finished with the mirror, she would follow him into the kitchen and put her arm around his waist while, with shaking hands, he carefully lifted her mother's best china cups from the wall unit and put them on the tray.

'I'll get Mum's sweeteners,' she'd say. He always forgot the sweeteners.

When things were on the go and they had cooled somewhat, there might be a few moments to talk over what had happened before the key in the door heralded her parent's return. Analytical it might have been but they hadn't the pleasure of the big picture so fragments of the unfulfilled became all there was.

'Phew, that was nice,' she'd say, stretching up to kiss him on the cheek. That kiss seemed like an act of gratitude and he would wonder about that saying 'It's better to give than to receive.' To him it seemed about equal.

He'd kiss her on the tip of her nose.

'I thought I was going to go,' he'd admit, using the word 'go' rather than 'come' because he didn't know the proper word and anyway 'go' seemed more apt.

'I heard you groan,' she smiled. 'But you mustn't you know. It might soak my skirt. They wouldn't let you back into the house if that happened. Besides, I might get pregnant.'

'I don't know if...'

'Yes,' she interrupted, her eyes widening to suppress any dissent, 'a girl in my class at school got pregnant last year. She was only fifteen. And she'd never had proper sex.'

'Really, I thought...'

She interrupted again. 'No, she said it was just a kiss and

he ejaculated over her school skirt and she was pregnant, just like that. That's what she told us anyway.'

'Did she have the baby?'

'Of course. She left school and went to stay with an aunt in Ireland. There was a place there for her. The baby was adopted. But she never came back to school.'

'That's a shame.'

'That *was* shame, I think. So, you see, you mustn't.'

'No,' he sighed.

He'd lift the kettle off the gas just as the whistle started and rip it off before filling the teapot. He hated that whistle.

'But what is it like for you?' she'd ask, filling the void in the conversation caused by the timely boiling and thoughts of the apparent dire consequences of ejaculation through umpteen layers of clothing.

'What?'

'Well, you are really big and hard. It was sticking into me a lot today.'

He'd have been proud of those words had they been said in the semi-darkness through the wall, but in the harsh light of the double kitchen strip while making tea, the only obvious response was to apologise.

'I hope I didn't hurt you?'

'No,' she giggled, taking the heat out of the moment. 'I suppose I'm made to cope with that hardness.'

'Yes,' he reasoned, as he put the bobbly knitted tea cosy over the teapot, the spout and ivory-effect handle sticking out through strategic holes. Everything in life was made to fit snugly if you thought about it.

'But what was it like?' she repeated.

'All exciting and throbbing and almost like losing control – not wanting it to stop. Everything seems so vivid and real. I just felt so alive.'

His memory is of a fairly advanced conversation late in

their relationship. In the early days, the questions had been more naive and certainly longer, though rarely posed, and the answers, if anything, monosyllabic.

She hugged him, knowing she was letting him do things he'd never done with anyone else.

'I want you, you know,' he said, clutching her to him clumsily and lifting her off her feet like a string puppet performing badly.

'I know,' she replied gently, reaching down to touch the floor with her stockinged feet.

'It's hard.'

'What is?' Now she was playing with him, knowing full well what he meant.

'The situation. Loving you. Knowing sex before marriage is wrong.'

'Yes, I know. It's hard for me too.'

'What's it like for you? I've told you what *I* think.'

'Sort of tingly,' she replied, distracted by a sudden need to check over the tray's contents.

'That's what you said last time.'

'Well, it was then too. Tingly. Nice.'

'It's just that I want to know *more* about what it's like for you.'

The Yale turned and her parents called out the obvious.

'We're home!'

The girl shouted a greeting and told them they'd bring tea through directly. He looked at her questioningly, engaging her eyes and turning his head slightly to one side. She put her arms around him and put her mouth to his ear. They could hear her parents pacing about noisily in the hall, scraping their feet unnecessarily on the doormat, sighing loudly, closing the door with a huge bang, hanging coats on the great wooden pegs and then going slowly through to the lounge, the air full of their inconsequentialities. They always made their presence felt at times like this, as though the embarrassment of the young people being caught in a compromising situation would be much the greater for them and adequate warning of their arrival must, as a consequence, be made.

She kissed his ear. 'It's wet down there!' she whispered.

He raised his eyes in amazement.

She smiled, nodded slightly and, lifting the tray, preceded him into the lounge . . .

Those of you familiar with London will know there is a cunning contrivance called a congestion charge in the city centre. David Grant won't pay the congestion charge. It is as though he doesn't see the signs or, if he does, it doesn't register. Instead he bounds on, crossing Waterloo Bridge as I have already said, turning left onto The Strand and working his way west and northwards to describe a large clockwise semicircle around the West End before ending up on Euston Road and then roughly following the Piccadilly Line out to the suburbs. The run out to Cockfosters is uneventful, even though he momentarily mixes up the road system with the more circuitous route of the Piccadilly Line and realises he is at the roundabout near their old house before he expected it.

His memory serves him well. It all looks the same. The trees are probably taller and the traffic heavier on the roundabout but he finds his way into the estate without a false move and experiences that foreshortening of the approach roads he more normally associates with memories of childhood locations. He's disappointed to see that someone has built a house on the once-manicured green space that gave rise to the developer's proud boast of the estate's 'village atmosphere'. He'd assumed, as probably everyone else had, that the grass was common land – it had certainly been treated as such when they had lived there. The children had played impromptu cricket matches on the rather too steep sward and he had once even seen someone using it for a child's birthday picnic. But no, greed and a lack of vision have spawned five or six linked houses that render the unusual and very nice quite ordinary and commonplace.

He parks the car and walks down past their old house, peering over the low wall and clocking on things that are familiar. The Japanese flowering cherry is much taller, its upper branches reaching to the tops of the windows on the first floor. The little rockery, slightly contrived on the otherwise flat front garden, is still in place with the rocks they had gathered from a short holiday in North Wales. He smiles at the memory of the car inclined upwards at an angle of about ten degrees all the way home and the fact that, try as they might, they couldn't get the feature to look right without using a lump of concrete left over by the builders. They had always promised themselves another piece of rock from another adventure but the concrete remained. He can see it still, incongruous amongst the slatey rocks from the lower reaches of Snowdon. There is the window for their bedroom, wide and matching the one for the through lounge/diner below. Beside it, above the front door which has been replaced by a uPVC double-glazed monstrosity, is what had been his mother's room. From the row of soft toys on the windowsill, its occupant is now a child – new life replacing one nearing its end. It would have made a much better children's room but not for too long. Children expand and need more space as they grow. His mother's greatest need in this house was on the day she arrived, shrinking her already modest world into the one tiny room. But within a week her limitations showed that even that small room was more than adequate for her and her rare need for clothes to go outside reduced her requirements to what would easily fit into half of the flat-pack wardrobe. They'd left it behind when they moved, tacked rather drunkenly to the wall with eccentric fixings

114

that implied a recognition of the frailty of the item on the part of the manufacturer and, for all he knew, it was still there. It was never possible to quite see it from the road.

He drives on to Potters Bar for lunch at a pub that deigns to serve roast beef, Yorkshire pudding and roast potatoes, it being a Saturday and thus, presumably, permitted. In spite of the size of the portion and the separate plate of boiled potatoes, cabbage, Brussels sprouts and slices of carrot so hard that they must have been sponsored by the greedy wing of the dental profession, he leaves nothing to be thrown away. It is precisely as he remembers it, curiously satisfying in a masochistic way – an English perspective on the process of catering where the objective is to provide pleasure from sheer volume and utter familiarity. This, in contrast to France, where regional tradition, a very learned clientele whatever their station in life, and the creativity of the chef, still satisfy on the basis of novelty and change, and certainly not quantity. He'd sought out the traditional fare in England, sought it out twice as a matter of fact, though only successful this time, and so he had fallen into the trap of preferring reminders to surprises. He finishes up with a treacle sponge and ice cream, a one-time favourite of his, and washes it down with a cup of what is described as freshly ground coffee.

When the waitress comes to collect his plates, she smiles at his not inconsiderable achievement.

'I can see you enjoyed that!' she enthuses. 'Have you been here before?'

'No. I don't think so.'

'Oh, because if you like, we can give you a Pub Grub Loyalty Card. Comes from the brewery but only some of their tenants subscribe to the scheme. You come here to eat ten times, get it stamped each time and the eleventh meal is free. Are you local?'

'Cockfosters,' he replies, without realising what he has

said. He expects the usual positive comments and curious enquiries when he explains where he lives but is surprised at the total lack of comment this time.

'Well then, that's local enough.'

What did the woman mean? It's a thousand kilometres away! But she is droning on with her sales patter so he is all rapt attention.

'I'll get you a customer registration card and you can put your name and address down. Then I'll give you the loyalty card duly stamped when you pay. Easy, isn't it? We'll send you details of all sorts of special offers and events, too. You married?'

'Yes,' he replies.

'What's her name?'

'Élodie. Élodie Grant.'

She smiles. 'That's a nice name; French, is it? Sounds French.'

That was the sort of response he'd expected when he told her where he lived. The waitress continues talking, sliding her tray gradually over the table as she takes mats, used napkins, plates and his cup and saucer out of the way of the advancing tray until she has effectively re-laid his place on the tray before removing it to the kitchen. It is well done. She pauses to complete her speech.

'Your wife might like our special ladies' lunch on Tuesdays. Very popular it is. Of course it's a very good deal, very inexpensive. Especially done for the Ladies Club. And we'll stamp your card if she comes on her own. There you are? Special deal cos you are nice and have got a very rewarding appetite. Still trim though, very trim. I'll make the loyalty card out in both of your names.'

When she brings the registration card, he takes his pen from his inside pocket and hesitates. Why is he filling it in when he lives three-quarters of the way down through France? He is about to hand it back and make some sort of an explanation when she asks, 'Whereabouts in Cockfosters?'

'Oh, just down near the roundabout at the bottom. Other end of the parade of shops. Sedgwick Road.'

'I know that road,' she replies, a smile crossing her face. 'I've got a friend lives in a new linked house near the top. The rest went up in the sixties, didn't it? I suppose you are in the older bit. What number?'

'Twenty-seven,' he obediently answers, shaking his pen and wondering why it has gone dry on him. Perhaps it needs the same approach as that adopted by the boarding-house proprietor. As he continues to shake his pen and scribble ineffectually on a corner of an unused paper napkin, he knows he is talking at cross-purposes with the waitress but can't quite see where the division in their understanding took place or what was and was not import-ant in the subplot, so he can't pause and rewind. Anyway, he's too deeply mired to be able to rescue himself.

'Here, looks as though your pen has dried up. Let me write it for you. Mr Grant, you said. Well, Mrs Grant, you said, so I assume it's Mr Grant?'

'Yes, David Grant. And Élodie Grant.'

'How do you spell Élodie. Like Melody without the M?'

'No.' He spells his wife's name; the waitress writes it down.

'See this pen?' She waves an expensive-looking biro in his face and clicks the point in and out a couple of times for dramatic effect. 'My husband bought it for me. Montblanc it is. That's French, isn't it? Birthday present with a differ-ence he said.' She laughs. 'It was his birthday, see? His birthday but my present. Can't be bad, I say! But I'm not allowed to let anyone use it, see? That's the rule. Twenty-seven Sedgwick Road you said?'

'Yes.'

'Postcode?'

'Pardon?'

'What's your postcode?'

'Oh yes, it's 07 . . .'

She interrupts.

'Is that EN07. EN for Enfield?'

'Umm . . .'

'Must be. Do you know the rest? It doesn't matter if you don't. The computer will find you. "Grant. EN07." That's all it needs to tell us your life story!'

She laughs as she walks back to the bar.

When he pays, she takes his credit card and thanks him for a cash tip. She writes out the loyalty card in both their names, spelling his wife's name like Melody without the M, dates it with the precious pen and stamps it with what looks for all the world like the block, type and ink pad from the John Bull printing outfit of his childhood.

Then he drives to North Wales.

In his mind, the most sensible thing to do is to get that missing rock and bring it back to the house in Cockfosters. He knows the people will be pleased and, besides, Élodie will find his quest extremely amusing. She even said on one occasion that they should put the rockery right before they sold the house. Well, it might be a bit late but it can still be done properly.

Setting off from Potters Bar soon after two o'clock, he reaches Conwy by nine and decides to run out to a spot near the start of the Watkin Path in the morning. That is where he and Élodie had found some good rocks within easy reach of the road. It would have been better to actually take them from Snowdon itself, but there was no way they could get the car near enough and they never claimed they had actually come from the mountain. Just some rocks from Snowdonia, that's what they'd always called them. He has eaten nothing more apart from most of a bag of mixed toffees bought on the A5. He finds a small hotel with a

118

vacancy for a night on the western road to Llandudno and explains his mission to the owner while he completes an entry in the visitor's book with his North London address. That seems to be where he's from in the context of his current purpose. The proprietor is a small round man who wears a cardigan buttoned practically to his neck over a loud checked shirt and sports a bad comb-over. He is wearing what look like Boy Scout shorts, well pressed and reaching several inches below the knee. This is a fashion that suits few people and certainly not the proprietor of this small hotel. His accent is softly Welsh, his tone critical.

'Don't let anyone see you. It's probably illegal to take the mountain away with you to London.'

'Really?'

'Really. How would it be if people came here taking all the rocks? London would end up looking mountainous and we'd end up flat and uninteresting.'

David Grant decides to say nothing more on the subject as the man is clearly deadly serious. After a moment of silence, while the proprietor studies the address details carefully and takes it upon himself to extend the tail of the 'd' in Sedgwick with a pencil tied to the desk with brown string, he asks, 'How will you pay?'

'Cash. I thought cash.'

'Just as well, see. We don't take cards and that. And cheques are so messy what with people's terrible hand-writing. Don't really like cheques, I don't.'

'What time's breakfast?' David Grant asks, keen to gain the privacy of his room.

'Eight to nine-thirty. Dining room to be cleared by five to ten.'

'Why?' he asks, curious at the precision.

'Hoover,' the proprietor replies.

He doesn't ask if the sullen response refers to a spookily dependable manifestation of J. Edgar, or a ritualistic clean-

119

ing of the carpet by someone obsessed by the clock. His powers of logic suggest the latter but, given the vivid imagination and slightly strange demeanour of the hotel proprietor, he decides it is evens that the old boss of the FBI is making his rounds after each and every breakfast in this corner of North Wales. Like Elvis, reliably reported serving in a fish-and-chip shop in Wigan.

'I'll be down at half-past eight,' he says over his shoulder as he picks up the key with the steel ball on the fob and makes for the stairs.

'I didn't hear what you are here for, do you understand? It isn't allowed, you know,' shouts the owner as David Grant clutches the handrail and juggles the key around the handle of his case before setting off up the slightly too steep staircase with its thick underlay and carpet sporting a loud pattern of autumn leaves. 'By the way,' the proprietor adds. 'Telly doesn't work. Aerial.'

'Doesn't matter!' David Grant retorts. Nothing matters.

'Here, you forgot your handbag!'

David Grant stops dead. He never forgets his 'handbag'.

In his room, shocked by his aberration, he puts the wallet beneath the pillow after carefully drawing the curtains. He can see a lighted room in a wing of the next semi-detached house with an elderly woman pacing back and forth and, he reasons, if he can see her, she can see him. But she doesn't look like the cat-burglar type. She is probably in her eighties and seems confused. When he first saw her, he assumed she was talking to someone beyond his line of vision but he can now tell she is on her own. Curious about the old lady and, with no working television to relax by, he reopens the curtains and watches the solo performance with curiosity. For her part, she paces back and forth and if he concentrates with the sash window open slightly he can hear her squeaky cackle. Even though she's speaking Welsh, probably a rarity in Llandudno, he can tell an animated

120

conversation is going on between her and herself and, from the changes in the pitch of her voice, one side of her personality is reasonable and measured while the other is argumentative and hysterical. She is standing most of the time with her profile to the window and, rather conveniently, when she faces one direction she is one side of her character, turning slowly with a suitable pause in the dialogue before reassuming her position in front of the window and becoming her alter ego. In spite of the argument, there are frequent outbursts of laughter and she seems overall to be happy.

That was not how his mother was. She was as quiet as a mouse. And she wasn't happy.

David Grant brews a cup of tea with the facilities provided in the room, making rather a mess opening the little plastic milk carton, and, driven by curiosity and very much against his better nature, draws the one upright armless chair to the window. With his curtains fully opened and darkness descending, and certain the old woman is either oblivious to her benign peeper or might even welcome an audience if she spots him, he turns off the light, perches the teacup on the narrow, painted windowsill and starts to watch the old lady again. Framed by her window and the brightly lighted room beyond, she will be his drama for the evening, a hint of television in the size of her across the narrow stretch of shadowed garden, a touch of theatre in the proscenium drapes of her curtains, her shabby props and the fact that her window is slightly uphill of him, as though he is sitting in the stalls.

Of her script, of course, he can understand not a word. This may be giving her more gravity, clarity and authority than she deserves. Even if she is talking gibberish and making no sense at all, he doesn't know. It reminds him of those early days in France when he would watch television and understand virtually nothing but gain a certain pleasure from the flow of words, the gestures and expressions, and his wife's spontaneous laughter at what was clearly a funny remark. When the panic set in and he despaired of ever learning the language, he would remind himself that human beings are the same the world over, thinking the same things, expressing the same emotions. It was just a question of learning the grammar, aligning the ear and relying on what was common to all. It would come in time.

And just as he looked for universal clues in dealing with an alien tongue, he now seeks the similarities between the animated old crone across the darkened orchestra pit and his mother. He had been witness to so much of her suffering, had locked away so many images and snippets of conversation and had been aware that, as she discarded her memories, she came into contact with more fundamental forces. But he never devoted the necessary time to explore the wisdom beyond insanity, the hints at what had been and will be, the illumination and revelation that only other-worldliness can disclose. In stepping outside the world and away from him, he was convinced she could see more but convey less because she had left him behind.

As he drinks the last of his tea and puts the cup down on the floor behind the velvet-covered chair in front, parks his programme in the gap between his tip-up cushion and the shared armrest to his right, shivers slightly at the draught coming from the double doors leading to the lighted foyer beyond, and smiles briefly at his companion, his concentration foreshortens the distance between him and the actress. His Thora Hird draws nearer, becomes a talking head that fills his vision, and speaks to him as his mother spoke.

'I remember how it was at the beginning. You never visited me, not like you used to. Very dutiful you'd always been, but then you stopped visiting. Not interesting any

122

more, I suppose. Stopped making shepherd's pie so you took your revenge by no longer visiting.'

The first inklings of trouble ahead were of a detachment from time. She would accuse him and Élodie of not being with her when they had been out of her house for the time it takes to trundle a trolley around a supermarket picking up essentials for a single old woman. The welcome meted out at the start of their visits can be imagined. Had they been returning for a ten-yearly visit from Canada, the reaction could not have been frostier. But she was still affectionate after the scolding and remembered everything about them. Then she stopped washing herself properly and forgot to prepare her meals. Something left in a pan to be heated after they left on Sunday evening would be found a week later, dangerously penicillined, and still in the pan awaiting heating up.

'You haven't been for ages,' she'd announce accusingly, looking over her glasses like an archetypal schoolmarm.

'We were here last week, on Saturday, just like today.'

'Nonsense. Was I here?'

'Yes, of course you were. We played . . .'

A look of triumph would cross her face.

'Ah-hah! Well there you are then! I *wasn't* here last week! I was away with Mrs Brough on a Scottish National Trust outing. I bought those place mats with the marquetry pattern, over there on the sideboard!'

'But, Mother,' he always called her "Mother", 'we bought those mats with you when we went out to the Palace last summer.'

She would walk smartly over to him at this and peer unblinking into his eyes.

'What are you trying to do, David? Do you take me for a fool? Are you trying to get me into a home or something?'

'Of course not,' he'd say. But in time that was exactly

what he was trying to do, for her sake as much as anyone else.

When she was finally taken to hospital, her complaints were about the institution as it affected her – the food, the fact that the place was too hot, and the way the young hospital porters used the wheelchairs as medieval jousting horses or as battering rams at the double swing doors placed at frequent intervals down the long corridor that connected the wards.

'I wouldn't mind,' she'd whisper, looking this way and that in case she was overheard and with a terrified look in her eyes.

'Oh, I don't think it's at all appropriate,' Élodie would say, quite shocked. 'If they want to play they should do it out of hours. Not in the hospital.'

'All young men need to let off steam,' his mother would reply, coming to the young porters' rescue. 'Only . . .'

'Only?'

'Only they shouldn't do it with the wheelchairs when we are sitting in them.'

David Grant told his mother he would have a word with someone in charge. Her bony arm stretched out to him and patted his arm as she implored him to say nothing.

'Why?'

'They'll take it out on me. I won't get anything to eat!'

'Are you serious?'

She continued the frantic patting, her eyes full of tears.

'Or worse,' she implied. 'Or worse.'

He remembers how he felt caught between a rock and a hard place. He wanted to bring her home again but knew that wouldn't work. She had paced the floor all night and went to the bathroom ten times every hour. Added to which, Élodie's company would not take kindly to any more extended leave, even if it was unpaid, and to take time off was impossible for him at the time. For all he knew,

124

wheelchairs were still converging at a combined speed of twenty miles per hour with screaming old ladies incontinently cowering into the innermost corners of their chairs as the porters whooped and then swung around at the end of the corridor for another tilt. He promised himself he'd write to the Health Authority the minute she was out of their grasp, but he didn't. With her death, the fight went out of him.

'You really liked your sister, didn't you, Mother?'

He was showing her some photographs when she was in the nursing home which she thought was a hotel.

'Yes, there she is, look. And there's me beside her.'

She could name and recognise people in photographs she hadn't seen for half a century but no longer remembered her son's name. And Élodie was that nice French lady who visited occasionally. She always seemed surprised when they arrived together.

'And what about this one,' he'd say, producing another family snapshot, posed and grey with everyone eccentrically overdressed and staring fixedly into the camera lens seventy years before.

'That's Minnie and me with Mother and Father,' she'd say, and then add, 'Yes, I was fond of my sister. We were very close but then we both died.'

Minnie *was* dead – she had been for ten years or more. But his mother? And this was a woman who, when asked by a family friend how old she was, answered truthfully, 'I am three years old,' and then added, 'In my fifth life.' Aunt Minnie had told David this story in her old age. She, much older, had been present and had never forgotten the incident. His mother had no personal recollection of what she had said but, of course, was rather proud of the celebrity it earned her on the odd occasion it was aired.

When he asked her to confirm her death, she did so, giving a date at the end of the previous year when she was still living in her own home. In fact, she became tetchy when he asked her to repeat the information.

'It's not interesting,' she said. 'Everyone knows. It was in the obituary columns at the time. And Mrs Brough knew about it, she told me she'd seen it and had cut it out to show me. I'll ask her to bring it next time I see her.'

When he asked her the same question on another occasion, she got the previously quoted date of her death precisely correct, even though as far as she was concerned, as he was the man on the desk in the hotel, he was being impertinent asking a guest personal questions and Élodie was a nice but nameless young girl she encouraged him to ask out on a date.

Were these just strange coincidental utterances from a slightly fey woman at each end of her existence, surreal book-ends to a library of a more or less conventional life spiced by tragedy? Or was there much more to it, new definitions of what life is, beginnings and endings outside the normal accepted span, a possibility that one can die and continue living, or be tremendously old at the time one is born, an explanation that expands and makes more problematical the narrow certainties of many conventional religions? Are the really important truths uttered by infants and geriatrics? Is all the rest, as a consequence, unimportant since perhaps we function within one of many parallel existences?

With his mother present on the stage he wants to ask her so many questions he omitted to frame on earlier occasions but how can he? You can't just stand up in the middle of a theatre and talk to the cast. He has felt that sense of frustration before, of needing to talk, to ask, to understand, but there was always something in the way. And as he tries to gather his thoughts and make a note on a little pad of things to ask later after the curtain falls, she moves on to another topic and the thread is lost.

He awakens stiff and cold and his head hurts. He is in

complete darkness. At first he cannot move his legs at all and decides to read the programme while circulation returns but, when he slides his hand down at the side of his chair, both the arm and the programme have disappeared. There seems to be no one in the audience either, the curtains are drawn across the proscenium arch and the stage is dark. His left hand has gone to sleep clutching the small hard-bound notebook Élodie gave him as a present a few months before.

'How could they leave me here?' he asks, as he returns the notebook to his pocket. He realises his companion has left, too. But who had she been? Indeed, was she, in fact, a she? He knows Élodie is miles away, so it couldn't have been her. Then he feels guilty that he took someone to the theatre without Élodie knowing and rather hopes it was a man.

He looks at his watch. It is ten minutes to twelve, midnight.

'No wonder no one's here,' he thinks. 'They'll all have gone home. But it's odd them leaving me here on my own like someone ending up in the sidings after going to sleep on the last train. Surely someone must have spotted me?'

But no one did, not even the object of his attentions. She has been tucked up in bed with hot milk, a sleeping draught, some light straps keeping her firm and safely attached to the mattress and a chrome bed gate as a last resort for hours, and she is wearing an outsized Pampers nappy to keep her and everyone else happy. Full house tonight. Everyone satisfied. Another show tomorrow. Twice-nightly. What a schedule. But who would have it any other way? Theatres should only be dark at ten minutes to midnight.

He tries to stand but his legs give way and he ends up on the floor. Pulling himself up again, he finds somewhere comfortable to rest and he falls asleep, dreamless except for an image of blonde hair soaked in blood accompanied by his silent scream.

127

Sunday

David Grant awakens by falling heavily to the floor. He strikes his head against the doorknob of the bedside cupboard on the way down and, when he reaches up to rub the sore place, he realises he's drawn blood. He drags himself to his feet and, in order to try to avoid getting blood on his clothes, he runs the cold tap in the washbasin and soaks the flannel before squeezing it dry and applying it to the rapidly expanding swelling.

He catches sight of himself in the mirror. He is fully dressed and more crumpled than he has ever seen himself. His hair is sticking out in all directions other than the blood-soaked patch on top which is flat and shining. He looks grey and ill, and his shirt, despite his attentions with the flannel, is flecked with blood and soaked with water. Feeling a little faint, he sits down in the chair inexplicably facing the window and concentrates on mopping his head. After a few moments he rises to his feet and surveys the scene from the window, clutching a paper handkerchief to his injury.

It is one of those bright, still, sunny mornings, frequently experienced in North Wales, that tempt the unwary into positive thoughts of a day of rewarding exercise a long way from shelter. The sky is a metallic slatey grey, in spite of the low, early sun, and the windows of the surrounding houses glint and dazzle as if absorbing as much light as possible before the rain to come. He knows this is the moment to wash his face, comb his hair carefully and go out for a quick walk in the early quiet; ozone filling his lungs and the cold air stinging his face and sharpening his senses. Already he can see small clouds gathering around the summit of the Great Orme, moving gently as if in passing but persistently reforming and increasing in size. To the east, lit by the sun, they appear white and harmless, but to the west, they are grey and more dense. He looks at his watch. It is not yet seven o'clock. He pulls the chair back from the window and sets it against the wall next to the shabby table with the non-functioning television and the tray of untidy tea- and coffee-making facilities.

He decides to take his walk before showering; even before washing his face and combing his hair. He won't be out long and the weather is changing even as he ponders his next steps, a sense of urgency compromising his usual high standards. He finds his room key and walks gingerly down the stairs, letting himself out of the front door which he bangs shut behind him.

It is exactly as he thought: a sharp, cool day with only a whisper of a breeze, the sun playing with the tops of the surf as it runs gently up the estuary. Across the railway line the shore looks inviting but he is not near a pedestrian subway or any level crossing he can see and thinks he might find an early-riser newsagent to sell him an English newspaper. Behind him, large banks of clouds are building up on the ring of mountains forming an amphitheatre around the deeply penetrating valley, and ahead the Great Orme is now wearing a fluffy grey hat.

A week earlier, David Grant would have put his experiences the night before down to falling asleep in a chair after a long tiring day. And, to an extent, as we know, that is just exactly what happened. But he would have rolled the whole package into his dream, everything from seeing the old lady as his mother, through to his mystification over being left in the theatre after everyone had gone home. Indeed, he would have been embarrassed by his peeping-Tom act, as shocked at his behaviour as he had been in his thirties when on the beach with his family he had watched a couple making love in a hollow in some sand dunes. There are times when, faced with bizarre, shocking or erotic behaviour, we all step out of our comfort zone of manners, routine and knowing how to behave, and risk reputation and self-respect because, at that moment, there is nothing we can do to save ourselves.

He had been innocently walking with his youngest who was running up and down the dunes whooping like a Red Indian (he was into cowboys and Indians at the time and always favoured the underdog) when he had seen the girl sitting astride a prone man, her arms outstretched, her face tilted up to the sun. 'Best way to make love in the sand,' he told himself later. 'Keeps the sand out of your bits as much as possible.' But that thought was subsequent to his embarrassment; when how he behaved at the time felt less shocking, after he had overcome his shame, convinced himself his response had been normal for a red-blooded male.

He had sent his boy on ahead to be near his mother and sister and had flopped down onto the summit of a dune to watch them, his face peering from between strands of spiky grass. He remembered the cool sand assuming his shape as he twisted himself into place. While he watched, the man, who was almost invisible, tore the bikini top from her breasts and she twisted around to release the clasp. He then kneaded her roughly while she rode him and shouted encouragement before succumbing to her orgasm. After it was over, he had wriggled backwards down the slope, the smell of semen filling his nostrils and sand sticking to his trunks in ways incompatible with someone who had not yet been in the sea. To overcome his embarrassment and protect himself from his wife altering her opinion of him

130

for life as a consequence of one totally out-of-character moment, he had run four hundred yards without stopping, ignoring the shouts from his family and roaring with theatrical laughter as he splashed into the sea for a great deal more than simply a swim.

When he emerged from the surf, he overplayed his affection for his family, hugging his children and kissing his wife in a way she thought slightly inappropriate in full view of the crowded beach.

'What brought that on, hurtling pell-mell into the sea?' she had asked, slightly surprised at his action.

'Oh, I don't know. Happiness, I suppose. Holiday. Being away from work. Freedom. Joy. My family around me.'

Everything, in fact, but the truth.

His wife looked at him and smiled.

'I'm glad you're happy. I've never seen you do that before, though, running straight into the sea. You usually take about half an hour to get in up to your waist! Daddy's usually a bit of a coward, isn't he, children?'

'Yes, well you'll never see me do it again, I can tell you,' he replied, towelling himself down and unkindly flicking sand into the face of his prone daughter, who twisted sideways, rubbing her eyes. 'It was so cold!'

But he meant it; they would never see him do it again. The need would never arise. He'd make sure of that.

And some time later, they had picked up towels and toys and ambled away from the beach for an ice cream and he had seen the couple approaching them from the other direction. He was slightly overweight and she had one of those white, blotchy, freckly skins that he found utterly unappealing. But it was her all right; he'd never mistake the shock of curly red hair. The sight of them, she particularly, surprised him. Even in those days, the cult of youth coupled to beauty and sexual athleticism, particularly on the screen, had consigned the plain to a role of passive, inevitable child production, home-making and DIY. Only the extraordinarily beautiful behaved like that – had sex that shook the earth and made voyeurs of the less fortunate. Now, sucking ice cream cornets and wearing Marks & Spencer T-shirts over their swimming costumes, they looked nondescript. They seemed hardly capable of love-making other than in the dark, and then it would have been a grunt from him and silence from her, other than a 'Feel better now?' But, out there in the dunes, she had been a goddess and reputations had been gambled, his most of all.

A week ago he'd have been similarly ashamed of his behaviour over the old lady, not that that stimulated him in any way like the time on the beach. But it wasn't nice, watching someone like that, especially when she was obviously deranged. But that would have been a week ago. Now he feels no shame because he isn't absolutely certain what happened. Some parts of his experience approach the inexplicable. His mother's appearance and the long monologue, for example, with his frustrated impatience to ask old questions again and pose new ones he wished he'd asked before. To know precisely when he was born would have been a bonus, but he really wanted to confine himself to subjects which most of us cannot experience but which, he was convinced, his mother had an inside track on. Then there was the extreme reality of it all, not at all like a dream with its trademark give-aways and conflation of events. He was most troubled by the interior of the theatre which, even as he walks in the direction of the town centre, he can feel again with the sensitivity of a cat whose whiskers are alert and trembling. The slight breeze from the exit doors with their round windows and the occasional bobbing face of an usherette; the difficulty of making his long frame comfortable in a seat he couldn't adjust with the floor a forest of cast-iron chair legs, braces and struts; his companion whose face was in darkened profile, intent on the lone player on the stage – he's sure it was a woman now; the theatre programme he felt down the side of the chair, staples at the bottom, sharp, cutting pages fanning up to his wandering fingers; the familiar smells and atmosphere of an auditorium. Then there was the odd business of being locked in after the performance and the notebook he had removed from his pocket and found in his hand when he awoke.

No, a week ago it would have been written off as a dream. Now, while he hasn't any answers, he is fairly sure it wasn't a dream. Just another of those odd experiences that he no longer feels need an explanation but is unable to rationalise. He has become willing to treat with equal credibility the plausible and the incredible.

Before he comes to the town centre, he arrives at a parade of shops where two men in jeans and paint-spattered T-shirts are parking their white Ford Transit and patronising a mini-supermarket. This, on a Sunday, a job running late or a bit of overtime, presumably. Moments later they emerge with bottles of Coca-Cola and milk, capped cardboard cups of coffee, packets of crisps and tabloid newspapers with appealing but inconsequential headlines, which they fold neatly and put in behind the steering wheel to be read later. David Grant crosses the road and saunters along the wide pavement to the shop. He nods at another couple of departing workmen as they juggle their purchases to get a quick swig from a bottle before bouncing off down the road to a building site. One of them holds the door open and looks at him strangely.

David Grant quickly spots the newspaper rack and selects a copy of the *Sunday Telegraph* before taking it to the counter.

'You all right, mate?' the man at the cash till asks in the familiar Liverpool accent of these parts.

'Fine,' David Grant replies, 'And you?'

'Oh, *I'm* fine. It's you. Your head's busted. Been in an accident?'

David Grant feels the top of his head and remembers that he hadn't washed the blood off before setting out on his walk.

'Oh,' he smiles self-consciously. 'Yes, bit of an accident. At home. Should have washed it but I wanted a paper.'

'Domestic, eh?' The man grins and shouts over to one of his regulars who is rummaging about in the chilled cabinet looking for the coldest bottle of orange juice with the longest sell-by date. 'See this guy? See how his wife treats him in the morning? Big whack on the head just to keep him in line!'

They both roar with laughter. David Grant smiles, trying to imagine Élodie hitting him over the head with anything.

'It's not like that. Hit my head on a cupboard.'

He pays for the paper and a Mars Bar – he always associates Mars Bars with long walks in the Welsh hills – and makes to leave.

'See ya, mate,' the shopkeeper says. 'But I'd get someone to look at that if I were you. It looks deep.'

David Grant stops and turns to him.

'It's not still bleeding, is it?'

The man strains to see the top of his head which David Grant inclines slightly.

'No, but it looks bloody sore.' He draws air through his teeth as he sees the full extent of the damage. 'It's all matted dark blood and your hair's all caught up in it.'

'Lucky him!' says the regular. 'If it had been you, you'd have had no protection at all, being a slaphead!'

'Only past-its-sell-by-date orange juice for you from now on, you cheeky article!' the shopkeeper laughs. 'See what I mean? The customer's always right, be buggered. And I get up at the crack for these fuckers and all they do is spend a couple of quid on nothing.'

'Lucky you, we take nothing and give you a couple of quid!'

'And bloody quick with their tongues too! Should be performing at the end of the pier.'

'There's no theatre at the end of the pier.'

'That's what I mean! Now bugger off!' He turns to a smiling David Grant. 'Sorry. Still an' all, I'd have it looked at by a professional.'

'Have you got any antiseptic?'

'I think so. I'll look for you. You stop here a minute.'

The shopkeeper crosses the shop and peers with a practised eye over a small section devoted to after-sun and mild painkillers.

'I've got this,' he says, brandishing something promising. He looks at the packaging. 'Says it's for minor grazes, which that isn't'

'Still, I'll take it. Thanks. I'll get a shower when I get back and see what the damage is after that.'

'Good idea.'

He walks quickly up the road reading the headlines in the paper as he goes. The sun has gone in now and the breeze has stiffened making him shiver in his blood-spattered T-shirt. He turns in at the gate and lets himself into the hotel. There is still no sign of life from other guests but there's a faint smell of bacon cooking in the deeper recesses of the house. He clambers up the steep staircase and lets himself into his room.

In five minutes he's in the shower and the warm water opens up the wound but cleans it at the same time. By turns he puts his head into the jet and winces when his head stings, and then stands with his head on one side as the blood trickles into the flow and forms a pink rivulet over

135

one shoulder and down his flanks. Gradually he begins to feel able to dab the top of his head with the flannel and some of the dried blood comes away. The pain increases but he feels he's making progress. A few minutes later he is towelling himself down and applying the antiseptic, looking in the mirror to make sure he's covered the whole area. 'Is this enough of a dire emergency to call Élodie, I wonder?' he asks himself, knowing the answer already. He sits for a while on the edge of the bed. His head is drumming badly but he puts it down to the injury. He really needs to bang his head with his record for headaches.

At just before half-past eight he is fully dressed in clean clothes and the wound, while still exposed and not a pretty sight, is only oozing slightly and what seems to be coming away is more like water than blood. He goes downstairs to the small dining room where he exchanges brief pleasantries with the other guests but receives a less-than-warm reception from his host.

After the other visitors have left, the owner seizes his chance before any other guests drop in for their breakfast.

'I've had a complaint.'

'Really?'

'Really.'

'What about?'

'Noise. That's what about.'

'Noise?'

'Noise. Bangs in the night. And slamming the door at the crack of dawn.'

'You can't shut your front door without slamming it.'

'Why do you need to shut it at six-thirty in the morning?'

'It wasn't six-thirty. It was at about ten to seven.'

'Still, people are trying to sleep 'ere. I don't encourage tradesmen for the same reason.'

'I needed to go out.'

'At six-thirty?'

'No,' he replies quietly, 'at ten to seven.' He takes a triangle of toast from the chromium rack and opens an individual pack of Welsh butter.

The proprietor changes his tack. He pulls up a chair from the next table and sits down to face his errant guest.

'Then there was a bang in the night and another this morning.'

David Grant pauses for thought.

'I fell over.'

'Both times?'

'Both times.'

'See,' the proprietor says, crossing his bare knees, 'we don't hold with drink in this house.'

'I wasn't drinking.'

The proprietor tuts and shakes his head slowly. He is clearly not convinced.

'Now, Mr Grant, to fall over once might be an accident, but to fall over twice . . .'

'. . . Might be carelessness. Yes, I know. I know. But that's what happened, believe it or not. See,' he bends his head forward and the little man winces, 'I did that on your bedside cupboard,' he adds.

The proprietor looks distinctly uncomfortable for the first time in the conversation.

'I hope you're not going to sue?'

'Why would I sue?' David Grant asks, surprised at the change of direction.

'Oh dear. Lots of people would try. Or threaten. Some-times I have to give them free nights. Happens a lot nowadays. A little accident, some threatening words, and the result? No money for me. I think some of them do it on purpose. In fact, I'm absolutely sure of it.'

'That's crazy. It was my fault I fell.'

'No one takes responsibility nowadays. It can be difficult in this business. Their word against mine, and the tourist office very twitchy about complaints.'

'Well, it was my fault but it wasn't drink, I assure you. In my youth, I have been known to fall over after a drink or six, but not nowadays. Not recently.'

'Of course, Mr Grant, of course. Can I bring you anything else?'

'Perhaps another cup of black coffee?'

When he goes back to his room he spends an anxious five minutes looking for his wallet. Normally when he is away from home he puts it on a bedside table, but it is not there. A frantic search results in him more or less stripping the bed and this reveals the wallet hiding under his pillow. His problem with his wallet is the thing that worries him the most. He knows his head will heal but he must get to grips with his new-found amnesia. Having spent a lifetime checking up on a wallet he's never lost, he has contrived to mislay it twice in the previous twelve hours.

'Going to get your stone, then?'

The tone is different, almost encouraging.

'Yes, it's only one. I need it to complete a rockery.'

'Nice you are using Welsh rock. Get a good one, won't you?'

'I'll try.'

'Good luck, and thanks for staying.'

'That's fine. Get the TV fixed, though.'

'It's the aerial, see? Seems to be on the blink. I'll get someone out.'

He starts the car and sets off southward just as the rain begins – a gentle mist of tiny droplets that covers the windscreen like clear sprayed paint. Within ten miles, he can barely hear the engine for the drumming of the deluge on the roof and the wipers, set at fast speed, move millimetres of water back and forth across the glass like a child creating tides in his bath.

An hour or so later, he is near the foot of the Watkin Path, one of the longer ascents of Snowdon, and the rain has abated to torrential. He drives slowly, peering out through the glass trying to identify where he and Élodie parked before. After two passes of the half-remembered spot he stops and kills the engine, winding the window down to confirm that he is within reach of where they found their other pieces of stone. Yes, here it is, a tiny quarry at the side of the road but now with very little loose stone visible. Clearly, others have had the same idea over time, and what had been comparatively easy fifteen years before now offers new challenges. There is nothing but some loose slivers of rock and clumps of luxuriant, springy Welsh turf giving off the beautiful scent of recent rain. Not recent rain. Current rain.

He struggles into his coat for the first time this trip and climbs out to look at the situation more closely. Raindrops pound onto his sore head and the blood starts to trickle down his face and into his eyes. Nothing. Nothing he can usefully use, anyway. He walks up and down, oblivious of the state he is now in, his face and coat, and no doubt his shirt, streaked with a weak mixture of blood and rainwater. He looks away from the quarry and back towards the road in the hopes of finding at least something.

On the other side of the road, there is a walled enclosure fringed with pine trees and protected by a large set of double gates. He looks and tries to work out what the place is. It could be a house, or something belonging to Welsh Water – a pumping station perhaps for one of their National Park 'stick an enormous pipe on a hillside' spoiling enterprises. The enclosure is high with a saw-tooth top, vertical stones placed at intervals of perhaps eighteen inches to help lock the top of the drystone wall and, at the same time, make climbing over it more difficult. Buck-and-doe coping, it's called.

It is his only chance. In his memory, the stone is about the right colour, but after rain all stone darkens. Still, it will do. The people back in Cockfosters will be so grateful, they won't mind if the shade is a little different. He walks over to examine the wall more closely and sees that there is a buck stone that he can wobble near the gate. He returns to the car and backs it across the road, stopping just short of the gates and opening the boot. He rocks the stone back and forth. It is wet and, being under a stand of dripping pine trees, mossy and covered in tiny lichen. Still he persists and after about five minutes of hard labour it begins to work loose, eventually falling with a clatter onto the half-buried cobbly stones at his feet. As he lifts it gingerly into the boot, the only car he's seen for ages slows down. With one hand on his rock, he waves to the occupants who do not wave back but drive off almost immediately. The rock safely stowed, he removes his coat and sets off, retracing his steps, entirely satisfied with his morning's work. Even his head isn't hurting so much, the cold rainwater anesthetising his wound. Still, his shirt will need to be changed, and almost everything else as well, as he is soaked to the skin. He thinks no more of the passing, pausing car, which is just as well.

But they are thinking quite a lot about him and have taken down his car registration number, shaking their heads theatrically and muttering angrily about Frenchmen and vandalism and asking what the world is coming to.

As he drives towards the coast he is well pleased with his morning's work. He has his rock safely stowed in the boot and he knows that it will be well received back in Cockfosters. He almost feels a sense of ownership about the house. It was his for so long and so much of what he and Élodie

140

had done is still there to be seen that it is almost as though he has never been away. He particularly admires the development of the cherry tree; how tall it has grown and how broad its branches! He has always liked cherry trees, reliable, rewarding and so extraordinarily pretty for that brief blossom time before the spring winds propel them into early summer. He even has one in France which is probably larger than the Cockfosters example even though the French one was only planted recently.

He puts the heater on and, while he begins to dry out, it does nothing for the blood on his shirt which is stained pink. Finding a small bus shelter on the way into Conwy, he stops, hauls his case out of the boot and changes his shirt and trousers quickly, looking up and down the road to ensure he is alone. He notices he is fast running out of clothes. His intention is to grab a bite to eat somewhere along the North Wales coast and then set off to the east and then southwards to his old haunts. The inland route would have been shorter but the choice of places to eat, especially on a Sunday, might be limited. Besides, he likes the sea and is deprived of it in the Ardèche.

As it is still early, he heads back into Llandudno for a coffee. Soon he is driving along the promontory towards the town centre, this time on the eastern road which sports a wide promenade. Although it is still windy, the rain has stopped and there are knots of people, arm in arm, leaning into the wind and working hard in one direction or skittering along propelled by the strong breeze in the other. He stops the car and crosses over to be near the sea. Four or five herring gulls the size of small chickens are standing on the wall eying the passers-by to see if anyone has boarding-house bread to feed to them. In the old days, maybe even now, if there was an excess of bread at the breakfast table, wise guests took it with them when they left. If not, it would be bread-and-butter pudding for supper every night.

A couple, arm in arm and pushing a buggy containing a small child, struggle with a small terrier who would give anything for freedom and the chance to kill herring gulls. Eventually the couple give him his chance and release him from his lead. The dog sets off at a run, barking wildly, but as soon as the gulls see him, they spread their wings, feathering them like Boeing 737 wing flaps, and rise almost vertically out of reach. The dog looks bewildered. It's as though they were there one minute, within reach, and the next vanished from sight. He didn't see their ascent. He trots quickly up and down the pavement and then hops on the wall for another look while, just above his head, the gulls, heads pointing downwards, circle and hover, rise and fall through the air, waiting for the dog to lose interest.

David Grant finds a café and orders a latte, which comes quickly with a cinnamon biscuit. Llandudno clearly sees itself as part of Europe. He stirs his coffee simply for the pleasure of it; he does not normally add sugar. His head still hurts and he winces as he explores his crown tentatively. The bump is still large and tender but it seems to be settling down. His coffee is too hot to drink so he goes to the toilet and re-anoints his wound with the antiseptic.

Having done a visual tour of the other guests and with his coffee still hot enough to strip the skin from his palate, he starts to think about taking the rock home and how he will present his gift to the present incumbents. As he puzzles over his approach, his mind is filled again with the house in Cockfosters and that cherry tree. He starts to hum quietly to himself without really knowing the song and then it begins to come back to him. The song fits his thoughts exactly. He stops, looks around slightly embarrassed hoping he hasn't been overheard, and starts again, forming silent notes by pressing his tongue up against his teeth and breathing in and out rhythmically. Something about cherry trees and their blossom and how their blossom is a reward for something. Now, what was it? 'Well done, everyone, well done.' That's what the singer had sung. 'We've travelled all around the sun; it's taken us one whole year. Well done, everyone, well done.' Memories flood back of smiling faces and flowing Guinness and wet nights in Dublin contrasting with the shabby intimacy of Mother Redcaps with its little stage and crazy lighting and the bar around the corner. And in among those faces, friends, long-known friends, friends with whom he and Élodie had travelled far.

'I think you'll like this,' he'd said. 'Knowing you, I think you'll like this.'

And he had driven them in from the salubrious Southside with its wide avenues and expensive houses peeking from behind high gated walls and trees in their spring foliage, through the darkened streets and water-filled potholes of Dublin 8; past prostitutes sheltering in doorways touting for passing trade that wasn't passing on that wettest of nights; past vagrants wandering uncertainly, one foot plashing the water in the gutter, the other by turns on the pavement or on the steep camber of the road, walking a few paces in one direction and then turning quickly, as if in fear, before resuming their journey, sometimes in the direction they had chosen before, sometimes as determinedly back the way they had come. The car turned this way and that along narrow streets of terraced houses with occasional illuminated plaster saints standing in elaborate Victorian cupolas, or blocks of poor flats with high walls and spiked railings and concentration-camp lighting; past market debris, rotten cabbage leaves piled sopping against dark brick walls and broken crates with blue tissue paper bleeding regally onto the pavement. And when they got out, checking their way and finally to park at Mother Redcaps, their noses were assailed by the smell from St James's Gate, the hops and the mashing and the brewing of Guinness.

They had climbed the stairs to the little theatre and sat

next to the stage and that's where he heard the song for the first time. John Spillane came on, self-effacing, making fun of his shyness, tongue-tied and awkward, but when he'd got himself through the ordeal of introducing the songs, he was in his element. Sometimes sitting, the guitar on his knee, sometimes standing, he sang his life in that winning Celtic mix of traditional storytelling song with a modern beat to an audience that knew practically every word. In no time they were all warmed up and the applause became deafening after every song. They knew every word but didn't sing along with him – just mouthed respectfully and listened to his expressive voice sitting inside its broad Cork accent. They were so proud of him that if he'd hinted he might stand for President, he'd be living in Phoenix Park by now.

'Sing the "Cherry Tree", John,' someone asked between songs and he had, fumbling nervously with his guitar as he pretended to struggle remembering the words. And when it was over, David Grant had a song in his head he'd never forget, not least because it was so simple and honest and uncynical. He couldn't imagine anyone in England writing or singing such a song other than in the narrow confines of the folk tradition, somewhere John Spillane didn't seem to belong. As the audience warmed, he warmed too, still jokey and self-conscious, but taking his time over his introductions. He seemed most comfortable singing in Gaelic, his language of choice, and brought the house down when he announced to his almost wholly Irish audience, who, with a few exceptions, could probably only use school Gaelic, that the next song would be sung in the 'language of the oppressor', meaning English.

It was a joke, of course. But not one without deep roots, without a history, without blood on its hands. For all its Celtic Tiger economy, its increasing numbers of high-powered, high-priced cars, its new-found confidence, Ireland's skin is thin and a mass of sensitive nerve-endings. Any conversation between a Brit and an Irishman about Ireland's history will soon lead to justification, shame and the revelation of two differently learned histories, of nations bound together by misunderstanding and injustice, truth and lies. Ireland is truly a young country with one of the longest histories in Europe.

They had ordered more and more beers, queuing them up on the spill-stained table, while the singer crouched over his instrument tuning it electronically and talking to anyone who spoke to him. David Grant was struck by warmth and generosity in a world growing cold and increasingly impolite, the bond between strangers in shared pleasure, and the sad recognition that this was unreal and largely confined to the past, a fleeting moment generously provided during a brief holiday.

And he wants more of it. More of the conviviality. More of the world of Mother Redcaps. More of the past, a place he likes because he knows what happened next.

At last he can drink his coffee. He spoons the dregs of foamed milk into his mouth and looks at his watch. It is just after eleven o'clock. He dimly remembers an afternoon ferry to Dun Laoghaire or Dublin and can think of nothing but the cherry-tree song, his fond memories of Mother Redcaps and, by extension, the sights, sounds, smells and ambiance of Dublin.

'This is real Dublin,' his friend had said. 'A link with the Dublin of Joyce and Behan. Literary, musical, pub-centric, characterful Dublin. It's under threat, the old Dublin, I'm afraid. But you can still find it in pubs like Mother Redcaps and the Long Hall. One or two others, too, but not many.'

He leaves the café and, thinking of Élodie, remembers that he is still travelling farther and farther from her. He returns to his car, finds his mobile by rummaging in his suitcase and decides to charge it in the cigarette-lighter socket. He might have to call her if he leaves things too late

but it is still only Sunday. If there is a crossing this afternoon, he could stay one night, return on the Monday and
still be back in the Ardèche by Wednesday, one day before
Élodie would be 'released' from the Vipassana. It would
mean a lot of driving but what a lot he'd have to tell her.

He swings the car around and heads quickly back for the
main road to Holyhead. The road has been improved since
he last used it, not least the conversion of the rail bridge
over the Menai Strait to include a road deck. He goes
around the back of Bangor using the bypass and crosses the
bridge, regretting the absence of sunshine. What can be
one of the great views of Wales just looks grey and uninteresting. The waters below are leaden and choppy and the
car rocks a little in the fretful wind. As he reaches the
Anglesey shore, the rain starts again. The wipers beat out
their monotonous rhythm all across the island with fog
banks building up as he traverses the causeway to Holy
Island.

He follows the signs for the port and parks in front of
the offices. There is a crossing at three-thirty with space on
board.

The booking clerk peers at his screen, hardly looking up
at David Grant as he asks, 'Do you want to take your car?'

'How much?'

The clerk quotes the price. It is not cheap.

'What are you going to do over there?' asks the man.

'Oh, just sightsee. Go around the city. I used to know it
quite well.'

'You won't really need a car, will you?'

'No. Not really.'

'There's the train from next to the port. Shouldn't need
a car. Plenty of taxis and buses around the city, too. Or you
could walk. Dublin's pretty compact, isn't it?'

That settled it. No car. Just a return passenger on the
high-speed ship.

146

'When are you coming back?'

'I thought tomorrow.'

'You won't have long, will you? You'll almost have to come back as soon as you arrive. Why not stay until Tuesday?'

'I could, I suppose. It would give me longer.'

'I would if I were you.'

Accordingly, he books his forty-eight-hour return and pays with his UK credit card.

'Where do I park the car?'

'Well, there's one near here but it is probably full. Then there's the municipal one but that's pretty expensive. Or you can go all around the dock and put it in the overflow. It's a bit of a walk back but there's a shuttle bus if you're lucky. It's free.'

'I think I'll get something to eat first.'

'Plenty of time,' retorted the clerk, his eyes still glued to the screen. 'Just as long as you are on board by three o'clock. There are restaurants on the ferry but it's rather a long time to wait.' David Grant thanks the clerk and bids him farewell but he is engrossed by the flickering screen and doesn't reply.

He drives off the dock and parks in a side street within sight of a fish-and-chip café. There is a carry-out counter to one side but he prefers to sit down. It is still raining, so the alternative would be sitting in the car and getting his hands greasy. His days of eating fish and chips from a paper were over many years before. Within half an hour he has consumed a large portion of fish and chips, to which he adds sachets of brown sauce (practically unheard of in France), with a couple of rounds of thin white bread crudely spread with something that only slightly resembles butter. He has drunk more than two cups of weak tea.

Next to the café is an outdoor shop, the window cluttered with walking boots, lightweight cutlery, dinners that heat themselves, cheap bags and rucksacks – the paraphernalia of doubtful pleasure. While his suitcase is not large, dragging it around Dublin for two days might quickly pall, so he goes into the shop and emerges with a sausage bag which costs him less than twenty pounds. This he loads into the car before following signs to the overflow car park around the end of the dock. It is a long way from the harbour, the signs pointing left and right past abandoned warehouses and rows of terraced houses, some with the lower windows and doors bricked up. The road surface deteriorates and then becomes practically non-existent as the car splashes through puddles onto an open space of gravel and broken paving lacking bay markings. Cars are parked around the perimeter like a Roman defensive strategy – facing outwards and shoulder to shoulder in a wide circle, the centre a pool of deep water the size of a bowling green.

David Grant packs his sausage bag with enough clothing for two days, plus his razor and toothbrush and then retrieves his wallet before returning the case to the boot, admiring the rock bound for Cockfosters, locking the car and running through the rain to a bus stop claiming to serve the shuttle to the ferry terminal. He looks at his watch and starts to fret – he has twenty minutes before he is due on the ferry. The place seems utterly deserted but, just when he reaches the point where he is resigned to a wet and hasty route march back to the terminal, a bus trundles around the corner and pulls up with a hiss of its air brakes. In no time he is getting off at the terminal with five minutes to spare.

The HSS ferry is splendid. It noses slowly out of the harbour, but then starts to shake, its engines whining like a jet aircraft, and it is soon lifting itself out of the water. In spite of the choppy sea, the craft churns along at high speed, taking just over an hour and a half for the journey. He hardly has time to look around the ship and wonder at the brute power of the jet engines churning the waters astern before the Dublin hills rise like a slumbering giant in the west and the coast lifts itself from the waters. Impressive cloud formations drift down the flanks of the hills like a fur stole on bared shoulders, while a shaft of sunlight strikes the summit of the highest hill, turning it into an intensely green oasis in a tract of grey that reaches from the turbulent waters ahead of the ferry to the lofty vastness of the sky.

David Grant congratulates himself. His actions have astounded him. A week before he had been in Le Crestet, seeing his wife off on her course and with nothing in his diary but a doctor's appointment and a grand plan, eminently flexible and not compulsory, to lay a path in the garden. As we have seen, in seven days he has done surprising things, with more to come.

Certainly Élodie will be surprised. David Grant has many good qualities but being surprising and impetuous are not two of them. She loves him because he is dependable and reliable, because he is courageous, and because he loves her, although, just occasionally, she might have traded a little of what he is for moments of unpredictability. He knows he will have to call her on Thursday as he assumes they will both be heading for home on the same day. He feels for the mobile phone in the inside pocket of his jacket but can't find it. He checks his other pockets and even his wallet before realising he's left it plugged into the lighter socket of the car. Worse, it is lying on the front passenger seat, in full view of any passing Holyhead hoodies looking for little ways of making a bit of extra cash. Then the loss of the phone moves into second place in his list of worries. Supposing they damage the car trying to steal the phone and then add hot-wiring and joyriding to their evening's pleasure? He remembers the sign exonerating the car-park owners from any responsibility for customers' vehicles and their contents. But, he reasons, the car park is remote and awkward; it would only attract a very determined thief who might be more interested in superior marques and more sophisticated technology than an ageing Corsa and a cheap French contract mobile. And if the phone has gone, it doesn't prevent him from phoning his wife. There must still be a few public phones that have not been vandalised.

Shouldering his sausage bag, he walks off the boat and past the minimalist security arrangements: a couple of booted Gardai resting their bones against a pillar and talking to a pretty ferry-company hostess. It is only a short walk up to the DART station at Dun Laoghaire and in no time he has bought his single ticket to Connolly station, fed the ticket barrier and gained access to the platform. The train comes in within a few minutes and he is soon making for the city centre. He remembers a number of small hotels in and around Connolly, the bus station and Abbey Street, and knows that a short walk is bound to result in finding a room. And so it does. Within a few yards of Connolly, he finds a dilapidated old Georgian house converted into a hotel and he is soon installed on the third floor.

He doesn't feel like eating but knows he should, so he lets himself out of the building and walks towards O'Connell Street where he finds a Thai restaurant up some stairs alongside the needle. There he eats a prawn soup followed by Thai chicken, washing it down with a pint of Tiger beer and a cup of coffee. He leaves the restaurant still elated by his behaviour and well satisfied by the meal. It is now dark and still, mercifully, dry. The streets are full of crowds brandishing furled umbrellas and walking purposefully. Many are on their way home but others, mostly young, are going to round off their weekend with a pub or two or a noisy nightclub on the other side of the river, queues of casually dressed lads and practically naked girls already

150

forming behind roped barriers while bouncers snarl or leer, according to taste. For the rest, noisy buses and clanging trams snake through the streets, whisking Dubliners home to the start of a new week. One shabby horse-drawn landau is standing at the side of the road, the horse chewing at its bit, its eyes shielded from the bright lights and fast-moving traffic behind blinkers, while its coachman helps an American couple down the narrow step to the ground. Money changes hands, the lad half touches his forelock and then clambers up onto the box before striking the beast with a short whip and driving him out into the traffic. He's had his last fare for the day. Perhaps a last quick run around St Stephen's Green to see if there are any late revellers that might like to round off their night romantically, but probably not. For him, it'll be back to a nameless gated yard in Dublin 8, the seat cushions put into a shed to keep dry, the carriage, exposed to the elements, stowed away beside a couple of old Nissan Bluebirds with taxi phone numbers, unlit, on their roofs, and the horse coaxed into its makeshift stable – a riot of second-hand timber and corrugated iron. The romance is in the minds of the hirers, bolstered up by a lad who knows just what the customers want – a tour of the sights, a tall story or two, a tilt at the English and a smothered swear word. But it is just a job to him. The lads run the carriages, the womenfolk the taxis, the older men hang out around the betting shop. That's how it has always been. At least since the carriages were the taxis and the spare money, and some that was not spare at all, was spent on drink.

David Grant peers down into the treacle-black invisibility of the Liffey from the Ha'penny Bridge. He can hear the water as it shoals against the wall but cannot see it. A young couple almost bump into him as they make for Temple Bar. Their careless progress is the consequence of the steeply sloping bridge, the pints already consumed and the fact that the lad has his hand thrust deeply down inside the girl's short skirt with its conveniently elasticated top.

'Sorry,' she breathes, before giggling. 'Locked already, I'm afraid.' She turns to her boyfriend and smacks his arm hard. 'Will you take your hand out from there?'

'See? Girls?' he pleads to the elderly stranger. 'She wears this skirt – knows what it does to me – and then she's giving out to me about being fresh!' They totter about uncertainly in the middle of the bridge, still coupled together but with two held hands rather than one G-stringed cheek clutched in his warm fingers.

'What's it tonight?' David Grant asks, half hoping they might be heading for Mother Redcaps.

'Techno,' she replies. 'There's a club with live acts most Sundays. You like techno?'

'I don't think I'd know what it was if I heard techno. Know the name of course. Anyone famous I might have heard of?'

'No, that's the point. Hardly anyone famous except for in the scene and the clubs.' He looks hard at David Grant as his undisciplined feet carry him within three inches of him before he, too, looks into the water. He uses his free hand to steady himself on the parapet.

'You're not Irish?'

'No. Scots, from England living in France.'

'Bit of a gypsy.'

'Yes, I suppose so. A bit of a gypsy.'

The girl pulls at her boyfriend's hand. 'Come *on*, Declan. We've got to *go*.'

Declan restarts his one-man show for David Grant.

'See, she's giving out to me again!' He puts his other hand around the girl's neck and clumsily draws her to him before kissing her under her ear.

'Go on, off you go. Enjoy yourselves.'

152

'We will. Perhaps we'll see you again.' The couple turn around slowly so as to face their original direction of travel.

'You might. You just might.'

'I'm from Donegal, all right. Do you know where that is?'

'Yes, I do. The north-west. Glenties. The Barnesmore Gap. Lovely, and desolate at the same time.'

Declan turns again while the girl sighs and shakes her hand away from his in frustration. She smiles at David Grant as if to exonerate him from any responsibility. Declan gives a whoop of pleasure.

'I'm from Glenties! That's amazing. Have you been there?'

'No, but I've heard of it. Seen it on the map.'

'You've heard of Glenties but I have no idea where feckin' France is.'

Declan pats David Grant on the shoulder as if, across the generations, they had been co-conspirators in the school-yard, before the girl grabs his hand again and he is yanked away towards the bright lights on the south shore. Soon they are lost in the crowd streaming through a line of gridlocked cars like water around rocks as the tide goes out, while unheeded pedestrian traffic lights change and count down the seconds before the authorities decide it will again be safe to cross.

The old bridge falls silent, save for the quiet murmurings of occasional passing couples and the forlorn attempt by a young girl armed with a plastic cup to beg a few coins. He had noticed her, dressed in a long shawl over a heavy coat that goes down to her ankles, her legs clad in thick stockings, solid shoes on her feet, sitting with her back to the parapet on the north side, her legs spread before her, a risky gesture to attract attention to her plight. She would have been recognisable to James Joyce or Jonathan Swift – the archetypal beggar of the centuries, Molly Malone in rags.

He rummages in his pockets and finds a few euros-worth of copper coins.

'Where are you from?' he asks her. He makes that assumption we all make when accosted by a beggar that we have the right to pose one or two questions – as though we have bought them for a brief moment. Misfortune alleviated awards us with rights and a curious intimacy.

'Iran.'

'Iran?'

'You been there?'

'No, but I know where it is. I've seen it on a map.'

The Ha'penny Bridge is a place of brief encounters for mapped people.

'Bad place. Might get better but bad place. Ireland good place. Not lot of money if not on the game. Me,' she interrupts herself by stabbing at her chest repeatedly with an index finger, 'not on the game. Beg all day and night. Not much money but good place. Good people. Happy people. Where you from?'

She carefully tips the meagre contents of her plastic cup into a gloved outstretched hand and funnels the money into a pocket. She stands beside David Grant and looks up into his face.

'France,' he replies.

'I heard you tell boy. Where in France?'

'You won't know it; it's in the Ardèche.'

'Near Lyon. I know it near Lyon.'

'You been there?'

'No, but I know where it is. I've seen it on a map.'

They both laugh, the young itinerant and the old man.

'Just one world,' she says, following his gaze, looking past him upriver, the black strip of naked water bounded by buildings, lights and endlessly restless traffic receding into the distance. He can see her eyes shining in the light from the street lamps. She might be crying. 'One world, one life,' she continues.

He rummages in his pocket for more coins but is stilled by her outstretched hand.

'No. Is enough. You don't look rich. And you soon be poor like me. Perhaps.'

'Perhaps,' he replies, unconvinced. Maybe it helps her to narrow the gulf between her and her benefactors.

'What will happen to you?' he asks.

'What, now? Or later?'

'Both.'

'Now, I stay until it get dangerous. Drunks need money too, you know. Then I go and sleep. I got a place below Connolly. I have a few friends.'

'And later?'

'Oh, I marry a rich man. A rich Irish man with big Mercedes. Bear him lots of childrens. Big house. Lots of flowers in vases. Forget this life. I will invent something to explain. Student, maybe. I *was* student once. Husband not ask to see degree papers, no?'

David Grant smiles. 'No, I shouldn't think so. Not unless he needs you to get a job and you have to show your qualifications.'

'No job. My Irishman very rich. Wife no work. Lots of childrens.'

'Then you should be able to keep your secret.'

'That would be good for me, no?'

'What? Keeping a secret?'

'No. Rich husband. Plenty childrens.'

'Is it what you want?'

'Yes, yes!' There is urgency in her voice, a curious desperation that unsettles him.

'Then it will be good for you.'

They are like two ham actors. Their lines are learned well

155

but they sound unconvincing. Unconvincing and unconvinced. The girl rests her chin on her hand, her elbow on the
parapet. Neither speaks for a moment, both listening to the
water boiling beneath them.

'It cold now.' She breaks the silence and shivers obediently like a line of italics in a playscript.

'Yes, I'm going now.'

'Back to big hotel?'

'Back to small hotel.'

She turns her head and looks at him.

'You go,' she says. 'I stay until all people with sympathy
go home. I suppose I'd be warm at nights if I was on the
game. But I good girl.'

David Grant opens his wallet and takes two twenty-euro
notes from it.

'Take these,' he says, stepping away from her to make
their expected rapid return impossible.

She doesn't quite know what to do with the notes. Her
method of working rarely has to accommodate folding
money. She folds them separately into half and then hesitates before putting them into an inside pocket of her coat.

'You are kind. Scotchman from England from France.'

'From the Ardèche.'

'Near Lyon.'

She grasps his hand and presses it to her mouth, making
a slight bow as she does so. He pulls his hand away and
yearns to be able to do something for her that would not
be misconstrued. He wants to take her in his arms and
make things better but knows any further contact would
bring disaster. He feels she is on the edge, vulnerable, and
her fragility is infectious.

'I here every night. You here tomorrow?'

'No,' he lies. 'I'm going back tomorrow.'

'Plane?'

'Ur, yes. Plane. Dublin Airport. Back to Lyon.'

'Lucky. France nice. Good to my country. Not hysterical like British and USA. Clever at handling regime. Nothing lasts forever. Good food, too, in France. I read about that.'

'Goodbye.' It is David Grant's turn to pat a stranger clumsily on the shoulder. She turns to look at the river again, placing her hand lightly on his wrist.

'What time is it?'

He looks at his watch, tilting it in the direction of a lamp to read the face properly.

'It's just after eleven.'

'You'd better go. Old men need sleep. One world. One life.'

He says 'goodbye' again as he makes for the north shore but she says nothing. He looks back to see her silhouetted against the bright lights of Temple Bar. She turns her head slightly to watch him go.

He can see her eyes shining in the light from the street lamps. She might be crying.

The Second Monday

David Grant awakens to the ringing of the bedside telephone and a terrifying image of stained gold fades with the
clattering of the bell. He has slept deeply and is barely
awake, functioning mechanically and seeking the receiver
with hesitant jabs of his hand like a blind man. He knocks
an empty drinking glass to the floor where it rolls slowly
under the bed, mercifully unbroken.

'Your early-morning call.' The voice is impersonal; perhaps twenty-five calls a day all exactly the same. In a good
year, it will be uttered nine thousand times. It's not even
that it is particularly early but something has to be said and
making the communication appropriate according to the
clock would require thought, make assumptions, and court
error and a response, as in . . .

'It's not early, it's eight o'clock.'

'Early-ish.'

'Not even early-ish.'

. . . or . . .

'This is your call for breakfast.'

'I don't eat breakfast. Never have.'

David Grant says thank you but hears the click at the
other end before he has uttered, his gratitude locked into
the wires and electronics and shabby fabric of the room.

His headache has returned with a vengeance and makes
him feel vomiting sick. He sits up clasping his head, swings

his legs onto the floor and rummages in his bag for the last of his prescription pills. He curses the hotel for not providing a drinking glass (he is not aware of its sudden descent to the floor or its curving shamefaced withdrawal to the furry darkness beneath the bed) and manages to swallow his pill by slurping tap water repeatedly, using the cap from his shaving cream as an improvised cup. He strips off his pyjamas before struggling with the en-suite shower door. It folds across the middle like one on a bus and, with his exhaustion and the drumming head, it defeats him for a moment as he tries pulling and pushing it by turns.

Carefully, he adjusts the flow from the two separate taps, hovering outside the booth until it is safe and comfortable to enter. With the water coursing over his body, he does what he has done ten thousand times before. He folds his arms at his sides and fists his hands up near his shoulders before stretching them backwards to unlock his muscles and enjoy a delicious morning yawn expelled by his exertions. As he does so, he feels a slight click in his left eye, as though he has burst a small blood vessel or even simply dislodged an eyelash that is now obstinately stuck to his eyeball. He rubs his eyes and thinks no more of it as he soaps himself and scrubs vigorously with the hotel-supplied flannel. His headache reduces rapidly to the slight discomfort of the place it once occupied. His feeling of nausea subsides and he quickly dresses. The sausage bag is not as crease-friendly as his suitcase and so, paradoxically, his garments are now full of creases. He looks in the mirror and is surprised at how scruffy he appears. He decides that creased clothes age a man and he is vain enough to resolve to get back to Le Crestet before Élodie, if only to regain his youthful good looks – or at least be as youthful in his appearance as he possibly can. He will sail back today from Dun Laoghaire and, with a bit of luck, be at home by Wednesday night. That would give him time to get himself and the house ready for her return. The imagined need to impress his spouse and avoid criticism is never far away.

Downstairs in the dining room, he spots an empty table in the window.

'Good morning, sir,'

A pretty waitress with blonde hair, high cheekbones and an Eastern European accent follows him into the bay brandishing a menu held in a greasy black-leather folder.

'What would you like for breakfast, please?'

David Grant opens the folder and sees that the bewildering list of ingredients could be summed up by the words 'You can have anything you like and, whatever you choose, it'll always cost the same'. He would prefer to be faced with precise items, scrambled egg on toast, bacon, egg and tomato, etcetera. Mix and match at this time of the morning requires consideration and a good deal too much thought.

Suddenly he feels very hungry and, rather than rove all over the page, orders a 'full Irish breakfast'.

'Tea or coffee?'

'Coffee please.'

The waitress hesitantly reaches out and turns his room key over to read the number which she jots down on her pad. He notices pale, narrow hands, clear nail varnish and short nails, practical and well manicured.

'You take whatever you want, cereals, yoghurt,' she pronounces it rather fetchingly without the 'g', 'juices, from over there.'

'Thanks.'

He gets to his feet and makes for the sideboard, takes a bowl from the stack and fills it with All-Bran from what resembles a dry optic, before pouring a glass of orange juice. Once again, the waitress follows him back to the table in the window, this time with a tray of coffee, toast and bread rolls.

'Is windy today,' she offers as she unloads the tray,

indicating the butter and marmalade, half to herself, half to David Grant. Everything present and correct. David Grant looks out of the window. It is sunny, but he can tell by the restless clothing worn by passers-by that the waitress is right. It is very windy.

'Did you notice it in the night?' she asks.

'No.'

'The windows was booming and it was whining through the cracks in the doors where I live.'

'Far away?'

'No. Not far. I live with my boyfriend. He works in Tallaght on the new apartment blocks in the centre by the Luas tram terminus. Is like a new town, Tallaght.'

'Where are you from?'

'Up near Phoenix Park. Near to Heuston Station. Is very convenient. He goes on the Luas one way. I come this way to city centre.' She smiles innocently at him and he notices little dimples in her cheeks. She is really very pretty. He smiles back at her, letting her 'dry' before reposing the question he was really asking.

'No, I meant where are you from originally.'

'Gdansk. Poland. There are lots of us here, working. It is good for us.'

'Good for you, good for Ireland,' he replies.

He can't overlook the irony of the nation that provided the builders in post-war Britain now being constructed by Eastern Europeans. He remembers the rather cruel use of Wimpey, the builders' name, back in the fifties as a mnemonic for 'We Import Millions of Paddies Every Year'. His gaze returns to the window where an airborne plastic supermarket bag, a thing of value in Ireland nowadays, streaks through the air and embraces a concrete lamp post. When the girl returns with his plate stacked dangerously with every conceivable fried concoction, he speaks again.

'I've decided to go back on the HSS ferry from Dun

Laoghaire today. Back to the UK. When I arrived last night, I booked for two nights but I think I'll just go today. Can you tell the hotel proprietor for me? If it's a problem, I'll pay for the two nights.'

'I'll tell him. I don't think it will be a problem. It is the high season. But it is his decision. OK?'

'Thanks.'

The girl returns to the kitchen with many pairs of eyes following her and some following the eyes of the ones glued to the back of her tight skirt. Wives and girlfriends are pleased to be on the receiving end of glances from their partners but then dislike the realisation that the glances are transferable.

While David Grant struggles manfully with his fried abundance, the girl returns.

'Not possible,' she says.

'Why? I'm very happy to p . . .'

'No. Is not possible. The wind. No sailing of the HSS today. Very rough. Mr Wong, he's the boss, says it was on the radio this morning.'

'Oh. Mr Wong.'

'Yes. Mr Wong. He very nice. I suppose ordinary boat running.'

'Don't fancy that, I'm afraid. Never was much of a sailor.'

'Please?' A slight translation is obviously needed.

'Never was much good on boats on long crossings – I easily feel seasick.' He clutches his stomach by way of providing a further clue. 'At least the HSS is quick. I can usually survive an hour and a half.'

'Oh.'

'I'll stay. Thank him for me, will you?'

'Yes. Thank you. You like breakfast?'

'Yes, but it's too much.'

'It called full Irish breakfast. It make you full, no?'

'Certainly does.' He cuts the rind off rasher number four

162

and couples a small piece to a generous slice of sausage number three and mushroom number thirty before giving up the ghost and putting his cutlery down. He pours another cup of coffee, though. Ireland is a good deal better at coffee than Wales, he thinks, even if it is simply 'coffee' here in the hotel, without the pretensions of the Italian for 'milk'. Plenty of coffee houses out on the streets of Dublin with lavish use of Italian though; he'd seen them on his walk the night before. He promises himself a cup or two later in the day.

Now David Grant feels stressed but to his well-deserved stomach pains must be added the return of his headache. He takes the napkin from the empty space opposite, removes a propelling pencil from his pocket and starts to do some sums.

'11.10 a.m. HSS tomorrow, Tuesday,' he murmurs as he writes clumsily on paper ill designed for the task. 'That should get me into Holyhead before one o'clock. In fact, if I'm lucky, I could be round at the car by one. Then what? Dover by midnight? It's a long way and I will have to go via Cockfosters with the rock, but I should be able to make it.' He sucks the end of his pencil as he puzzles over the logistics. 'I should be able to be at the house when some-one's in even if they go out to work. Early evening would be a very good time I would think. Then, a night crossing on the boat. I might get a short sleep in the car waiting on the dock and another one during the sailing. After that, I could take it slowly down through France and still be home by Wednesday night. Or, I could stop on the way, as close to home as possible, get a good night's sleep and be home by Thursday lunchtime. It's a long way and my head hurts a lot but at least I'll be home. I might go down to the doctors on Thursday morning. Then I can whack some more pain-killers in before Élodie gets back.'

He is setting himself, if not an impossible task, a difficult one. He had taken six days to make a journey he now intends to repeat in a mere two, and with very little change to his original route. He'd done that sort of thing in his youth, of course, even driven all night so that he could sing the Orbison song to a sceptical two-timing girlfriend who had dumped him soon afterwards. Funny how being romantic in one person's mind can be deeply embarrassing in another. He might have been better to check she was alone before he'd started singing in the garden beneath her window. But now he isn't as young as he was, even though a lack of realism is fully compensating for his limitations.

So, he is free to visit Mother Redcaps after all. He will go up at lunchtime and, if he is really lucky, there might be a gig on in the evening. What a culmination to his trip.

'What have you been doing?' Élodie will ask in her unpacking-the-car distracted way.

'Oh, I've been to Mother Redcaps to see' (Who? Could it be possible?) 'John Spillane. Remember him?'

'John Spillane? Wasn't he in Ireland?'

'Yes.'

'What's he doing here in the Ardèche?' she'll ask.

So he'd have to tell her his story all over again. And he knew he'd have to prove it, so unlikely would it seem to her. Part of it would be incontrovertible, though. As David Grant is folding up his calculations and putting them into his pocket, his French bank statement is dropping through the letter box of the empty house in Le Crestet. Amongst all the normal domestic items, the weekly ordeals to the supermarket, the occasional visits to the petrol station in Tournon and a couple of meals at La Terrasse, there is a short list of expenses marking his inexorable travel across France – two more full tanks of fuel and one hotel bill in Dijon, plus his lunch north of Lyon, and, if the system is very efficient, another from Calais, although that might be withheld until later. And when the credit-card bill arrives at

164

the end of the month, he will be able to show her his visit to a cash machine and the hotel bill from Laon. The British cards would fill in the gaps. It's not as though Élodie wouldn't believe him in the end; it's just that his behaviour in her absence has been totally out of character.

At this moment he realises he hasn't yet drunk the orange juice. Although he is full to bursting, he supposes that it might act as a counter to the fried-fest recently concluded. Unfortunately, he carelessly catches his hand on the coffee cup as he reaches over it for the juice. If the gods were to be kind, the empty cup would, at the most, tip over, spilling the dregs into the saucer with no collateral damage. But the gods are not always kind. The cup is inexplicably lifted into the air by his thumb and thrown ahead of his hand so that it reaches the glass of orange juice first. In spite of its chunky appearance, the impact shatters the glass and the juice flows out of the ruin and back in David Grant's direction, dividing neatly around the Dublin pub place mat and showing no sign of reducing its flow. In fact, it moves a great deal more quickly than David Grant, who stands up just as the juice pours over the side of the table like a miniature lazy Outspan-coloured Niagara and comes to rest on his chinos.

'Damn,' he cries, and then overcomes his embarrassment at his outburst by shaking his head, rubbing frantically and ineffectually with his paper napkin and avoiding eye contact with the rest of the guests. The waitress comes to his rescue with a fistful of napkins and promises to return quickly with a damp cloth.

'I'm not usually careless,' he mumbles, nodding in agreement with himself.

'Accidents can happen,' the waitress observes with a smile, nodding because she has been told that the customer is always right.

David Grant returns to his room and changes into his only

other pair of trousers, some dark-brown corduroys. He holds the chinos under the shower until the water runs clear and hangs them, soaking wet, on the shower door. Then he goes out of his room, down the stairs and out into the city. He wanders along Abbey Street past the Methodist Central Hall and joins the throng in O'Connell Street. A watery sun reflects off the bottom twenty feet of the Spire of Dublin as it is officially called – a supremely pointless point – which soars promisingly to the sky and leads the eye to oblivion. Before, in its place, stood a statue: Nelson on the top of his fluted pillar. However much the Irish disliked that most English of references, to blow it up was, to some, a rather dangerous case of vandalism; while to others, it was an act of self-determination that reflected a kind of distorted democracy and even heroic independence. Once blown up, there was no question, practically or politically, of repairing it. So, what should take its place? A statue of one of the Irish heroes, perhaps, or some extraordinary sculpture that the great and good decide will represent the new Ireland? David Grant looks at the spire and sees only confusion and muddled thinking – a replacement of something that stuck in the craw of many Irishmen with something no one could be offended by and many would not even notice. A bold opening at the foot, a burnished effect reflecting the sun, that quickly dulls at the roofline of the surrounding buildings and then leads on forever to nowhere, like an interminable sentence spoken by a voice that fades before the full stop, like a joke without a punchline, or a song that no one knows how to complete and so fades to grey – just as, frequently, the Dublin Spire fades to the grey of the sky. In a city full of good sculpture, the needle appears to David Grant as an anachronism, an opportunity lost.

He obediently crosses the road by a pedestrian crossing and dips into Eason's to browse the bookshelves for a while. This is a real luxury for him, something he misses in France.

Not that he doesn't go to bookshops in France, go and buy, but the authors and titles have a familiar ring here in Ireland and the shop smells right. He buys nothing, though, and stumbles badly as he descends the steps to the street, dropping his coat and wallet. He is on his knees and takes a moment or two on all-fours before attempting to stand up.

'You all right?' A girl comes to his aid, hooking her hand under his armpit.

'Yes, thank you.' He dusts himself down, clutching at his wallet, as the girl picks up his coat.

'The steps can be tricky,' she commiserates. 'Worse than this, sometimes. They can be clogged with people who have said, "Meet me under Eason's clock at such-and-such a time" and they don't and the people get tired and sit down to wait. It's like people queuing for a sale sometimes. Here's your coat.'

'Thank you,' David Grant replies. He rubs his knee and then realises he's torn a small hole in his corduroys. He ignores the hole and, to make light of the event, moves the conversation away from the particular as he speaks to the girl. 'They say that, for men, it's a sign of growing old when girls come to their rescue.'

She smiles but doesn't reply.

'I'll be fine,' he emphasises. 'Been a bit careless today – not the first time. Thank you again.'

He throws his coat casually over his shoulder, smiles at the girl and they go their separate ways, she into Eason's where she will forget him as she glides up the escalators to visit the music shop on the top floor.

Partly to nurse his sore knee, he goes to a coffee shop off Henry Street via a chemist where he buys the strongest painkillers he can get over the counter. He finds a private table in the café, and discreetly rolls up his trouser leg to survey the damage. His knee is feeling stiff and is already

167

bruising nicely. He has cut his knee slightly just under the kneecap. 'Another job for the Welsh antiseptic,' he murmurs, wondering if it is still in his case in the back of the car and not thinking of buying another tube. The hole in his trousers, however, is only small, hardly noticeable, and, other than buying another pair, he is down to his corduroys with the hole or the chinos that are soaking wet back in the hotel. His head is still spinning and the combination of an overdose of paracetamol and a double espresso do little to improve things.

Thinking the fresh air will help, he decides to find Mother Redcaps. Looking at his watch he realises he will probably be early for lunch but that might be all to the good. Might get busy, he reasons.

He wants to avoid an encounter with the Iranian girl on the Ha'penny Bridge. He had told her he was going home today and might even have done so if the weather had been better. But he'd told a lie; said he was flying out to France that morning. There's no way he would be stumbling around the city at close to lunchtime if that had been true. Why had he done that? If he had said he was going to be in the city, would she have asked if he'd come to see her? And if she had, would he have been ashamed of her for her situation, or himself for talking to a beggar in broad daylight? What if he'd said he was going to be around, what was there to fear? That he and she would, in some convoluted, theatrical, clichéd way, have filled the gap between their farewell and an anticipated meeting the next day . . . together? Besides, he had never been with a prostitute and she was not on the game. Or would she have asked to come back to the hotel for a proper night's sleep with the attendant logistical problems of getting her into and out of the hotel unseen? If she had, how could he have refused? And how would that have looked to anyone with half an imagination if it had not remained unseen?

168

The acid test was always 'Could he tell Élodie?' He knew he could not. Why had appearances mattered so much to him? Was that it? Appearances? He had always thought that what mattered was the truth, not people's constructions on a situation. Even if she had come back, nothing would have happened. Would it? She had her principles and he his. He was happily married and she had her dreams of wedding-day virginal blood on the sheets with her rich Irish husband. That was all she could bring to him that was true and verifiable. The rest – the gaps in her life, the degree she didn't possess, even the right to be in the country – was a fabrication. But there was a spark, perhaps only in his imagination, but he thought there was one. He had only spoken to her for a few minutes but he felt he knew her better than many people of long acquaintance. Not only did he feel he knew her, he felt comfortable with her and that, for him, was an extreme rarity. And she seemed to have wisdom, second sight, perhaps. Above all she was interesting. Mostly, the beer- and spittle-stained alcoholic bags of bones begging on the streets seemed so lost behind their assumed identities, their personalities – for they must have had personalities once – discarded as a useless luxury in the battle to survive. They were like soldiers, individuals remodelled into identical machines, perfect for their new role. But she was different. Maybe it was her extreme youth, the patina of hopelessness not yet fully formed; hope still the stressed syllable on the journey she found herself on. He wished there was something heroic he could have done for her but his only achievement was to tell her a lie.

And so he carefully avoids the Ha'penny Bridge, walking instead along the quays on the north side of the river before crossing on a traffic bridge and working his way up the hill to where he remembers the shabby grandeur of Mother Redcaps.

Of course, he gets lost and dips into a Centra mini-supermarket to ask the way. The man behind the counter, presumably the manager, looks confused.

'Mother Redcaps? What is this?' he asks.

'It's an authentic Irish pub,' replies David Grant. 'Puts on traditional music at nights.'

'Don't know it. I don't know this area well. Only been here in Ireland for a while. You don't mean big nightclub on Thomas Street? With Harley Davidson in window?'

'No, it's just a little place.'

'You can answer this man's question?' he asks his assistant who out of curiosity, emerges from behind the hot and cold lunch counter, ignoring a small queue of hungry customers. He removes thin plastic gloves as he makes his way across the shop and stuffs them into the pocket of his white coat. In appearance, people in the catering industry look more and more like surgeons.

'What is it?'

'I'm looking for Mother Redcaps.'

'In Christchurch Back Lane?'

'Might be. Worth a try.'

The assistant provides detailed instructions and David Grant thanks him as he leaves.

'Round to the right, you said?' he asks over his shoulder as the automatic door opens to let him leave.

'That's right. To the right and then right again. You can't miss it.'

'Thanks again.'

'No problem.'

The assistant grins knowingly at the manager as he walks back, pulling his plastic gloves on again before serving the first of his customers.

'It's a good place?' the manager shouts through the shop.

The assistant smiles again as he puts a generously filled bacon, lettuce and tomato baguette together before answering.

170

'No.'

'No good?'

'Not now.'

'Why? It gone downhill or something?'

'No, it's closed down.'

'You should have said!'

'He didn't ask. Just wanted to know where it is. So I told him.'

And so it is.

David Grant sees the pub name first, closely followed by the 'For Sale' sign. The place seems shabbier than he remembered it. Then it had been honestly shabby, well used, well loved but in need of a lick of paint. Its character would have been diminished if it had been otherwise. Now, it is boarded up and seemingly out of time and place, a tatty vestige of old Dublin, a well-remembered dinosaur.

'It's a shame.' A young man addresses him as David Grant stands looking at his memories.

'I came here once,' he replies. 'Years ago. With friends. Good friends. I know they moved but I don't have their address with me. I didn't know I was coming to Dublin you see. They're in Wexford or somewhere. Semi-retired.'

'I did, too. I mean, I came here once, so I did. And I live in Dublin, so I've no excuse now. You're not local. I can tell from your accent.'

'No, but not the England you might assume from how I speak.' There always seems to be a need to separate oneself from England during casual conversations in Ireland – that is if you have a right to. In early days, David Grant had always stressed his Scottishness and courted fragile fraternity by describing the Highland Clearances if the need arose. Even so, he felt he should apologise for the multitude of wrongs heaped on the country by those over the water. Close examination of either history would quickly identify the culpability, or at least involvement, of fellow travellers, however. History is never cut and dried, them and us clearly identified, the blamed and the blameless conveniently defined by nationality, colour or creed. Without willing black men seduced by gold and the chance to settle tribal scores, arguably there would have been no significant slave trade. But the conversation did not continue along those old, well-trodden lines.

'Perhaps, if I'd come more often and drunk Guinness until I was legless, it would still be open.' The man's gaze rises to the upstairs windows, thick with grime. There is a strong smell of damp emanating from the building. 'They used to hold concerts up there, you know.'

'I know. I saw John Spillane when I came.'

'John! Oh, he's a big shot now. Got his own TV programme on the Gaelic channel – something to do with postcards. Still sings, of course, but he's more likely to be at the "Point" now than in places like this. Mind you, he still tours around the more remote corners so it's probably still about good craic and songs and pints down-country. He's getting a new album out – all in Irish, but he's still got that beat and the expressive voice and that freshness. You might just get a copy before you leave.'

'I might do that,' David Grant says, and then asks, 'Why did it close, apart from your culpability in not going more often and drinking loads of beer?'

The young man laughs.

'I don't suppose anything I could have done would have altered things. Have you seen Dublin lately, I mean really seen it? It's all cranes and apartment blocks and the young people have had their eyes opened to other influences.' He smiles wryly. 'I suppose drinking cocktails and alcopops and going to nightclubs and listening to garage, hip-hop and rock music is more exciting than an evening in a run-down pub with a pint or six of the black stuff and a few guys playing traditional music on a fiddle, a guitar, a bodhran

172

and a set of uilleann pipes. Maybe the owner saw no future in it. Maybe they'll tear it down and put up another apartment block with an underground car park for five hundred cars and no roads to drive them on. They'll probably call it Mother Redcaps Towers or something.'

'But it's history. It's tradition.'

'If you want history, they'd say, go to a museum. If you want tradition, go down to Temple Bar. It's like Disneyland to me, mind, but the tourists love it.'

'Well, there's no point in standing here, I suppose. And it looks like rain.'

'Yes, wind's dropping so rain's pretty inevitable. Happy days, eh?'

'Thanks for filling me in.'

The man nods ruefully and walks away into the tangle of brick-terraced streets while David Grant walks back in the direction of the city. He ends up in Temple Bar, busy but not jumping as it will be tonight, every night.

Lunch is the next requirement and he quickly finds a pub that serves meals. He orders Irish chicken and chips, whatever that is, and a pint of Guinness and pays with some of his remaining cash. The food comes in moments, just like in England, and he even gets the mindless 'enjoy your meal', even though it is at least spoken with an Irish accent. After his huge breakfast, one of Centra's sandwiches would have been more than enough, but a light drizzle was falling at decision time and, besides, he wants to toast the ghost of Mother Redcaps and its loss that he knows must be keenly felt by too few to make it commercially viable. He finishes his pint, having almost spilt it when replacing it on the table clumsily, but makes a very poor attempt at the food, stripping the meat carelessly from the leg bone so as to release as little as possible and picking at the generous pile of chips, first with his fork and then his fingers, dipping them without enthusiasm into a pile of ketchup. He smiles as he

173

tries, having eaten his fill, to define the ingredient that made it Irish. He assumes it refers to the nationality of the donor chicken and the potatoes and has nothing to do with the recipe.

He goes to the toilet after his meal and washes his hands, looking at his reflection in the mirror. He still feels groggy and his head is now reaching the stage where, although he will be exceeding the recommended dose, another administration of the paracetamol is becoming inevitable. He clutches absent-mindedly at his forehead with wet hands and the water courses down his face and into his collar. Rather than simply dry his face, he decides to wash it too. Perhaps, he reasons, the warm water and soap will help to revive him. As he does so, in spite of closing his eyes, he gets soap in them and dabs first one and then the other with warm water to relieve the stinging sensation. It is at this moment he realises there is something wrong with his eyesight. He closes one eye and then the other, peering into the mirror as he does. Then he covers one eye and then the other with an open palm, still looking at his reflection. The realisation is undramatic and unsensational. It insinuates itself upon him quietly like the moments before a road accident impact – that slow-motion silence where the strongest sensation is one of utter calm. He does not cry out or clutch the sides of his face, he doesn't grimace and he doesn't rush from the conveniently empty toilet. He tries again, shaking his head slightly before he does so. First he covers the left eye and is rewarded with normal monocular vision. But when he covers the right eye, he can see nothing. He tries again. His right eye is working normally but the left has closed down completely. He is blind in one eye.

The door opens. A man of about forty enters the toilet in something of a hurry.

'How's it goin'?' He says as he wrestles with his flies.

'Oh, fine,' replies David Grant. And in an odd way it is fine. Without his headache he would be completely fine, and the realisation that he has gone blind in one eye is no more than an explanation for his clumsiness today. He remembers the broken glass at the breakfast table and the stumble on the steps of Eason's, not to mention the near miss with the pint of Guinness fifteen minutes before. To David Grant it is almost more important to discover an explanation for his clumsiness than it is to accept he has lost a vital part of his senses. He even remembers the incident in the shower and that odd clicking sensation. Perhaps, he reasons, that was when it happened.

'A bit kitsch this pub but they serve a decent pint.'

'It's OK,' agrees David Grant as he shakes his hands over the washbasin and pulls the roller towel out a few notches before drying his hands and face. He dries his left eye tenderly as if he is caressing a dead pet – just as he and Élodie had stroked Queen Elizabeth that dreadful day a few years back.

'Handy for me,' the man continues as he turns towards David Grant, draws breath and makes an exhibition of zipping his fly vigorously and at great speed. David Grant is always more cautious. He once knew someone who did that habitually until he needed a painful and embarrassing visit to Accident and Emergency. 'I'm working on a building site nearby. I'm an electrician. You on your holidays?'

'Yes.'

'Pity about the weather. It's turned wet again. Nothing happens in Dublin when it's wet. Still, at least I work under cover, although those apartment blocks can be feckin' cold in winter. And the pay's good – no complaints. Needs to be, though. Eight children and a ninth on the way. I only have to look at her and she's telling me what she calls "good news". I'll tell you this,' the man wags his finger at David Grant in a friendly way, a smile breaking out across his face,

'Leinster winning the rugby final. Now that's good news. If things go on like they are, I'll begin to forget their feckin' names and then there'll be hell to pay all right.'

Chance encounters with Irishmen in public toilets are often enhanced by autobiography.

'My name's Pat by the way,' he says, holding out his hand. The byline, the only part of his life story that's missing.

David Grant shakes his hand without telling the electrician his name and holds the door open for him.

'See ya,' the electrician says happily as he makes for the door. His audience nods and then returns to the bar.

'Could I have a glass of water please? It's for some paracetamol. Bad head.' He fumbles in his pocket for the medicine in a vain attempt to prove the purpose.

'Sure,' is the friendly reply and he returns to his chair with the water.

He rummages in his pocket for the analgesic and bursts three pills from the pack. 'One or two,' it says on the box but 'one or two' was what he used the previous time to little or no effect. He puts them in turn into his mouth and takes a gulp of water after each. He is feeling rather pleased with himself. After walking the earth for almost sixty-six and a half years, he is finally getting the hang of pill-taking. Not with the consummate skill of his father, it's true, but without the vast consumption of water necessary hitherto.

He looks around the pub, at the utter normality of it. Everyone is quietly going about their lives: the barman is lifting clean glasses from some elaborate mirror-backed shelving at the back of the bar, carrying on a loud conversation with a regular sitting twenty feet away; a young couple are facing each other over empty dirty plates, one hand clutching a glass, the other each other. An older couple, probably tourists, are slowly eating in total silence, he with his head down concentrating on his Irish chicken and chips and studiously avoiding eye contact, while she watches him between mouthfuls, a look of consuming hate on her face, while three or four tradesmen stand around a piano that serves as a prop for them and a shelf for their drinks. The piano is shabby and closed, giving the impression of not being played since the Troubles but it contributes to the 'kitsch' mentioned by the electrician, along with the old theatre posters and advertisements extolling the virtues of travelling to the United States on the split-new *Titanic*. David Grant smiles wryly at his choice of hyphenated adjective. Well, it's a bit ironic, isn't it?

David Grant begins to experiment with his new situation. He looks around the pub and realises how inferior monocular vision is. He can't put his finger on it but he realises he will have to relearn hand–eye coordination. Everything looks flatter, no depth to it, like a bad painting or the photographs he used to take with a Kodak Brownie 127 camera in the 1950s. There is also a definite reduction in his field of vision to the left, rather like driving a car at night in the dark when one of the headlamps has failed. He's surprised at how much he *can* see to the left, but also how much he's lost. He does not consider the possibility that his situation is temporary. Although his predicament is a novelty, he assumes this is his new normality.

This period of self-analysis does not go unnoticed in the pub. Even the young lovers' eyes stray from each other towards the dishevelled but rather distinguished man gazing around him and occasionally covering his eyes one at a time. David Grant catches sight of them looking at him and he turns his attention to his wallet and then the little notebook into which he makes irrelevant notes with his propelling pencil. At times like this, it is best to look normal and the most normal thing in the world is to look busy. Having discreetly scribbled a short list of Dublin pub names he has seen on his travels, he shuts the notebook with a flourish and returns it to his pocket, together with the pencil.

Out on the street, he hurries along as he has no umbrella and it is certainly umbrella weather. Knowledge is power and he quickly learns to take extra care over kerbstones and steps and consequently reaches the big shopping arcade at the top of Grafton Street without mishap. Not the first person in the world to find himself eyeless, he thinks. For a start there was old Nelson, he of distant memory on the top of his pillar in O'Connell Street and still acting as a landing strip for pigeons in Trafalgar Square. He assumes the IRA's definition of democracy will allow that one to remain. In fact, *his* blind eye proved to be of material benefit when he chose not to see a signal to withdraw, and it arose from a much more dramatic incident than a stretch in the shower.

He finds a coffee shop and orders a latte and a chocolate muffin. He knows they are probably not good for his head, which seems to be oblivious to the hard-working paraceta-mol, but he needs to find a way to fill the time. He sits down and picks at the cellophane that covers the cake patiently but ineffectively for a moment before resorting to tearing at it with his teeth. He breaks crumbs from the cake and drops them one by one into the cup before spooning the sticky mess into his mouth. You can take a Scotsman out of England but you can't take France out of a Scotsman. He stirs the last of the cake as it absorbs the dregs of coffee, each mouthful more solid than the last. Absolutely delicious.

'We should advertise that,' says the man who served him and who is now clearing tables.

'Sorry,' David Grant mumbles. 'Dirty habit. Don't know where I learned that,' he lies.

'I knew a French teacher when I was at school that did that with a Mars Bar.' Funny how quickly little deceits are

178

exposed. The man takes David Grant's tray and loads empty cups and cellophane wrappers onto it whilst wiping the table next to him with great speed and dexterity. 'He would dip it again and again in his coffee until it looked totally phallic. He said it was the high spot of his day.' He pauses in his work and laughs. 'He was training to be a priest so I suppose it might have been the high spot right enough. Or perhaps not. They seem to have lost the plot recently, in Ireland anyway. There was never a government health warning on taking your children to church, was there?' He looks at the sludge in the bottom of David Grant's cup. 'What could we call it? A Frenchie? Latte in, let me think, a tall glass, with a muffin submerged in it and a long spoon. Worth five euros of anyone's money! If you come back one day and see it on the menu, don't be at all surprised. Remind me it was you who gave me the idea and I'll give you one for free!' He returns to the servery and starts washing up. 'Good name, too. A Frenchie. That should stop them walking past! "Come in for a Frenchie!"' He laughs loudly.

David Grant finishes the last of his coffee-and-muffin soup and thanks the proprietor, who emerges from behind the counter and quickly clears the table.

'Remember now; come in for a Frenchie and we'll give it to you for free.'

David Grant leaves the café and walks around the shopping centre for a while before braving the elements. It is still raining but it is only a shower and his lack of an umbrella doesn't single him out in quite the way it did when he arrived. He goes quickly down Grafton Street, past Trinity College and across the O'Connell Bridge before reaching the hotel. He nods at the man he assumes to be Mr Wong, collects his key and goes up to his room. There he finds the bed carefully made and a drinking glass on the bedside table. His chinos are still hanging on the shower cubicle just where he left them. He takes off his coat and carefully hangs it on a hanger before hooking it onto the back of the bedroom door.

He feels tired suddenly and lies down on the bed, fully clothed. He stares at the ceiling and carries out his eye test once again. Left eye covered, no change at all. Right eye covered, no sight at all. He repeats the procedure, sighing at the lack of improvement he knows will never come. His head aches like it never has before and what he really needs to do is to pull the curtains and blot out the light but he hasn't the energy or the inclination. He finds his body actually moving to the throbbing in his head like an old-fashioned sports car idling powerfully before the off.

A slow realisation of what lays ahead of him – having to get to Dun Laoghaire in time for the ferry tomorrow, the journey home, the diversion via Cockfosters, the long drive across France, explaining things to Élodie, the unmade path that will have to be made – crowd in on him. He realises that retirement has made him less able to cope with too many things at once. He knows that he tends to leave the day-to-day things to Élodie, a thing of necessity when they first moved to France and his French was inadequate but now one of selfish convenience. What he has not realised, however, is quite how much this laziness has reduced his capabilities. He realises he probably couldn't work on contract in London again. The *work* wouldn't defeat him; it was like riding a bike, he could do it with his eyes . . . eye . . . closed. But the logistics, the booking hotels or finding accommodation, the travelling, the catering for himself, the separation; all would make life impossible. He also knows that, while he sometimes resents Élodie's suggestions as to how he should fill his day on little bits of DIY and gardening, or accompanying her to the supermarket, without her egging him on he would probably retire to the nearest chair – inside or outside according to the weather –

and read his life away. Even spending time with friends is becoming more of a trial to him; the irony of at last being able to understand and be understood at the same time as preferring his own company not lost on him.

He rolls over onto his side and draws his knees up to chin, wrapping his arms around his shins and linking his fingers. He wishes he could get up, pack his bag – damp trousers included – and head for the ferry. But he knows he must wait, hoping the wind will have dropped by the morning. He loosens his trousers but then resumes the foetal position and starts to sob quietly to himself. He so wishes Élodie was with him and it is thoughts of her that linger as he falls asleep . . .

He finds himself standing at the side of a long lane which is little more than an unmade track. The image is more real than life; the colours vivid, the air warm with a slight breeze, the sky blue and cloudless. He is about ten feet away from the only tree he has noticed, other than a stand of pines at the top of a long low hill that climbs steeply from beyond the field opposite. The tree, an ash, is dressed in clean, young leaves – it must be late spring or early summer – and a small flock of sparrows is chattering in one of the lower branches. The fields to either side of the lane are showing row upon row of green shoots. He is too much of a townie to know what it is and the crop is too young to have the give-away clues of oat beards or corn ears. He is sure it is not maize, or sweetcorn. He knows what that looks like – ugly, thrusting and fast-growing. This is more gently familiar.

There is no sense of intensive farming – the edges of the fields ploughed in straight lines cutting off the slight corners of the lane to leave a border of up to twenty feet in places, twenty feet of long grass and wildflowers. Into these, insects constantly circle and swoop: honey bees working by colour – seeking out reds, blues and yellows by turns; beetles blundering carelessly into everything and each other; bumble bees fighting to gain height with hopelessly overladen pollen sacs; butterflies lacking concentration and overwhelmed by their own beauty, and dragonflies – one step up in the food chain – looking for careless flies pausing on flower petals.

He longs to lie down in the grass, to stare at the sky. He used to do that at every opportunity, sometimes in the company of others but mostly alone. It was a pleasure undiminished by solitude. Staring at the sky, he would soon become dizzy, his head swimming at the light and the silence and the vastness of what he observed. If he closed his eyes, his head would still swim with the memory and the anticipation. When his companion had been another boy like him, they would talk about hobbies and school and parents, about the pleasures of hobbies and the injustice of school and parents. And if his companion had been an adolescent like him, they would talk about hobbies and school and parents and girls they had met or seen on the tram, bus or train, or at the youth club. By this time they knew their hobbies well but were confused and often disappointed about everything else. And if his companion had been a girl, he and she would have been very young of course. Older girls on the whole lost interest in intimate contact with the natural world. From the age of about twenty, women invariably want a blanket between them and the grass and whatever creepy-crawlies nature could muster, and blankets usually meant a thermos flask and a Tupperware box of sandwiches, a banana for each of them, hand wipes for cleaning hands and a 'Don't do that – someone might be watching!' He could only remember lying in the grass on rare occasions with an older girl and that had always ended in sex, which was probably the objective all along.

He remembers how, on an early adventure, he had been

out cycling with a girl on a hot summer's day. He was probably about fourteen at the time, she perhaps a year younger. They were on a lane remarkably like this one, unmade but as hard as iron after many long warm days, sharp stones restricted to the verges and crown of the lane, the ruts smooth with dried mud and safe for bicycle tyres. Just such a lane as this, treeless except for a lonely ash, the lane level but threading a shallow riverless valley, a low hill rising beyond, ploughed over except for a stand of trees against the sky.

They were hot and tired but he had brought a bottle of Tizer and a tube of Spangles and she had a packet of KP nuts and a couple of apples. Her mother had looked apprehensive as she waved them off but gave him a formal hug after kissing her daughter on her curly blonde head.

'Want to stop now?' he encouraged. 'It's very hot and we could shelter for a few minutes under that tree.'

She didn't reply but dismounted that strange way girls did in the fifties when they always wore dresses in summer and rode girls' bicycles without a crossbar. Through the gap between handlebar and saddle went her right leg, her weight, such as it was, supported by her left leg still on the pedal. She pointed her right foot delicately like a ballet dancer before it landed effortlessly on the ground just as the machine stopped – so different from his leg-over-the-back, rear-wheel-locked emergency stop. She came to a halt just ahead of him, beyond the shade of the tree, standing in the lane facing ahead of her and away from him, taking in the beauty of it all and the seemingly endless road of her life before her.

He leant his bike against the tree and then offered to do the same for her. The treats were removed from the saddle-bags and he strode out into the sunshine, stamping his way through the long grass, like a big-game hunter hoping to disturb something worth shooting in Ugandan grasslands.

'Nowhere to sit,' he observed, hoping for a gate or at least a bit of a log. Although he knew where he was, about five miles from home and six more if they went on instead of turning back, he was in unknown territory. He had no television; boys' magazines were always about worthy subjects, women's magazines reflected a life of homemaking and cooking, knitting patterns occupying the pages that now concern themselves with keeping your man interested or trying to regain interest in your man. He didn't know what to do or, indeed, if he should do anything. In fact, he knew he shouldn't do anything. It was just that girls were different and he knew he'd kick himself afterwards if he just treated her as a surrogate boy, talking about hobbies and school and parents, about the pleasures of hobbies and the injustice of school and parents.

They drank from the bottle and, with a shriek, she opened the nuts carelessly and lost about a quarter of them in the long grass. He bent down to try to retrieve them.

'Don't do that,' she had said. 'It's dirty.' Already that long separation of women from the realities of the world they lived in was beginning.

He retrieved one, a small triumph in all that long grass and a breach of her wishes out of devilment, and put it ostentatiously into his mouth, holding it out in front and above him like Yorick's skull before plunging it between his teeth and catching her eye. She frowned at his lack of hygiene and smiled at his theatricals, all at the same time.

'We'll keep the Spangles for later,' he announced. They were his after all. 'We could sit down in the grass for a few minutes as there is nowhere else to sit.'

He sat down and she sat beside him without saying anything. She spread her legs out in front of her, being careful to draw the skirt down to mid-calf. It was a flowered print, quite full, which rustled to her touch. She was wearing short white socks and brown leather sandals with big shiny metal buckles.

'Ah, this is great,' he enthused and released a sigh of contentment. He looked at her and offered another sip from the Tizer bottle. She declined but smiled at him. She was beginning to feel comfortable in this strange situation, all alone in the countryside with a boy.

She offered him one of the apples and he took it, putting it to his mouth and sinking his jaw into the thick green skin, feeling the acid stinging the nerves in his teeth. As he did so, he lay back in the grass, sighed again and said, 'Lie back down here.' It must have sounded like an order, as though this was par for the course for him. What was he saying? He had never seen a woman lying down in the flesh, other than his mother when she had flu and looked dreadful. Even in photographs, his experience was restricted to a couple of illustrated books of pre-war film stars that his parents had anachronistically kept in the bookcase with the lifting glass doors. The male actors he dismissed: Clark Gable looking pleased with himself, Edward G. Robinson looking sinister, Fatty Arbuckle giving hope of celebrity to the ugliest boys. The women were the ones who interested him. Mostly they were standing leaning against doorposts in period costume looking sultry and slightly scary or just full-lipped head-and-shoulders portraits, but there were one or two distinctly disturbing images of the likes of Betty Grable and someone called Jane something. One was lying down on a carpet in an improbably luxurious sitting room, fully dressed of course, but with a leg drawn up, arms down by her side, defenceless, looking deeply into the camera lens. A glass of something alcoholic was lying on a coffee table within reach of her hand if she felt thirsty. The other was worse, or better whichever way you looked at things. She was lying on a hay bale in a barn wearing what looked like a gypsy skirt and white blouse. One leg reached down to the floor and she was flat on her back although her shoulders and face were lifted and turned to the camera. She had long, luxuriant hair that tumbled from her head in a stream over the edge of the bale and almost to the ground, and her feet were bare. There was more than a hint of breast peeping from the partly unbuttoned blouse and, in David Grant's prepubescent mind when he had taken the books from the bookcase as a child, she looked as though she was about to eat the cameraman. As he matured, he knew her expression was sexual and that's what frightened him – she looked as though she might eat her lover, like some arachnid – a dreadful gamble with life, the recent memory of extraordinary sex uppermost in the mind of a dying victim of cannibalism. Pleasure followed inevitably by pain. So different from the docile creatures he imagined as future lovers for himself.

Whatever she thought of his last words, she lay down beside him, obediently or because she wanted to. Her trust melted him and, with a rush, he knew he loved her at that moment. He stared at the sky, listened to the birds and insects, felt dizzy for more reasons than one and stretched out a hand to touch hers. When their fingers entwined, her grip was unexpectedly strong. He turned to look at her but she still stared at the sky, motionless except for a slight clenching and unclenching of her hand in his.

He lifted himself up and looked into her face. She focused on his face and smiled. He brushed stray hairs from her eyes and slowly kissed her mouth. It was dry and barely moved but she smiled when he pulled back to look at her again. He had kissed a girl!

He lay back again and stared at the sky.

'Does that mean we are boyfriend and girlfriend?' he asked.

She tightened her grip on his hand.

186

'I suppose so, in a way. But not serious. My mother says I don't have time for boys. I have to work hard at school. I hope to go to university and I have only a few years before doing my lowers.'

He leant up again and kissed her once more. It was the same. She didn't turn away, seemed quite happy for him to kiss her, but it was again unresponsive and unyielding. He had kissed a girl but a girl had not really kissed him.

'I'll say I've got a girlfriend,' he said confidently. 'I'll say you're my girlfriend.'

'Don't do that,' she said anxiously. 'It might get back to my mother and she would be cross. And I don't really have time for boys.'

He resented 'boys' in the plural. There was only one she should be thinking of . . . him. He would only think of her, not 'girls' from now on. And they could practice on the kissing – it probably took practice. Or full red lipstick, he surmised. Perhaps that's why Jane what's-her-name was obviously a good kisser. Maybe lipstick lubricated things and made girls feel more like it.

Soon afterwards they stood up and became children again, he wresting her bike from her in mock battle and she shrieking with pleasure. Then they wolfed the Spangles down and set off home. When they got back to her house, her mother appeared in the front garden and pointedly pulled a piece of grass from her daughter's hair, giving him an angry glance. But he, all innocence, carried off the moment.

They soon parted – ceased to be the boyfriend and girlfriend she denied from the start. He didn't trust her to put all boys out of her mind for years and then reward him for his loyalty. And he was impatient for something, even a little, more.

And as he stands in his maturity in what appears to be the same place, a long hay cart pulled by a red tractor

187

comes bouncing down the lane. The back is filled, not with hay but with a crowd of people, all laughing and chattering. One or two are even singing, a ragged noise that starts and stops and starts again but is not taken up universally. When it comes alongside, the tractor stops, the engine idling and the driver using the moment to take a tobacco pouch out of his pocket and roll a thin cigarette.

He half recognises someone on the trailer, her face turned away from him, half in shadow, her hair hidden by a headscarf.

'Is that you, Élodie?' he asks. He hopes it is.

'Think again,' she says, but does not turn towards him. The others on the trailer laugh at his discomfort.

'No, of course not,' he chides himself. 'It's Jennifer.'

'Think again.' The girl still faces away, a dark shadow falling across her features. She folds her arms awaiting his next attempt. Once again the laughter, a tinge of cruelty insinuating itself into the sound.

'Elizabeth?'

'Think again.'

'Joan? Gillian? Helen? Sandra?'

Again the same voice, denials matching proffered identities.

'Think again! Think again! Think again! Think again!'

And still the laughter, savage and malevolent, louder and louder, drowning out the voice of the girl, itself flinty and merciless. Then, silence. Total silence. The others on the trailer are waiting for something. The only sound is the contented chugging of the tractor.

Then, slowly, the girl looks straight at him, her face distorted, expressionless and covered in blood.

'Think again, David Grant. Think again! Now do you recognise me?' She wrenches the scarf from her head to reveal golden hair stained red.

And he wakes up as if from a nightmare. He is sweating

188

and knows he has cried out. He is still breathing quickly and moaning in terror, his heart pounding in his heaving breast. He is uncomfortable and cold and his clothes are constricting him. He turns on the bedside light and reads the time on his watch.

It is five minutes to midnight. In order for this end-of-the-day event not to spill into tomorrow and another chapter, you must accept that he achieves the practically impossible – he changes into his pyjamas, relieves himself and climbs into his bed, still with a drumming head, before midnight strikes on some church or municipal clock outside the window.

Perhaps his watch is wrong, perhaps the clock is running fast, set early to make sure stragglers get to work on time.

Not that precision in matters of time is too important to you and me, but, as you know, he is a stickler for these things.

The Second Tuesday

David Grant awakens again. He knows it is not long since he went to sleep, the drift into unconsciousness a promising betrayal from which he emerges too easily. Once again he looks at his watch and sees that it is just after twelve-thirty on Tuesday morning – an early night for many in Dublin. The streets are full of pedestrians; the red traffic lights have gathered small herds of impatient cars and taxis, exhaust rising like empty speech bubbles in the cool air; there are still a few buses around, not to mention the trams on the Luas with their rhythmic warning bells and sharp hooters for those who do not heed the ringing. The clubbers are clubbing, some even still arriving at narrow doors to basements and darkened spaces far back from the street, going through the humiliating rigmarole of drugs and weapons checks.

'We don't entertain weapons here at all, you know that,' says the man on the door, not particularly tall, but square and mean, the kind you bounce off if you walk into them by accident. 'The only drugs allowed inside the club are the ones we provide. Tell you what, seeing as you are a regular, if you want these back, talk to Conor inside. You know Conor. He knows you. You never know, he might even give you a discount. Fancy getting caught with them on you! You should know by now, I always check the back pockets of lads' jeans.'

David Grant is awake for one reason and one reason only. He needs to vomit. He is not just feeling like it this time; it is the real McCoy, the upcoming technicolor yawn. So he hurriedly exits his bed, hurtles across the room and throws up down the toilet pan. In fact, he is in such a rush that he performs this rite in the dark, kneeling on the floor, heaving and spitting and wiping his mouth with a handful of ill-torn toilet paper and flushing before he turns the light on. This is just as well, as there is an unmistakeable trace of blood in amongst the half-digested food. He cannot taste it as the ratio of blood to regurgitate is not high but, if he'd had the light on, it would have given him just one more thing to worry about. Thinking about it, no matter how projectile or violent vomiting is, blood is rarely one of the ingredients. So, he might have had cause to be anxious had he known.

'Oh shit,' he exclaims, an understandable expletive but grossly inaccurate. It was almost everything but shit. Ever since he was young, being sick, physically sick, has been one of the things he is least courageous about. For years he would scream for his mother and then it was for one or other of his two wives. Between wives, a period of nearly seven years, he was never physically sick at all which might be significant. It is as though, without an audience, he never felt the need.

He does now turn on the light, not being familiar with the geography of the room. He needs to clean his teeth and rid himself of the acid taste of bile in his mouth. He looks at himself in the mirror and realises he is shaking, presumably from shock and the relative cold of the room. His skin is grey, his hair unkempt, and he looks as though he has lost weight, this in spite of the recent readjustment of the contents of his stomach which can hardly have been a match for the huge breakfast, the Irish chicken and chips and his unpatented cake-in-coffee concoction. If it is poss-

191

ible, his face looks thinner and more gaunt than ever. He has left Jeremy Irons far behind, half a generation behind. At this rate, he will soon resemble Jeremy Irons' father, so long as father and son resembled each other.

He cleans his teeth and swills his mouth around with water using the glass from the bedside table. He catches sight of himself again and looks hard at his eyes. For a brief moment he thinks his eyesight is restored. The combination of being tired and dealing with his reflected affliction convinces him that all is well. But it is his left eye that no longer functions and he soon obtains confirmation by turning around and looking at himself backwards in the mirror, aligning true-left over his left shoulder. Besides, he needs to practically imitate an owl to actually see in the mirror over his left shoulder without binocular vision. His neck is cricked but his handicap is confirmed.

'I wonder how long before my eye realises the truth and doesn't bother to open at all,' he wonders. 'It's doing all the right things at the moment: opening, closing, being blindly expressive' (he raises his eyelids as if the recipient of a serious shock), 'watering, blinking' (presumably – this he cannot confirm on his own if you think about it), 'but everything is now unnecessary. When do the lessons of sixty-six years start to be unlearnt?'

He takes comfort from the memory of a cat he had once owned. She had gone stone deaf after a clueless veterinary surgeon had carried out a minor operation and overdosed on the anaesthetic but, from that day until her death, the ears had pricked and twisted around to the sound of silence. Even when she was asleep, the cat's ears had never been at rest. Perhaps it would be the same for him, his eyes obediently behaving normally on the outside even though messages remain unconveyed on the inside. Appearances count to David Grant.

He switches off the light and returns to his bed, taking

the glass filled with water with him. Twice more within the next hour, he returns to the bathroom to be sick, each time turning the light on but each time being cheated on the visible presence of blood. Of course he is still shaking, presumably from the shock and cold as before, and of course his head still hurts abominably. But then, heads do hurt when one is being sick; it's normal. This is what he tells himself.

For most of the night his mind wanders. He sleeps only fitfully and his waking imaginings resemble dreams. They are as vivid as dreams with as many characters as dreams but with one big difference: he is in control. So Élodie comes to him and is how he wants her – not angry, nor dead, nor in the arms of another, nor unable to comprehend him in a place full of noise and endless coming and going, nor indifferent to his earnest impatience. She soothes his brow and is sympathetic, even while he cowers over the side of the lavatory pan. She is pretty as he is handsome, smart with just that hint of sexual allure in her strappy long dress with the slit up the side, to his sleekness in his pale Armani jacket and the matching trousers she extravagantly bought him for his sixtieth birthday. She is ten years younger than when he had first known her to his evergreen good looks he thought would last for ever. He longs to be with her, to see her clattering happily around the kitchen in Le Crestet, to hear her long explanations of short stories, to smile at the cement of her words in the wall of his silences, to feel the sleep weight of her arm over him, to know her lying sleepily on top of him, to experience her beginning to be playful, to her moving her hips around and asking what that must be that has come between them, to reach the moment that filled him with curiosity when who a woman is with ceases to be as important as what is happening.

'When we make love,' he had told her more than once,

'it is as though there is a moment when it no longer matters that it is me at all. To start with it is you and me and that is uppermost in both our minds. We talk and look at each other and do all those familiar things that we have never done in quite the same way with anyone else. We are simply confirming our love for one another by making love. What could be simpler or more normal? But then there comes this moment when you are making love and that – simply the act – becomes what is important, not with whom. I can tell from your eyes. If I were to move aside and someone else take my place, there would barely be a moment's hesitation. You would reach your orgasm with anyone, be as familiar with a stranger as with me.'

'It must be the same for you,' she had retorted snappily. 'Anyway, I don't like you talking like that. It's a bit, you know, weird. Besides, isn't it the same for you?'

He had agreed with her. Probably it was the same, he'd confirmed. Trading a serious point for peace, appearing mildly deviant the price to be paid. But he didn't believe in his heart it was the same. He would know full well that a substitution had taken place and he would probably stop, push the interloper away and ask what the hell was going on. She would have to be very quick and very convincing if he were even to continue as before and achieve an orgasm for both of them, and he would have been frantically seeking Élodie's approval for this uncharted circumstance. Even with it, he would probably have stopped the process, realised it was all probably a dream and tried to shake himself awake to recover normality. But Élodie would not let a stand-in ruin her game. Hers would not be like a substitution in a football match with its slight delay, its play-pause, indication boards held aloft, illuminated signs broad-casting the development to the whole ground, and the cameras picking up the slow trot of the replaced back to the benches, deliberately drawn out to allow the new man to pump blood through his muscles so as to hit the ground running. He imagined she would move from one to another without pause, without change to her breathing pattern, without a hiccup in the rhythm of her groin. Only afterwards would truth dawn and it would be difficult to anticipate her reaction after the event. Women only feel guilty before a sexual misdemeanour, while men keep feelings of remorse for later.

He hears the invisible clock outside in the street ring one, two, three, four o'clock, his mind travelling through space and time as he wishes for sleep and, in spite of himself, does all in his power to prevent it. All the time his head drums and his stomach turns over but mercifully without another session of physical sickness. At six o'clock he gets up, mechanically shaves and showers, and gets dressed. His chinos are almost dry, although extremely badly creased. In spite of his efforts to wash them through, there is a noticeable orange stain from fly to mid-thigh on both legs, the right worse than the left ... but not much worse. In his mind, however, there is a reason why the corduroys cannot be worn but he can't exactly remember why.

He looks around him and no longer knows where he is. He had shaved and showered like a car irretrievably broken down but still coasting forwards under its own momentum. Now he has come to a halt on the hard shoulder of his life, sitting on the side of the bed quietly looking around him. There is his bag, open at the side of the bed. He remembers the bag, knowing he bought it without Élodie being present, but not sure if its purchase had been before or after he had met her. He lifts the bag onto his knees and looks inside to find one pair of unused underpants and a pair of clean socks, a pullover, a T-shirt, a thick dressing gown, an empty toilet bag and a Champion supermarket plastic shopping bag containing used pants and socks rolled into tight balls.

195

He slowly removes each clean item and holds it up to the light. Each garment is perfectly acceptable. Nothing outlandish, inappropriate or even too bland – just nice, good-quality items that might be owned by a man in his sixties. A man such as David Grant.

Excepting the fact that he doesn't recognise any of them. He studies the pullover again. It reminds him of one he had owned at school, although its piping had been in the school shades of navy blue and yellow. It also reminded him of some white trousers he had bought that looked for all the world like cricketing trousers.

'I'll never pair these with a white pullover. People will think I'm going out to bat for England!' he had said.

'In your dreams,' someone replied. 'If you were to go out to bat for anyone, it would be the second team in a village of three hundred inhabitants with a strict "locals only" policy!'

He could still hear the person's laughter at the quick wit – a kind of whooping, kind sarcasm. It was a woman, at least the laughter was that of a woman, but who was she? And perhaps, after all, the remark even came from someone else and the woman's role was only one of an amused bystander.

But although the garment triggered thoughts of the one he had owned at school and the trousers that might mistakenly have been paired with something very similar, this one, this pullover with the red piping, is a stranger to him. He shrugs and puts the items back into the bag, folding each one carefully. He has to repeat the process when he realises he has left the dressing gown until last – its size and weight threatening to crush the rest.

His eyes rise to the long walls leading up to a shabby picture rail and on to an elaborate cornice with a later plaster rose in the near-middle of the ceiling from which hangs a grubby chandelier on a twisted and rusty chain threaded with plaited electric wire. Nothing is familiar to him; not the pictures of mountain and flood and brooding clouds in their plain wooden frames, not the shabby furniture with its splayed, turned legs and its laminate surfaces in mock dark oak, not the silver-grey television staring blankly and reflecting the sun and dust on its screen, not the large orange rug laid upon the treacherous laminated wood floor doing its best to part company with whatever lies beneath.

He takes the bag from his knees and puts it gently on the bed before he stands up. He puts on his shoes and leaves the room unlocked, forgetting to take his key with him. At the foot of the stairs, still totally unfamiliar, he hears the sound of voices emanating from behind a closed door.

'You all right Mr Grant? You look not well today.'

A pretty girl with blonde hair, high cheekbones and an Eastern European accent, emerges from the room. She is wearing an approximation of a waitress's uniform with a black shirt and a rather too short skirt with a white pinafore. As David Grant has no idea where he is, she seems incongruous and out of place, a remembered face in an unfamiliar setting, like the time he was walking along Oxford Street and saw Frank Muir heading towards him. Frank Muir was mostly a voice, sometimes an erudite and amusing quiz show contestant and never a face on Oxford Street. Accordingly, the tall man had passed almost unnoticed, kept his anonymity, even though David Grant, and, no doubt, dozens of others had spun around with a 'Wasn't that?' to themselves or their companions.

'Do you want breakfast?'

David Grant nods. This is an appropriate non-verbal reply to a question which he assumes is in isolation, although the uniform would indicate some possible connection. So he continues to stand there, looking at the girl, trying to place her. 'Do you want breakfast? Yes. Do you have a headache? Yes. Do you enjoy fish and chips? Yes. Do you live abroad? I

197

beg your pardon. Could you repeat that?' He can only answer questions about subjects at the very front of his mind.

'You want to come through?' The girl puts her head on one side, conveying concern, sympathy and a pause for a rhetorical answer in the one, gentle movement.

David Grant nods again. The girl opens the door, propels him ahead of her and he finds himself in a restaurant. A shabby restaurant but a restaurant nevertheless.

'You sit at your table, Mr Grant.'

He hesitates.

'My table? I haven't got a table.'

'The one you sat at yesterday. Over there by the window.'

More by luck than design, he aims for the table she means as it is the only one he can see that is empty. As he crosses the room, several pairs of eyes follow him; his stained trousers, crushed shirt and bewildered expression are even enough to divert almost all eyes from the waitress's bottom. The waitress catches sight of the glances and shakes her head subtly in their direction – a movement that firmly says 'Don't stare'.

'Tea or coffee, Mr Grant?' This is the waitress again, once he has sat heavily in the chair.

'Tea, please.'

'Oh. You had coffee yesterday.'

'Did I?'

'Yes. I'll get your tea . . .'

'No, I would like coffee,' he says firmly.

She heads for the kitchen where Mr Wong is gathering calories and flavour in his huge frying pan. The spatula spins and turns, burrows and flies as food sizzles angrily.

'That Mr Grant, he the one going on the ferry yesterday but couldn't because of the storm. He acting very strange.'

'Is he trouble?' Mr Wong snaps.

'No. Not trouble. But strange.'

198

'How strange?' Mr Wong drops the pan on the gas with a clatter and makes for the door. The girl restrains him with a hand lightly brushing his wrist.

'He just ill, I think.'

'He drink too much perhaps?'

'I thought so . . . to start with. But not now. He seems lost.'

'What he want for breakfast?'

'Don't know yet, just getting coffee and toast.'

'Find out, eh?'

'Yes, Mr Wong.' She gathers the bread and toast warming in an oven and fills a one-person coffee pot from a huge coffee machine that resembles a leaky steam engine. Ireland certainly takes its coffee seriously.

After the girl has made a number of suggestions, David Grant settles for scrambled eggs on toast.

'You want cereal?'

He nods again and makes to stand up. The eyes are on him again. She presses him back into his seat and bends her mouth to his ear.

'I'll get it for you,' she whispers. 'You want flakes and orange juice?'

'Yes,' he whispers back to her. 'Thank you,' he adds, still in a whisper. He nods to himself as if he has just learnt that speaking very quietly is appropriate in these circumstances.

The girl moves swiftly and as subtly as possible, not wanting her kindness to be treated as a precedent. She visualises other guests ordering cereals and juice from what is, after all, the self-service sideboard. She knows Mr Wong wouldn't like that.

'You going on the HSS ferry this morning?' she asks as she carefully sets the cereal down and moves his coffee cup to make drinking from the glass containing orange juice as accident-free as possible.

'Am I?' he asks, his eyes boring deeply into the girl's as

he seeks more detail about this development in their conversation.

'Yes. You wanted to go yesterday, but too windy. Today it look calm. HSS will sail today, for sure, all right. I'm certain.'

'Oh.' He puts his spoon into the cereal bowl and spoons dry cornflakes into his mouth. The girl looks at him, an expression of alarm spreading across her face. She helps him to milk and motions towards the sugar. He nods and she sprinkles it onto the moistened flakes, the crystals momentarily reflecting the early-morning sun before they dull and slide on a milk piste towards the bottom of the bowl.

'Here, you drink the juice.' She stands between him and the rest of the diners, interspersing her gentle instructions with inconsequential references to the weather and the odd comment about passers-by. He nods and replies with a 'yes' or 'no', the two of them in an impromptu conspiracy of normality which works, as the other guests' attention strays from the man's curious entrance and the girl's solicitousness to other matters more important to them. From time to time, as the juice is slowly drunk and the cornflakes consumed, the girl makes quick return trips to the kitchen, spinning the circus plates of her profession as she caters for thirty or more guests. Each one has to have their room number taken, each one has to be asked what they want to drink and what to eat, each one has to be directed to the sideboard (all except David Grant for this one day only) and each one has to be served their drink, their toast and their (almost invariable) cooked breakfast. Then the tables have to be cleared for the next guests. But after each trip, each gentle direction, each table cleared, she returns to David Grant, increasingly worried by what she sees. He is crouched over the table, spooning mechanically or sipping at the juice as if it is scalding hot. When the scrambled eggs arrive, he cuts the toast with difficulty, forking little piles of egg onto squares of toast before stabbing it and moving it clumsily to his mouth.

'He must be unwell. He's like someone in an old person's home. I know. I worked in one back in Poland. He looks the same. I think he need doctor.'

Mr Wong looks around the door of his kitchen. He can just see David Grant, but his back is to him and nothing appears out of the ordinary.

'Perhaps it better if he go on the HSS this morning. Problem if doctor come and he say he not well and must stay. Room let for tonight. Very complicated.'

The girl's gaze follows Mr Wong as he returns to his cooking. The morning rush is over and he can take a little more time over his task. He started out in a take-away, went on to a restaurant and now has twenty-five bedrooms in a listed building in the centre of the city, but cooking is his real pleasure. He has built a small empire around his fryer.

'But he doesn't know where he is,' she pleads. 'He won't find the ferry. He'll just wander off and come back here again maybe. And his room will be gone.'

Mr Wong is a man who doesn't like loose ends. Never has.

'Tell you what. We call him a taxi. Then he go to the ferry for sure and he on his way home. That's the best thing. If he really ill, someone will sort him out nearer to home.'

'Do you know where he lives?' she asks.

'Of course, he told me when I swiped his card on arrival. He lives in France.'

'Wales nearer to France than Ireland, I suppose.'

'What you say?'

'Nothing. It doesn't matter. I suppose you are right, but he does seem odd.'

'Perhaps fresh air do him good, anyway. Perhaps he recover on the ferry.'

'Do you mind if I see him off? He's not finished eating but I'd like to and it's getting quiet in the dining room.'

'Yes. Why not clear his room? Here,' he expertly spatulas half a dozen ingredients from his huge frying pan onto two warm plates and adds some creamy scrambled egg from a small non-stick pan, 'take these two full Irish to Table 12 first. Then, if you bring his luggage down, he don't have to climb the stairs again.'

Mr Wong is glad his scheme has gained favour – scepticism and emotion overcome by practicality. The girl is good, he says to himself, but she does sometimes get 'involved' with the customers.

The girl serves Table 12 and then returns to David Grant.

'Have you got your room key, Mr Grant?' she asks.

He looks at her as though she has asked him for the answer to the world, the universe and everything, and him never a reader of Douglas Adams.

'Key?' He searches the table and then rummages in his pockets.

'Perhaps the key is still in your room.' She nods and he joins in, as though nodding has become a ritual alongside whispering. She takes this as a 'yes' and goes quickly out of the dining room and up the stairs. She remembers his room number from yesterday. The door is slightly ajar so the presence or absence of the key is immaterial.

In moments she packs his toiletries and puts them into the sausage bag, along with his pyjamas. She is about to leave when she spots a pair of corduroy trousers hanging in an otherwise empty wardrobe. These she folds carefully and places on top of the pyjamas. She finds his room key on the bedside table and takes it with her, together with a large Continental-style wallet, and returns to the dining room.

David Grant has finished eating and is sitting quite still, looking straight ahead of him.

'I've got your things and your wallet. Do you think the ticket for the ferry is in there?' David Grant motions her to open the wallet. This is probably what Mr Wong means by getting 'involved'. She would probably have assumed its presence from the conversation the day before but she must check to make sure. After a couple of false starts – a few photographs of family members and a London Tube ticket – she finds the paper folder with the HSS return. David Grant seems to recognise it and the girl feels better. She leaves him for a minute and walks over to the kitchen to report progress to Mr Wong.

'OK,' he says, 'Almost done.'

'Has he paid?' she asks.

'No. I swiped his card but that's all. I'll make up his bill and then he can do it properly. Did you see his credit cards?'

'Yes.'

'He used a French one. A euro card, of course. French bank. Visa, I think.'

'I'll see if I can find it. I suppose it's all right me looking.'

'Of course. He trusts you.'

She shrugs, returns to the dining room and soon David Grant has paid. She had worried about the pin number – how would he remember it in his present state? – but he just does, the number going in and being confirmed correct before the possibility of a calamity had fully registered in her mind. She even sees that he has about seventy-five euros of cash in his wallet – enough for the taxi ride to Dun Laoghaire even allowing for the atrocious Dublin traffic and the loosely regulated cab charges.

'Come on, Mr Grant. I get you a taxi for the ferry. No don't . . .' she motions him to just make his own way to the door, '. . . I'll bring your bag. That's the way, Mr Grant.'

On the street a breeze is blowing but it is a light breeze, enough to fan the face and blow miniscule pieces of grit into eyes but not much more. The sun is still shining and the two of them squint four eyes to protect three. Around the corner from the hotel there is a small taxi rank and the girl links arms with David Grant to steer him in the right direction. She tries to talk to him but he seems incapable of responding. He smiles and tightens his arm against his side but never looks at her and contributes nothing other than a 'yes' or a 'no' to her otherwise one-sided conversation.

An old Japanese car, painted black with a yellow taxi sign on the roof is at the head of the queue. A woman in the driving seat leans stiffly across towards the open window as the unlikely-looking couple approach. The girl ducks her head through the window.

'Hello. This is Mr Grant. He is going on the HSS ferry from Dun Laoghaire this morning. Can you get him there in time?'

'That's what we're here for all right,' the woman says, a smile breaking out across her face. Dun Laoghaire from the city centre is a good fare and much more satisfactory than the to-and-fro to the Guinness Centre or, perish the thought, the airport. The girl leans in further and talks quietly.

'He is rather deaf, so he don't say much. He's got cash, though, in his wallet, for the fare.' She extracts herself from the window and turns to face David Grant, still miraculously waiting quietly by the car. To keep up the story of David Grant's newly acquired deafness, a kindly meant device to protect him from idle curiosity, the girl raises her voice. 'Show her your wallet, Mr Grant.' David Grant holds his wallet up and smiles before opening the rear door and letting himself into the car. The girl swings the sausage bag in after him but puts it onto his knees to make sure that when he comes out, it comes out too.

'Goodbye, Mr Grant.'

'Good-bye, Justyna,' he says, patting her hand as she closes the door.

She does a double-take. How does he know her name? Perhaps he's not as bad as I thought, she thinks, as the car revs up and swings out into the traffic in a cloud of blue smoke. His last word to her gives her hope; exonerates her from pressing harder for calling a doctor. There is no magic, however, because, although there is clearly something wrong with David Grant, he can still read. And, although she has quite forgotten it in the context of this parting, Justyna has her name stamped onto a badge and pinned just below the collar of her high-buttoned blouse.

When the taxi draws into the setting-down point at Dun Laoghaire's International Ferry terminal, his actions and slow responses are explained to the satisfaction of the taxi driver by his reported deafness. She even helps him, having taken what the meter says, including a hefty fixed sum for the little sausage bag, plus a tip of ten euros ('It's normal for people to pay me ten euros as a tip for such a long trip'), followed by the nodding which David Grant copies to confirm his approval of the sum, plus a rounding-up to match the notes in his wallet ('I'm sorry but I don't have any change on me'), by removing his ticket for the ferry and putting it into his hand.

'You'll be needing that next, Mr Grant,' the taxi driver roars into his ear. If he were deaf, he might have appreciated the decibel level but not the implication that deaf people are somehow very stupid as well. But he is not deaf, maybe just a little stupid, so he obediently takes the ticket and his wallet and his sausage bag and thanks the taxi driver before heading off into the terminal building.

'Odd-looking fella. A bit of an untidy person,' she says to herself as she contemplates whether to look for a long fare back into the city or risk a possible falling-out with the local cabs while she looks for someone on the street wanting to go to the Dundrum Shopping Centre.

David Grant is swept along by a flotilla of luggage trolleys with family outriders: the casual vandals with their folded-arms, lean-on-the-handles action who change course only by physical contact with walls, furniture and other travellers; the frightfully correct couples who spend their time peering around the perimeter of their moving space gauging the best direction to choose next; the children insisting on standing between their parents' arms to push and tripping the adults in the process . . . David Grant manages to get through security by doing exactly what he is asked and is soon on board the high-speed ship. It sails on time (it always sails on time except when it doesn't sail at all) and an hour and a half later the white familiarity of South Stack light-house signals an imminent arrival at Holyhead. He could have eaten on the boat but he isn't hungry and therefore eating never occurs to him.

The sun has now gone in and grey clouds billow over the cliffs like a child's painting, one step on from an intensely blue sky, a round smiley-faced sun and flying birds like lower-case 'm's. David Grant leaves the ship, joins the queue and finds himself through customs without incident. Two policemen dressed like cops from an American television series pace around arrogantly, half a dozen leather pouches hanging from manly leather belts, radios nestling affection-ately at their necks and machine guns poised at the ready. Had David Grant been more aware he would have revisited his oft-aired opinion that they achieve two own goals in addition to the bonus of looking ridiculous in the melee of human holiday flotsam. He knew they'd never actually use the machine guns owing to the near-certainty of killing half a dozen innocent bystanders in picking off a single terrorist, and their ability to pursue would be severely compromised by the dead weight of the weapon in their two hands. Better to have a small pistol in one of those pouches than the silly machine gun. Still, this is the age of statement over substance, image over common sense, machismo over discretion, and we are living in dangerous times. That man with the pot belly wearing a T-shirt saying 'Mine's (another) Lager, Ta' propelling a trolley, an improbably fat wife and two ugly children, is a terrorist for sure.

But David Grant is not aware so we are spared any frustrated ranting. He is travelling light so he doesn't have a trolley and cannot join in the trolley marathon. The crowds pass through the door and fan out in different directions towards the town, car parks and the railway station. A few are met with exaggerated greetings and hugs and step-back stares as if the greeter expects some physical change in the greeted after – what is it? – a week in Ireland. But there are few of these. Arrivals in Holyhead for the most part go unnoticed.

Over in the long-stay car park, a pair of rather more practically dressed police are standing with a public-spirited woman of about thirty-five. She is wearing a rather old-fashioned flower-printed dress that is full and billowing in the seashore breeze. She wears flat white shoes, rather scuffed, and no stockings. She has gone slightly beyond beauty, her body thickened by childbirth, a poor diet and the loss of dreams. Nevertheless, she is smilingly animated, and follows the police's gaze as they look into the car and around the front at the number plate.

'I thought I ought to tell you,' she repeats, needing to fill the air with sound.

'Glad you did, Mrs . . . ?' The policeman raises his voice into a question.

'Moffat. Mrs Geraldine Moffat. Just call me Gerry, everybody does. We're on holiday on Anglesey. We've got a caravan on a Caravan Club site on the other side. It's very nice, the pitches are all generously spaced, nice toilet blocks – not like the old days, and it's great for the chi . . .'

'. . . You parked here too?' The policewoman sees Mrs Moffat's life story as immaterial to their present investigation.

'Yes, John, my husband, has gone off with the boys for a walk; taking the dog. He's called Rags on account of his colouring. Just like one of those old rag carpets, he is! He doesn't like being shut up in the car for too long, poor love. He throws up and do you know how bad dog sick smells? I thought I'd look at the shops and then I saw it. Thought I'd get onto the mobile. It's a shame for someone.'

'You did the right thing, Mrs Moffat,' the policewoman confirms, following her partner's gaze as he looks again through the broken front window. A police radio in their parked patrol car crackles but is ignored.

'Foreign, isn't it?' The woman is getting curious, a sense of proprietorial involvement propelling her onwards. This is her discovery, in a way it is her story, and one she will certainly tell everyone she knows, probably more than once.

'French, I think. Yes, French. No country sticker but the 'F' is on the number plate so I suppose that's enough,' the policeman says grudgingly, taking his notebook out of his top pocket and scribbling a few details with a cheap Biro.

'Do you want to report back, or shall I?' asks the policewoman.

'You do it,' her colleague replies.

The policewoman takes her mobile from the harness on her jacket and quick-dials the police station.

'Duty desk please,' she demands, scuffing her feet in the crumbled window glass on the ground. 'Yes, hello Sian. Yes, should be back within half an hour. Yes, all right. Look, we've got a car been broken into in the ferry overflow car park. What? Yes, like I said, the ferry overflow. No, it doesn't look as though they wanted to drive it away. Well, they'd have to be desperate – it's more of a wreck than yours! Looks as though they wanted something . . .'

'Looks like it might have been a mobile,' this from the policeman who is now inside the car. 'Look, there's a charger in the cigarette lighting point.'

'Did you hear that, Sian? Right. Has the phone gone? I'd think so, hold on.' She raises her eyebrows at her colleague.

'Of course it's gone,' he whispers loudly. 'Does Sian think they broke in, used the phone and then left it on charge?' He shakes his head, smiling.

'Yes, I can confirm it's gone . . . It's a Corsa. Nope, not Vauxhall. It's an *Opel* Corsa. It's French registered. It's 7698UO07. Got that? All right, I'll say it again.'

She repeats the number. The policewoman covers the phone with her hand and then talks to Mrs Moffat who is thoroughly enjoying her experience.

'As the owner is probably in Ireland, it is likely we'll be asked to make the car as secure as possible and put a sticker on the window asking the owner to contact us.'

Mrs Moffat suddenly looks crestfallen. She rather hopes the owner will appear around the corner and jump about in an agitated manner gabbling away in French. A string of onions around his neck would just complete her mental image. So far, this hasn't happened but she hadn't considered that the owner is probably blissfully unaware of the little drama on the Welsh coast. Why, he might be a week away from his car, and the Moffats have only got another three days before they set off home to Dudley. The best of her story may already be over.

There is a long pause. The wind gusts about the serried ranks of parked cars while, from time to time, new arrivals off the HSS arrive, open boots and load cases. Some fretful children stand about dejectedly while others sidle off and hide behind neighbouring vehicles to indicate their disapproval of the next leg of their journey. One proud couple take an age to unstrap a baby from a buggy and install him or her into a backward-facing child's seat before folding up the buggy and spending minutes arranging the luggage in the boot. Parenting makes ditherers of the formerly quick and efficient. One overweight man with 'Mine's (another) Lager, Ta' emblazoned on his T-shirt shepherds his overweight family through the lines of cars. As they approach, they are making an awful lot of noise but the man spots the police and suddenly falls silent, shushing his family in the process. They take a wide detour before, unnoticed, they unlock the door of an old Ford Granada and quietly stow their luggage and themselves.

'Yes?' This from the policewoman who has been pirouetting around with the mobile stuck to her ear. 'What? Well, how should I know! I don't know. Hold on.' She covers the phone again and turns, this time, to her colleague. 'Mike, Sian's asking if you can get into the boot.'

He looks surprised.

'Why?'

'She thinks you might find a rock in the car. There's not one in the cabin so, if there is one, it can only be in the boot.'

'A rock? What's that about?' He tuts before continuing. 'I'll have a look and see what I can do. You can get into the boot from the back seat in these babies.'

He folds the front seat forwards and eases his huge frame into the back.

'Mind your head!' Mrs Moffat helpfully advises. Her advice goes unacknowledged.

A few grunts later, Michael the Policeman is folding seat swabs, trapping his feet and tugging the seat back forwards to reveal a couple of warning triangles, a regulation yellow emergency coat, a good quality suitcase . . . and a rock.

'What is this, "Treasure Trail" or something?' Michael asks.

His colleague gets back onto the radio.

'Yes, there's a large stone in the back. How did you know?'

The voice at the other end crackles and they both laugh before the policewoman signs off and puts her phone away.

'Apparently our Froggie friend has been reported seen stealing a rock from a wall in Snowdonia.'

'Is that illegal?' Michael the Policeman starts to reassemble the Opel Corsa.

'It is if the rock belongs to someone. No one took it very seriously, especially as the car was reported to be French, but here we are, Starsky and Hutch, on the case and apprehending the thief. Now, when he comes back, we'll be commiserating with his loss of a mobile phone and criminal damage to his car and then we'll be fingering him for knocking down Welsh Water's precious wall!'

'Why on earth would a Frenchman, on holiday presumably, pinch a rock from a wall?'

'Beats me.'

'Perhaps he wants a little bit of Wales for his garden, and pinching a rock from a wall is a damn sight easier than quarrying one for himself.'

'Or perhaps he thinks it's rightfully his. Don't the French own most of the water companies in Britain?'

The show is over. Mrs Moffat looks slightly disappointed. She looks around and sees some more people approaching the car park, this little band brought by the free transfer bus, but no one approaches the scene of the drama.

'Do you want my home address,' she asks hopefully.

'No,' the female policeman replies, 'I don't think so. It's

211

not as though you were a witness or anything and we might have come across the damage as easily as you. No, that won't be necessary. Thanks for reporting the incident, though.'

Mrs Moffat smoothes down her dress against the breeze for the one hundredth time since we encountered her and she smiles, but shrugs at the same time.

'Oh well,' she sighs. 'Glad I was of some help.'

'Oh, you were. Identifying a crime that leads to us clearing up another. Very helpful, I'd say. It'll just be lads stealing the phone. Bet they had trouble with it, though. If it's a French phone, there'll be all that international dialling to do before you can get through to your mates!'

The police clamber into their patrol car, fire up the engine and, with a subtle salute to Mrs Moffat, drive off.

'That Ford Granny looks a bit weird,' Michael the Policeman says as they slip out of the car park.

'No you don't!' his colleague says firmly. 'I don't care if he's a bloody terrorist, I want my lunch!'

Mrs Moffat walks slowly away, absent-mindedly adjusting the broad shoulder strap of her flowery-printed dress. When she straightens her arm, a red line stays momentarily in the white folds of flesh at her elbow. She watches it gradually disappear, sighs and, not looking where she is going, bangs her shin on the tow bar of a parked Audi.

Had she waited for her thieved, thieving Frenchman, and she did look around more than once as she made for the town, trying to pick a likely suspect without really knowing what to look for, she would have sighed a good deal more often. David Grant did not go to the car park for one simple reason.

He does not remember he has a car.

David Grant is standing outside the terminal building with his sausage bag in one hand and his wallet in the other. The cool air is making him feel more alert than at

212

any time today, and he even manages to smile and nod at one or two stragglers who walk past him, but his head is drumming fit to burst and he doesn't know what to do.

'Train station's over there, mate,' a man says helpfully, 'unless, that is, you've got a car.' You'd think the mention of the alternative form of transport might have rung a bell, however distant, in David Grant's mind. But no. He ignores this last clue and, as a result, squanders any chance of getting back to Le Crestet before Élodie.

'Train? Yes, a train will do. Always liked the train.'

'There's one going in about fifteen minutes. It's a Manchester but you can change at Chester for the south.'

'No, Manchester will do me fine.'

'Going north then?'

'I come from the north.' David Grant nods to himself as his mind wanders away across the miles to the lost world of his youth.

'Well, that's why you'd be going back.'

David Grant looks at him closely before answering.

'Yes, I would be going back there, wouldn't I?'

The man looks confused and not a little miffed at the curt response.

'Don't take on, mate. Just trying to be helpful.'

David Grant takes a few moments to reply, during which time his new contact makes to leave.

'No. Sorry. You have been helpful. Manchester would be good for me.'

The man relaxes and falls into step with David Grant.

'I'm going to Chester. Well, I'm not, but I get a train into the Wirral for New Brighton from there. I'll come with you as we don't now have much time, especially if you have to buy a ticket. Come on, mate.'

The two walk at David Grant's pace towards the station booking office. The man from New Brighton chatters on, glad of an audience. After his initial display of sensitivity, he is affable enough and helps David Grant with his ticket, especially when the clerk unhelpfully replies 'Piccadilly?' to his request for a ticket to Manchester and there is a moment's confusion over the 'other' Piccadilly.

The two find a seat on the train and David Grant sits down, putting the sausage bag on his knee.

'Want that up on the rack, mate?' the man asks, making to rise to his feet.

'No thank you.' He clutches the bag to him and knits his wallet in amongst the handles of the bag for added security.

Within a few minutes, the warning buzzer for the doors sounds and the diesel engines wind up to a whine before the train moves off. It accelerates across the causeway to what Holy Islanders call 'the mainland'.

'Always like the view from here,' David Grant's companion observes, his neck twisted away from him as he scans the horizon. 'See? There's a few people out there sailing today even though it looks like rain. A bit of a breeze, though. Not like yesterday! You could hardly stand up in Holyhead yesterday – horizontal rain, too. Ever seen that? If you're out in it, you get soaking wet but the ground stays practically dry. Odd that. My company's putting in some new sewerage pipes in the town. They have to put me onto jobs I can get to by train on account of a problem I had with too much beer, a driving licence and a bloody cop. I'll get it back in six months but I quite like the train. You meet interesting people; always someone to talk to.'

David Grant nods but doesn't say anything.

The train gains the other shore and motors quickly across the island. The two fall to silence except for the odd interjection from the pipeman as he points out places of interest. They cross the Menai Strait after a short explanation of the longest station name in Britain – something David Grant already knew about but didn't let on – plunge

214

through the tunnels each side of a station stop in Bangor and then regain the coast for miles.

'That's Llandudno over there,' the pipeman says, pointing northwards after the train clatters through the walls of Conwy Castle. 'Do you know Llandudno? That's the Great Orme – the big hill, look. Do you know it?'

David Grant follows the man's pointing finger.

'No, I don't think so. It looks very pleasant.'

'We used to come here for holidays when I were a kid – here or Rhyl. Great for children it was then. Probably not changed much but kids want more now, don't they? That's why Rhyl and Prestatyn have got all its funfairs and attractions. Mind you, it's foreign holidays they want now, isn't it? Do you go abroad for yer holidays?'

David Grant screws up his eyes to think.

'No, I don't think we do. We tend to stay at home.'

This, of course, is the true answer but somewhat lacking in precision. He doesn't go abroad but he lives abroad. So his 'abroad' is not the pipeman's aboard. Anyway, let's move on.

The pipeman peers at his companion who is looking troubled, but neither man says anything more on the subject. David Grant's demeanour is due to a detail of his response to the pipeman's last question. He used the word 'we' in his reply but he cannot remember who or what caused him to respond in the first person plural. The more he thinks, the more the answer seems to elude him. He has been here before – trying to remember things that just won't come. He knows that the best thing is to let it go. It'll come back in time. 'You'll remember what it was,' his mother used to say, 'and if you don't, either it didn't matter or it was a lie in the first place.'

The train skirts the coastline for most of the journey to Chester, at which the pipeman gets off.

215

'Mind how yer go,' he says as he stands up to make for the door. David Grant starts to follow him.

'No, you're going to Manchester so you don't get off. This train'll take you all the way.'

David Grant sits back down, placing his bag with its embraced wallet back on his knee. The pipeman bids him farewell but David Grant just nods without smiling. 'I stay on this train,' he says to himself as he watches the bustle of the station and hears the bing-bong-bing heralding station announcements. Soon it is the warning for the doors closing that he hears and the train is off again.

Without the cheerful distractions of the pipeman, David Grant dozes, clutching his luggage for comfort and safety. The swaying of the train and the monotonous roar of the diesel engines drive him deeper into sleep. He is unaware of the train frequently stopping and starting as it crosses Cheshire.

He is awakened by a member of the public tapping him on the arm.

'Wake up, mate!'

'No, I am to stay on the train. Thanks very much, though.'

'But this is the end of the line,' the lad says. He is wearing a hoodie and clearly attempting to appear tougher and more cynical than he obviously is. 'This is Manchester Piccadilly, the terminus.'

'Oh, right.' David Grant stretches himself. 'Thank you.'

'That's all right. Can't have you going back and forth all day, can we?'

David Grant smiles and struggles to his feet. It is just before four-thirty in the afternoon. The train is almost on time. His head is drumming as usual and he feels a throbbing pulse in his temple with his left hand.

He leaves the concourse and walks out onto the station

216

approach. For once Manchester seems to have lost its trademark. It is not raining.

He feels hungry, so wanders around the city centre looking for somewhere to eat. The only place he recognises is a MacDonald's. It is quiet and almost empty, with just a few customers ramming buns carelessly into their mouths. As they do, green and red gollop squirts from between their fingers and from the corners of their mouths. It's no wonder burger advertising rarely shows their consumption. Little chimneys of fries lie overturned, their contents spilling coldly onto the Formica surfaces. Small children propel bent worms of straws into their mouths before noisily slurping sugar-water into their swollen cheeks. The slow progress of the dishevelled traveller is watched by a few without interrupting the process of refuelling, working jaws following swivelling eyes like cattle cautiously observing ramblers on an across-the-field public right-of-way.

'Yes?' a spotty girl asks, her lapel a constellation of good-behaviour stars. 'Can I help you?'

David Grant puts his hands on the counter and stares heavenward at a menu that is made seemingly generous by endless repetition.

'I'll have a Big Mac please.' He continues to look up at the menu.

'Large fries with that?' the girl asks, wiping her nose on the back of her sleeve and sniffing loudly to complete the task. Her fingers are poised over the till, like an athlete under starter's orders.

'Yes. Thank you.'

She is off, clattering buttons. He continues to stare up at the illuminated menu.

'What do you want to drink with that?'

He cannot quite pick out the drinks from the display. Perhaps he is looking in the wrong place. He pauses.

'What do you want?' the girl asks in an irritated voice, her fingers momentarily frozen by his indecision. 'Coke? Orange? Coffee?'

'Coke please.'

'Regular or large?'

'Regular,' he replies, not quite knowing what that means.

She is at the winning post. The machine clatters happily, the score taken, race over – almost. She takes his money and puts his change on the tray.

She starts to assemble the meal. Everything is long made, the wrapped burger on a sloping stainless steel slide endlessly refilled from the kitchen beyond, the gaggle of little chip pokes standing around under a lamp to keep warm beside the fryer. She crosses to an ice dispenser.

'No ice, please,' David Grant intervenes. 'I don't want any ice.'

The spotty girl sighs and fills the cup to the brim anyway, adding a plastic lid with a single blow from her flattened palm. If you want to adversely affect MacDonald's profits, always ask for no ice. They still fill the cup.

'Enjoy your meal,' she intones as she looks beyond him to a woman who has come up to form a queue of two.

He carries his tray clumsily, with his left hand still holding his sausage bag and wallet which swing about crazily without the constraint of their normal close proximity to his leg. He makes for an empty table and unwraps the bun. It nestles in the opened paper, lukewarm, damp and a very poor reflection of the image on the menu. He pokes it and then lifts it carefully to his mouth. In no time he, too, is spurting mucus and gore down his face. It is then that the needful routine of leaving the counter for the table via the shelf fitted with napkin dispensers and straws becomes apparent. He rectifies his situation and spends the rest of his meal providing props for a criminal investigation television series. Eating the fries provides a blessed relief from the squirty,

218

dangerous beef burger, while the Coke, drunk with the lid torn off and the absence of a straw, profoundly chills him. Obediently, he empties his tray in the bin, the blood and snot-soaked napkins sticking to everything as they pass into the darkness. He retires to the toilet to wash, burping at every breath. Burgers, he decides, are designed for the young and those with robust constitutions. After a good wash he takes his pullover from his bag and puts it on. He doesn't know it but, apart from his stained trousers, he looks smarter than when he left Dublin in the morning. He even manages to find a comb in his toilet bag and, by frequent use of the tap, brings a semblance of order to the top of his head. A plastic Ronald MacDonald sees him off the premises, exhorting him to hold his next children's party in the establishment.

There are distinct advantages to growing old, he thinks.

He looks at his watch. It is almost five-thirty in the afternoon and he has no idea what he should be doing. He knows he must find somewhere to stay but, beyond that, nothing seems to beckon. His memory is fading fast and his future plans reduced to short-term necessity. He is like a mole caught in a mole trap, his world restricted to a pace behind, two paces in front, his prison not a wire frame but of his own incognisant making and infinitely more imposs-ible to leave.

He walks around for a while and into Peter Street, dominated by the solid pile of the Midland Hotel. He walks in and up to the reception counter before anyone spots his shabby trousers or hesitant stroll. And so he books into one of Manchester's finest hotels ('You're lucky, sir, we only have one or two rooms that are not already reserved'), which, as you will read later, is probably fitting.

Oh, just one more thing.

Although I've not mentioned it much today, his head is still giving him a lot of pain. In fact, on his way into the

219

hotel, he managed to buy lots of very strong codeine and paracetamol compound tablets by visiting several chemists and telling the same story in each. He has getting on for a hundred tablets in his sausage bag when he goes up in the lift and lets himself into the immaculate bedroom. He watches television for a few hours, quietly sipping water and, from time to time, swallowing painkillers as though they are going out of fashion. After he changes into his pyjamas, he continues the process until he gently passes out, his head on the pillow and his body on top of the bedspread.

David Grant is dead to the world.

The Second Wednesday

David Grant does not die. His night is full of vivid dreams that exhaust him, but their plot lines, the characters that populate them and their outcome, if any, elude him when he awakens. For most of the night his head is spinning and he rises twice to be sick. Although there is again a trace of blood in his vomit, he doesn't see it in spite of the fact that he switches the light on each time. The line between reality and his sleeping state is crossed and recrossed so often during the night that, had he been able to recall anything, he might not have been able to say to which side of the line any event belonged. As he can't remember what he ate the afternoon before, he doesn't unfairly impute MacDonald's for his condition. We can be sure most of the blame should be laid at the feet of an excess of the codeine-laced compound; with tiredness, his recurring headaches and the long day bearing the rest of the responsibility. But, as the adage goes, 'It's an ill wind . . .' and vomiting probably saved his life, bringing up half-digested analgesics together with everything else.

When he awakes, he does not rise immediately but lies motionless on his back, legs spread outwards so that they form a wide V. He is under the bedcovers and strangely serene. He is smiling for no apparent reason and tracing a hairline crack across the ceiling. It is almost too faint to see but with his one good eye he can focus clearly on the minute imperfection. It runs in a long curve from a light fitting to a corner near the window. He remembers doing the same when he was a child, although the cracks on his ceiling at home were very much wider and more complex than the example on the ceiling of the Midland Hotel, Manchester. At home they had resembled spidery tree roots, but to him they were roads down which he could ride his bike or even drive a car, a means of transport unavailable at that time to his family. He had even dragged a table under one part of the pattern, perched a chair on top and clambered up to link two lines together with a balsa knife so that he could trace the movement of cars from one side of the ceiling to the other without having to take to the imaginary fields.

Had he been able to shield the world from his eccentric behaviour it would have been better for all concerned but, while no accident had befallen him during his attack on the plaster and his parents would scarcely have noticed an extra few inches of stria in a hundred feet of multi-threaded fissures, they found greying dust on his blunted balsa knife. To David Grant, coming at the event from the uncomplicated world of an eight-year-old, the explanation was simple and, seeing it as a necessary step to satisfy his insomniac imagination, entirely justified. But from his father's point of view, a young child clambering on a pyramid of furniture to mutilate a ceiling was made all the worse by the explanation. If it had been simple vandalism, that would have been one thing, but in order to complete a network of chimerical roads? That was something else altogether and did much to sow the seeds of misunderstanding that characterised the relationship between father and son from that day forth.

He tries to lift his head but it is like a lead weight that is somehow detached from the rest of him. He can even move his neck muscles and everywhere else on his body seems

222

capable of mobility, but his head is far too comfortable in the pillows to respond. On other occasions, such a situation would have propelled David Grant to a state of panic but he is strangely resigned to the dilemma he is in. For the first time in his life, he is unable to rise. And so, for the time being, he doesn't. Instead, he stares at the ceiling enjoying not being able to do anything at all.

He drifts in and out of sleep without any change to his condition, dreaming and forgetting what he has dreamed, staring at the ceiling and remembering his childhood. At one moment he thinks he hears someone at the door; even that it might have opened, but he could be mistaken. During one of the periods when he is asleep, the bedside telephone rings. After four rings, he manages to lift the receiver.

'Mr Grant?' the voice enquires.

'Yes, this is he,' he replies. He adopted his telephone-answering technique from an American film he once saw. He felt it particularly set an energetic tone to the start of a business conversation and still uses it when he is uncertain of the caller's identity.

'Mr Grant, we've been trying to get hold of you. It is two o'clock in the afternoon.'

What goes through his head is a facetious reply such as 'And your point is?', but he says nothing.

'Mr Grant,' the voice continues. 'Are you still there?'

'Yes,' David Grant replies.

'It's just that you have to clear your room by noon on your day of departure and it is now two o'clock.'

David Grant says nothing again.

'Mr Grant, would you like to stay another night? We could do that if it is more convenient for you.'

'Yes.'

'Would you like that?'

'Yes. Yes please. Do that.'

'We have a credit card voucher for you here. Just settle your bill in the morning but please vacate your room before noon.'

David Grant does not reply and the phone goes silent.

Although he has not lifted his head off the pillow during the discussion, he has turned it slightly in the direction of the handset and this encourages him to attempt further movement. Although it takes him nearly an hour to summon up the energy and inclination, he finally manages to sit on the side of his bed, his hands between his knees and his head slumped almost to his waist. He feels very dizzy but for the first time in memory he does not have a headache. He attempts to stand up and the dizziness transforms into serious vertigo. He feels he is going to vomit again and does so down the toilet bowl, making his way there partly on his feet and partly on his hands and knees. He kneels beside the bowl for some time, spitting and wiping his mouth with toilet paper before flushing. Each time the bowl looks fresh and unclogged, another mouthful comes up and he has to go through the same process all over again. He breathes in clear air through his nose, which makes him light-headed but, in the end, has the right effect. His vomiting fit is over. He flushes one final time and then runs a bath, dropping the entire contents of a bottle of bubble bath under the streaming hot water. He lies back and has a thorough soak before drying slowly with a large bath towel, one hand gripping a conveniently placed towel rail for support, and dresses in his last-remaining clean clothes. He decides to try the corduroys and is delighted there is no recognisable reason for their rejection. While he is in the process of dressing, he finds a set of car keys in a pocket. They are equipped with an Opel fob and a tag with a car registration number printed on it in neat writing. He and Élodie used to hang the keys for the cars on hooks in the kitchen back in Le Crestet and Élodie had thought it more practical to identify the keys clearly. He had doubted this approach, warning that any burglar could break into the house, read the detail on the car keys and, since they had only one garage, take the car that had been left outside.

Élodie had rather scoffed at this.

'With our security system – shutting shutters, leaving lights on and so on no one would ever seriously break in and, if they did, they wouldn't take the car – it makes such a noise getting it out of the drive and up the slope,' she had said.

And, so far, she has been proved right.

David Grant cannot imagine why he would have car keys in his pocket. He even wonders if the trousers are really his or if, somewhere along the way, he has acquired them, together with their contents. There is a coin in the pocket as well and he takes this out and turns it over in his hand. It is a one-euro piece with a harp prominent on the obverse. 'Irish,' he says, and then shrugs. Coins from all over Europe seem to turn up all over the place. It must have been given to him in change at some time and he had set it aside as a sort of keepsake – if indeed the trousers are his. He knows he likes Ireland, loves the people and the particular friends he had made there. 'I quite want to go back,' he muses. 'It has been so long. What is it? Three years? Four?'

He looks at the car keys again, knows the registration is French by the juxtaposition of letters and numbers, but the rest of this little scene in the theatre of his existence – his wife, her writing the car registration on the tag, the name 'Opel' on the fob, and all the minor events – the key-nails on the wall, the gentle argument about security – all have gone from his consciousness.

He no longer remembers his wife or his life in France.

The bath and getting dressed refresh him and he decides to go out of the hotel for a walk. He slowly packs the sausage bag, including a drinking glass, a part-drunk bottle of still Malvern water, a leather place mat, as many of the bathroom accessories as he has not used, a towel, and the leather room welcome-binder complete with envelopes and headed notepaper, together with a large number of codeine tablets, some still in unopened boxes, some in plastic bubble packs and some burst already and scattered on the bedside table. It is as though he is programmed to pack, and pack he will – everything that is moveable. By way of a fair exchange, he leaves the car keys on the bedside table, returning the coin to his pocket.

The process takes about half an hour so it is nearly five when he makes his way down to reception and, unnoticed, out of the main door clutching his wallet in one hand and the sausage bag in the other. For the moment, he knows he has the hotel room for another night but his memory is very short. Even Ireland, the country he awakened in the day before, has faded like a dream, the space filled with the certain knowledge of something forgotten. His chances of ever returning to the tolerant and dependable magnificence of the Midland Hotel seem slight.

It is a warm afternoon and the streets are busy with late shoppers and early office leavers. With his slow, stumbling walk and the sausage bag in his left hand, he occupies a wide, ponderous space on the pavement. Mancunians divide and rejoin around him like fast-moving wildebeest avoiding an injured or elderly individual in the endless stampede around the African plains. And like that singled-out, doomed wildebeest, David Grant is expressionless, his very normality hiding a deep malaise, purposed but purposeless, seeming to be focused on some known-only-to-him goal but mechanical and lacking any urgency in his movements, cautiously moving with the crowd who are and are not going his way. But behind that deadpan face, that unimpassioned stare into the middle distance, that sense of remote intention, there is despair and fear. He is lost but knows he is lost, isolated by his span of consciousness which has reduced to no more than three hundred minutes. He is still just aware of himself, aware of mechanisms by which one measures the quality of one's life: happiness, fulfilment, purpose, satisfaction, hope. Equally, he is aware that he cannot apply those mechanisms, cannot find the levers and switches and buttons that order his life and reward effort with reason. Instead he moves forward sluggishly, neither resenting nor approving his direction. Thus he is propelled and coaxed across the city centre from south to north until he finds himself approaching a vast shopping mall. He feels tired, and that old companion, his headache, begins to make its presence felt. He sits down on a public bench and watches the ebb and flow of the pedestrians. From time to time his view is obscured by large single-deck trams that pass with an easy-going hiss and fold themselves around the corner at the top of a slight hill before disappearing. He remembers other trams in another city, trams that were day-to-day, matter-of-fact. They had been taken from him when he was about fifteen years of age, victims of supposed progress, but until then had been an essential part of life; his journey to school, weekend visits to that other city centre or down to the sea. Just normal and everyday. From the focus on the trams and the essential difference between the ones plying their trade in front of him and those lurching through his memory (the vehicles from his past were double-decked), he nevertheless recognises similarities: the way the vehicles move in straight lines on their tracks, their sway as they grow closer, the slight whine of their electric motors, a faint smell of hot oil mixed with warm brakes, a biting, discordant squeal as the flanges resist the change of direction on the tight curves, the hiss of the overhead wires. And those very similarities awaken in him a pleasure that extends far beyond a conscious comparison of Manchester trams versus Edinburgh trams; the trams of today set beside the trams of yesteryear. Just as with Proust's Marcel, who was offered a cup of tea into which he sank a morsel of *petite madeleine* and thereby not even the simple fact of the cake or the tea, but its taste and smell alone, conjures up what he calls the vast structure of recollection, dead people, broken and scattered things, the ruin of the past, and rebuilds and recalls in infinite detail a better, lost time, so for David Grant it is the fragile ephemera of sunlight dancing on the windows as the vehicle rumbles past, not the fact of the tram with all its attendant brutish thrusting habits and characteristics, that makes him sigh deeply while trying to grasp a universe that can only be approached using the key presented to him by that fleeting phenomenon, the dancing light constrained by wheel and rail but released by the rocking and swaying motion of the tramcar. And, just as with Proust, the moment repeated diminishes the effect and puts the key progressively out of reach, so the phenomenon of sunlight and glass repeated by the passing and repassing of the trams banishes the moment and restores fear and wistfulness born of loss. David Grant turns away from the material and instead concentrates on himself, what is inside, to try to recover that which was lost, found and is now lost again. The key, signalled by an external force, is his and his alone, its precarious residence his own fractured mind. But, by concentrating on what the shivering, capering light had triggered, and then thrusting aside the treachery of visual repetition, he recreates first the immediate familiarity of his home. This, a first-floor flat approached by a stone stair leading from a dark corridor behind a massive wooden door flanked on either side by columns of six brightly shined brass bell-pulls, each with the family name on a brass plaque alongside is, in comparison with the elementary facilities provided in the common areas, the proud reflection of his mother's good but unfathomably safe taste. With its polished parquet, patterned fawn carpets and long gold curtains hanging at deep bay windows, its accent on upholstery, dark polished wood, and the constancy of family heirlooms, its clean white tiles in the kitchen and bathroom, its order and permanence, it has what used to be called a 'woman's touch'. The family played out their roles uncompromised by the theatre in which they performed. There had never been words about it being too small, too cold, too noisy, too bland, too awkward or too shabby, because it was none of these things. From time to time, his parents would announce that they would be decorating this or that room and all would be upheaval as furniture was stacked or covered and almost-forgotten step ladders produced from the large, dark press near the door. By the time the smell of paint or the damp acid smell of the paper paste had dissipated, however, it would be as though nothing had changed – the flat would return to its reticent self, the furniture replaced in its proper place, the pictures and mirrors rehung on the same nails carefully drawn by his father before decoration and placed in a small ashtray kept in the kitchen, seemingly for this purpose and no other. He could picture his father, head twisted upwards, one eye glued against the newly decorated wall, using the light to identify the slight unevenness that would betray the hiding place of a mirror's nail hole, and his cry of satisfaction as he found it and marked it with a stub of pencil produced from a pocket in his jacket. His father always wore a jacket, be it a suit jacket for work, church or the Lodge, or a Harris tweed hacking jacket with leather elbow patches for all other occasions. He wore his tweed jacket to the beach.

The singularity of the tenement flat remained, but further concentration set its self-satisfied, smoke-stained sandstone in context. The other tenements above, below and behind, the row that stretched the length of the street, the St Cuthbert's Co-op on the corner with its milk crates and vegetable displays, the elegant dark reddish-brown and white trams (there are those trams again) whining and clanking briefly across the end of the street on their way to the West End or the even-smarter residential districts that gathered around the foothills of the Pentlands, the school a few pennies away on the swaying upper deck, the proud conservatism of Princes Street with its bazaar of canvas blinds on hot and wet days, the grand portals of Jenners, his red sandstone school and the shabby wonder of the sea at Joppa and Portobello. David Grant remembers his home and the city as it was, but, to him, was and is are the same. In fact, to David Grant there is only an is, a now of a few hours at most, but while he takes Manchester for what his eye can see, Edinburgh can only be how it is in his memory, how it was before he left it. Furthermore, as his reliable memory shrinks and travels away from him back in time, he only thinks of his native city as he remembers it at fifteen or less, not even as it was when he departed the city for England when he was approaching thirty. Edinburgh is mightily hip, mightily grasping, mightily 'now', but in the early nineteen fifties it was proud of the genteel, conservative and God-fearing face it showed the world, even if that face was as inaccurate and incomplete as it was possible to be. But he was caught up in the deception, the location and style of his home, the good fortune of his education and the instinctive good manners of his family reflecting what Edinburgh portrayed as its universal image.

And this is what he now sees; clean uncrowded streets, elegant and overdressed women, lifted pinkies as finger and thumb grasp the cup in the shabby elegance of innumerable tea shops before nervously adjusting fox-fur stoles retaining anatomical features around pearled necks, columns of smoke marching east and west from locomotives hidden from view by the wrought iron and arborous boundary at the foot of Princes Street Gardens, the Gothic paraphernalia of Edinburgh and its Greek pretensions, and the horse-drawn milk floats where the horse knows each door-step destination without bidding from the white-uniformed, peak-capped milkmen.

Sees, but also hears. The accents, as familiar and comfortable as a mother's caress, the shout of the newsvendors with their daily headlines flapping in the breeze, the rattle and hum of the trams with their loud foot-treadled bells, the one o'clock gun that daily scatters pigeons with short memories, the skirl of the pipes as kilt-swaying soldiers march by in the summertime, the green SMT coach with luggage perched on its roof, its gears grinding as it turns into St Andrew's Square, and the oompah of the brass in the bandstand on a Sunday.

Sees and hears, but also smells. The distinctive scents of Edinburgh, the curious blend of the breeze off the sea and the heather from the hills, the stone and damp of old tenements, the brewing near Haymarket, the sulphur from ten thousand open fires, the barrels and vegetables from the warehouses and markets, the rush of eye-watering tobacco smoke from men-only pubs, lily of the valley and eau de cologne wafting around the ground floor of Jenners – in short the reeks of Auld Reekie.

Now his search for lost times, for times past, is becoming ever more complete, the thrum and murmur of the city infilled with ever more precision. A forgotten advocate's sign screwed to New Town pillar with a woman in a flowered pinny smearing it with Brasso and then polishing it until it shines, the stain of the product forming a ragged clean halo on the surrounding grime-stained stone, or a gap between buildings from which a large Clydesdale, led by an old man in leather chaps and a flat cap with a neck flap reaching to his shoulders, emerges dragging a coal cart and swings ponderously into the traffic before the man jumps lightly up and backwards to catch the slowly passing cart and ends

231

up sitting one leg bent, one almost straight on a perch backed by sacks of Fife Cobbles and Newtongrange Doubles, reins in one hand and a short whip in the other, a guttural roar geeing the horse onward. Dobbin, too, knows where he is going, knows when he must abandon the relative safety of the granite setts for the traitorous tramlines, his hooves picking their way carefully as he peers secretly downward behind blinkers to avoid skidding and falling, or on dry days takes the weight off the skid brake, sparks flying from beneath steel shoes as he fights for adhesion on the self-same granite blocks. Then David Grant sees a crocodile of uniformed schoolgirls, wide-brimmed hats, tweed jackets, plain thick skirts – kilt-lengthed, deathly white bony knees, long socks and button-over shoes – filing across the road at the Belisha led by a straight-backed Jean Brodie who never looks at but always sees beyond.

And to the familiarity of the city, remembered faces emerge. Alongside his parents and sisters, there are uncles and aunts and grandparents, each one an Edwardian or a Victorian with their Edwardian and Victorian certainties, their instinctive knowledge of what is right and wrong without the conflict of greater experience, self-doubt or standpoints unexpressed in *The Scotsman*, the comfort and security of not seeing another's point of view, a churchgoing faith made strong by a total absence of emotion. Here the uncle, back from the war, back from his second war, who might have had something to say but who never spoke easily of anything other than his career in men's outfitting and spent all his spare time at the Willowbrae bowling club where the grass was as green and smooth as a perfect lawn photograph in a gardening magazine. David Grant remembered his hands, peeling and infectious – 'It's his nerves,' his wife would say in hushed tones, mouthing 'the war' without a sound leaving her lips – and the way he called him 'son' even though he wasn't his son and, anyway, for

232

some reason he said it more like 'san' than 'son'; his favourite aunt, busy and round and elegant with the most silver hair he had ever seen on a human being, she who had the timing on a pelican crossing extended by proving to a councillor that, well into her seventies and pulling her little two-wheeled shopper's trolley, she could just make it to the crown of the road before the 'wee green man' went out and the traffic started to edge forward like boxers looking for an opponent's weak spot. That was after the trams had gone, of course, when the comparative security of the fifteen-foot-wide ribbon of the tracks was replaced by a white line the thickness of a pack of butter.

To David Grant, his Edinburgh is more real than life itself – more real than Manchester and his growing hunger, more real than anything else he has ever experienced. It has gone from that tenuous link with the shuddering sunlight to dominate his entire existence. And with recall and resurrection comes need. All that fills his mind is his return home, the only home he knows.

His head is aching again so he rakes around in his bag for his painkillers. Some he puts in his pockets, others he bursts from bubble packs and gathers loose in his hand. These he washes down with the remains of the Malvern Water. One or two passers-by see the crumpled man overdosing enthusiastically on pills – one or two even look back over their shoulders as they retreat into the distance – but no one says anything. Refreshing live-and-let-live in a society where no one is allowed to think for, or be, themselves any more.

Rather as we expected, he does not return to the Midland Hotel. Instead he stumbles off in the direction of Victoria Station (Manchester is so confusing and lacking in imagination with its Victoria and its Piccadilly), clutching his wallet in his hand. The sausage bag is left, forgotten, under the bench where it lies unclaimed for precisely seven minutes.

For five of those seven, a tall lad with long hair, unwashed blemished skin and an unkempt beard, and wearing a hooded anorak, tracksuit bottoms and elaborate trainers with yellow reflectors, has been slouching against a wall watching the bag. He didn't see its previous owner but the bag looks useful, might contain a few goodies and, if it isn't claimed pretty quickly, well, it's finders keepers, losers weepers. David Grant does not return and Mister Hoodie makes his move, quickly crossing the paved area between the wall and the bench and sitting down where his extended fingers just reach the handles of the bag. He touches it briefly but possessively, and then withdraws his fingers as a young man approaches, smiles and sits down.

'All right, mate? Just rest me legs for a minute.'

The new arrival might just be the owner of the bag, so Mister Hoodie bides his time, nodding at the greeting but saying nothing.

The new arrival, hair cut short and parted severely on the right-hand side low down on his temple, is curiously conservative in his dress for someone who cannot be more than twenty. He is clad in a cheap suit with worn turn-ups but his shoes are highly polished. He turns to the would-be thief.

'Say, friend, do you love Jesus? Praise the Lord! Do you realise He died for your sins? Have you accepted Him as your saviour?'

'Fuck off,' intones Mister Hoodie, certain now that he is about to become the owner of an inexpensive piece of luggage. He will complete his mission just as soon as he can get rid of the celestial salesman.

'No need to be aggressive, friend. That's the Devil talking, you know. He doesn't want to lose a single soul to Jesus. For the moment, the Devil talks through you. That's his voice – I recognise it. But one day, Jesus will speak through you, just as He speaks through me.'

Mister Hoodie's reaction explains his frustration at being

engaged in a religious debate just as he is about to perform a heist.

'It ain't the Devil talking. It's me talking. And I said "fuck off".'

'OK, I'm going. But remember: "No one cometh unto the Father but by me." That's what the Bible says and the Bible is the Word of God, you know.'

Mister Hoodie turns to his unwanted companion and hisses, 'Well, here's the word of Ralph Biggins for what it's worth. Fuck off.'

The smart young man shakes his head sadly and, just a little patronisingly, pats Ralph Biggins on the shoulder, thereby nearly inviting a clout from a fisted hand. He stands up and smiles at the object of his concern.

'Jesus will be back for you one day, Mr Biggins. Oh,' he pulls back slightly, 'I know what you are going to say. It's all right. Goodbye Mr Biggins. I will pray for you tonight at our Wednesday-evening prayer meeting.' He notes the Devil's Disciple's name in a small gold-coloured notebook with a little old-fashioned diary pencil.

Ralph Biggins watches the young man go, shakes his head, picks up the sausage bag and saunters off into the early-evening crowds. At night, back in the squat over in Salford, he opens up his treasures and, it is fair to say, is reasonably disappointed by what he finds. The drinking glass might prove useful, but even people living in squats are usually well equipped with drinking glasses, although they are usually pint-sized. The leather place mat will add a certain je ne sais quoi to the splendours of the rooms above the disused funeral parlour, while the bathroom accessories might get him a free shag from a grateful fellow-squatter he has had his eye on for a while. The towel might generate the same outcome. But the leather welcome-binder complete with envelopes and headed notepaper, boldly and deeply embossed with the name of the Midland Hotel, will

235

need to be thrown in the canal as soon as possible – a police raid might result in even more awkward questions than usual. The codeine compound tablets are something of a bonus as they might cause a bit of a rush for someone new to the world of drugs, but the rest, recently worn clothes and badly stained trousers, are not a pretty sight, and what he had hoped for, things to sell mainly, are absent. The best thing about the sausage bag holdall is the holdall itself. If he ever has to move sharpish, the bag will really come into its own. Most of Ralph Biggin's miserable life will fit comfortably inside the sausage bag.

But the young man calling on Jesus to once again suffer on the Cross to save the lost soul of Ralph Biggins, and Ralph Biggins himself, are not really our concern. They occupy mere walk-on parts in the dramatic production where David Grant is the main actor, and who is, at this moment, playing a walk-off role. We left him tottering down to Victoria Station with only one thing on his mind.

'Need to get to Edinburgh,' he mumbles, clutching his head again as it pounds to the point where he is visibly shaking with each pulse. The accent of his birth, flattened and diluted by years of being out of his own country and a degree of conscious engineering, is now restored.

'Too late tonight, mate,' says the electronically enhanced voice through the spittle-stained booking-office glass. 'You'll not get all the way tonight. You can go to Newcastle at a pinch, although York might be better. Catch a train in the morning from there to Edinburgh.'

'All right. York will do. It's on the way. How much?'

'Single?'

In every sense of the word, David Grant affirms the question. Single ticket, single in the sense of being not married. He wants a single ticket back home and he is sure he is single in every other way. He has no memory of being married, once or twice. In fact, if the man behind the glass had asked him if he had a student railcard, he wouldn't have thought it odd and would have spent a few minutes searching his wallet for the requested item. He does not have the benefit of a mirror but would be quite shocked if he had, as the reflection would not match up to his image of himself. In his jumbled world, he is imprecisely young again, not sure of his age but certain of his youth. From memory, he will not yet have grown into Jeremy Irons.

'I'll just sell you the ticket to York. There might be a good deal in the morning from there to Edinburgh and a single over two days issued here? Well, it's complicated.' He quotes the price.

'Can I pay with a card?'

'Course you can.'

David Grant proffers his French card, more by accident than design – it is topmost in the pocket of his wallet devoted to credit cards.

'Put it in the tray,' orders the man as David Grant waves it ineffectually in the air at the glass partition. As soon as he does so, there is a clank and a spinning and David Grant nearly loses a finger.

'French,' mutters the booking clerk as he takes the card.

'No,' replies David Grant truthfully.

The transaction completed, David Grant shambles off following platform instructions issued by the booking clerk. He finds the subway and eventually stumbles up the slope to wait for the train. He looks at his watch and the train information board and realises he has nearly half an hour to wait. To his pounding head he must now add an ache in his stomach. He realises he has no memory of ever eating at all and struggles back down through the subway to find something to eat. He buys two sandwiches, one being cheese and pickle in a conventional plastic triangle and the other a recipe for disaster in the form of a so-called baguette oozing chicken in a thick and generous sauce relieved with leaves of irregularly arranged lettuce. A packet of crisps and a small brick of orange juice with a little droopy straw stuck to its side complete his meal for the day. With these in a paper carrier, he returns through the subway.

In due course the train sidles in a shamefaced manner into the station, so unlike the grand entrances he remembers as being normal in Edinburgh, and he climbs aboard as soon as sirens, lights, pressed buttons and unruly passengers admit him. He finds a seat and sits down, putting his sandwich bag on the little table in front of him . . .

'There now, that's fine. I do like to face the engine. How long is the journey, Daddy?'

David Grant looks on as his mother and father shuffle and fuss; he and his sisters too young to help and knowing their best plan is to sit down and keep still. Brown leather suitcases are hoisted with a swinging action and the requisite grunt to the strung racks above their heads; coats are removed and folded carefully before being put one by one on top of the cases, the presents for their cousins near Montrose are propped upright in the corner and patted backwards affectionately against the partition wall. David's mother's main contribution is to sit down and look inside what she calls her 'lunch basket', which is really a tartan canvas shopping bag that only sees the light of day on picnic days, and move the contents around inside like the letters on a word puzzle to ensure everything made it to the train. As she does so, she talks quietly to herself as if the objects in her bag are old friends she hasn't seen for a while, which, in a sense, they are.

'There now, there's the thermos with the tea and the extra cup to go with the thermos lid. And, wait a bit, ah yes, there's the wee bottle with the milk. And here's Daddy's sugar in its wee screw-top jar. And here are the two apostle spoons we use on picnics for stirring the tea. Oh,' this is almost uttered as if it is a surprise, 'there's the greaseproof paper bag with the egg-and-cress sangwidges'. David's mother always pronounced the word that way. 'Oh, and yes, there's the mashed banana and sugar sangwidges. You particularly like those, don't you, Maggie?' David's younger sister nods her head and smiles. It's a trick she learned very young and in no way confirms that she has heard the question. With her mother, affirmation is invariably the right road to take. 'Here's the packet of petticoat-tail short-bread. And the juice for the children with the, let me see, one, two, three beakers. And, yes, here are the Jammie Dodgers. You like those, don't you, David?'

She then lets out an exclamation.

'Oh, no!' The 'oh' and the 'no' are drawn out to an immense length but uttered quietly. David's mother is, above all, dignified.

'What is it, Ida?' David's father looks up from filling his pipe, laying his special penknife with the pipe ram on his knee.

'I've forgotten the paper napkins!'

No one is unkind enough to point out that she always forgets the paper napkins. The solution, as usual, comes from the head of the household.

'We'll just have to be especially careful when we eat, that's all, Ida. Isn't that right, children? If we don't eat too quickly, we'll arrive nice and tidy. And if there are any spills, we can walk them down to the lavatory at the end of the carriage and tidy them up. It's not a problem at all.'

'That's right. Can't think why I'd forget those napkins, though. Be a love, Jim, and put the lunch basket on the rack. We'll have it back in a wee while.'

With immense care, David's father puts the tartan shop-ping bag on the rack, eases it back for safety, and finally drops his wife's umbrella down behind the rail at the front of the rack ahead of the biggest case. This is always the last

239

movement of the luggage-stowing symphony, the final build-up as he spreads his hands like a conductor and pats everything into place. He is probably doing what his wife has done, counting and checking. Hopefully he hasn't forgotten the baggage equivalent of the paper napkins.

David's father addresses the elder of the two girls.

'Don't let me forget your mother's umbrella, Jeanie. If I do, there'll be hell to pay.'

'Jim, language!' Ida Grant is not amused.

David's father winks at him, with his mother neatly out of eyeshot.

His mother, sitting resolutely facing the engine, becomes the eye of the typhoon, a still figure in a pale-beige suit, her hands clasped on her lap and with her silk scarf still around her neck, while the family restlessly shuffle up and down the seat cushions around her. David has taken up position by the window beside the seat selected for his father, while his two sisters jostle for a place opposite, next to their mother, the elder, Jean, lifting her mother's large handbag onto her knees. The five of them have the compartment to themselves and Jim Grant slides the door shut in a proprietorial way. This, he seems to be saying, is the Grants' compartment. The one remaining seat is quickly filled with *The Scotsman*, the *People's Friend* and the children's papers, while Jean completes the task by carefully laying her mother's bag down beside them.

Whistles blow, someone is saying farewell at the door and the train moves off. David Grant had thought they were just one carriage behind the engine but he cannot hear the locomotive get a grip of the train, nor can he feel that slight fore-and-aft motion as the train accelerates. He can't see the clouds of smoke or smell it either, just a low hum that doesn't really belong. He opens his copy of the *Hotspur* and starts to read, while his sisters chatter and argue briefly over who should read *Girls' Crystal* first.

240

He must have been engrossed because he has no recollection of the tunnels or the short run through Princes Street Gardens. All he sees through the window is factories and houses and, although it is beginning to get dark, the architecture seems all wrong. Still, this story of derring-do in the *Hotspur* is exciting and he is soon thoroughly absorbed. After half an hour or so, when he should at least have seen the Forth Bridge and felt the train rumbling through the vast iron diamonds, his mother speaks to her husband.

'Is it lunchtime, Jim?'

David Grant's father pulls a pocket watch from his waistcoat. Without revealing the information about the time, he replies, 'In about ten minutes.'

The family know it is ten to one without being told. Lunchtime in the Grant household, even when the household is on the move, is always at one o'clock.

David Grant's focus wanders. His stomach is rumbling and he cannot concentrate on his boys' paper any longer. He wishes his mother would for once look at her own watch; she wears one but rarely consults it, often leaving her sitting room at home to peer at the great grandfather clock in the hall instead of merely looking at her wrist. So, the senior Grants have had their usual exchange and the children, their appetites awakened by the imminence of their repast, know they must wait for ten whole minutes before lunch will be served. As you will remember from your own childhoods, keen anticipation makes time stand still. Only on the rarest of occasions is the inevitable question posed by Ida Grant answered by a 'Goodness me, we're late'. Then, and it is extremely rare, there is a frantic retrieval of the tartan bag from the rack as though a crime has been committed by the act of being late, and there is no time for stomachs to rumble or concentration to lapse in the face of pleasure postponed as sandwich bags are opened and passed around, and the juice and tea are assembled on the rocking table. David Grant cherishes those moments of lapse for the resultant speed of gratification and the keenly felt sense of somehow being wronged.

Unable to read further – he has just arrived at a new story about a footballer – he looks out of the window. By now it should be Kinghorn through the window with the blackness of Fife's interior to the north or perhaps the sprawl of Kirkcaldy with glimpses of the sea and the distinctive smell of Nairn's linoleum factory. But instead of rural Fife, with its low rolling countryside and small twinkling lights from the isolated farms, or the oily black of the Firth of Forth to the south, he sees nothing but Kirkcaldy after Kirkcaldy – town after town – with a carpet of lights thinning as they climb to great heights on both sides of the line; too high and too far from the sea for Fife. He asks his father to his right why he cannot see the sea but a woman's voice replies that they are not near the sea before getting up and leaving the seat some distance between stations. When he looks again, his father has taken up his rightful place and is puffing contentedly on his pipe, the blue smoke curling aromatically from the bowl for long periods, the only interruption being when the tobacco glows red and the faint sound of gurgling emanates from the stem before his father releases the smoke from his mouth around the teeth-gripped mouthpiece. David Grant watches, fascinated. He is intrigued by the yellowness of his father's teeth and the way that two top and two bottom teeth on the left-hand side of his mouth are worn into an oval to receive the stem. His father is a left-handed pipe smoker.

Jim Grant removes the pipe from his mouth, opens the pipe-cleaning spike from his penknife and, in so doing, looks at his watch.

'I think that's ten minutes,' he says as he propels the

spike clockwise around the bowl before tapping the contents out into the ashtray fitted under the window.

Immediately, pandemonium breaks out in the compartment. Papers are discarded, chattering breaks out like a classroom after the bell has rung, Ida Grant removes the 'lunch basket' from the rack and the children do their best to speed up the process at the expense of haste. Now it is Jim Grant's turn to be the eye of the storm, quietly clearing the last vestiges of ash from his pipe and extracting a pipe cleaner from his jacket pocket while all around him is frantic animation.

David Grant is expecting egg and cress or crunchy, sugary mashed banana between thin slices of pan bread. Instead he finds he is eating hard English cheese and brown pickles and the greaseproof bag has somehow transmuted into rigid plastic. He feels a need to comment. He addresses his mother, sitting opposite.

'These are nice.'

'Good,' replies a man's voice.

'I wasn't expecting cheese, though. We normally have egg-and-cress or banana sandwiches. And they are usually in a greaseproof poke, not this fancy see-through plastic package.'

'A change is as good as a rest,' the man's voice continues in a detached way.

'Thanks anyway, Mother.'

The man looks across at David Grant. He must have misheard him so he says nothing but watches the strange-looking man. David Grant is eating his sandwich like a child, nibbling the crust from two sides of the triangle so as to retain as straight a line as possible. He then sucks the pickle from between the bread and cheese.

'I will be careful, Mother' he says, 'I won't dirty my trousers as I know we don't have any napkins.'

243

The man remains silent but watches as David Grant turns a triangle into a hexagon by biting off the three points and then looks at the sandwich and smiles with pleasure at his handiwork. No spills so far. He finishes the sandwich and then turns his attention to the baguette, turning it over and over in his hand. He has never seen anything like this in his life.

'Yummy!' he says appreciatively, grinning at his mother. 'This looks good, too!'

His mother nods. So does the man. Neither speaks.

'You aren't eating?' David Grant asks.

'No, I'm not hungry,' comes the reply.

'You always eat your lunch.'

'I do, but it's not lunchtime.'

David Grant laughs, perhaps a little too long, a little too loudly.

'Well, it is a bit late, I suppose!'

His compatriot grunts in agreement. The sandwich-eater is clearly handicapped. His whole countenance is haggard as though he is in considerable pain. The dullness of his expression is exaggerated by a strangeness in his left eye. It seems to follow the gaze of the other like a subservient sibling. His clothes are crumpled, although of good quality. His hair is unkempt and his hands shake as he tears at the packaging and opens his mouth to accept the end of the chicken baguette. Immediately, disaster strikes. The sauce leaks from each side of his mouth and drops over his fingers to his knees.

'Oh, jings!' he cries.

He looks frantically but knows he doesn't have a napkin. He picks chunks of chicken from his trousers and licks his fingers, clearly in some distress.

'It doesn't matter,' comes a concerned voice.

'I could go to the lavatory and wash my knees,' he wails.

'That's what to do. Finish your sandwich because you

244

might have another spill. They are difficult to eat, I know. Then you can get washed up.'

David Grant does what he's told. He finishes the sandwich, bursts open the packet of crisps and eats them after first complaining that, 'as usual', the little twist of salt is missing, and even drinks the juice after someone helps him to open the bendy straw and poke it through a silver circle in the box. Then he scuttles along the carriage, puzzled at the fact that he doesn't open a compartment door and lurch along, one hand on the rail over the glass, the other clutching at individual compartment doors but, instead, goes hand over hand down the middle of the coach with seats on either side. When he gets to the lavatory, he is disappointed by the fact that, when he uses the flush, he cannot see the tracks at the bottom of the bowl. He likes that bit, pulling the lever and hearing the roar of the wheels on the rails as his plops and the toilet paper slide off the metal plate. He would usually mess about with the flush ages after it was strictly necessary, watching the tracks and the slow curve of the rails whenever they came to some points, hearing the syncopation as the four beats to the bar stumble and pause before resuming their monotonous clatter. Perhaps this carriage is new and you can't see the tracks any more. Perhaps the rails are welded and the clickety-clack is no more. Even when you are ten, you are a witness to change and, if you are that way inclined, you learn the bitter-sweet taste of nostalgia, of unshared loss.

By judicious use of the water he washes most of the food from his trousers, although he is surprised that he must be wearing his Sunday best as they are his only long trousers. All the more reason for anxiety back in the compartment. Why is he wearing his Sunday best when he is on his way to his cousins in Montrose?

He makes his way back down the train and rejoins his family, greeting them warmly and showing off his soaking trousers proudly. To David Grant, the reaction is positive, his family murmuring their appreciation while his mother tidies the lunch away and returns the much lighter tartan bag to the rack. His sisters giggle behind open palms and his father refills his pipe before igniting it with his lighter tipped to one side, his cheeks bulging and flattening like a trumpeter as the tobacco catches fire and the compartment is filled with cold smoke and the smell of lighter fuel.

But David Grant is alone. The other passengers took his sudden visit to the toilet as an opportunity to make their escape and, by the time he returns, the bay is empty. Two lads sitting opposite make a couple of insulting comments on his return but he seems not to notice them. Instead, he sits with his head bent forward and turns imaginary pages. He mouths the words of forgotten stories, accompanying his pleasure with raised eyebrows and occasional smiles. He is so engrossed that he completely misses the Tay Bridge, the slow run through Dundee and the scenic coastline towards Arbroath. But then, contrary to previous experience of visits to his cousins and at odds with the meal just consumed, it is quite dark and, disconcertingly, from time to time large towns crowd into the railway line on both sides, high buildings with winking lights like the superstructure of a liner, shopping centres with immense empty car parks, neon signs in every colour of the spectrum, some steady, some flashing on and off, dual carriageways carrying heavy traffic picking out the road with powerful headlamps, an advancing army of white, a retreating army of red, lofty street lights on wide over-bridges turning night to day and making the countryside between the towns impenetrably black.

He combines his reading with looking out of the window, no longer questioning the loss of his bearings. The train is still going; his parents and sisters seem unconcerned so it is not his place to say anything to the effect that they are on

246

the wrong train or they've gone too far, that Aberdeen must be next and the cousins will be worried. He must just stay on the train until they get to Montrose and then all will be well. And if it is not, never mind. At ten years of age, someone else will make things better. They always do. In fact, he is beginning to feel tired so he folds his *Hotspur* carefully away and curls up in his seat for a nap.

The train comes to a standstill and a disconnected voice asks him to make sure he doesn't leave his belongings on the train on leaving. He still has his eyes shut. His parents will tell him if this is his stop. At the same moment, a man touches him on the shoulder.

'End of the line, mate.'

'No!' David Grant knows for sure that Montrose is not the end of the line.

'It's not going any further.'

'Really?'

The other traveller is not in the mood to engage in conversation. He has seen some of the strange man's antics throughout the journey and telling him when and where to get off is the limit of the support he is prepared to provide. So he walks away.

David Grant realises he is the last person in the carriage and rises stiffly to his feet.

'You getting out? This one's off to the sidings now.' A railwayman looking for a quality newspaper – it must be all he needs as his arms are full of red tops – stands in the doorway and addresses the swaying traveller.

'I suppose so.'

'You'll be down to the sidings if you don't move sharpish. Quick as you like!'

'All right, I'm coming.'

He stumbles stiffly to the door and steps off while addressing the railwayman.

'I'm going to Edinburgh. Got to get back tomorrow.'

'I was going to say. Not tonight you're not. But tomorrow's a different thing. Plenty of trains tomorrow. Where are you staying?'

'I thought I'd wait for the train.'

'Can't do that. You'll have the police onto you. Staying here overnight is against regulations.'

David Grant pulls a face.

'But I thought I'd wait for the train.'

'You got a ticket?'

'No.'

'You'll need to get one tomorrow. But you can't stay here in the station. It's not allowed.'

But that's just what David Grant does. He finds a bench and stretches out, using his wallet as a pillow. During the night he swallows some more pills and goes to a public toilet but otherwise his night is trouble-free and he hardly moves at all. And just to keep the record straight, his rising to relieve himself during the night happens just before midnight. A visit to the public conveniences on York railway station is hardly the way to start the next chapter

Of course, David Grant has no idea where he is. At least, if you were to ask him, he'd probably say so or he might just ask if he is in Montrose, his recollection of his mysterious journey still clear in his mind. But we know he is curled up on a bench on the wide outermost platform of York station. It is mercifully warm and there is only the slightest breeze funnelling through the immense curved cathedral of an overall roof. Late travellers come and go and a few people stare at the rumpled figure, but nobody pays much attention. There are shabby David Grants on every busy railway station and in every town and city centre in the world.

A couple of railway policemen come over the footbridge and one of them spots the prone figure.

'We'll move that tramp on, shall we?' the younger one asks, eager for a bit of action.

'Nah! Leave him to it. Where would we move him on to? He's not causing any trouble. Besides, if we touch him we'll probably have to go and get defumigated. You know the rules. Touch one of them and you'll get lice or crabs, like as not. Then it's you and your bloody clothes as well. It's a nightmare. Let someone else deal with him in the morning. If he's dead, it won't be our responsibility. If he's alive, he'll probably just shuffle off for something to eat. He's probably drunk, come to think of it. So you'd only get abuse for your trouble.'

They descend the steps slowly, wander around the back of the newsagents and take a closer look.

'Don't touch him. I told you!' the older one snarls. 'Looks a bit of a mess, doesn't he?'

'He's all wet . . . his trousers. Oh no! It looks as though he's wet his-self!'

'There you are, then. I told you. Leave him alone. Nothing we can do. It's a caring, sharing society, so let society, whatever that is, look after him. We don't have to care. Come on. Teatime.'

They walk off leaving the prone figure, knees slightly drawn up and head sideways on what looks like a small black pillow, to sleep it off – or die in the attempt. The younger policeman looks back once.

'He could be my grandfather.'

'So he could, my lad. So he could. But he isn't, is he.'

The Second Thursday

David Grant sleeps badly. Even at night a large railway station is seldom quiet and never deserted. There is still traffic well after midnight and even after the passenger trains stop running, one or two freights headed by roaring diesels tread noisily around the curve under the beautiful roof heading north and south into the night. At about two in the morning someone has thoughtlessly scheduled maintenance work on the track and this involves the attendance of a large red diesel locomotive that demonstrates its 2000-plus horsepower for a couple of hours while men shout, shovel and whistle. Asleep, when the maintenance work is finally over, the absence of the big locomotive with its attendant noise awakens him. He must now try to sleep surrounded by silence.

At about five in the morning, cold and weary, he gives up but at least he now knows where he is. His condition seems to retreat after sleep, only to reinvade and reinvigorate during the day. He merely remembers a vivid dream of a childhood visit to his cousins in Montrose and nothing of the certainty of that experience with its crude superimposition on his journey from Manchester. True, if asked, he could not say where he was yesterday, but his trek to Edinburgh, and York being a staging post on his odyssey, is clear enough in his mind, and any interested enquirer would be answered correctly as to his future intentions although there would be no precision to his answer. He is going to Edinburgh, full stop. Any further enquiry of a detailed nature would be met with a blank expression. And while he is still very dishevelled and his trousers have not quite dried from the frantic washing on the train that some ill-informed people assumed was urine, it is far from unlikely that an elderly man would be travelling light to Edinburgh at this time. The Festival is still on and that means lots of strangers in the vast crowds of tourists who are going to be in the city.

His first thought this Thursday morning is for something to eat but the station facilities, although well illuminated – the windows full of tempting offers and encouragements to enter – are empty and locked. He shuffles out of the station through an iron gate at the side of the main entrance and works his way out onto the street. There are a few early-risers and a bus or two but he has the road towards the city centre largely to himself. His head is starting to hurt and his subconscious tells him he must return to the station in good time, buy his ticket and get on a train soon. It is as though he realises he has but a few hours of clarity of mind and that complicated activities must be accomplished quickly. Still, his stomach is empty and he has a little cash for food. He crosses the river and up into the old city. The Minster, visited long ago before faithless bishops and thunderbolts from Heaven became good career moves for the place as a tourist attraction, the target for his impromptu hajj. At the same time, his nose is keenly alert for the smell of cooking. When he arrives at the Minster, he remains unfed and finds that loss of faith and vandalistic greed have made the cathedral retreat behind stout locks. He circles the building, trying doors and peering upwards at the stone retreating towards heaven, but finds no way in.

For a few moments he stands at the door feeling the power of the vast pile. Even deserted, without the clicking

251

of heels on the flagged floor, the subdued Babel of a hundred languages and the merry jingle of cash registers, the building is not entirely hushed. David Grant feels its domination, the unimaginable pressure on its frail foundations, the tension and suspension of arch, buttress, roof and wall as an aural presence. He can hear God's House, knows its voice and wants to be consumed by it. If only it could all stop. He finds himself envying the stone figures.

He is panicked by his feelings and, rather than do the sensible thing and return to the station to wait for his coffee and breakfast, he skirts around the city, passes back through the city wall and finds himself in a sprawling commercial-vehicle parking lot. Over to one side, smoke curls from a large brightly lit mobile home which provides a contrast to the forest of silent trucks, their cabs curtained around sleeping drivers and grey in the early-morning light. A badly painted sign over one of the mobile home's windows provides a byline for the hard-working soul within and another painted board leaning beside the closed door details the menu 'Sam' provides for his captive audience. Around the door stands cheap garden furniture that must have started out white many years before. Dining at Sam's alfresco. The thing that first attracted David Grant's attention, the scent from the galvanised chimney leaning drunkenly, Pisa-like, and topped by a Chinese coolie's cap to prevent the ingress of rain, tells him all he needs to know. A few yards of tarmac and a modest sum of money are the only things standing between him and a good old English fry-up. He walks across the broken road surface and taps at the closed door.

'Yes?' comes a muffled reply.

'Are you open?' David Grant asks.

'Come in. Close the door behind you.'

David Grant opens the fragile door, which bends alarmingly as it tears itself reluctantly from the aluminium frame, and enters a world of damp steam and pungency.

252

'I keep the door shut to keep the cold out. And the dogs. A few of them about at this time of day. Like bloody tramps, they are, wanting to eat for nothing.' The man in the tiny kitchen behind the counter cuts cold lard from a jar with a cooking knife and drops a brown curl into the spitting violence of the frying pan. 'I hope *you've* got money?' he asks as an afterthought, looking back at David Grant as the lard writhes, sinks and disappears into the molten mass.

'Yes. I've got money. Some money.'

'You going far?'

'Edinburgh.'

'Road should be quiet at this time of day.'

'I'm not going by road.'

'How you going? By train? You'd be daft to go by train if you can get a lift from here,' Sam replies. 'Too bloody expensive. Usually someone goes across to the A1 from here in the morning. What day is it, Thursday? Silent Fred normally pops in here for a bacon buttie on his way north on the chocolate run.'

David Grant nods but says nothing of his travel arrangements. He wants to change the subject, move attention back to the speaker from the spoken to.

'Are you Sam?'

'That's me. Mind you, it was me dad as well. I suppose I'm Sam-Son.' He laughs. It's clearly not the first time he's run that past a customer. 'Been here forty years we have, father and son. Can't carry on no more, though. Named me eldest daughter Samantha thinking she'd take the business over and like to keep the name into the third generation but she's got ideas above working in a truck-drivers' caff. She wants to be a hairdresser when she leaves school.' Sam minces about and twiddles extended fingers in a balletic motion to emphasise his disapproval. 'What you wanting? One of Sam's fry-ups? Doesn't matter what you ask for, that's what it'll turn out like. It all goes in this big bugger,' he lifts and waves the enormous frying pan which hisses angrily at him, 'and it comes out tasting the same. I have people in here saying "Oh, I don't like tomatoes" so I don't put one in but they tell me it still tastes of tomatoes.' He looks at the pan and there is a pause before he continues. 'I'm a bloody slave to this thing. Every morning I come in and it's sat sitting there and I light the gas, bung a load of fat in and off we go again. Slave to it, though.'

'I'll have one of your fry-ups,' David Grant confirms, adding, 'And I like tomatoes.'

'Just as well. As I say, you'll taste the tomatoes anyway. Some fella once said I should wash the bloody thing and then it wouldn't taste of everything. But you don't want to do that, do you? When it gets really bad I scrape out the thick but you give it a proper wash and they'd all be saying "I can taste the washing-up liquid", wouldn't they! And that's carsinomowhatsit, isn't it! Gives you bloody cancer. That's what I've been told anyroad. Just sit yourself down and I'll bring it over. No, try over there at the back. Outside's too cold this time of the morning. That's why I keep the door shut.'

David Grant sits down and, with nothing better to do, watches Sam at work. He certainly lives up to the Samsonian appellation. He must be well over six feet tall, such that his shaved head is grazing the roof over near the side of the van, and his clean white cut-away vest reveals arms the thickness of a strong man's thighs, white and bulging, as first one and then the other takes the strain of the vast frying pan. With his back turned to him, David Grant can see that he is as broad as a sideboard and completely hairless. When he turns he sees his face: beetle-browed, round-cheeked, pudgy-chinned, smooth-skinned and largely expressionless. He is exactly as he was when he was a baby, round and fat – just grotesquely bigger.

With an angry sizzle, the gas is turned off. Sam tips his

frying pan at a steep incline and with great dexterity allows the food to slide onto a plate while preventing as much as possible of the fat from joining it. He brings the plate over to a seated David Grant.

'Here you are, bread and marge coming up. And tea. Everyone likes my tea. I should have asked you if you prefer instant.'

'No. Tea's fine.'

Sam brings over the bread and tea and produces a couple of knives and a fork from the counter. Too early for his normal trade, he stands over the one customer rubbing his hands on a tea towel.

'If you come again you'll know the form. Cutlery's in the box on the top there.'

David Grant ignores the mild reprimand and slices up the fried bread into small squares. He adds a wedge of hard fried egg and some crisp bacon with the rind still in place. Before putting it into his mouth, he asks Sam for a glass of water to take his painkillers. Sam walks in behind the counter and fills a glass from the sink tap.

'Got a hangover?'

'Feels like it,' David Grant admits.

'Food'll help. That and the tea.'

Sam's tea is as pale as death but it is hot and sugared. David Grant doesn't like sugar in drinks but, for some reason, it seems appropriate in this case and he sips the tea happily. He feels comforted by it. It is forever since he drank sweet tea.

'You don't talk much, do you?'

David Grant has his mouth full so he confirms the observation by saying nothing.

'If someone going to Edinburgh comes in, say Silent Fred for instance, do you want me to ask if they'll give you a lift? He'd be a good choice for you. He got his nickname for obvious reasons. You can sit together for hours saying nowt.'

255

There's something about the traveller that touches Sam and makes him search within himself beyond his routine of frying and boiling and passing the time of day. They have hardly exchanged two words ... Oh, Sam has talked a lot but few words have actually been traded ... And yet David Grant stands out. Perhaps it's simply because the caravan is empty and he is made memorable by being alone. Perhaps it is simply that he is not like most of his customers; he doesn't give off the scent of burned rubber, ingrained diesel fuel and too much hair cream, or pace around like a caged animal released from restrictive incarceration. This man is different. Sam's regular clientele move about restlessly, stretch their legs kicking chairs and table legs in the process and flex their stiff arms constantly, but this character is very still, shrinking in on himself, absent and vulnerable.

'You got a name?' Sam asks, tipping his head skywards to stress the question.

'Grant,' the seated figure mumbles, his mouth full of sausage. 'David Grant.'

'Where are you from?'

'I told you. Edinburgh.'

'Oh, I thought that's where you are going.'

'It is. From and to Edinburgh.'

Sam shrugs before he continues. 'Got any family?'

'I don't know. I think so.'

'Wife?'

'Possibly.' He sounds unconvinced, almost as though he hasn't heard the question correctly. He clears his throat before contradicting himself. 'No, I don't think I do.'

Sam snorts. 'Most people know if they've got a wife!' he replies. 'It's not something most people easily forget. If you were to ask me, and quite a few do by way of making conversation, I'd say, "Yes, I've got a wife, she's the mother of my children." "Three girls," I'd add ... Well, I'd know. Not easy to forget that. Not that you should read anything

256

into a clear memory. I'm very fond of my wife. But, well, you don't forget a thing like that, do you? Most people carry a photograph, as a matter of fact. If I had a pound for every photograph of a wife or girlfriend I've seen in this café, well, I'd be a rich man, that's certain. No danger. Not got any photographs?' Sam motions to David Grant's wallet, resting on the table beside three untouched slices of bread and margarine. 'Want a spot of jam with those?'

'Yes please. Thanks.'

Sam's jam pot is as sticky on the outside as in. It has no label but resembles the strawberry jam David Grant ate just after the war when it first came back. But he doesn't spread the jam. Instead, he has been triggered by Sam's curiosity over photographs and he clumsily unzips his wallet and begins searching. Eventually he finds a small envelope containing photographs and carefully lays them out face-up and deliberately on the Formica-topped table, like a card sharp or someone about to do a Tarot reading. Sam moves around the table and sits next to David Grant, leaning over proprietarily and snatching up a picture of a couple.

'That's you there, isn't it? Few years ago but it's definitely you.'

David Grant looks at the photograph. He recognises himself but cannot place the woman. He nods his head and makes to move on. Sam is not so easily distracted.

'So if that's you, who is the woman. Your wife?'

Of course it is his wife, but the slim woman in the black pants and T-shirt, smiling with just a slight squeezing of the eyes against the sun, is a stranger. Sam looks again and asks again. David Grant takes the picture in his hand and stares at it thoughtfully but the pretty face means nothing to him.

'I'm not sure,' he admits. 'I don't remember.'

Sam widens his eyes and sighs, blowing tea breath at his companion.

'Let's look at the others. Here are a couple of younger

257

people. Your children perhaps? And,' he picks up a black-and-white snap, 'this must be from longer ago. Recognise anyone?'

'Yes,' replies David Grant with more certainty, 'My mother and father and my two sisters. Maybe I took that one as I'm not in the picture.'

'They're pretty, your sisters. What are they, late teens in the picture? That one,' he points to the taller of the two girls, 'is a real looker.'

David Grant follows the line of Sam's finger.

'That's Jeanie. Jean. My sister Jean.'

'She looks almost Chinese with those slanting eyes. She's beautiful, isn't she? She doesn't look like anyone else in the picture.'

David Grant says nothing but looks sadly at the image. They are on a beach somewhere; it could be down at Portobello or over in Fife. There's not enough background detail to place the scene accurately. His mother is wearing one of her flowery dresses pulled in at the waist by a broad black belt. His father is, as usual, wearing his tweed jacket and his shoes are shining in the rare sunshine; his one nod to the obviously hot weather being the absence of a tie and a single button undone at the neck. Maggie is like a miniature version of her mother, round and happy, and with a broad smile and short curly hair. She looks about fourteen in the picture.

Sam is right; it is Jean who stands out. If Maggie is fourteen, Jean would be about seventeen – sixteen or seventeen, depending on exactly when the picture was taken. She was born in June so she'd be just either side of a birthday. She is tall and slim with long fair hair down to her shoulders. She *is* beautiful with those sloe eyes and high cheekbones. She is wearing a white blouse and a skirt that's kilt-length and has on one of her first pairs of stockings. In

short, a nice, well-brought-up girl on the eve of woman-
hood. The other thing that distinguishes her from the
others in the shot is that she is not smiling. The group is
too far away and the photograph too grainy to see her full
sensuous lips clearly, but the picture brings secret memories
back to her brother.

'We lost Jean a long time ago.'

'Oh, I'm sorry like.' Sam looks embarrassed.

'She died.'

'How did it happen?'

David Grant does not reply but slowly gathers the photographs together and puts them one by one into their
envelope before clumsily reopening his wallet and zipping
the pocket shut.

'Sorry, I shouldn't have asked. A loss, though. She was a
fine-looking woman.'

David Grant nods, sighs and then turns his attention to
the sticky jam pot with its colourless strawberries. At just the
right moment the door opens and Sam doesn't have to
think of what to say next.

'Bloody hell, it's parky out there!'

'Go on with you. You should have been up at five this
morning. It were really cold then. Usual, John?'

'Aye,' the new arrival answers, pulling his fleeced coat
around him and then, as quickly, taking it off with a 'Mind
you, it's warm enough in here.'

'We aim to please,' replies Sam as he lights the gas and
sets to work with eggs, bacon, sausage and the controversial
tomatoes.

'Here, Dave?' Sam bellows up the van, 'I'll get you
another cup of tea.'

David Grant takes a moment to respond. Hardly anyone
ever called him 'Dave'; he was always 'David', especially at
home. His sisters were always abbreviated and pet-named,

259

but not him. 'Thanks,' he eventually replies, glad of the offer. He spreads another layer of jam onto the bread, primarily to try to mask the flavour of the margarine.

There is now a steady flow of lorry drivers into the van, each one seemingly familiar to Sam, who is too preoccupied with small talk and wielding the frying pan to exchange more than a few words with David Grant. The second cup of tea is followed by a third and then a fourth. The drivers come and go, shovel food into ample bellies and then push their plates away with a satisfied sigh or burp; sometimes both. Many of them produce pouches of tobacco and papers and delicately, amazingly delicately with those round fat fingers, roll full and even cigarettes before lighting them up and then setting off out into the park. Each time the door is opened, powerful truck engines can be heard contentedly idling or revving in first gear as the big vehicles snake slowly out of unmarked bays and head for the exit.

A small man enters and stands at the counter.

'Ah, Fred! I thought you might come. You off to Scotland?'

Fred nods once. Sam rummages around in the warm drawer beneath the rarely used grill and produces about six rashers of cooked bacon which he slaps between two thick slices of bread and then wraps in greaseproof paper. Fred proffers some coins.

'You want some company on the road up?'

Fred's expression doesn't change as he picks up the sandwich and slides it carefully into the side pocket of his donkey jacket.

'. . . Only, there a bloke over there going to Edinburgh. I think he'd like a lift.'

Fred looks over to where Sam is pointing. David Grant has not heard the conversation or even spotted the new arrival. He has his tea between two cupped hands and is sipping the liquid slowly. Fred sighs and shrugs before shaking his open palm at Sam.

'Oh, sorry, Fred. Your change.' He opens a drawer, grabs a fistful of coins before carefully counting out the correct change and placing it on the counter. Fred pockets the coins. And waits. This, to Sam, is the signal he has been looking for.

'Dave?'

David Grant looks up at hearing his foreshortened name.

'This is Fred. He'll take you to Edinburgh.'

There's a small part of David Grant that would like to be left to his own devices. There's a large part of Silent Fred that would like to be left to his own devices too, but Sam has brought them together and neither has the will or inclination to argue. Fred, it seems, does not even have the wherewithal to argue. He stands watching as David Grant drags himself to his feet, pockets the packet of codeine he has been sampling with the tea and moves through the pinball-machine hazards of chairs and tables, lorry drivers and swirling cigarette smoke. He thanks Sam and, in true French fashion, proffers his hand. It is Sam's turn to be taken aback but he wipes his greasy hands on his tea towel, takes the hand and shakes it warmly.

'Have a good trip. Don't let Fred do all the talking.'

There's a subdued murmur of laughter at this but it disappears into the general conversation as Fred gazes frostily at the throng.

David Grant follows Silent Fred out through the door and down the rickety step into the park. The air is filled with the smell of cold burnt diesel oil and the sound of idling engines. Fred does indeed earn his nickname. He says nothing at all but leads the way to a short rigid van advertising drinking chocolate. There is no sense of ani-mosity or irritation at having a passenger foisted on him,

261

just a reluctance to say anything. In fact, the only thing he says is 'no' when David Grant suggests that his lorry carries drinking chocolate 'like it says on the tin'. As with everything to do with Silent Fred, he is cloaked in mystery, misunderstanding and inaccurate conclusions. Sam's assumption and David Grant's concurrence about the load he carries weekly to Scotland is dismissed by that single 'no'. It is merely advertising and, for all he knows, Silent Fred is carrying electric cables, powdered potato or, for that matter, cheap tin trays.

Safely installed in the cab, and with Fred pointedly pulling at his seat belt to indicate David Grant's next task, the van rolls slowly out of the lorry park and ponderously gains a short road of terraced houses before turning onto the main road. David Grant is surprised at how clumsy the vehicle seems. Cars have a degree of finesse that lorries do not possess. They bounce and judder into and out of every pothole, go around corners in a series of tightening segments, their engines roar with little effect and each change of gear is accompanied by clanks, rattles and sudden changes of speed. Added to these normal but unattractive characteristics, Fred's cab seems only nominally attached to the chassis with the effect that it squeaks and rocks fore and aft like a small boat in a swell.

But David Grant is increasingly absorbed by the rising tide of his headache and he worries less and less about the choices as to his method of travel made for him by the well-meaning Sam. He is also grateful that Fred is a man of few words. They make their way north via Thirsk, Northallerton and Darlington before they join the A1 and stop at the first service station for a natural break. Fred just stops the truck, holds up his hand with his fingers spread indicating five minutes and drops down through the cab door. David Grant struggles with his seat belt and, as a consequence, follows a little later. He goes to the lavatory and then buys a sandwich for lunch, knowing that Silent Fred has his cold and greasy bacon sandwich in the pocket of his donkey jacket left hanging in the cab.

It is nearly ten o'clock on the Thursday morning, which is really of no importance at all, leastwise to David Grant, that one-time keen observer of time and schedules, the man who hated to be late and hated most of all being in a position where he didn't know if he was late or not. David Grant is on his way to Edinburgh and for him the time doesn't matter at all. Fred's lorry runs to its own timetable – there is none of the clock-watching associated with travelling by train, and David Grant's deteriorating condition makes the destination the only requisite – the where but not the when. Even the why may be slipping away, beyond recall, beyond question, like the soldier who no longer considers why he is fighting, only that fighting is beyond doubt, incontrovertibly certain; the thing he must focus on if he is to remain alert and reduce the chance of his own premature death. But back in Le Crestet, in the little house off the village's main drag and below the tiny bypass where, incidentally, it is raining unseasonably; along the road from La Terrasse where Michel is standing in the doorway of the little bar talking to a young Arab carpenter who is helping with the refurbishment of a house belonging to a couple from Paris and who acknowledges a cheerful greeting from Madame Blanc who is rescuing her baguette basket from a trickle of rain pouring through a small hole in her awning, the telephone rings.

It is eleven o'clock local time and, parked down the road from the unprepossessing Vipassana Centre, Élodie is telephoning from her mobile phone to speak to her husband to tell him she is on her way home and that she loves him. But the phone is unanswered and, after a few rings, France Telecom invite her to leave a message, which she does, more or less along the lines mentioned above. She assumes

263

he is down at the supermarket in Tournon or just possibly down the garden laying the little path they had discussed, but gives a quick call to his mobile all the same. She shakes her head and smiles. It would be just like him to be frantically working on his civil-engineering project at the last minute. Once again, after a few rings the service invites her to leave a message, which she does, adding an 'I hope you're all right' to her overall sentiment already lodged behind France Telecom's message service. Then she snaps her phone shut, looks at it, shrugs and drops it into the pocket ahead of the gear lever and sets off on her long journey.

At the same time, the little yellow La Poste van stops in the lane, the post lady with the scarf around her permanently stiff neck clambers out and an envelope overprinted with the Société Générale logo plops through the letterbox, gliding to a stop on the tiled floor. The bank statement has arrived.

David Grant makes his way out of the service station complex and over to the lorry. Fred is already sitting in his cab with the engine running.

'Sorry I'm late,' intones David Grant. Fred shrugs, but not unkindly, and engages gear. Soon the little truck is moving sluggishly down the slip-road and joining the slow lane northbound. The curious rocking of the cab and the noise, coupled with the strong smell of diesel fuel, take no time to lull David Grant to sleep, his head drumming despite the overdose of codeine and Sam's generous repast – or perhaps because of it.

The next time he awakens they have crossed the border and Fred is bouncing the truck over an unmade entrance to a small roadside lay-by. With a hiss the brakes are applied and the engine is switched off. Fred turns around and releases his bacon sandwich from its resting place. For a moment David Grant expects Fred to share but then finds his own chicken version in its plastic triangle. He bursts it open and eats quickly. The more you eat for breakfast, the hungrier you are at lunchtime.

He picks threads of chicken flesh from between his teeth, rolls them on his tongue and swallows them in silence. The last thing he is thinking of is any existence outside the confined lorry's cab and the certainty of his return to the city of his birth. But, beyond his reason and memory, a much-loved house is awakened from its slumbers again by the ringing of the telephone bell. Élodie Grant knows he should be home by now. She is running out of excuses for him – he can't still be at the supermarket, he can't be out of earshot down the garden for the whole of the day – and as she eliminates the possibilities, something much more serious begins to fill her thoughts. But she is still miles away and, even with her vivid imagination, could never in a million years envision the truth about her absent husband.

Before David Grant has finished eating, Fred screws up his glistening sandwich paper and throws it onto the top of the dashboard before he starts the engine and guns the accelerator. Soon they are on the open road again with brief glimpses of the sea and the familiar forgotten names of childhood at every road end and hamlet. David Grant smiles as it all comes back to him: that recently swept look on country pavements, the preponderance of iron post and rail fencing, the little houses crouched by the roadside sinking into tarmac and concrete, the big ones hidden behind high stone walls and impressive gates. Soon the road broadens and traffic increases, new estates open up on either side and David Grant is lost and disturbed. Only when they find the coast again and judder through Mussel-burgh does his panic abate. The familiar is back, the tall houses modulating into tenements as they move towards the city centre, Joppa and Portobello, Piershill and Abbey Hill, before the lorry takes a sharp right turn onto Leith Walk and stops.

Fred nods at the door. David Grant smiles but does nothing. The link between the familiar streets and the purpose of his journey is now lost to him. He is enjoying the ride and sees no good reason for it to end. Once again Fred nods, this time more insistently. David Grant follows the driver's eye out through the door window as though he wants him to see something, but sees nothing untoward. Speech not being a means of communication between the two men, David Grant tips his head quizzically onto one side, at the same time raising his eyebrows.

Fred waves at him to leave and makes his feelings so clear that David Grant gets out, still not sure what the intentions of the truck driver are. As a consequence, he doesn't thank Fred for the lift as the latter leans across to pull the door shut. Instead, he stands with his wallet in his hand looking quizzically up at the cab as Fred guns the engine and sets off down Leith Walk in a thin plume of mauve smoke.

David Grant watches the vehicle go and continues to peer down the broad road long after it has disappeared in the direction of the docks. Slowly he turns and takes in the scene of fragmented familiarity, some buildings imprinted indelibly on his mind, others strange and unknown. He is surprised there is no friendly queue of trams clambering up the hill, merging with those from along London Road and then dividing again as some take a breather along York Place while others continue bravely uphill into Leith Street. Their dignified and courteous progress always pleased him. Then he realises there is no track in the middle of the road – the trams are no longer there. Most would simply accept the situation and move on, but David Grant is torn between what his eye sees and how things should be and he makes the complicated and irrational assumption that it is he who has made a mistake and at some time, when he looks again, they will be back where they should be. But he doesn't look again, his mind occupied by another distraction.

There is a man on the other side of the street who resembles his father. He is quite tall, straight-backed and carries a brown raincoat. He wears a pinstriped blue suit (although the stripes are not visible from this distance and especially with only one eye) and is walking briskly uphill towards Princes Street. David Grant forgets his mental exercises over the presence or absence of tram tracks and starts to walk uphill, keeping the familiar figure alongside him although divided by streams of traffic. Again and again he looks and still he believes he is his father. As the road narrows into Leith Street the suited figure draws closer but his relative proximity does not invalidate David Grant's conviction. He is about to cross the road to greet him when he sees a woman approaching the man, who smiles in recognition. They embrace briefly but with familiarity and then, holding hands, continue up the hill towards Waterloo Place. She swings a shopping bag in time with her steps and, from time to time, lifts it to face-level to look inside. Clearly she is pleased with her purchase. Unfortunately for David Grant, while the man is his father, the woman is emphatically not his mother. She bears no resemblance to her at all, being slim and tall and very fair. What he had intended to do, cross the road and speak to his parent, is simply not possible any longer. Think of the embarrassment and the shame? How would they be able to go home, together or separately, to face his innocent mother with both males knowing the terrible truth – that Jim Grant is clearly having an affair and his son knows about it!

David Grant looks again to see the woman kiss his father on the cheek, a gesture both innocent and provocative at the same time. The kiss hardly makes contact but is surrounded by coquettish moves; her head on one side, the back of her hand grazing his cheek, broad smiles from both of them. The woman is the opposite of his mother: extrovert where she is introvert; high-heeled where his mother always wears lace-up brogues or fur-lined ankle boots with zips up the inside; openly demonstrable in her affections in contrast to his mother whom he never saw hold his father's hand or even kiss him – her limit was to take his arm briefly when crossing the road or negotiating a difficult step. Why, this woman has a bottom where his mother has only ever had a seat.

David Grant lets them overhaul him. He drops back as they turn sharp left at the top before disappearing and then crosses the road uncertain of what to do. As he crosses Waterloo Place he is comforted by the feel of tram track under his feet again. He had been certain his not seeing the track earlier had been some carelessness on his part. He knows that if he waits a few minutes he will see the trams again but he doesn't have time to wait – even for a few minutes. He must go along to the Gardens to sit down and think through his next steps, so he crosses the road leading to the North Bridge and makes his way along Princes Street to the point where he can drop down into the Gardens. It may simply be because of his blindness but the piece of track still in the road in Waterloo Place is preserved there. It is only a few yards long and hasn't seen a tram in fifty years.

His mind is churning over with his new and terrible discovery. The pavements and neat paths in the Gardens are awash with people, the normal numbers of shoppers needing to rest for a minute or two vastly increased by the presence of thousands of tourists. The numbers of ordinary holidaymakers are swelled by culture vultures and alternative theatre and comedy anoraks armed with sheaves of flyers imploring them to visit this, that and the other venue to be entertained, challenged, shocked or just plain-ordinary abused – a favourite occupation of fringe entertainers. The lawns sprout sprawling young people arguing over what to see and dialling their mobile phones one-handed to book seats. Their evenings planned, they use their phone-cameras to capture the moment: pictures of the Scott Monument, the dark bulk of the Esplanade at the Castle or hitherto unreported boyfriends to send back to anxious parents in California, the Causses or the Caucasus. 'Can you climb the Monument?' (Yes) 'Did you?' (No) 'Can you visit the Castle?' (Yes) 'Did you?' (No) 'Is he a nice boy?' (Yes, what a stupid question!) 'Was there a lot to see at the Festival?' (Yes) 'Did you see a lot at the Festival?' (No. Too busy screwing the boyfriend.)

Eventually, dodging through the crowds like a basketball player, David Grant finds a half-occupied bench and sits down to decide what to do. He is extremely agitated and silently mouths his preoccupation while the bench remains only half-occupied. In fact, the other people resting there soon find they have something urgent to do and leave the man to his torment, looking back in some alarm until they have put a safe distance between the bench and themselves. There's always some weirdo to spoil a happy holiday moment.

David Grant, whose head is splitting with pain and possibilities, is still able to see that his options are limited and none has that instinctive feeling of being right, of working out for the best.

If he goes home straight away, he might beat his father back to the house. He imagines the scene as his mother calls from the kitchen.

'Is that you, David?'

'Yes, Mother.'

'I'll just put the kettle on. Your dad is still out. He said he had a few messages to get but he's been gone a long time.'

'Oh, I expect he'll be home soon.'

And when he does come home, he'll come into the house all the innocent and hang up his hat. He always wears a hat when he goes into the city centre but, oddly, he wasn't wearing one in town today. Thank goodness he didn't cross the road and confront him but it will still be embarrassing.

'Where have you been, Dad?'

'Oh, just away out to get some shopping, son.'

'Shopping? And what did you buy?'

'Just another pouch of shag, David. Just as I always do of a Thursday. Why the cross-examination?'

'Ha! You have a nerve! *Buying* a pack of shag or simply *having* one?'

Or.

He could wait until he knows his father will be back and then go in as quiet as a mouse and say nothing to start with. In fact, he could try to extract a confession. His dad will be sitting in his favourite chair at some stage in the pipe preparation, smoking or cleaning process, looking completely unruffled.

'Hello, David,' he will say, only looking up if he has reached a suitable juncture with his pipe. He has vivid memories of his father's slightly balding head bent low as he concentrates on the repacking of his tobacco in the briar. Another odd thing, his father hadn't looked the slightest bit bald on the pavement in Leith Street.

'Hello, Dad,' he'd retort. 'Been out this afternoon?'

'Yes, as a matter of fact I was. I went into town for a bit of a walk around.'

'On your own?'

'Yes, son. Your mother had her things to do so I . . .'

'. . . Went out to meet someone?'

'What?'

'Oh Dad, don't pretend.'

270

'Now listen, my lad . . .'

Or.

He could keep the awful secret but devote time to spying on his dad to see what his movements are.

See where he goes. And when. And with whom. Become a sort of private-eye character transposed from forties Los Angeles to fifties Edinburgh, 'David Grant' in gold leaf on the frosted-glass door of a tatty short-lease rented office three floors up in Dalry, the Grassmarket or Pilrig, a six-castored revolving chair behind a grubby desk strewn with papers, a Colt 45 in the drawer for emergencies, the air blue from chain-smoked Passing Clouds. Passing Clouds? Well, you need a bit of style in the private-eye business.

A devoted woman in her forties taps the door respectfully and enters.

'Oh, Mr Grant, there's a Miss Shagnasty here to see you.'

'Show her in, Mish Jones.'

(It's important to sound like a Scottish Humphrey Bogart at times like this. Think Humphrey Bogart meets Sean Connery.)

'Right you are, Mr Grant.'

'And, Mish Jones?'

'Yes, Mister Grant?'

'Jusht keep yourshelf behind the door out of shight and lishen to this. I may need you as a witnesh later.'

'Oh yes, Mr Grant. Certainly Mr Grant.'

A slight pause and a long willowy platinum blonde in high heels is shown in. Miss Jones gives a knowing look to her boss around the back of the new arrival, camera three.

'Now, Mish . . .'

'. . . Shagnasty. Miss Easy Shagnasty.'

'Right, Mish Shagnasty. Shit down, won't you?'

She looks around woodenly, sees a bentwood visitor's chair and flops down, dropping her head into her hands somewhat melodramatically.

271

'Now, what sheems to be the trouble.'

'Oh Mr Grant, I am so frightened. I think I'm being followed!'

'Thatsh right, Mish Shagnasty. You *are* being shadowed. On account of you having an affair with my father!'

Easy Shagnasty reaches inside her handbag for a roll of banknotes, not having fully understood the implications of what has been said. Beauty and brains never seem to go together in black-and-white Hollywood. Sorry, Edinburgh. However, David Grant, Private Eye, is pretty pissed off with the affair this woman has been having with his father and is in no mood for taking risks.

'Now, what are you doing in your pursh!'

'Why I . . .'

'Take your hand out of that pursh!'

He removes the Colt 45 from his drawer, camera two, and the next ten minutes of the film are taken up with the Private Dick and Miss Jones disposing of the body. Jolly good job too.

But, as you can appreciate, nothing rings quite right.

And, so often when faced with what are, to him, insurmountable problems, David Grant decides there is nothing to be done. So, he does nothing. Instead, he sits quietly on the bench in the Princes Street Gardens of the Athens of the North while his head slowly begins to cloud and confuse his every thought. It is five o'clock in the afternoon, a dangerous time for him.

The crowds slowly thin. Shoppers reach the time where a return home via the multi-storey car parks or one of the crocodile of buses jiggling along Princes Street is preferable to a pause in the Gardens before assaulting the shops again. Besides, shopping in the best-placed street in Britain is more and more about tourists as Edinburgh succumbs to the scourge of out-of-town shopping malls like everywhere else in the world. The tourists, too, leave, as the upcoming temptations of the evening usurp the simple pleasures of the Gardens. A few people hang around the floral clock, a tall lad dressed like harlequin juggles clubs with a donation box on the ground, his eyes flitting up and down the path watching out for park attendants. He doesn't do well. He'd have been better to stay near the galleries at the foot of The Mound where people expect to be entertained. Even the lone violinist has had enough. After constantly interrupting her theatrical playing – eyes closed, vibrato overdone, generously bared cleavage crushed and released by the movement of her arms, shoulders weaving and bobbing in time to the metre and the piano and forte of the piece – to adjust the music on her flimsy stand before battling on with Bruch, Bach and Bacharach, she sees her market disappear. She lays the instrument down carefully before she scrapes the coins thrown into her violin case together, pockets them and puts the instrument to bed. An overlooked piece of rosin lies for moments on the path after she has gone before someone steps on it and reduces it to crushed brown glass.

The sounds of the traffic change too. If anything it is louder as it encounters reduced resistance; fewer cars means faster cars and more noise. An ambulance scatters jaywalkers and renders other vehicles obsequious as it sirens its way from the West End before turning up at The Mound, its blue lamp writing a rising S, before disappearing behind blackened stone onto the George IV Bridge. David Grant cannot place the sound as he is in a place where beep and bell are the only audible traffic warnings.

He sits for about an hour barely moving, the turmoil in his mind and its begotten indecision freezing him to the spot. He is a still Darby to Élodie's animated and anxious Joan. After driving for most of the day and phoning with increasing frequency, she drives too quickly up into the hills from Tournon and makes her way along the little main street of Le Crestet. She waves at Madame Blanc as a final batch of baguettes are dropped into her faithful basket. The sun is out again and as she jostles the bread into place she quickly forgets the essential repair that needs to be done to the blind. Every time it rains she makes a mental note. Every time the sun comes out, the mental note fades in the bright sunlight. Élodie toots at Michel as he struggles up from the sunken garden carrying a paint-encrusted step ladder. He stumbles a bit with the ladder, which pirouettes around on a single grounded leg, and waves back cheerfully.

Everything is normal: delightfully, dependably normal.

She even scolds herself for getting worked up and regrets losing her temper when a car took unnecessarily long in the *péage*. She had left the Vipassana completely mellow and had stayed so until just north of Lyon where that brief encounter brought her back to the reality of self and the world.

She turns down into their small road and through the opened gates. 'He's not far away,' she thinks. 'In fact, he'll probably be in – either in the house or down the garden.' She parks the car, kills the engine and, instead of taking her case out of the boot, lets herself into the house, shouting 'Je suis là,' as she walks through to the kitchen. But the house is silent except for the chattering of the refrigerator compressor. 'Oh, wo!' she cries, checking the ground-floor rooms before running up the stairs. From a window at the back she looks out over the garden and the land falling away to the bottom of the valley before it climbs beyond the river to the hills opposite. She never tires of the peaceful scene and allows herself a moment of reflection before returning to the matter in hand. Concentrating on the garden, she can see that there has been no progress on the path – everything is exactly as she remembers it, other than the grass being longer and the weeds more profuse.

Now she is beginning to worry. She flies downstairs and

lets herself into the garage through the door leading off the kitchen. His car is missing and the wheelbarrow, always a badge of office when he is doing one of his projects, is standing in its usual place in the alcove, still clean and washed from its previous employment. The two bags of cement, which he would presumably have used doing the edging to the path, are standing beside the barrow. Only one thing is out of place. She and David keep their suitcases Russian doll-like, one inside another, from the largest suit-case, known to them as 'Number One', rarely used owing to its colossal size, right down to the smallest rucksack they use on short walks. Usually the only case to be seen is 'Number One', the repository of repositories, but Élodie sees that it has been opened and there are now two Russian dolls. 'Number Four', which must contain all the smaller ones, is standing beside 'Number One'. A quick look inside the large one reveals its next neighbour. The third case is missing.

Fear dissipates and is supplanted by irritation. If the case is missing, his absence is intentional but he had said nothing to her about going away before she left. 'If he had planned this before, why didn't he tell me?' she asks herself. 'And if it was a last-minute thing, why isn't there a note?' Then she realises she hasn't looked for a note, so walks quickly back into the house. She looks behind the clock on the shelf above the fireplace in the living room, a favourite place for unopened letters and little reminders, but there is nothing there other than a request for funds from the Croix Rouge which she remembers from before she left. She returns to the kitchen and puts the kettle on while she retrieves her case from the car and locks it up. Everything is uncannily normal but utterly still.

She spoons Mariage tea, enough for two, into the teapot and pours the water, leaving it to infuse while she retraces her steps all over the house and down the garden. There are no clues as to David's whereabouts. It is as though he has just popped down to the village for a few minutes. As this thought crosses her mind, she forgets the tea and, grabbing her keys, drives down to the village. Madame Blanc is still inside the *boulangerie* wiping down the surfaces with a damp cloth and soapy water. Élodie buys a last baguette but when she asks Madame Blanc if she has seen her husband she shakes her head. She thinks she saw him about a week ago but not since then. In fact, she assumed they were both away together, having forgotten that Élodie had explained her visit to the Vipassana Centre.

Élodie crosses the road and pushes the door of the hotel bar open. There is no sign of any staff although there are one or two early customers looking at menus and sipping aperitifs and there are sounds of activity at the back. Élodie walks through the restaurant and turns towards the kitchen calling, 'Is anyone here?' Michel appears carrying cheeses for the display. He smiles and kisses Élodie lightly on both cheeks before holding her back from him and studying her troubled face.

'You have a problem?' he asks.

'I can't find David. I'm just back and the house is empty.'

'No problem,' he replies, grinning. 'Mister Grant said you were away and we had a little talk and I encouraged him to take a little break.'

'You did what?'

'Yes. Well, he was in here and said he had nothing much to do. When would that be, now? Let me think. It was the night of the rugby match. Or was it the night after? No, I think it was the Monday night. That's Monday a week ago, not the Monday just gone. St-Étienne did really well. Only one thing, though. He said he was going for a few days only. Said he had a path to lay in the garden and that he'd come back to do that before you returned. Has he laid the path?'

276

'No.'

'It's a long time to be gone.'

'Yes. It's a very long time.'

'Perhaps you should call the police? They might know something.'

This sound advice raises pure dread in Élodie's mind. It is, of course, the right action to take but shifts the scenario from the banal to the serious. In one sentence, a silly old man might now be a victim of a road accident.

'You're right. I should call them.'

'I'll ring later on to see if you've found anything out. Just as soon as the rush is over.'

Élodie spreads her hands in a gesture of impotent resignation and thanks him.

'Don't worry. There'll be a perfectly simple explanation. There always is.'

But there isn't, is there? We know that.

Élodie goes home to drink her cool tea and sits at the kitchen table. The irritation at his absence has all gone, replaced by heightening anxiety. The only thing she finds is a squashed coin which she thinks they placed on the railway line several years before. And as for the post lying below the letterbox, she picks it up, ruffles through it, realises it is mostly bank statements and credit cards, and leaves it behind the clock for David to deal with.

When Élodie unhappily prepares dinner for one, the police, in the form of a single officer on shift in the sprawling police station in Tournon, together with his faithful computer terminal, are making enquiries and repeating Michel's message of consolation. Late in the evening, Michel rings back, as does the policeman, but there is nothing to report.

'No news is good news,' they both say. Élodie just grunts at the policeman but has a tearful response for Michel.

'No news is just that, Michel. No news is no news.'

277

And back in Edinburgh, David Grant has been shooed out of the Princes Street Gardens by a parkie who wants to lock the gates, or at least that's what he says, and, unable to go home to face his innocent mother and guilty father, curls up on a bench in The Meadows and falls asleep. The night is blissfully dry and he has found himself a place to rest that is away from the most frequently used paths. David Grant is at relative peace. The only problems he has are the dilemma over his family, his recurring headache and a slight trickle of blood from his left ear.

The Second Friday

David Grant is awoken at about one o'clock on Friday morning by someone kicking him in the ribs. It is done with a flying kick, rather like one he saw deep in his memory, but this time, instead of a cold underground-railway tiled wall, it is his defenceless body that is on the receiving end. As he is asleep at the time, he doesn't see anything coming but just feels the impact. The force of the blow bounces him off the back of the park bench and he falls in a crumpled heap on the paved footpath. He clutches his sides and draws his knees up to his chest, letting out an awful groan that seems to come from someone else. The sound frightens him.

A voice shouts from so far above his head as to seem other-worldly.

'Fuckin' nomad!' it says as the boot goes in again, this time hurting his shins and the hands clutched under his knees to protect his damaged ribs.

'Hold it, Hamish,' another voice warns. 'He doesnae' look like a tramp. No' enough plastic pokes and he doesn't even have a coat.'

'Still behavin' like a tramp, all the same.'

'Leave him alane!' This phrase, issued like an order by a female voice, introduces us to the third in a gang of young people on their way back home from a pub in Rose Street. They are in their early twenties and, it is fair to say, their evening has not gone according to plan. They had an appointment with a dealer in the pub – just a bit of weed and maybe a line of blow they could share if the price was right. None of them has very much money so they tend to pool their resources on most things. But, hey, as bloody usual the dealer didn't turn up, did he? So, rather than stick to the point and go in search of another pusher, they bought whisky, pints of heavy, pork scratchings and fish suppers on their way home and spent the lot. So, no drugs, awfully pished and stomachs churning with cooking fat, vinegar and a shared bottle of warm chippie Irn-Bru, they are not in the best of spirits. Then there was the down-and-out drunk who cornered Catriona – the girl's name is Catriona by the way, the guys are Hamish (he's the one with the red hair and freckles who is good with his feet) and Wee Wullie (he's the dark-haired one who detects tramps by the presence of an overcoat and fistfuls of plastic shopping bags) – and put his hand on her crotch as they were coming out through the narrow pub doorway. 'Put his hand' is a wholly inaccurate and sanitised way of expressing it. He grabbed her like a cricketing outfielder catches a ball and could only be encouraged to let go by a right hook to the cheek from the gallant Wee Wullie. That incident, of course, put tramps a long way down the gang's 'I love you' list. In fact, it's reasonable to say Hamish, particularly, has been looking for a down-and-out to work over ever since the event. Catriona's crotch is very much Hamish's property and it's he who decides who can touch it. When he's feeling benevolent or just plain stoned, he lets Wee Wullie have a feel and, just occasionally, and when Catriona's in the mood, a bit of a shag, but that's not often and no one, repeat no one, is allowed to grab her on the street without a by-your-leave. What is the world coming to?

At first sight David Grant fits the bill. An old man curled up on the bench in a public space in Edinburgh at night is either drunk or homeless or both, and their anger at themselves for their misdirection of funds as well as the sense of impotent frustration at not seeing Catriona's assault coming, puts them into a place dangerous for anyone who crosses their path, even if a sleeping man does very little crossing. But the possibility that their act of revenge has been misdirected, plus the pathetic sight of the old guy lying at their feet and the fact that the attack in some way settled the score and took away the anger, has a mollifying effect on the gang. They help David Grant to his feet and sit him back on the bench. He sinks until his head is almost in his lap and he threatens to fall to the footpath again. They prop him up and Hamish sits down beside him on his left, a restraining hand on his shoulder.

'Sorry, old man,' says Hamish. 'We thought ye were somebody else.'

Catriona sniggers and whispers 'bollocks' to anyone who is listening. She's a girl who can't abide lying, even though a bit of violence, as long as it's by proxy, is fine by her. She sits on David Grant's right and Wee Wullie joins her. What with his chivalry outside the pub and her eagerness to point out Hamish's hypocrisy, he may be in the ascendant again after a few weeks's enforced celibacy. The truth is, Wee Wullie loves Catriona, and they have a lot in common. They both did arts degrees at university for a start, whereas Hamish's degree was in computer science. See, no clichés in this story or a harping back to 'trainspotting' days when wit, drugs and hopelessness were bedfellows. These three will get it together when they take responsibility for their lives. Parental ambition got them to and through university, but now the task is to take control and there's a strong urge to delay conventional life for yet another year. Besides, their arrangement largely suits them and they all know that the acquisition of proper jobs will either split them up geo- graphically or handcuff them to lives travelling at three different speeds, instead of the no speed they currently enjoy.

Catriona told Wee Wullie once that he was a more sympathetic lover and Hamish warned him about making her too happy.

'Treat the bint mean and that'll keep her keen,' he'd said after Wee Wullie and Catriona had had a particularly noisy and clearly satisfying session. Come to think of it, that was the last time Hamish had obliged and that had been four weeks before. Wee Willie smiles to himself as David Grant takes another lunge groundwards.

'Fuckin' silly name, Wee Wullie,' Catriona had said, taking his penis in her hand after he had withdrawn and the two of them were resting on the living room sofa-bed after their exertions. She had sighed through clenched teeth before continuing. 'Not appropriate, not appropriate at all.' It was this that had made him smile at an inappropriate moment; plus the fact that her gently admiring and exploratory caress had prepared him for re-action in record time.

At the sound of a regular footfall they look up to see two policemen walking towards them. It is too late to run, so they sit stock still, hardly breathing. They hear the click of a torch and are blinded as the stream of light weaves across each face in turn. David Grant sinks slowly forwards again and Hamish's quick action prevents complete collapse to the pavement.

'Well, well, well, it's Hamish McIntyre. What in the name are you doing here?'

Hamish smiles up at the policeman, an expression that is barely skin-deep.

'Hullo, Mr McNab. It's a free country, eh? No' trespassing, are we? '

The policeman doesn't reply but shines his torch in the faces of Hamish's other companions again.

'All the usual suspects, eh Hamish? How are things, Catriona?'

Catriona shields her eyes before replying.

'Oh, you know, officer. The same as usual. Just gettin' by.'

'Can't think why you hang out with these ne'er-do-wells, Catriona. Your faither'll be turning in his grave.' McNab turns to his colleague who is nothing but a tall dark silhouette in front of a street lamp and behind the glare of the torch. 'Young Catriona here's dad was an officer at Tollcross. A good man, he was, a good officer. Sadly he got the cancer, didn't he, Catriona? A tragedy. But this one's not turning out well so far. No' exactly a chip off the old proverbial, are ye, Catriona?'

Catriona bristles. 'Oh come on, Mr McNab. Just a bit of harmless fun,' she barks, righteous indignation emboldening her. Cracks about her upright father and his down-wrong daughter are just not fair.

'Hamish beating up that Hibs supporter a bit of fun? That was the last time our paths crossed, wasn't it, lassie?'

'Well, it wasnae' me. Just Hamish getting carried away.'

'He's a bit too easy with his bits, though, aren't you, Hamish? University degree, all that privilege, and then what does he get? A criminal record for ABH. Terrific achievement, isn't that right? The "Flower of Scotland"; don't you just love it?'

Hamish sighs. 'It was self-defence, Mr McNab.'

'Like buggery it was self-defence. Court didn't buy that one either, did they? A record for "Actual" and a wee visit to Her Majesty's Holiday Camp into the bargain.'

Hamish shrugs. The torch moves from him to David Grant.

'Who's this old guy?'

Hamish looks up at McNab and then at the slumped figure. 'He's ma uncle, Mr McNab.'

283

'Your uncle, eh? He looks in a bad way.'

'Just a bit too much of the booze, that's all.'

'Too much of the booze?'

'Well, you don't need to say it as if it's a totally new concept, Mr McNab. This is Scotland in the twenty-first century, just another millennium of Scotland's love affair with the drink.'

McNab crouches down on his haunches and shines his torch up into David Grant's face. He has a cut over his right eye, a small wound on his left cheek and his lips are swollen as if from a hard punch. He is also bleeding a little from his left ear. His eyes are closed.

'He looks bad, ye ken? He might need hospitalisation.'

Hamish interjects with a voice that exudes calm.

'No, no, Mr McNab. No' at all. He's just a wee bit pished. We'll get him home and he'll sleep it aff. We'll clean him up and he'll be as right as rain in the morning.' Hamish laughs an easy laugh and blows through his lips before a partial contradiction. 'Well, maybe he'll have a gae sore head, eh Uncle?' Hamish pats David Grant affectionately on the back. Wee Wullie and Catriona look on in silence, wondering just how much further Hamish can dig and whether the fallout will affect them all.

McNab continues to look into David Grant's face and, at last, his eyes open. His left eye stares blankly into the torchlight but his right eye closes quickly, followed by the raising of a hand, palm outwards, against the glare.

'You OK, sir?' asks McNab in a loud, deliberate voice.

'You're fine aren't you, Uncle?' asks Hamish. 'Just a bit of a skinful.'

'Can he speak for himself, Hamish?'

'Of course he can. Sorry Mr McNab.'

'Can you hear me, sir? Are you all right?'

Wee Wullie and Catriona hold their breath and stare into the middle distance. Only Hamish seems to have learned

284

his lines well. He pats his relative on the back by way of encouragement.

'Yes,' replies David Grant. The sigh of relief from Wee Wullie and Catriona is audible.

'Had too much to drink, have we?' McNab shouts at old people as though they're both simple and deaf.

'That's right, isn't it, Uncle?' Hamish encourages.

'Yes,' says David Grant again, his thickened lips giving him an authentic drunken slur.

'How did he get injured?' McNab is looking at Wee Wullie or Catriona for an explanation. None is forthcoming from them as they don't seem to be singing from Hamish's hymn sheet. But Hamish can be relied upon for the developing story.

'He fell. Oh we tried to prevent it, didn't we, Wullie? But down he went like a pack of cards. In fact, he did it a second time straight after the first when we weren't looking. Slap down onto his face the second time. What a mess! Used his hands to try to save himself, that's why the backs of his hands are all chapped and bleeding.'

When telling lies, it is said that it is best to remain as close to the truth as possible. Most of David Grant's injuries to his face are, indeed, the consequence of a fall, the only straying from the truth being the cause of the fall in the first place. And by drawing attention to his injured hands, a condition McNab had not spotted during his cursory examination, Hamish adds authenticity to his tale. However, if the policeman had been more of a detective, he might have been puzzled by the presence of shoe polish in the grazes.

When he first arrived on the scene, McNab had the whole truth under a heading called inspired misgiving. He dreaded his intuition, of course, on account of Catriona and her late father, but he harboured a suspicion that he and his colleague had interrupted a piece of gratuitous violence and that Hamish had been covering up all along.

285

The other two were odd, too. Strangely quiet and sober. However, Hamish's story and the easy manner of its telling convince McNab otherwise, and the bit about his hands plus the monosyllabic answers of the victim push him even further off the track of truth. He believes Hamish but has one or two more questions.

'Where's he from? I might visit to see if he's OK later on today.' As you can tell, McNab is a policeman from the old school.

'Oh, you can't do that!' Hamish's answer is a bit too hasty but he quickly recovers himself. 'He's staying with us tonight. He's over from Fife. Mustn't let his wife know about this, either. She'd kick up if she thought we'd got him drunk. And she's told him more than once she won't let him in the house if he's ever plastered again. That'd be terrible – cause all kinds of trouble.'

McNab nods slightly and turns to David Grant again.

'What's your name, sir?'

'Robert . . .' interjects Hamish.

'. . . David,' replies David Grant almost simultaneously and in a soft, slurred voice.

'We always call him Uncle Robert but he is actually David Robert.' Hamish is indeed able to think quickly on his feet as well as being handy with a pair of boots. 'David Robert McIntyre. I think he's a remote relative on my faither's side but he's always known as Uncle Robert.'

'David,' repeats the hapless victim.

'I know, Uncle,' says Hamish, patting him affectionately on the back.

'David Grant,' expands David Grant. The company freezes.

Hamish clicks his teeth. 'That's his wife's maiden name! Oh dear, Wullie, we've got him into a hell of a state tonight!' He laughs loudly and the other conspirators join in, if a little weakly.

It's getting late. If McNab and his colleague leave now, they'll get across to the police office in Tollcross in not much more than ten minutes. And that will be just ahead of their tea break.

'Just you make sure you look after him, Hamish. That's all. I don't want to see him face down in the grass when I come about these parts again later on!'

'Don't you worry, Mr McNab. I'll look after him just as if he were family . . . which, of course, he is!'

'Right, get on home then.'

Hamish looks at his new charge and then replies, 'I think we'll give him five more minutes. Then we'll set off. He's a good bit better now than he was but another five minutes should see him stronger on his feet.'

'OK then,' mutters McNab. 'I'm giving youse the benefit of the doubt now. By rights I should call an ambulance on account of his injuries . . .' The three young people stiffen, '. . . But seeing as it's Catriona, we'll say nae mair aboot it.' He extinguishes the torch which puts the others considerably at their ease.

'Thank you, Mr McNab,' says Wee Wullie. 'You can rely on us.' Wee Wullie thinks, rightly, that a contribution from one of the others will reduce McNab's suspicions still further.

The two policemen walk off in the direction of Tollcross. Hamish waits until they appear and disappear in lamp light all the way down the path before he gets to his feet.

'What a bastard!' he says. 'Close shave, eh?' He laughs.

'Fuck,' says Catriona. 'I thought we were all going to end up in Tollcross police office with them. What a fuck!'

'Come on, let's gang hame.'

Catriona gets to her feet and puts her arm around Hamish, leaning her body into his. He puts his arm around her shoulder and turns her in the opposite direction towards their apartment in Marchmont. It is beginning to

287

get cold and the trees rustle in a rising breeze. Catriona shivers and grips Hamish even closer.

'What the hell are youse doing?' Wee Wullie explodes.

'Goin' home, ye idiot. What else would we be doing?'

Are you leaving him here?'

'Of course!'

'You are quite mad, the two of you! Old McNab'll be back, find the old fart and we'll be up before the beak. Then they'll find out you aren't related; never even seen him before, and they'll put his injuries down to you. Rightly.' The sight of the two of them arm-in-arm doesn't please Wee Wullie.

'What do you expect us to do, take him hame with us?' Hamish hams up the sarcasm in his reply as if the suggestion is too ludicrous to take seriously.

'That's exactly what we must do. The alternative doesnae' bear thinking about.'

'That's daft. We cannae' start taking old tramps in.'

'He's not an old tramp. He's an old man who was attacked by us; by you, actually, and he can get us into a heap of trouble if we don't get him out of sight sharpish. And the safest place for that, for the night at least, is the flat.'

'Daft!' spits Hamish, making to walk his clinging girl-friend off home. But she stops and wheels the two of them around.

'He's right, ye ken,' says Catriona, at which Wee Wullie's heart misses a beat. If he could just keep to the wise, he'd win Catriona. He wonders what she sees in Hamish at all, but her loyalty augers well for the future so long as he can make that future a Catriona and Wee Wullie production. Catriona continues, 'We could get him hame, clean him up a bit and then think about what to do with him in the morning.'

'Daft!' repeats Hamish, but he knows he's lost the argument.

288

Wee Wullie stands up and pulls David Grant heavily to his feet. As he does so, something falls to the ground.

'Hold him a minute,' he says to Catriona and Hamish. 'Something fell off the bench.' Hamish and Catriona link arms with David Grant on either side while Wee Wullie gets down on his hands and knees under the bench. At first he finds nothing but the first fallen leaves and what feels like a discarded ice cream cone but his blind man's wandering hands are rewarded. 'Got it,' he whispers.

'What is it?' Catriona asks.

'Don't know. Some kind of book or wallet or something.'

'I wonder whose it is?' Hamish asks.

'Well, bit of a coincidence if it isn't Mr David Robert McIntyre Grant's. We'll take it home and see what we've got.'

'This is *daft*,' says Hamish, not so emphatically.

'You're right. It *is* daft. When are you going to stop picking fights and getting us all into trouble?'

'Oh shut the fuck up, Wullie,' Catriona barks. 'It was Scottish Literature you studied, not bloody ethics or divinity. We're where we are and we've just got to get on with it without preaching at each other.'

Wee Wullie is crushed. Just when things were going so well, too.

David Grant walks bent forward, holding his aching side, the two young people's arms linked through his. His shins are smarting and he can tell that sticky blood is chafing on the trousers. His hands hurt too and one of his fingers feels sprained at best.

He realises they are heading towards Marchmont and he stops walking.

'Can't go here,' he pleads. 'My father and mother are here. They'll both be angry. Can't go here.'

The three young people look at him. They know that about twenty-five per cent of the population in Edinburgh is about one hundred and forty years of age on account of the cold crisp air, the ready availability of blue rinses and stimulation by self-important disgust, but he has to be seventy-odd, so how old are these parents, ninety, one hundred? And why do they hold such fear in the heart of David Grant?

'He must be havering,' answers Hamish, urging them onward. But David Grant holds his ground.

'Can't go here. I told you.'

'Look, there are loads of flats here. Can't be the same one, can it? Let's get on!'

They more or less frog-march David Grant onwards, cross the last of The Meadows and take to the roads of elegant terraces that anywhere else in Scotland would be called tenements. These, however, are far too grand for the general term.

It's not the same flat but it *is* the same entrance and David Grant is shaking when they arrive at the door.

'Not the first floor!' he pleads. 'Not the first floor.'

'No, it's on the fourth. Come on!'

'Must be quiet on the landing. We have to be quiet on the landings – that's the rules. But must be especially quiet on the first-floor landing. Mustn't awaken my father and mother.' David Grant murmurs his fears as he reluctantly lifts his feet from step to step as he is dragged ever upward.

When they get to the first floor, Catriona cannot overcome her curiosity. She looks at the doors on the landing and can tell by David Grant's terror which is 'his' door. She bends down to read the name on the little door plate. 'Khan', it says. She looks back at the little party and shrugs her shoulders.

'Was it his?' Hamish asks as they go on up the stairs.

'Not unless his is a very complicated family,' she replies. The name says "Khan".'

'I knew he was havering,' Hamish confirms.

When they reach the fourth floor, Catriona unlocks the door and all four stagger in.

'He'll have to share the sofa-bed with you, Wullie,' Hamish commands.

'Oh, Jesus, no!' wails Wullie. 'That's no' fair!'

'Who's flat is it? *Mines*, I think,' says Hamish. 'And you wouldn't have him share with Catriona? Besides, if he's got fleas or whatever, it'll be easier to get the sofa-bed cleaned.'

Wee Wullie shakes his head. 'Fucking great,' he adds as they put David Grant down into an easy chair. Paradise postponed again.

The friends do very little to repair their handiwork. They take a brief look at David Grant's chest and find it bruised purple. No one wants to remove his trousers to examine his legs but take courage from the fact that he goes off to the toilet on his own and seems to manage by himself. Catriona washes his facial wounds and the backs of his hands and then finds some disinfectant and applies it generously.

'Oh shit,' she whispers after working for some time on his face.

'Whit?' ask the two lads.

'He's bleeding from his ear. Look.'

They both stand up and walk over to Catriona to see. There is very little blood and Catriona wipes it away with some cotton wool.

'See? It's gone,' says Hamish. 'Superficial wound like the rest of them. I didnae' kick him hard, you know.'

'No, watch,' she says and, sure enough, a little trail of blood begins to ooze from his left ear. 'What have you done, you stupid bugger?'

'I've done nothing,' whines a clearly upset Hamish.

'Well, I know nothing about first aid but bleeding from inside the ear doesn't seem like nothing to me. What if you've given him a tumour or something? Can you get that from falling to the ground?'

291

Hamish is suddenly terrified. 'We've got to get rid of him! If he fucking dies on us, we're finished.'

'You're finished you mean!' snarls Catriona, her practical wisdom down in The Meadows shaken by the developing facts of life.

'Just let me remind you, Catriona my love. You were with me and, by your lack of a contribution during the visit by Mr McNab, corroborated my story. You are an accessory after the fact or whatever. If he dies, we'll all go down.'

There are a number of 'shits' and 'fucks' at this accurate revelation of their legal position.

'Anyway,' continues Hamish, glad that his rightful position of clan chief has been restored, 'he doesn't look too bad. How are you feeling, old man?'

David Grant nods.

'There you are, you see? Get him some toast and tea, Catriona. He's probably hungry. Then we'll get him to bed.'

'My bed,' moans Wee Wullie.

'No, not your bed – my sofa-bed, the one I let you sleep on, you lucky person.'

'I pay rent!'

'Aye, but it's my flat, remember.'

David Grant eats his toast with relish, nods his head to the offer of a further slice and slurps his tea noisily.

'Look how he eats his toast!' exclaims Catriona. 'Like a wee bairn. He's nibbling the crusts off all around. I used tae do that!'

After he has finished eating, they tear off a large piece of tinfoil from a kitchen roll, place it on the sofa-bed near where David Grant's head will be, spread an old sheet folded up treble and put it on top, and Catriona puts a plug of cotton wool into the leaking ear. David Grant seems ready to sleep, but the rest of them don't get the feeling he is going into some kind of coma or anything. He just seems tired. They cover him in a blanket and deep breathing soon tells them that he is sleeping.

'At least there's one thing,' Catriona observes. 'He's no' a tramp. Look at his manicured hands, and his clothes are of very good quality. Designer stuff, some of it.'

'It's a bit damaged,' observes Hamish.

'Well, I don't think you should go there,' snaps Catriona. 'This is your bloody fault in the first place and I bet his clothes looked a good deal smarter before you decided to have a go at him.'

'He's a bit of a mystery all right,' muses Wee Wullie. 'A tramp that's not a tramp. A rough-sleeper who has manicured fingernails. What's the story, I wonder?'

'Well, we can soon find out. Where's that wallet you found?'

'Good point,' observes Wee Wullie. 'I put it on the hall table when we came in. I'll get it.'

Wee Wullie comes back into the room clutching the wallet in his hand.

'Bloody hell, that's a big one!' observes Catriona, pulling a chair up to the table. 'You could keep your life in one of those.'

And, after ten minutes, Catriona is largely proved right. There are banknotes, sterling and euro, but no Scottish notes yet. This makes them suspect he hasn't been in Scotland for long. There is his passport, his Carte de Séjour and a *carte grise*, which fox them, a quantity of credit and bank cards, some receipts and a London Tube ticket mightily out of date, an envelope of photographs, his driving licence, a couple of cheque books from French banks, insurance certificates and various other bits and pieces. They open pockets and unzip zips like children opening their stockings at Christmas. Eventually it is all spread on the dining table, while David Grant sleeps on. Once he turns over and moans and they all freeze guiltily but he is soon still again.

'We've got to get rid of most of this stuff. It's incriminating evidence. If something bad happens and they trace it back to us and they find any of this stuff here, we'll be in the papers.'

So, they pocket the money and Hamish produces a metal waste bin. Then they start to carefully burn everything incriminating – driving licence, official papers and the photographs.

'Look, this is him,' says Catriona. 'Must be his wife with him. She looks nice.'

'Nice or no', she's got to go,' observes Hamish as he snatches the photograph and lights it with the burning remnants of the insurance papers.

'And *she* is very pretty,' remarks Wee Wullie as he looks at the picture of a couple on a beach with two grown daughters.

'Show it me,' commands Hamish. Wee Wullie hands the picture over. 'Jesus, she'll be old enough to be your granny, I'll bet. That must have been taken before the war.'

'No, the clothes are all wrong. Nineteen fifties or even sixties, I'll bet.'

'The old man isn't our Mr Grant, is he?'

'No. Not like him. Anyway, it's too long ago. Might be his faither, though.'

'You mean the one who lived downstairs?' asks Catriona, and then adds, 'That's a wee bit creepy.' She looks carefully at the photograph and shivers as though she is cold.

'We'll have to get rid o' the credit cards, too,' says the ever practical Wullie.

'Pity,' says Hamish. 'Might have been a way to get some money.'

Wullie just shakes his head in disbelief but says nothing. He's only really hanging on for some change in the dynamics, for Catriona to stop saying all the right things and doing nothing for weeks on end. It's as though she and Hamish are in some sort of conspiracy that keeps Wullie loyal and truculent. He is an emotional prisoner awaiting the release of commitment, the freedom of responsibility and the chains that might at last order his life. Suddenly, he wants to be in a different place.

But Hamish is just thinking out loud about making easy money and, without argument, he cracks open his lighter and holds it to a corner of the first credit card. It melts and drops waxy plastic into the bin.

'Oh, Christ,' he exclaims and then shrieks as his fingers are burned. The others tell him to pipe down. David Grant grunts but turns over.

'For fuck's sake open the window,' Hamish hisses. 'We'll be buggering poisoned in here with that gas!'

Wullie opens the window and flaps like a swan getting ready for take-off. After which, they change tactics and line the bottom of the bin in paper hankies. Then they start the process again with more success this time. Blobs of molten plastic drop to the tissues which brown but don't catch fire and, when it is all done, they put the mess into the toilet bowl. After a couple of tries, David Grant's life has truly been flushed down the toilet. Only the wallet remains.

'That'll no burn,' Wullie observes. 'We'll have to take it with us when we get rid of him in the morning.'

'It fucking *is* the morning,' Hamish informs them. It's nearly four o'clock. 'Bed,' he orders. 'We'll decide what to do with him when we're fresh.'

'Let's hope he's still alive,' Catriona says, getting to her feet. She looks at him. He looks at peace and the only problem seems to be the ear. The cotton wool is saturated with blood. Catriona carefully prises the wool out and replaces it, David Grant conveniently lying on his right side for the entire operation. The sight of his ear angers

Catriona. If it weren't for that, this whole incident could be cleared up tidily. But what would the morning bring? What if he ends up dead?

'Coming, Catriona?' Hamish asks from the door.

'I am but you are not!' she announces. 'This is your problem so you can sleep with him on the sofa-bed. Come on, Wullie!'

Wee Wullie gets to his feet in indecent haste but his hopes are soon dashed again.

'Oh, and if you think we're going to exchange bodily fluids tonight, Wee Wullie, you are sadly mistaken. I have done all the anatomy and making men feel better for this night already. Sleep means sleep.' She looks back as Hamish as she leaves the room, closely followed by an obedient but somewhat frustrated Wullie. 'Hamish, one more thing.'

'What, for Christ's sake?'

'You'd better have a foolproof plan for the morning when we get up or we are very much through.'

'I'll think of something. Only . . .'

'. . . Only what?'

'What if he dies.'

'He'd better not die, that's all. But, if he does, then you'll be sleeping with a corpse. Sleep well, lover!'

At a little after seven, Hamish cannons into his bedroom to find Catriona lying, fully clothed, on her side, with Wee Wullie naked except for a pair of pants beside her. He has an arm possessively over her body in the cleft of her waist.

'Get up!' snarls Hamish.

The two sleeping beauties rub their eyes, look at each other in surprise and then darken as they remember the events of the night.

'You've got five minutes to dress. Coffee's on. Cereals and toast are ready. Our guest is already eating . . .'

296

'You're very cheerful today.' They awoke with no memory of their shame and fear; then it returned like a black cloud but now, almost as quickly, Hamish's happy spirit seems to be giving the nightmare scale and proportion. Perhaps things are not so bad after all. As if to justify his cheerfulness, Hamish delivers his parting shot as he leaves the room.

'I've got a plan,' he reports, his eyes raised and his mouth fixed and unsmiling.

Catriona comes through first, having peed and cleaned her teeth. Remaining dressed gave her an advantage and eases Hamish's mind somewhat. She takes a moment or two to steal a look at David Grant. He is sitting up at the table, eating mechanically and even thanks Hamish when he passes him a cup of coffee. The only disconcerting aspect is the blood which still seeps from his left ear and the quantity of dried and drying blood on his cheeks and neck.

'You might have had a go at his face. Have I got to eat my breakfast seeing him in such a state? I think not!'

Hamish shrugs as Catriona gets a dish towel from the sink, runs it under the hot tap for a moment and proceeds to clean off the worst of the blood. David Grant grimaces like a child and pulls away as the dish towel is rubbed vigorously over his face. Catriona looks sorry for him as she finishes her handiwork. He looks like a boxer who has done fifteen rounds with someone who is, at this moment, glorying in wearing the belt of victory. Hamish indicates the damp and bloodstained dish towel.

'We'll have to take that with us . . . and the sheet,' he adds. 'At least the tinfoil worked. There's no blood on the sofa-bed. We'll take it all with us, plus his handbag, and dump it somewhere.'

Wee Wullie takes longer to get up but looks ragged when he comes through.

'After breakfast, you will tidy yourself up, Wullie. Smart

clothes. Shave. That sort of thing. We don't want to draw attention to ourselves on our wee journey.'

'Journey? Where are we going?'

'Well, we said he was from Fife and Fife is where he is going.'

'What?' Wullie runs his hands through his hair and rubs his eyes before pouring himself a cup of coffee.

'Monimail,' mutters David Grant, before slurping another mouthful of coffee. His head is hurting fit to drop.

'Money Mail? Is that some kind of a cash transfer?'

'Dunno,' replies Hamish. Catriona shakes her head. She hasn't a clue either.

'Monimail, Fife,' David Grant volunteers helpfully before taking a nibble from the crust of his thickly buttered toast.

'Monimail? Never heard of it.'

'Look it up on the map, someone.'

Catriona jumps up from the table and walks over to a laden and untidy bookcase next to the window. After a moment or two of shuffling with the inevitable cascade of books to the floor, she has a road map in her hands. She looks at the beginning of the atlas for the sheet number, flicks through the pages and starts searching for the obscure settlement.

'It's tricky. Fife runs into two sheets and, of course, they're over the page from each other.'

'Oh, look in the index at the back for goodness' sake. We'll be here for ever,' bellows Hamish, buttering himself another piece of toast.

Catriona does what she is told and soon has it located. A moment or two later, she has her finger underneath a place called Monimail. It looks to be little more than a road-end, miles from anywhere.

Hamish turns to David Grant. 'So, what's the story about Monimail, old man?' David Grant turns his battered head and smiles weakly at his interrogator. 'Have you got family there? Friends?'

David Grant shakes his head.

'So why did you say "Monimail"?'

'Graveyard,' he replies. 'Lots of the family in the graveyard. My daddy took me there once to see the stones. Went on the train. Graveyard.' His voice trails off as if he is recalling an event years ago, one he cannot share with anyone in the room.

'Well,' says Hamish, sighing, 'It's as good a place as any. And he doesn't have family or friends there in a position to know him, so he won't be recognised.'

'So,' says Catriona sarcastically. 'How are we going to get him there? By train? There probably aren't any trains nearby anymore and we'll be spotted on the way, even if he is anonymous in Monimail. Think of all those bloody cameras! What you going to do, get a taxi from somewhere nearby?'

Hamish nods his head, impatient to get a word in edgeways.

'Didn't I tell you I had a plan? If I had said "We're going to Fife", that wouldn't be a plan, it'd be a destination. I have a *plan*.'

'What is it, then?'

'Black Bob's Ford Ka.'

'Black Bob? Will he lend it to us?'

'He already has. While you two were sleeping . . .' he looks angry for a moment, '. . . I was on the phone. Result? Black Bob's wee Ford is outside the door at this moment awaiting a little romp into Fife. And good old David Grant has provided us with a precise destination.'

Catriona spots blood trailing down David Grant's neck again and gives it another wipe with the dish towel. As she hasn't run it under the warm tap, David Grant jumps at the cold touch.

'My head is sore,' he says, as he pushes extended fingers into his forehead above his eyes melodramatically.

'I think we should get this over with as soon as possible,' Catriona observes, getting a glass of water as David Grant removes painkillers from his pocket. 'He isn't right, you know.'

'Ach, some injuries take longer to clot than others,' observes Hamish. 'Don't worry about it.'

Wee Wullie looks troubled. 'Do you think it's a good idea to go to this Monimail? It might be a trap or something.'

'Trap? Look at him,' scoffs Hamish. 'He couldn't trap *The Sound of Music* in his condition. Like as not if we go to Kirkcaldy or Dunfermline or somewheres, *we'll* meet someone we know or we'll walk into his ancient granny or something. God knows how long the Grants survive! If his own parents are still alive, why not all the ancestors? I think Monimail sounds just the place.'

'What will we do?'

'Just take him there, drop him off, get rid of all the stuff – his wallet and the bloody bits and pieces – and come back as quickly as possible. Then we think no more about it.' He turns to look at David Grant. 'Look at him, he'll be fine.'

Catriona and Wullie are less convinced. Most old people are just old. Fully compos mentis (unless, of course, they're not), but David Grant seems very far from being normal. He says very little and behaves like a child, eats his crusts like a child and uses the name 'Daddy' like a child. Catriona and Wullie look at Hamish and marvel at his indifference, his ability to separate himself from the here and now and his probable culpability. They, of course, know nothing of David Grant's history, his steady deterioration, his pinball-machine bounce around Europe moving this way and that on a whim, his reducing history, his withdrawal into his childhood, his profound suggestibility and his flawed and fractured memory. All that fills Catriona's mind particularly is that this injured cretin may be these things solely as a result of Hamish's unprovoked attack. Her cold feelings towards her lover are more acute than the sympathy she should feel for David Grant, but she is the product of the modern 'me' society which has the effect of subjugating almost everyone else into a state that is effectively subhuman. One could not be so indifferent to others unless they are lesser mortals, so lesser mortals they must be. The blinkered reasoning of the concentration-camp guard is alive and well in the Britain of 2006.

For David Grant's part, these three young people are his friends. They have taken him in after some sort of a situation he cannot remember and, while even the events of the early hours now escape him, he is surrounded by an aura of care. Coffee and toast and sympathy and somewhere warm to sleep are all he knows and the girl, particularly, administers to his every need. It is almost as though she is Jean, long-lost Jean, who was always his favourite. They look quite alike, from the slim figure and long legs to the sloe eyes and the full mouth. Catriona and the others didn't spot the similarity when they ransacked his wallet and now, flushed away to the sewage farm, Jean is the fond memory of David Grant alone. But he is in his soap bubble on the wind state, moving where and when doors open to him. And a few minutes later, with an old coat wrapped around his shoulders against a stiffening breeze and a considerable drop in temperature, the raggle-taggle party descend the stairs with David Grant frantically shushing them on the first landing and the door of the silver Ford Ka is opened for him. He is guided into the back and, with a final wipe of his ear with a tissue afterwards consigned to a plastic bag of incriminating evidence, Catriona pulls a floppy woollen hat down over David Grant's ears and the others clamber in.

'Like that knocks years off you!' exclaims Catriona who is

301

sitting beside him. She puts an arm around him and he turns to look at her adoringly. To her, he is an old man who is passively dangerous. To him, she is Jean, full stop.

'I'll keep to the quiet roads to avoid as many cameras as possible,' Hamish says as he starts the engine and moves away from the kerb.

Wee Wullie laughs hollowly. 'You'd have a problem nowadays avoiding cameras on the way to your bathroom.'

'Oh,' says Hamish, still jovial, 'but I told you I had a plan. I told Black Bob that, providing we don't have any encounters with the police or that, I'd tell him exactly where we went and he'd swear on his mother's grave that it was him that went for a spin in the Kingdom.'

'Is that necessary?' asks a troubled Catriona. 'It all seems to be getting too complicated. It would be fine for us just to be taking him back. Anyway, he's in the back and no one will see him. Even if, *you know*', she says this quietly and pointedly, 'happens, they'd find it difficult to link this old man with the one we were sitting with on The Meadows. After all, it was very dark on that bench.'

'Look! Who's running this show?'

'Oh Christ, *you* are Hamish.' Catriona is getting very pissed off with the way her week is ending and cannot avoid a degree of sarcasm.

'Well then, play by ma' rules.'

They drive in silence in a long arc around the south of the city avoiding as many large junctions as possible. They then travel westwards to the Kincardine Bridge to avoid the toll and, no doubt, the cameras on the Forth Bridge, and then travel due east until they stop for petrol in Leslie having taken minor roads to avoid the complications around Kinross. Hamish gets out to fill up the car, part of the deal he struck with Black Bob, opens the boot, extracts a spare can and fills it too before disappearing off in the direction of the kiosk. He has a spring in his step. Everything is going to plan. Although it is very windy, a sprinkling of rain lands on the windscreen.

'Oh, great!' moans Catriona, 'Just what we needed.'

'Well, he's got Hamish's old coat. He'll be fine.'

Catriona sighs and the two remaining men in the car look at her. David Grant merely smiles at his elder sister, but Wee Wullie turns around and touches her knee lightly. It feels warm and secret and she makes no attempt to remove his hand. He squeezes her knee slightly and feels it tremble.

'What d'ye think about all this, Cat?'

'No' a lot,' she says. She is miserable and feeling vulnerable.

'We don't have to keep doing this, you know. What is this, the fourth time?'

'Aye. McNab only knows the half of it. That guy at the disco ended up in hospital. It was in the papers, remember?' Catriona sighs again.

'You know I love you, Cat.'

She puts her hand briefly on his shoulder.

'I know.'

'Why don't we just move out when this has all died down? We'll need to behave as normal for a few days but, after that, we could find a place of our own. I've been looking out for jobs I could do and there's quite a bit about at the moment. We might not even need to leave Edinburgh.'

'You're full of surprises, Wee Wullie,' she says quietly, her voice deep and resonant.

He says nothing but squeezes her knee again. She places her hand on his and holds it there for a moment before easing it gently away with the words 'Be careful. He's on his way back.'

Wee Wullie exaggeratedly hands Catriona a box of tissues and she keeps up the charade by administering to David Grant's ear. It works, for Hamish suspects nothing.

He puts the spare can of petrol in the boot, lets himself into the car and slams the door hard. 'Fuck! Even this little fart on wires costs a bomb to fill up. Twenty-two quid including the spare!'

'What would the train have cost for all four of us?' asks Catriona, her voice betraying a sense of the beginning of the end and the end of the beginning at the same time. 'Besides, why are you filling his spare can of petrol?'

Hamish says nothing but looks at her, taps the side of his nose with an extended index finger, starts the little car and heads off into the Lomond Hills; the wiper clattering back and forth on too little rain. After crossing the main road at Falkland, he heads up through rich farmland to Auchter-muchty and turns right onto the A91 signposted for Cupar and, by default, Dundee.

'See, even the rain's stopped.' To Hamish, this whole adventure is a small matter that, by the minute, is getting smaller. Just a few miles to go and then back home. That wee bit of money they 'inherited' might just enable them to rescue the weekend. He could always swap the euros in a bank near to home in the afternoon but it would hardly be worth it, the sum is so small.

A few miles out of Auchtermuchty they see the sign for Collessie and Monimail and Hamish turns the car off the main road. Around the church and hamlet of Collessie they spin, and out across the fields to Monimail on the straight road linking the two.

'Here,' David Grant says, short of what passes as a village centre.

'There must be more than this,' observes Catriona. 'A pub or a shop . . . Something.'

Wee Wullie looks around him. 'Doesn't look like it. The place is as quiet as the grave. No one's about.'

'Well, we'd hardly want it to be fucking Mardi Gras, would we?' storms Hamish. 'This is a perfect place. It's quiet, there's no one about as you say, our friend here wants out at the cemetery and seems to be very vague. He won't remember us, will you, Granddad?' He turns to David Grant who nods, but this is interpreted as being in agreement with the question rather than the sentiment. 'There you are, you see? Well, here we are, old man. You can get out now.'

David Grant pulls the coat around him and the three young people all get out to say their goodbyes. Catriona gives him a hug and David Grant hugs his sister back. Then, while Hamish heads back into the car and Wee Wullie hovers, she takes his arm and walks with him slowly into the cemetery.

'You'll be all right here? I expect there's a café or something. Or you could go to the pub. Everywhere in Scotland's got a pub, hasn't it? Or you could get a bus.'

'All right,' the old man says mechanically, his feet retracing ancient steps, his one eye recognising what his two eyes had seen years before.

'You'll be all right, won't you?'

Catriona thinks less and less of the scheme the more time she spends with the old man. It even looks as though the rain will start to fall again and there seems to be no life in the village at all. She comforts herself with the idea that things are largely as they were when they found him, sleeping rough, a bit confused and contradictory in his appearance. At least, she figures, there'll be no one like Hamish out here to give him a good kicking. If someone finds him here, they'll take him in and he'll probably get the hospitalisation he so obviously needs. She even begins to convince herself that, in an odd way, they have helped him. Cities are dangerous places.

David Grant is a man on a mission. He steps more quickly than before, almost towing Catriona along. She ignores Hamish's shout to 'get going' but keeps up with the old man, noting that his ear is still bleeding. Now the blood is soaking into the woollen hat and running down into the collar of Hamish's old coat but she does nothing about it. It's too late now, she decides. It's up to the hospital to mend him. They've got the facilities. And someone will come along or he will go out into the village and be spotted.

'Where are you taking me?' she asks.

'Come on, Jean,' he urges. 'It's just over here. I remember it.'

She is intrigued, so once again ignores a shout from Hamish and another gentler one from Wee Wullie. Calling her 'Jean', whoever she is, makes her feel better. He must have heard her real name bandied about scores of times in the previous eight or nine hours but here he is calling her Jean. Fine, Hamish was right, he won't remember us.

That was something else that would need careful thinking about, she reasons. What to do in the future, a life of domesticity with Wullie or a return to the status quo. Has this latest incident been a warning? Is it time to choose to settle down, or should she read nothing into their close encounter of the criminal kind. She likes Wee Wullie very much but Hamish still has that irrational authority and wildness that she finds so attractive. Perhaps there is a middle way; she moves in with Wullie while he pursues a sensible career and she spends some time with Hamish for those moments of raw excitement. Mind you, she can't see Hamish buying that arrangement. Too proud . . .

'Here it is!' David Grant spreads his arms, nearly knocking Catriona over in the process. There's a look of pure joy on his face.

They are looking at a gravestone with the name 'David Grant' carved on it.

Catriona runs, spooked, from the graveyard, leaving her erstwhile companion peering down at the stone with his

306

arms outstretched, the coat flapping in the breeze like the wings of some huge shabby cormorant.

'Get the fuck outa here!' she screams, jumping into the vacant passenger seat in the front, Wee Wullie having been encouraged to climb in the back.

'What's up?' asks Wee Wullie. 'You look as though you've seen a ghost!'

'Don't jest!' she cries. 'I think I just may have!'

It is approaching eleven o'clock in the morning in the Kingdom of Fife and midday in Le Crestet, Ardèche. Élodie is in bits. Still no word from David. She has been along to La Terrasse again to talk to Michel, who is long on sympathy but short on answers because there are none. Madame Blanc hugs Élodie in a matronly way and tells everyone who comes into her bakery that 'L'anglais est disparu'. The word is soon out and little knots of people form and disperse with much head-shaking and almost as many theories, from the tragic to the sinister, as to the reasons for his disappearance. In no time, his name has become familiar in Le Crestet to four times as many people as knew it twenty-four hours before. By his absence he is known.

A detective from Tournon has an appointment to see Élodie the following morning and he has told her to stay by the phone in case her husband rings. He comforts her by telling her on the phone that absolutely no reports have been made concerning accidents to his car or him and that there are many leads they can follow which he will explain to her in the morning. She is briefly comforted but cannot find a way to endure even the next minute.

So she returns home and weeps at the kitchen table, turning the flattened coin over and over in her hand. The detail has become almost obliterated by the passage of the train; only the date remains clearly recognisable. This she looks at carefully and realises it is 2006. The coin is less than nine months old. It cannot be the same one as the one they had squashed together. She remembers Queen Elizabeth frolicking about on the track as David placed the coin on the rail.

The little Ford Ka bounces off down the road retracing its steps from the Howe of Fife, its passengers silent and deep in thought. Only Hamish seems to know where he is going. He fiddles with the car radio and sings along to an old Elton John number, peering around affectionately at Catriona as he intones, 'Blue eyes, baby's got blue eyes.' Catriona peers at the sky through her green eyes as the rain begins to fall again and sighs.

Sensing the cause of her concern, he says, 'He'll be fine,' as he squeezes her leg proprietarily. Wullie notices that she doesn't remove his hand from her leg, even when he slides his hand slowly away upwards from her knee.

'Where are we going?' she asks, Hamish's intimacy ignored.

'You'll see. It's just the last part of my plan.'

She sighs again. Perhaps being with Wee Wullie would be better. Perhaps.

Eventually the grey expanse of Loch Leven appears on the right, its leaden surface disturbed into small waves by the westerly wind. Hamish drives more slowly now, craning his neck and searching for a suitable turning. Eventually he finds one and steers the small car onto a narrow tarmac lane that quickly deteriorates into a gravel and mud track. At the side of the loch, the track broadens and then peters out behind a low reedy embankment. Beyond is nothing but troubled waters without a bridge in sight. To the left and to the right there is nothing, only farmland and occasional trees. The one or two houses are too far off to matter.

Hamish kills the engine. 'Come on,' he says, letting himself out of the car. 'Last stage!' He takes the spare can of petrol out of the boot and motions Wullie to bring the plastic bag of bloodied sheets and dish cloths, the screwed-up tinfoil, the paper tissues and the famous wallet. Over the strand they clamber, bending into the wind and wincing in the cold draught. 'This'll do,' he exclaims, finding a small hollow. He piles the debris into the hole, adds some paper he found in the boot of the car and pours about half the petrol onto the pyre. Taking a twist of the paper, he lights it with his lighter. Ever since he gave up smoking he has always carried his lighter, rather as a Boy Scout carries a pocket knife – 'just in case'. Never has it been more useful than in the last twelve hours.

'Stand back,' he cries. He touches the soaked sheet with the burning paper and it explodes in a ball of flame. Hamish barely has time to throw himself backwards. When the fire has died down a little, he moves forward cautiously to examine the remains. 'Whew! It's almost all gone. Just a bit of the wallet and your dish cloth left. I'll add a bit more petrol . . .' He does so and jumps back again. 'That stuff fucking burns, eh?' he chortles. Wee Wullie and Catriona look on miserably: her head full of her final image of David Grant; his as confused as ever over Catriona's mixed messages. This time there is nothing recognisable in the fire. Even the screwed-up piece of tinfoil seems to have disappeared, melted and with the blood boiled off into oblivion.

'Just bury what's left, Wullie, while I get rid of the last of the petrol.' This time he pours it into the sandy soil. Wee Wullie kicks the soil about rather ineffectually and eventually there is nothing to show for the campfire other than a few singed reeds and some fabric ash which, even as they watch, blows away into the grasses and reeds on the edge of the loch.

They get back into the car, Wullie in the back, Catriona in the front beside an extremely cheerful Hamish. Wullie is once again confused, both by his boldness at pushing his hand around Catriona's seat and laying it along her thigh, well out of sight of the singing Hamish, and by her reluctance to prevent him from massaging her upper leg and the left cheek of her bottom. This can be done by a passenger in the back without alerting the driver if the passenger is extremely intent on the scenery through the window and, of course, the passenger in the front seat is willing to let it happen. Catriona is willing to let it happen but implies nothing by her passivity. She hasn't decided what to do. And Wee Wullie is extremely intent on the scenery.

This is the last we'll see of Hamish, Wee Wullie and Catriona. They take their chatter and restless commotion out of our story and make it back to Edinburgh without further incident; Hamish returns the car to Black Bob and tells him where he was until early afternoon; Black Bob is not sure about the bonfire but is convinced by Hamish that there will be no follow-up on that one; the three stay in the flat for the rest of the afternoon and Hamish cracks open a hitherto undisclosed bottle of Lagavulin; they eat a Chinese takeaway collected by Wullie and polish off a six-pack of beer. It is as though their curious experience with David Grant never happened. Even Catriona relaxes and starts to smile again. Then, partly out of curiosity on the part of Hamish as to how it is between Wullie and Catriona, they enjoy their first threesome – strictly heterosexual. The only conclusion Hamish draws from the experience is that he should have been last with her, since he gets the very clear impression – as clear as things can be after at least a third of a bottle of single malt and a couple of big cans of beer –

that he did all the work warming Catriona up while Wee Wullie got the benefit of a very well turned-on girl. Also, he couldn't quite get the joke after it was all over when Catriona said Wee Wullie's name in her post-coital dreamy way and they both burst out into fits of uncontrollable laughter. What *is* so funny about the name Wee Wullie?

David Grant looks around after a while but Jean has gone. He thinks he hears a car turning and moving off past the graveyard wall but it is too high to see. Anyway, Jean never had a car. The only one ever with a car was himself. He walks out to the gate and looks up and down the lane. To his left, the long road back to Collessie, to his right the lane drops down to a cluster of houses that have been smartened up. Most appear to be empty but that is just until tonight. Monimail is within easy commuting distance of Edinburgh and many other places. He cannot see a pub or shop anywhere.

It starts to rain again and he returns to the graveyard. Water begins to drip down the inside of his coat collar and he buttons it up before looking for shelter. The trees provide cover for a short while but, in the end, the rain slips from one bough to another before finding the old man and using him as a channel to the grass below. His head is giving him serious trouble but he has nothing to swallow his pills with. He finds a discarded bottle and fills it with water from a standpipe used for irrigating the grave-yard during the rare Fife droughts. He swallows a number of pills – far more than it says on the packet. Now thoroughly wet, David Grant searches for better shelter and finds a shed in a corner of the graveyard with clamps of cut grass and a midden close by. It is easy to prise open the door and he sees that the shed contains garden implements: a small digger, wheelbarrows, a lawnmower and some small garden tools. There is also an ancient armchair, damp, discoloured, but extremely comfortable, placed conveniently under a cobwebby window. He pulls the door shut behind him and finds his way to the chair in the gloom. The damp of the chair soon soaks through his already wet coat but it feels warmer than outside and at least he is out of the wind. There he sits and waits. He has no real idea of what to do. Things just seem to happen, and the set upon which the theatre of his life is unfolding is constantly changing. Now he is in a darkened place sitting in a comfortable chair but there is no noise, no coming and going, no tea and no hot buttered toast. He imagines whoever they were will return and the whole process will begin again – change, movement, pain even. But it doesn't. The only pain that is constant is in his head. In fact, it has become so much a part of him that he is learning to go with it, to rock his head in time with the pulses that he can feel when he puts his extended fingers to his left temple and ignore the flashes of light and elaborate floaters that criss-cross his vision like an uncountable shoal of minnows in a slow-moving stream.

His head reminds him of a boil he had long ago. *That* he remembers as a huge lump on his leg like an alien being clutching him, throbbing and red, unfamiliar and hostile, its claws buried deeply into his diseased limb, something separate and unnecessary, yet conveying acute pain to the core of his being. He could feel this newcomer, this colonist, this interloper more palpably than the limb from which it had grown, a quiet, unassuming member that went about its duties unnoticed and largely ignored.

So too his head, constant in size, appearance and function, but become the custodian of broken glass, sharpened blades, fire and a rampant animal blundering back and forth, the ongoing damage and vandalism within confirmed by the thin trickle of blood that fills his left ear and then drips slowly down his neck.

By early evening this has been joined by another from his right nostril, but he is not aware of it as he has been sleeping for some hours. When he awakes, he wipes his nose and the crusting flow with his sleeve and sniffs as he did when he had nosebleeds as a child. He again experiences the metallic taste and remembers remedies from keys dropped down his neck on a piece of string to lying on his back for ages with parents and relatives peering down at him defenceless on the floor, his hands protecting his genitals and hiding any embarrassment this awkward position might reveal. He can see again the red lump of gore and mucus in his handkerchief when, contrary to advice to 'leave it alone a little longer', he would blow his nose cautiously. Sometimes he got it wrong and, to a chorus of 'we told you so', he would have to repeat the remedy of the day. But he knew his own body and mostly he would time it right, clear his nose and make himself comfortable without the damaged vein giving forth again. He used to go deathly pale after a nosebleed and the traumatic event was almost worth the care and consideration it occasioned. One aunt used to say it was caused by high blood pressure, which would generate even more concern, but David Grant knew that having a probing finger well up first one nostril and then another also had something to do with it.

Still no one comes, and David Grant sits on in his comfortable chair, his only illumination emanating from a moon squinting through the dirty window and throwing delicate shadows onto the wall opposite when not frequently obscured by white-edged scudding clouds racing forever across the world like the Flying Dutchman. The wind rattles the pulled-to door from time to time and flows through the branches of the trees with the sound of running water. A small invisible creature scuttles across the floor, pauses for a moment and then runs back behind the chair, aware of an alien in its own nervous world. The wavering and intermittent cry of an owl penetrates David Grant's consciousness as it marks its territory ready for the lean months of autumn and the famine of winter. First the cry is almost overhead, making him jump with fright at its first shriek, but then, after a pause, it repeats its cry from half a mile away to the north, then again in the west close by Collessie. Without a defiant answer from a competitor, it gives up for a while, taking a couple of mice home to feed the family, leaving the world of sound to the wind and the occasionally rattling door.

Somewhere out in the darkness a church clock chimes midnight.

The Second Saturday

'David Grant, will you help me or no'?'

Jean, at eighteen years of age, had let herself into his bedroom. After pacing around for a few moments, she sprawled on his bed, her long legs drawn up in a foetal position, her body twisted around so that she was lying on her side, her beautiful face anxious and pleading.

He sat cross-legged on the untidy floor where she found him studying. Near to hand lay a couple of jotters – one for lecture notes, the other for essay drafts and questions for the lecturer. They were both broken-backed and folded with their covers together, seemingly discarded but in fact vital to his labours. An Edinburgh-published *Chambers Twentieth-Century Dictionary* and fifteen textbooks made an untidy Tower of Babel just out of reach. By the end of his degree course they might all speak his language, might merge and combine to make sense of it all. A couple of Biros and a pencil, ruler and eraser completed the tools of his trade.

The story she had just told him had driven the outline for his essay to be handed in on Monday morning from his mind. In fact, it had driven everything from his mind.

'How did it happen?' he mumbled weakly.

'Oh, for goodness' sake, David! What do you mean "How did it happen"! You must know how it happens?'

David Grant nodded frantically and, despite his nineteen years, blushed.

'You're just a boy, aren't you, dear brother? I shouldnae' have asked you.' She made to get up but he put a restraining hand on her ankle. She sat back down on the bed with her hands on her hips.

'No, Jeanie, no! Sorry. It's just a shock. Couldn't it have been prevented or something? I mean, this is nineteen fifty-nine. I thought . . .'

'. . . Contraceptives? Yes. Well, it was his responsibility, wasn't it? I asked him but he said it'd be all right. It's no' as though it was the first time but usually he's very careful.'

'You mean you've done it before? Made love?' Again David Grant coloured up.

'Haven't you ever made love, David?' She was almost smiling at him in spite of the precariousness of her situation. He could smell her scent, saw the swell of her breasts under her blouse, marvelled at the long, straight smoothness of her brown summertime legs, imagined only vaguely and inaccurately the secrets beneath her skirt, and contradictory emotions flooded his mind. Even without anything really happening, brothers and sisters often share momentary intimacies, brush and nudge, squeeze and feel, walk past open bedroom doors and see, walk past closed bedroom doors and imagine, enter in error unlocked bathrooms and gaze in spite of themselves, sit side by side on a narrow settee and feel trembling thighs, indulge in childish horseplay year on year until it ends with the two of them locked together breathing heavily and he feels her breasts and she his stiffening penis and they know they must stop for ever. But now his Jean, his elder sister a twelve-month younger than he; the one with whom he had always felt closest; the one with whom he had laid chaste on his or her bed while they whispered and talked and held hands and shared secrets and put the world to rights; the one who had given him theoretical anatomy lessons without ever asking the same from him; the one whose feet were never still but

316

wriggled and writhed, stretched and flexed in time to a secret tune; the one who lay on her back while he looked guiltily at her breasts, watching them rise and fall as she quietly breathed, and even saw the perfection of her final nipple mounds; the one who lay smiling and telling while he watched her mouth open and close, her lips full when in repose, expanding and contracting in speech; the one whose fleeting dimples he waited for, trying to anticipate the words that formed them, had utterly and irrevocably changed.

He felt betrayal, jealousy, and a keen sense of bereavement. Why couldn't it have gone on for ever just as it was? Oh yes, it had changed as they had matured. The horseplay had had to stop two years before and he was more careful when using the bathroom after he realised that one of his sister's fears was to be behind a locked door, but the lying side by side and the virtuous intimacy, the trust and secret sharing had gone on unimpeded. Until that moment. Now she had someone else with whom to whisper and laugh, with whom to touch fingers; someone else who would drink in her beauty from the fountain of blonde hair exploding from her head to her long narrow feet. And so much more. Someone who had, in a single moment in time, crossed the line of their abstinence; learned first-hand all that he had imagined; stroked and pressed and stimulated all that he had admired from afar; penetrated that which he cannot even describe accurately. And she, presumably, had encouraged it. Him. Billie Ravelston, presumably. And in so doing she had grown and he remained a little boy. She had carnal knowledge while he only had carnal thoughts. And because of where he was, vis-à-vis his inconvenient Christian faith, he felt an overpowering righteous indignation that, given free rein, would destroy his relationship with his sister for ever.

'Well?' She looked deeply into his eyes awaiting an answer

while he seemed lost in his own thoughts. 'Have you?' The question regarding brotherly support had been set aside temporarily in the face of new sibling discoveries.

'No. My beliefs ... God ...' His voice trailed away, his thoughts a confused turmoil of restraint and longing.

'Oh dear, I really shouldn't have told you.' Jean sadly shook her head.

The image fades and he hears the owl again, high overhead and no more than a few feet away. The sky is dark now, the moon lost behind thick cloud. There is just enough light to see the black boughs, branches, twigs and leaves fanning restlessly back and forth in the invisible swell and tumescence of the wind. His back is sore from his sitting position and he is desperately cold. He tries moving but that crushes his bladder and he needs to pee. He struggles to his feet and makes it just as far as the door, which he throws open. It is all he can do to wrench the zip down before he adds a trickle to the river of wind flowing through the trees. He rocks and sways like someone drunk and tries to shape the words of his dilemma but can't. He can hardly say his own name. He tries but it has lost the valley between the two syllables. He tries again but it comes out the same. It sounds like 'Da-ed' and the next time 'De-ad'. He feels hot tears on his cheeks but when he wipes his face the moisture brushes his lips and he tastes metal and salt; blood and tears. He tries to remember where he is and why he should be outside on such a cold night but cannot grasp a single hand-hold or iron ring in the harbour of his memory. He reaches out to grasp anything that might be solid but everything is tossing and restless and unreliable. There is nothing he can tie up to that might give him a starting point, no stone steps to the jetty where he might discover, no anchor that might give him time to take stock, to swing

318

around and around to gain his bearings, to allow vision and recognition and, above all, a sense of security. He tries again but still cannot pronounce his own name. He cries aloud in frustration, his scream subsiding into uncontrollable sobbing. He zips up his fly and supports himself with the door. The wind rises again and somewhere behind him he hears the dry pistol shot of a breaking branch. He shouts out loud again, a long low cry that catches on the wind and sends shivers down his spine. Then the shout is repeated and takes shape.

'Why have you forsaken me?' he cries, the words clear and unequivocal and in very great contrast to his lost name. The words come from long ago, a verbal arrow from his youth, from a time that mattered, from simple certainties, from unquestioning faith long since doubted, from the hooks of an old popular song, from the sound bites of a religion. And the question is unanswered; the only sound other than David Grant's uncontrollable crying the rise and fall of the wind moaning through the trees and the sudden flapping of powerful wings as the owl moves off to a quieter place. He turns and stumbles back into the shed, falling over a wheelbarrow and cutting his leg. The injury goes unnoticed, a bagatelle in his compendium of problems, and he drags himself to the chair that is now his home. Slowly the anguish on his face recedes and he regains the blank expression of recent days. This outward change reflects the return of a sort of inner calm and in no time he is asleep again.

'Have you told him?' he asked, and then added, 'I assume it was your boyfriend, Billie Ravelston?'

'Of course it's Billie Ravelston. What do you take me for? And no, I haven't told him.'

'Do you love him?'

319

Jean looked shocked. 'Of course I love him. Do you think I'd let him do . . . it . . . if I didn't?'

'No, of course not. I'm sorry, Jean. Only, sex before marriage . . .'

Jean calmed down and smiled at her brother. 'You'd be surprised how many girls, even down at the kirk, get married in a wee bit of a hurry, David! It's happening all the time. Remember Moira Fraser?'

'Of course. But her baby was premature.'

'Aye, so everyone thought. Don't tell, mind?' Jean laughed gently. 'I won't be the first. And, anyway, Moira's very happy. She and David, her David, teach in the Sunday school as you know. And they have a nice flat in Bruntsfield and the baby's beautiful. They named it for her mother, Mary. He works at Scottish Widows so he's set fair. And they've got one of those huge Silver Cross prams with the big wheels.'

David knew Moira and her husband and, in the face of more pressing problems, didn't need a potted history of the perfect couple.

'You are sure you're . . . ?'

'. . . The word is pregnant, David.' She knelt down beside him and gave him a hug. He let her, but now the tables had really turned as he folded himself into her just as he might have done with his mother years before, while she took him around the shoulders and gave him a light kiss on the cheek. He could smell her perfume again. Her face suddenly distorted in pain.

'David, can we sit up on the bed? Only this is all a bit uncomfortable on the floor amongst all your books.'

They sat on the bed, side by side.

'Will he marry you?'

'Of course. He'll do the decent thing. He loves me. I know that.'

In middle-class Edinburgh in the nineteen fifties, and lots

of other places too, if young people lost control they jolly well made everything right with their family and friends, if at all possible. Invariably, pregnant equalled married shortly afterwards. Of course, if they were under-age, the solutions were more discreet. That was all part of Edinburgh's sanctimonious face to the world.

'Does he know?'

'Not yet, no. I wondered if you'd help me to break the news to him? Then, when that's done we can tell the parents. It's just that you have a car and it would be easier to do with my big brother than on my own. We two going out together in the car won't raise any suspicions.'

Now it was David's turn to take control. 'Of course. I'll drive you over to him. But he's still at school, Jean. It's not the same as with Moira. Her David was about twenty-five when they married. Billie's head boy at the Academy. He'll be headed for university and goodness knows what after that. Isn't his father something big at the General Assembly of the Church of Scotland as well as being a minister out in Corstorphine?'

When the sun rises in Fife on this cold Saturday morning, it does so with muscular Scottish reticence. The clouds are too thick and too low to give way at all, so the light filters through in slow stages. First, the rise and fall of the land appears featureless and ghostly grey with the scattering of houses emerging falteringly from the soil they'd much rather be beneath like inhabited rocks on a lunar landscape. All appears abandoned, the only sign of life being a curl of smoke from one of the few houses still burning fossil fuel. Then, as the light gathers confidence, subtle colour, so subtle as to be like an old tinted postcard rather than a colour photograph, begins to stimulate the cones of the eye, a wash of grey–blue for a slate roof, a touch of green in the peeled paint of an old window frame, a variegation of greys and browns in the stone of the houses and, finally, enough definition to know that a doorknocker is brass and not base metal and that, in bright sunshine, it might just glint. As if to labour the point, the clouds thicken and drop like smoke to facilitate the rain that must inevitably follow. By six o'clock it is as light as it will ever be today.

But in Le Crestet, where it is seven o'clock, France always being just that little bit ahead of Britain in so many things, the sun is shining and an early-rising hoopoe is flying from tree to tree, crossing and recrossing the valley, filling the air with his distinctive song and then dropping silently into fields and large gardens to walk elegantly back and forth, his crest in direct line with his beak, as he forages methodically for food. Élodie has been up since the sun rose. Her eyes are ringed black and her hair needs to be brushed. She is wearing a short, white dressing gown tied tightly at the waist, a trim contrast to her wasted and troubled face. She is drinking her fourth cup of coffee and the coffee machine is hissing, smelling slightly burnt and running on empty. At the sound of every passing vehicle, she rushes through to the living room to see if her David has made an appearance. However, the cars and light vans never stop, and most of what she hears is not on the little village road at all.

She looks through the window at the back of the house and sees a neighbour's cat spring onto the fence and creep carefully paw-over-paw along the top. Every few steps it pauses, turns its head first to the left and then to the right in a quest for something to destroy, and then, with a defiant lick of a paw, continues its safari. The cats have made the garden their territory ever since Queen Elizabeth died. She would have none of it, tearing down the garden barking furiously at even the scent of a cat. But it's as though they know. As soon as the owner is away or gone forever, the squatters move in.

Élodie stands up, crosses to the window and bangs the glass, but the cat simply looks at her, gauges the distance to the ground to prepare for a quick getaway if it is required and, instead of jumping, looks back at Élodie to see if the danger is real. It isn't, so the cat shows exaggerated indifference for a moment or two, looking firstly at Élodie and then upwards at the sky to trace the flight path of a little flock of gossiping sparrows before jumping down in its own sweet time. It even has the audacity to scrape a small hollow and squat for a moment before elaborately burying and smelling the area. Satisfied that its passage cannot be traced, it crosses the lawn slowly and resumes its stalking in the rose bed.

'I'll ask David to go around with the pepper when he gets back,' she says out loud. 'He's good with it.' Élodie is allergic to pepper, particularly when it is on the wind. But then she realises what she has said and the tears well up in her eyes.

Everyone is telling her there must be a perfectly simple explanation but as time passes her imagination for the positive is beginning to fail her. She's heard of people driving off the road and turning upside down in steep-sided ditches which inconveniently hold all the doors shut. Then it's only a matter of time before lack of water and food take their toll or the ditch fills with storm water and the occupants drown. She's heard of these things and they make her blood run cold. She knows death is inevitable but not now, not yet and, please God, when it comes, with dignity.

She tries to pour another cup of coffee but the wretched machine spits at her and delivers a puddle of saturated grains to the bottom of her cup. Before she goes for a shower, she refills the machine. The detective is due at nine o'clock and she knows she must make an effort. Oh, and look at her hair!

David Grant awakens with a start. He has been dreaming but, although he knows the content troubled him, most disappears like the boiling wax from an extinguished candle. All he is left with is an image of his mother crying her heart out and his father telling him to leave the house. His sister Maggie is there too but she has faded with his dream to the role of expressionless bystander. He tries to rekindle her image to give him a clue but all he can see is her turning her back on him.

He opens his eyes and is struck by how terrible he feels. Nothing seems to work. His head is screaming and every joint, muscle and tendon feels paralysed. Only his bladder glows and whines for relief. He knows he must get up as he has a hundred and forty thousand times before but nothing moves and all of a sudden that which has always seemed vital has lost its importance. So, without going into explicit details, the warmest part of his body, albeit temporarily, is his left thigh. He sighs, mostly with relief, and goes through a long painful process of unblocking digits and then the extremities of his limbs to the point where he believes he can stand.

Bad call. He falls again, this time without collateral damage, and being prone helps in the healing process. He lies face down on the compacted earth inside the shed and moves each limb one by one until he feels able to attempt to move all four together. His stiff movements resemble a child learning swimming strokes on dry land. In time he rises and works his way to the door by using both hands along the wall. At last he can push the door open and steps outside into the rain.

Twice, while she is taking her shower, Élodie thinks she hears a car draw up to the house. Both times she throws a towel around her and runs to the window on the top landing but each time she is disappointed. The road is deserted and so, each time, she unwraps the towel and steps back into the shower, closing the door behind her. It is all taking much longer than she had planned but on seeing her hair in the mirror she decided it was beyond redemption and in need of a wash. The police inspector will see Élodie at her best.

David Grant makes his way slowly across the graveyard, using the stones as impromptu handrails where possible. If anyone sees him, he will appear to them to be both concentrating powerfully and utterly expressionless. To avoid falling is his main preoccupation but his mind is on other things, the vacant mien a theatre drape disguising the turmoil within. Eventually he finds a flat stone against the wall which is sheltered from the prevailing westerly and he sits down. He is out of breath and feeling faint. Slowly his head tips to one side and he passes out.

They stood in the Ravelston drawing room, a room so large David had been in it for fully five minutes before he saw the eight-foot grand piano, lid raised, musical score open on the rest, the instrument placed safely over in the back corner away from the window and any damaging sunlight. The walls were papered in tasteful Regency stripe and the intricate cornice had been picked out in a deep green and gold-leafed by the man who refurbished Holyrood Palace. One could have seated a small charabanc of passengers on the many settees; there was evidence of genteel female preoccupations, such as an embroidery frame and patience cards neatly stacked on a little table; and on the walls hung a number of Victorian and Edwardian portraits each showing remarkably similar facial features. They looked a lot like Billie Ravelston, at least the normal, confident, rather smug, success-guaranteed, head boy, Billie Ravelston.

The Billie Ravelston standing before David and his sister was deathly pale and shaking from head to foot. He was but a pale shadow of the images caught forever in oil. Jean stepped toward him smiling, still confident of the outcome, talking, talking, talking, the little dimples at the sides of her mouth deepening and filling from syllable to syllable. David Grant remained near the door where he and his sister stood as soon as they were admitted to the vast drawing room. Luckily, the front door was answered by Billie whose first reaction was to gather Jean in his arms while greeting him cheerily. For only a moment David pictured Billie and his sister naked. Making love. Doing it.

'It'll be fine, Billie. I know it's no' what we wanted, but it's happened and that's that. We'll be fine. Mum and Dad'll be a bit shocked but they'll help, I'm sure of it. I've missed two so we have to get on, but there's plenty of time.' David had no idea what she was talking about but he watched Billie. While his sister was making the best of things and sounding incredibly mature, matter-of-fact even, he was poles apart from her. He looked as though he was about to burst into tears. At last he spoke.

'What a mess,' he whimpered and then he did burst into tears.

Jean stepped back slightly, tipping her head to one side and then drawing it backwards.

'I didn't expect that reaction, Billie Ravelston!'

The object of her desire stood slump-shouldered and sobbed. 'Oh my goodness. What a thing to happen. Look, I'm sorry. I need to speak to my father. He's upstairs in his study. I'll speak to him now. You wait here. I'm sorry. I'm *so* sorry.'

He quickly crossed the room, avoiding eye contact with either of them, and closed the door behind him. Jean looked at her brother and opened her hands imploringly. David feared the worst but comforted his sister with 'He's a bit shocked. That's all. When he's had a moment to think about it and spoken to his father, he'll feel better. The same as us, he does need to speak to his parents, so at least that's one thing accomplished.'

'I thought he might talk to me first,' she replied, clenching her fists in frustration. 'I don't know what I expected. I thought we'd come in here, I'd break the news to him, and you'd be here to back me up, and then you'd go home and he and I would have a long talk. Even make plans. I don't know why I thought that. It's what I would have assumed. He's such an honourable chap, so upright and good. I had pictured it all as being all right in the end. Not like this, anyway. But, like you say, it's a bit of a shock. It'll be fine in the end.' She gathered herself a bit and managed a nervous smile. 'I'll love being his wife, you know. Think of it, David, your sister an old married lady!'

When news is broken to people, the only certainty is what is said in opening the conversation. It isn't even worth wasting time anticipating the other party's response. If you do, their true reaction might astound you.

They stood for a short while and then Jean, still comfortable and confident in familiar surroundings and only disappointed to the point of her boyfriend's initial reaction, invited David to sit down. This he did without question, sinking into upholstery with the consistency of quicksand.

When he comes round, David Grant has an earache from lying on cold stone and he is stiff again in all sorts of different places. He is desperately hungry but tea and toast are not forthcoming. He thinks it should have come by now. Jean always looks after him so well, washing his face, cleaning up whatever it was on his head, but she seems to have become sadly neglectful. After several attempts, he rises to his feet and makes his way back to the shed. It is still cold and windy and the rain looks as though it's set in for the day, so he pulls the shed door shut and sits in his chair waiting for something to happen. If he'd stayed outside, it might have, because an elderly couple park their car and bring a bunch of flowers into the graveyard. It's an annual ritual and they stick to the day religiously. The old man's mother died giving birth to him and, although they now live in Bathgate many miles away, they drive over with a bunch of flowers to put on the grave. It will get harder. He has arthritis and she doesn't drive but they keep up the tradition. He carries the flowers while she brings a shiny pot and a small trowel. They walk past the shed in silence and David Grant has now sunk into his catatonic state again staring into the middle distance, not hearing, not seeing, strange thoughts running through his septic brain. At closest they are a mere ten feet apart but neither party knows of the other.

He doesn't need to press the doorbell. She hears the car, looks at her watch and knows that this is the one that will stop and throws the door open to a short, stocky man in plain clothes. He introduces himself and she leads him into the living room, offering him coffee on the way. This he accepts with gratitude and small talk flows back and forth while she makes yet another pot. Élodie is looking well with her hair newly washed but her stomach is upset from worry and too much coffee. Still, when it is made she pours herself another cup to keep the detective company. She sits opposite him after putting an occasional table, complete with a coaster, in front of him. He asks if he may speak in English.

'I ave been learning at night school. But I know no English people so it is difficult to practise.'

To Élodie, the detective is here on a matter of the gravest concern to her, so she is slightly taken aback by the trivialisation of the moment by it becoming an impromptu English lesson. However, she needs this man on-side so feels she can hardly insist on their precise method of communication.

'You, ah, tell me when I say it wrong. Zat would be good. Zen I get best . . . better. Zat is so?'

She nods and then makes to ask a question. He interrupts.

'First zing. We know nozzing more. He is missing but we ave no records of problems, accidents or nozzing. Is zat English good?'

'Perfect,' she replies.

'It is strange. He don't have no reason to be away, do he? He done zis sort of sing before?'

'No. My husband is utterly predictable. Dependable would be a better word. He is so reliable. I can't understand it.' She bows her head and shakes it before wiping her eyes with the backs of her hands.

We needn't listen for too long to the conversation between Élodie and the detective as it follows the course you will have seen on the goggle-box, from *Dixon of Dock*

Green to that great series with Helen Mirren. Of course she has to explain their entire history in France, the fact of her being away at the Vipassana Centre, what the Vipassana Centre is, the two cars, justifying why neither is French-built – all the usual stuff. You already know most of the answers and would probably respond with a 'Mind your own business' to the others. No, the only interesting part was when the detective asked if she had received any mail since his disappearance.

Élodie puts her cup down and says, 'No,' and then changes her mind. 'Sorry, I was thinking in terms of a ransom note . . .' You see, she has watched too many police stories, from *Dixon of Dock Green* to that great series with Helen Mirren, as well. 'There has been post, of course, but most of it was just bank statements and so on.'

'Where is it?'

'Behind the clock. Over there.' She indicates across the room. 'David deals with those so I just put them there for his return.'

'Can I look, please?'

'Of course.'

She stands and walks over to the clock. The detective's eyes follow her. This vanishing David Grant certainly has good taste in women. She produces two sealed envelopes. 'Here you are?' she says.

'Shall I open zem?' he asks.

'By all means,' she replies, curious as to what the bank statements might reveal.

The first looks like an attempt to sell insurance to account holders in a *caisse d'épargne* so he leaves that one. He slides his nail under the flap of the second envelope and tears it open expertly.

'That's from Société Générale,' she says unnecessarily.

He doesn't reply but looks down the list of detailed entries.

'I see you use ze garage in Tournon for essence.'

'Petrol,' corrects Élodie.

'Pardon?'

'Petrol. The English word is petrol. You asked me to correct you.'

'Voilà! Excellent. Petrol. Precise!'

'Yes, we use that garage. We know the people.' She smiles briefly. 'I think David likes to see little Cécile. She is very pretty.'

'Mais oui! Elle est très jolie.' You will have noticed that even when a Frenchman is determined to use the English he has learned at night school, he resorts to his native tongue when the subject turns to love and female beauty.

'I see you used ze garage on ze 7th. When was zat, let's see. Ze Monday before last. Two weeks ago next Monday. My English is good, isn't it?'

'Yes, it's good. Well, it wasn't me on the 7th. I told you I was at the Vipassana Centre then. It must have been David. It's normal. He probably fills up his car once a month.'

'And again on ze Wednesday.'

'Well, that's possible. Michel at the hotel said he thought he might go away.'

'Zis was at a petrol . . .' He laughs at the progress he is making. '. . . station near Dijon.'

'What?'

'Yes, and look . . .' He stands up, crosses the room and sits down beside her, spreading the bank statement out for her to see. He catches a brief waft of her perfume. It is Chanel No. 5. Frenchmen know these things. He points to the items in turn. 'Here is a restaurant bill on ze motorway between here and Dijon and anozzer for the Campanile 'otel. Zey are both for ze Tuesday.' He stands up. 'I sink, Madame Grant, as you say, your 'usband 'as gone on a little trip.'

'It doesn't make sense for him to go north, though.

Michel said he'd mentioned Switzerland. Oh, and he likes Provence. Could someone have stolen his card?'

The detective feels he has fulfilled the function reflected in his job title and is now anxious to leave. 'It is highly unlikely, Madame Grant. If credit cards and bank cards are stolen, zere is usually a big rush to get ze money out in case ze loss is reported and ze card stopped. In zose two or tree days, zere might be six or seven hits on cash machines, normally. Quick, but for modest sums. Two or zree 'undred euros each time. Different machines, all local; Tournon, Tain, for example. Not a leisurely trip across France with a modest night in a Campanile and a little lunch. He is, I sink, a careful man, your 'usband, no?'

'Yes, very careful.'

'Zis,' he waves the bank statement with a triumphant flourish, 'is the 'istory of a careful man.'

'What about any other entries.'

'Zey are ze last, Madame Grant. You should ask ze bank for an up-to-date statement. You on internet?'

'No.'

'Pity, you could look at your account on line. No, Madame Grant, zere is nozzing suspicious in zis. It is not a police matter.'

She shows him to the door, more confused than ever.

'If I can be of any furzer use, Madame Grant, give me a call. Ozerwise, telephone family, friends and relations. Ask if zey have seen 'im. And try to remember any strange conversations you ave ad wiz him recently.'

He turns to look at her as he walks to his car. She stands with her hands clutching the front door, watching him. She must be much younger than her husband, he thinks. He half hopes the husband has run off with someone and that he might be able to provide a shoulder to cry on. He has been a lonely man since he lost his wife to a stroke five years before. There have been one or two dalliances but nothing serious. Besides, we all travel hopefully.

David Grant hears footsteps and muted conversation as he sits stock-still in his chair. He assumes it will be Jean with that nice young man fetching some warm buttered toast and tea.

'That's it for another year, Rab.' It's a woman's voice, but older-sounding than he was expecting. 'Aye. And I've got the old pot to give it a clean and bring it back next year. It's so nice how they keep the graveyard. So tranquil and nothing ever out of place. Just a wee spot o' weeding and the clean pot with the flowers and everything's fine and dandy again.'

'What I like is it's unchanging. It's a good place to be for ma' mother.'

'Would you like to be put here, Rab. You know, when . . .'

The old man laughs briefly. 'Now, we have this conversation every year,' he says gently, putting an arm stiffly around her shoulders. 'I want to be alongside you, you know that . . .'

Their voices trail off as they move uncertainly towards their car. After their annual ritual they always go down to the shore and throw a few pebbles before having fish and chips in a restaurant in Pittenweem that's only open for the summer months. Then they'll make their slow progress back to Bathgate where they'll play Harry Lauder and Jimmy Shand and he gets morose over the loss of the never-known and she puts a protective arm around *him* before making a cup of cocoa.

David Grant looks this way and that, straining his ears but there is no further sound, other than the wind and the rain pitter-pattering on the roof of the shed. He is alone again.

*

After a very long time, Ravelston *père* walked into the room, closely followed by his son. Billie still looked white and had added 'deeply ashamed' to his demeanour, but David Grant sensed it was not strictly on account of what he had been doing with his sister. He feared a bombshell.

Ravelston was one of those scrubbed-looking Church of Scotland ministers; skin pink and soft, hair silver, chin clean-shaven to the point of perfection, with hands immaculately manicured. He wore a dark three-piece suit with a Scottish regimental tie tightly drawn across his neck beneath an old-fashioned stand-up collar. He was about five feet nine inches tall but had the build of a defensive rugby player. The only thing out of place was a broken nose, no doubt won on the field of play in his youth. He sported rimless half-spectacles over which he peered at his visitors with steely resolve.

David Grant jumped to his feet and his sister walked over to her future father-in-law with an easy familiarity. Her warm greeting was not acknowledged.

'You will both sit down, please. Over there, on the chaise longue will do fine. William? You sit here.' He indicated a settee opposite the two Grants. 'I shall stand. Come along now; sit down as I have asked.' They all sat in their allotted places but no one was comfortable. David Grant couldn't take his eyes off Billie who was sitting crouched forwards with his white and shaky hands on his knees. 'This won't take long.' Billie's father turned away from his son towards David and Jean. 'Did I not tell you on one occasion, Miss Grant, that I did not want William to get involved seriously with any young women at this time? These are crucial years for him if he is to fulfil his full potential.'

'Yes, you did. But that was a long time ago. I thought . . .'

'There is no simple way of putting this so I'll just say it *sans phrase,* just as it is. There can be no question of William getting married. After all, he's barely eighteen years of age

334

and in no position to take on the responsibilities of a family.'

David Grant looked sideways at his sister who had gone grey. Her strong young frame had collapsed into the settee as though there was not a muscle or tendon in her body, just like a discarded rag doll. She looked at Ravelston and his son by turns, unable to believe what she had heard; the betrayal, the indifference, the finality of it. She was utterly despairing and David Grant was in despair for his beloved sister. He knew he must speak out for her.

'But this is down to your son as much as to Jean? He should do the right thing!'

'Did I give you permission to speak, young man?'

'I don't need your permission to speak in support of my sister. I'm sure we never suspected this response from you. I know it's difficult . . .'

'. . . On the contrary. It's not difficult at all, young man. It's not difficult at all. Your sister knew my views on the subject. She has admitted as much. So she seduced my son thinking he'd be an excellent catch.'

'What?' this from Jean. 'Me seduce *him*? It was he who seduced *me*. Here, in this house. Upstairs in his room. Billie, tell him!' Billie Ravelston slowly shook his head and tried to steady his hands by putting them both clenched together on one knee. 'Billie?' He averted his eyes and shook his head again.

Ravelston walked slowly across the floor, tripping slightly on a corner of the valuable Turkish carpet. 'From what he tells me, young lady, it was you who tempted him. He tells me it was only the one time. It is surely surprising to fall pregnant after a single sinful escapade. Perhaps you've been doing this with others, Miss Grant? Finding yourself with child, you took steps to better your situation.'

David Grant stood up quickly and moved across the room, his fists bunched.

'How dare you say that about my sister!'

Ravelston took one small step backwards – only one. 'I don't advise you to strike me, Master Grant. Firstly, I would not bet much money on your prevailing over me in any fisticuffs. Nor would I expect to have any problem with the constabulary if I had to call them. But you, I suspect, might.'

Jean was crying and looking imploringly at Billie Ravelston who seemed preoccupied by a hair on the back of his hand.

'It wasn't only once. We made love . . .'

'. . . Enough, young lady! Don't be ridiculous! And don't give what you did the dignity of the term "making love". Come now, would I believe you over my own son? He may be impetuous and subject to all the temptations thrown at him by this world but he is honest and, of course, I believe *him*.'

'You've not heard the last of this!' David Grant roared, jumping to his feet.

'I would advise caution, young man. As they say in all the best detective novels, it is your word against ours. I think with my standing, William's impeccable record to this time, and your sister remembering my advice about friendships with William, there is no case to answer. On the other hand, your sister's reputation, such a fragile thing, surely, will be sorely sullied if this ever gets out. Take my advice, since she has brought you along for – you'll forgive my sense of humour – moral support? Advise your sister to cast back to see who else might be the father. Then she has three courses of action. One: Marry *him*. Two: go the full term and have the baby adopted. She could go some way away for that. I'm sure you have remote relatives who can be trusted to be discreet. Or, the third way, which I will not put into words, but there would have to be a reckoning with God and the authorities if that one is chosen.'

'I am horrified!' David Grant said. 'And you a man of God.'

'Do you not attend the kirk, Master Grant?'

'Until now, but never again!'

'Then that is sad. All my life has been devoted to winning souls for Christ. But God's chosen flock have to imitate him here on earth. The body is the temple of the spirit, Master Grant. I pray that, one day, the church will welcome you again into its fold. Now, please leave.'

David Grant and a tearful Jean did leave, but not before Billie Ravelston had felt David Grant's fist in his guilty face.

The telephone rings at about eleven-thirty and Élodie runs from the kitchen to answer it.

'Allo, Madame Grant? Is Bouscarel here, from the police.'

'Oh, Monsieur Bouscarel!'

''Ave you 'eard anything? 'As he telephoned?'

'No. Nothing.'

'We ave 'eard something.'

Her heart jumps. At last. She prays for good news.

'What have you heard?'

''Is car. It has been found.'

Her moment of unbridled hope drops into a deep shadow of despair. She suspects the worst.

'What? Tell me!'

''Is car has been found in a place called Holyhead. It is in England, no?'

'Yes.' She corrects herself, 'No. Wales, actually. Pays de Galles.'

'Ah, it is beautiful, no?'

She doesn't believe this is an appropriate moment for a discussion about the beauties of Wales. 'Why?'

'Ah, why is a big question, Madame Grant. It is vandalised. A window broken, something stolen perhaps, they think. Maybe a telephone. But he is in trouble with the local police also.'

'Why? Have they got him or something?'

'No. He is disappeared. But he took a big stone. It is not legal to take big stones in England? Anyway, he has big stone that is stolen in his car and it has been vandalised.'

David Grant stood outside the manse with his arms around his sister who was crying uncontrollably. 'Come on, Jeanie, we'll just go home.'

'No! I can't. I can't face them!' She buried her head in his shoulder and sobbed her heart out. Nothing he did seemed to stem the flow of abject despair. It was as though she would never stop crying.

'We'll have to tell them sometime. But we could leave it until the morning if you like? Perhaps we need to think about things. There's no hurry to go home.'

'No. I'll tell you what I want to do. Don't be angry or sit in judgement of me, only, let's buy a bottle of wine. We'll go down to Silverknowes and have a drink. Maybe we'll think what to do there.'

'Jean, I didn't know you drank?'

'Another thing Billie taught me.'

David Grant wished his blow to Billie Ravelston's spoilt face had been all the harder. He could now picture it all. As far as he was aware, Jean had never taken a drink in her life. Their father was a fully paid-up teetotaller, his only dependencies being his pipe and vast quantities of tea. So, that's probably how it happened the first time. Empty house, bottle of wine, up in his room, head swimming, groping fingers . . .

'I don't know if it will be easy to get a bottle. Are the off-licences open?'

'Let's find out, shall we? I know one quite near here.'
David Grant didn't doubt it.

'What on earth are you doing here?'

David Grant shields his one good eye against the light and breeze swirling through the newly opened door.

'You gave me the fright of my life! Jesus!'

A man wearing dark-blue overalls is standing at the door of the shed, visibly shaking. Understandable, finding a shabby old unshaven tramp in your place of work.

'You shouldn't be in here, really. It's not a good place for you. Where are you going?'

'Don't know,' David Grant slurs.

'You should move on. I've got to get the lawnmower out, but first I've to get a can of petrol from the car. You should be gone when I get back.' His shocked reaction to his discovery subsides and he feels more generous. 'There's a bench over on the other side if you want to rest. It has at least stopped raining. Go over there before you go on your way.'

The man leaves without waiting for an answer. He is thinking that he'll have to burn the easy chair now and his resentment increases. He likes that chair and often, when his work is done, he does just what the tramp has done – while away an hour or so in the calm privacy of the shed. But his unexpected guest has changed all that and he'll have to replace the chair. Well, he reasons, tramps have lice and fleas and all sorts of awful habits, don't they? And, as we know, the gardener is not entirely wrong.

David Grant pulls himself to his feet and makes his way out of the door. The gardener turns around halfway to the gate and, seeing David Grant, points to a hitherto unseen bench which he obediently makes for. He sits down and lolls over to one side before vomiting over the side and onto the grass. He makes no attempt to clean himself up, other than wiping his mouth with the back of his coat sleeve. He spits a dozen times into the pool of pink vomit to try to get rid of the taste and then lays his head back with his mouth slightly open. A bee, attracted by the unaccustomed smell emanating from the stranger, does a couple of circles around the prone head before drifting slowly off on the wind.

David Grant bought a bottle of cheap Spanish wine and a corkscrew in an 'offie' near the zoo and twenty minutes later he and his sister were sitting on the wall overlooking the beach on the foreshore at Silverknowes, down below Lauriston Castle and the farm policies. The Fife coast drew a wavy green line between the solid mauve of the Firth of Forth, creamed by wavelets and given scale and perspective by sailing boats and one or two cargo ships, and the pale blue and off-white of the sky, empty save for the scream of invisible gulls. To their left, one red elbow of massive proportions betrayed the presence of the Forth Bridge, ahead lay the Inches, Inchmickery looking like a low-in-the-water warship full of silent, still menace, and to the right the Firth opened out past the necessary clutter of Granton gasworks. The air was warm, the water advanced, folded and retreated with the sound of steady breathing, and the scents of the shore – salt water, a trillion corrupted crustaceans, wet sand and sun-dried seaweed – all contributed to what should have been a perfect afternoon. From a distance they could have appeared as lovers, seated closely together, comfortable and animated. Wild lovers, though, with their bottle of wine and she with her mane of unruly blonde hair.

He had drunk the equivalent of a glass but she was swigging the rest of the bottle as quickly as she could between bouts of hysterical crying. She simply could not come to terms with Billie Ravelston's cowardice and treachery. It was as though the one man she had ever loved, the one man she had trusted beyond all others, was a complete stranger. She realised she didn't know him at all. Looking at her situation with him centre stage, a short-term period of embarrassment and need for quick action would have been followed by a very happy life, all she might ever have wanted. With only a few short years behind her, and those spent in a family that was solid and safe, she had every reason to trust the future and make few demands on life. Now, with him firmly out of the picture, she could not see any way forward.

'I'm finished,' she sobbed, and then squealed as a thought re-enters her head, 'What will Mother and Father say? Oh, this is terrible!'

David put his arm around his sister and patted her to comfort her. 'It'll be fine, Jean. You should dry your eyes and stop greeting. We'll go home and pretend nothing's afoot. Then, when you feel stronger, you and I will go off somewhere quiet and decide what the best plan is. It needn't even be today. But you must stop crying first!'

She was hardly comforted. It was as though she lived through all the possible scenarios in a series of subliminal flashes, each one more hopeless than the last.

She waved the empty bottle in the air. 'Well, that's finished. Just like me. What'll I do with it, throw it on the shore?'

'No, just put it in the car. The back seat will do.' They walked back up the grassy slope to the parked car. 'I'll get rid of it when we get back,' he added. He unlocked her car door and she climbed in, doing what he suggested with the bottle. 'Look in the glove compartment,' he said. 'There's a packet of Polos in there. Best to have a few so that Mother and Father don't know we've been drinking.'

341

'If they take one look at me, they'll know *I've* been drinking! No Polos are going to hide that!'

David Grant shrugged and started the engine. He was nervous and terribly upset for his sister.

On the way home, David Grant ran into the back of a Number 8 bus. He had pulled out to overtake while the bus paused at a bus stop but it set off and he had to swing in sharply to avoid oncoming traffic. At the inquest he was found guilty of driving too quickly but charged with nothing owing to the tragic loss of his sister. The coroner used the case as an opportunity to draw attention to the danger of driving with glass bottles left on the back seat.

From that day forward, David Grant relived the moment almost daily when, with the bonnet of his small car smashed into the back of a Corporation bus and steam rising from its smashed radiator, he turned to his sister smiling with relief at the limited damage to check she was all right and saw her beautiful face through the windscreen but turned toward him, expressionless, with the broken bottle projecting from the back of her neck. She was stone-cold dead.

As is David Grant when the gardener returns with his can of petrol five minutes later. At noon.

Cadit Quaestio

You might like to know the outcome of a few of those loose threads, those pieces of unfinished business, those shards of colour in the stained-glass windows of lives brought together by happenstance.

The begging girl in Dublin ended up on the game. She was really too pretty and too naive to recognise the silky words of one of Dublin's many drug dealers for what they were and there was no other way she could pay for her resultant habit. She was picked up in Dublin Bay one night by a fishing boat but she hadn't drowned. There was a bullet hole the size of a pea in the back of her neck – neat, professional, terribly final. The exit hole in her throat could have accommodated a clementine. An execution, the Gardai had said. But no one knew who she was, so for her there were loose ends spanning a continent – a family in Iran who knew everything about her but not where she was, and a mortician in Dublin who knew where she was but nothing about her.

Billie Ravelston was shown the story in *The Scotsman* the very next day by his father. He took the news badly, even blaming himself briefly for complicity in her death. Having gone into deep shock, he had to be kept away from school and confined to his room. His parents called the doctor and he was sedated for a period of four days. Persuaded that the Hand of God indeed works in mysterious ways, and reminded that the Ravelstons always face setback with courage and fortitude, common sense won the day and, as a consequence, his absence from school was explained by his contracting a viral condition. The secret was kept by all the family and was quickly set aside. For a while, it is true, Billie's father wondered if he would receive a knock at the door indicating that David Grant had told his parents everything. But, as the weeks went by without any contact, he realised a conspiracy of silence that suited both families had prevailed. Clearly, the young lady's parents were never informed of her pregnancy, her death already quite unbearable without the addition of her shame. The truth of Billie's ardour and how he took passionate advantage of a lovely, innocent girl was, as a consequence, never revealed. Billie went on to win a double first at Oxford where he rowed victoriously in the Boat Race. He managed to impregnate the daughter of a government minister while he was at Oxford but they were a rather more sophisticated family so she had a termination conducted by a family friend in Harley Street. Billie had learned his lesson about informing parents and losing his nerve with the Jean Grant episode, so Ravelston senior never knew and Billie kept his cool over the affair. After Oxford, he became a top barrister and took silk. He married satisfactorily and had four children, all boys. The last time he entered the headlines was when he chaired an ethics committee for the UK government a few years ago.

David never told his parents why they had been out that day and took the blame for his sister's death by reckless driving. As a result, relations with his parents became increasingly strained and his flit to halls of residence, followed by a hasty and unsuitable marriage as soon as he qualified, satisfied everyone concerned. He had two children, a girl and a boy, but this fact has already been touched upon. His mother never really recovered from her loss.

Maggie Grant resented the disproportionate grief for her sister's death and blamed David for revealing the true dynamics and distribution of affection in the family. She married a newly qualified doctor and had three children but didn't encourage the children's uncle to keep in touch. So, after a while, he didn't. David's father died when David was twenty-nine, which was why, with nothing holding him to the city of his birth other than his children and a host of resentful adults, he divorced his wife shortly afterwards and went to live and work in London.

You will recollect the coat David Grant was wearing when he died? It was Hamish's old coat, remember? In fact, it was Hamish's last *school* coat, gabardine and with a rash of buttons and flaps that, if fully understood, could make him look a lot like Humphrey Bogart. Hamish's adoring mother had sewn a Cash's name tag inside the collar. So, the coat and the old man and Hamish were once again united in the minds of the police . . . but not in a seamless way. In spite of computer systems and all the ballyhoo of modern life – cameras that record crimes for the Roman amphitheatre of the television news but don't, however, prevent crimes and all that sort of thing – the truth was never fully discovered.

The Fife police found Hamish quickly enough. He had a police record after all. They contacted the Lothians and Borders Police and asked them to obtain an explanation from Hamish as to why an unidentified corpse in a Fife graveyard was found wearing his old gabardine school coat. When the police visited Hamish, they didn't volunteer anything about making a connection between the discovery of the old man in Monimail and the incident in The Meadows a couple of nights previously. Clearly McNab, the Edinburgh policeman, had been true to his word and left the curious incident in The Meadows unrecorded for the sake of loyalty to an old, dead colleague. Hamish said nothing either. The story of the coat, therefore, was hugely simplified. It had gone from Hamish's back to that of the unknown man in Monimail via a charity shop in Leith Walk. His girlfriend, a pretty thing named Catriona, vouched for his charity-giving.

Élodie's detective made his move but it was too soon for the grieving Madame Grant. She didn't even know what had happened to her husband for sure at the time and she rejected his advances. He is now married to a widow in Tain and spends a lot of time fishing.

As to identifying Élodie's husband and piecing together what actually happened, in time she got to know so much but without absolute certainty of the conclusion. His credit- and bank-card transactions took him to England, then to Wales and Ireland. He then caught a train the very day the police found his car in Holyhead and stayed a couple of nights in a fancy hotel in Manchester. As he didn't sign his bill, they had to present it unsigned to Barclaycard and it was met. After that, he bought a single ticket to York and then the trail petered out. No more hotels, train fares or restaurants. A stroppy letter arrived from the London con- gestion-charge people that sat neatly between his stays in Canterbury and Dublin, and the London police of course took a dim view of his speeding on the road into the capital. Élodie paid both for peace.

Hearing of his death, David Grant's doctor called Élodie in for a meeting and revealed details of his slowly develop- ing brain tumour. He even showed her the X-rays of his brain, obtained at an alert hospital on the other side of the river. The tumour was little larger than a cherry at the time but was in an area of the brain considered inoperable. The doctor had advised David Grant to tell his wife but he had decided that, as it was slow-growing, he'd wait until there were conclusive signs of his deterioration. The doctor sus- pected that his request for strong painkillers was an indica-

346

tion that the tumour had grown, advised another X-ray and the revelation of his condition to his wife, but David Grant had seemed unconvinced about either course of action. Besides, he had told the doctor that his wife had gone away for a fortnight.

The post-mortem of the man in the graveyard revealed a brain tumour as the cause of death but it took an age for the missing people's bureau to make any connection. And then it was his watch and wedding ring that finally convinced Élodie. The authorities had held the body for a while but some confusion had taken place and it had been disposed of. They kept the unmarked ring and watch, though, and one day, a year later, the trail having dried at Manchester Victoria station, Élodie finds herself in a small police office in Dunfirmline, Scotland, sitting at a polished pine table and looking at her husband's wedding ring and cheap Festina chronometer.

'No identifying marks on the ring I'm afraid, Mrs Grant. And those watches are very common in France I've been told. However, it's got the number 16069 on the back and on the bracelet. I don't suppose you've got the guarantee with you? When we spoke to you on the phone, you seemed to think it was out of date and disposed of.'

'It was. He'd had it for about three years. But my husband was a very methodical man, officer. He kept records of everything he bought in a little notebook. Look, here.' She produces a black pocket book with a little diary pencil down its spine. She opens it at a Post-it note and reads from it. 'Festina Chronometer. 16069. Bought from Aubry, rue d'Antibes, Cannes. September 2003.'

'Well, that's it, Mrs Grant. The mystery is solved. I'm sorry to have to confirm that the man found in the graveyard in Monimail was your husband.'

The news is almost a relief. She sighs and wipes a single tear from her eye but her time for crying is largely over.

'I'm sorry you won't be able to bury your husband, Mrs Grant. His body should have been kept but sometimes things go wrong and we often cremate unidentified people too hastily. He had clearly hit rock-bottom when we found him, although, from what you say, he was completely normal a fortnight before. Strange.'

'It *is* strange. Everything about it is strange. I found out he was actually rather ill but was keeping the news from me.'

The policeman sighs before he replies, 'That is *so* common, Mrs Grant. Oh so common, believe me. The closer the relationship, the bigger the secrets.'

'I feel there's so much I don't know about a man who has died when, in life, I knew precisely what he was thinking and guessed pretty accurately what he was going to say next.'

'Did he have any connections with Scotland?'

'Yes, he was born here. He was brought up in Edinburgh but I never knew his father. He died a long time ago. I knew his mother but they had an odd relationship, she and David. I always felt she didn't really like her son. She fell ill with Alzheimer's disease eventually. We had her staying with us in London for a while to give his sister a break from looking after her – she stayed on in Edinburgh and married and had children. She and David didn't seem to get on very well, either. We exchange Christmas cards but that's about all. I thought I might go over and try to look her up before I return the hire car and fly out of Edinburgh the day after tomorrow. I told her about his disappearance at the time it happened but she wasn't very "involved" if you know what I mean. He never told me why they weren't close and I didn't probe. Oh, and he had another sister but she died when she was a teenager. He never said much about her either. I got the impression they were close.'

The policeman gives her the last remaining possessions

of her dead husband in a small brown envelope and she leaves, thanking him for his kindness.

There's one more thing she needs to do. On the way back to the city, she makes a detour and, after a couple of wrong turns, finds herself in Monimail. Because she's tired, she can't find the graveyard but knocks at the door of a terraced cottage to ask for directions. In no time she has parked the car and is walking into the tranquil space. A robin is singing the evening in, hopping from bush to tree and keeping her company on her stroll. She, of course, knows nothing of the drama on that windy night a year ago, the screeching owl, the trees lurching and groaning, her husband's ponderous peregrination from shed chair to gravestone and park bench. All is at peace on this still sunny evening.

There is no one about so she feels she can spend a little time exploring. She walks along each pathway between the stones, reading the inscriptions redolent of controlled Victorian emotions and Calvinistic resignation to the inevitability of predestination and the transience of man. She notices a number of stones dedicated to members of the Grant family and then almost knows what she is going to find before she finds it.

On a tall and slightly drooping slab, a nineteenth-century inscription records the birth and death of a man called David Grant.

Ignotum per Ignotius

This book is not really about Élodie, or Jean, or Fat Sam shackled to his frying pan, or the flawed Hamish, Catriona or Wee Wullie, or the sad begging girl on the Ha'penny Bridge in Dublin, or Justyna and her new life on the Emerald Isle, or Ralph Biggins with his sharp eyes and light fingers, or Cécile with her fragile certainties, or David Grant's memories of loves lost or never won. It is about an ordinary life's close. All right, it is slightly unusual in view of the fact that the hero of the story went away on a trip. It's also unusual in that his wife, who would under any other circumstances have been there for him, knew nothing of his slow-developing tumour that suddenly decided to be slow-developing no longer, hadn't an inkling that there was anything wrong, and happened to take a very rare retreat at what turned out to be a critical time in his life.

As lives go, however, his was fairly ordinary. His fair share of tragedy and joy; the space to be conventional and eccentric when he chose, even though he was not himself when true eccentricity took hold; the imagination to dream and therefore see his faults and disappointments with equal clarity; a keen curiosity about the world and those he met within it; a satisfactory balance between wealth and poverty that many would envy; and a health record that rewarded him for his avoidance of excess even if his life didn't achieve Shakespeare's three score and ten (and certainly not his four score). He even had an average sort of terminal decline. For everyone fortunate enough to be taken in a second by heart attack or unexpected death in their sleep, there are many that endure, for the most part with great fortitude, a year or two of painful and humiliating decline. David Grant knew about his tumour six months, give or take, before his death – not a bad situation to be in.

I have never been one for precision in terms of time and am not much concerned with the start of life but, so that you get a clear picture, David Grant was born on the 18th of February, 1940. The date of his demise, which is much more important to me, was the 19th of August, 2006, precisely at noon – twelve and a half days or three hundred hours after our story commenced. A pedant might point out that we met him a full ten hours into the first day and that the tale should be called 290 Hours or somesuch. But, as I have said, I am not that concerned with the Alpha. Only the Omega interests me. And 'Three Hundred Hours' has a certain ring to it, don't you think?

You will forgive the formal identification of the man as David Grant throughout this book – it's a mark of official-dom and my own respect for mankind in general. A habit I simply cannot shed. To his employers, the tax office and the pensions people he was also always David Grant, so why should I diminish him by implications of a familiarity that never existed – at least not until now. Only his wife and a few friends called him David whilst, outside the family, he was always 'Davie' in his Scottish childhood. As you have read, 'Dave' was so rarely used as to be a shock when uttered by Sam in his greasy spoon in York just as dawn was breaking.

So, David Grant – David – joins the minority (since it is said there are more people alive in this world today than have ever died) and he may yet be useful to us. We are always extremely busy and there will almost certainly be an 'adjustment' in the near future that will make today seem like a party.

Oh, who am I, the little commentator putting in his pennyworth from time to time?

We haven't met yet, even though we have mutual acquaintances and have almost certainly been close to encountering each other from time to time. Perhaps I should introduce myself. That would be the polite thing to do.

My name is Death.

I'll see you all quite soon.